A Different Place to Die

The following work is pure fiction. All the names, characters, locations or incidents are works of fiction created by the author. Any resemblance to people, whether living or dead, is a coincidence.

This is dedicated to my mother Kathryn "Joan", who has always been my biggest fast fan. This is only fair, since I have always been hers.

And to my father, Jasper, who I'm sorry didn't live to see this. This book is about his time, not mine.

Table of Contents

CHAPTER 1

It all started when I shot that guy's dick off.

No, I'm too far ahead; that came later and technically I didn't shoot it completely…that's beside the point and it started before that. It started when I entered that dive bar. It was a nasty place where you could expect nasty things to happen.

That's still wrong.

It should have been obvious when things went sideways, because I had been going through the same routine for almost a year. During the week I worked as a construction laborer for a crew of brick masons. I worked mostly downtown hauling and mixing sand, mortar and cement as well as carrying bricks and blocks all day long. The job was rough as hell but it made me feel a little better when I wore myself out working that hard. Unfortunately for me it didn't make me feel good enough.

After the horn blew for quitting time on Friday, something inside me threw my self-respect into the nearest trash can and inflicted me with the overwhelming urge to get knee-crawling drunk and tour the ass end of Chicago.

It was early that Friday morning when things started to change. That's when the doctor warned me something was coming. He didn't tell me what it was but that wouldn't have mattered because if he had I would have assumed…no, I would have *known* he was crazy as hell. Who would be mentally deficient enough to buy into that nonsense? Of course what I knew then and what I know now is different altogether.

I started the day in 2017. If the doctor had actually come out and told me I would finish the weekend in 1947 I would have written him off as bat shit crazy and that's precisely the reason I don't talk about it.

I'm getting ahead of myself again. As I said, everything started during my regular therapy session with Dr. Nichols and that began at 8:00 every Friday morning. Instead of going straight to work on Fridays I went to the VA for a session with the doctor and that morning began the same as always.

Dr. Nichols was sitting in his chair, just like he had every Friday before, reading my file as if he had never seen it but this time it turned out a little different. When he finally laid it down he said, "Jake, you seem determined to be a piece of shit and I can't do anything about it."

1

"Is 'piece of shit' a psychological term?" I asked in a flat tone. Standing six feet two and weighing in between 220 and 230 pounds I didn't usually have to put up with that type of exchange. It didn't deter the doctor any. He went on.

"No, it's a street term. It means that if I should see you on the sidewalk I should step around you, because I wouldn't want any of what you are on my shoe."

"They teach you that in school?" I asked, allowing a little grit to show in my voice.

"No, I picked it up on the job. I've seen a lot of pieces of shit come through here."

"So what now, are you going to send me to a new therapist?"

"I'm going to send you to someone else, but it isn't a therapist."

I raised an eyebrow and waited for him to continue.

"No one has been able to help you because you refuse to be helped. I can usually get through to people with enough time and effort but you're kind of a stubborn asshole so I'm going to pass you on."

"Pass me on to who?" I asked, ignoring the asshole reference.

"To whom," he corrected.

"Wow," I said, trying to sound surprised. "You can actually double down while you're being a prick."

"Look who's talking. The VA has been trying to help you for a year now, and you haven't bothered to put forth any effort whatsoever."

"You could always put me back in the Corps."

"Believe me, I would if I could but I don't have the pull."

"That puts us back to square one."

"You can't go back; you never left the damned square in the first place. You sit and gripe, because you can't be a Marine anymore. And in the meantime, when you're not sitting on your ass pissing and moaning about it you're working a backbreaking job which you find demeaning and you spend your weekends treating your growing depression with Vodka."

He was hunched over with his forearms across his knees and his hands were clenched together so tight the knuckles were white. He stared down at them and said, "Your file is amazing; I truly like reading it."

"You must," I said, "you read it every week."

He didn't look up, but I could tell he smiled. "I knew you thought that but your actual file is huge. I only bring a piece of it in each week and read through it."

"I've seen my file. It's only this big," I told him holding my hand up and pinching my fingers together.

"That's your medical file. I'm your therapist. I have access to a lot of other information that no one else is allowed to see."

He raised his head up and looked at me. It was a sad look. "You have done some amazing shit in some bizarre places."

"I haven't done anything special," I told him earnestly.

"Like hell. You've been to countries all over the globe and done a lot of things that I know you're not allowed to talk about, but some of these things are amazing."

"I had a job to do and I did it."

"So part of your job was rushing into a burning school outside Kandahar to save a dozen small children."

"The Taliban had put an RPG into the propane tank next to the school. What was I supposed to do?"

"According to the file you were supposed to secure the area and keep moving."

I had trouble looking him in the eye and I turned away when I said, "The area isn't secure when a building full of little girls are screaming for their lives."

I could see the doctor nod out of the corner of my eye as he said, "Four men in Zimbabwe were trying to rape a girl in an alley. You fought them off with your bare hands."

"I would have preferred that my hands weren't empty," I told him.

He smiled. "I'll bet that's true. When you were extracted, the corpsman dressed multiple knife cuts and stab wounds. You were admitted to the hospital upon landing, and it was just dumb luck you didn't bleed to death."

I waved my hand at the file he was holding as if it were a fly or mosquito and mumbled, "None of those guys offered to loan me a gun or a knife so I didn't have much of a choice."

"The hell you didn't. You were supposed to be keeping a low profile until your unit could be extracted. Saving a civilian girl from local non-combatants was not in the job description. You could have easily chosen to stay out of it."

I looked up at him and I could feel my eyes narrow and the skin on my face burn but before I could say anything the doctor did it for me.

"You can't make that choice, can you?" He closed the folder and said, "This file is full of stuff like that. The only reason you don't have a medal of honor is because the government can't openly admit you have been in half the places where you did these things."

"I don't want a medal of honor. I just want back in the Corps."

"Of course, you do. You're a gallant knight that can no longer perform valiant deeds."

I felt my face wad up. "Now you're just being weird."

"The hell I am. I can read and what I read says that you're chivalry incarnate. You're Galahad or Lancelot or Dudley Dogood or whoever the hell's supposed to come riding in on a white horse to save the day and now that you can't do that it's eating you up inside."

I didn't know what to say so I didn't say anything.

Doctor Nichols brought his hands up and for a moment I thought he was going to pray; but then he pushed his face between them, stretching the skin tight all the way back to his ears. He released the tension and looked down as he pushed his hands around the back of his head and interlaced his fingers. He stayed that way for a moment and the silence became uncomfortable. I still didn't have anything to say. If he wanted anything said he'd have to do it himself.

He finally untwined his fingers and looked up. "Someone will come to visit you tonight."

"The ghost of Christmas past?"

The doctor didn't even blink. "I have no idea who it is. I just know that once I release anyone to these people we never hear from them again."

The conversation had gone from odd to insulting to ennobling and then to bizarre and I'm sure it showed in my voice when I asked, "You're having me put down?" I didn't ask, because I was kidding. I had worked around people that did that sort of thing but I couldn't believe it was worth the time and money to send one of those guys after a broke-dick Staff-Sergeant that had been turned out of the Corps on a medical.

3

My therapist didn't even break stride. "I don't think so, but I won't swear to it. None of the people I have sent to them have ever turned up in the news, but then again, they have never turned up around here either."

"What are these people supposed to be doing with me?"

"I'm told they take you to a place where you have opportunities and can live better."

In a sour tone I told him, "This sounds like the Rainbow Farm where my mother told me my dog went when I was five."

The therapist looked at the floor for a moment and when he looked up he said, "Believe it or not, I want to help you I just don't know how.

What I couldn't believe was that we were having that conversation. I was curious to see where it went from there but it didn't go anywhere. He stood up, tucked my file under his arm, stuck his hand out, shook mine and wished me luck. He seemed very sincere and looked me straight in the eye when he said it, but I could see that he wasn't confident about what was going to happen. I could only see the wishful sincerity that he had already conveyed. He spun on his heel and left without another word.

He walked out and left me sitting there staring at the door. I'm pretty sure my mouth was hanging open.

I waited in his office for a while to see if anyone came in with more information but no one did so I finally got up and went back to work.

At this point, I should mention that Dr. Nichols was actually a pretty good doctor. I gave him a world of shit, and I was as bad a patient as he said I was. It was his recommendation that I start keeping a journal which is why I am writing this down. He said it would help, and it does. I pray no one ever finds it because they would think I'm nuttier than squirrel shit, and there would be no convincing them otherwise. I couldn't blame anyone for that. Who would believe my story about a new world or the little old man, but I'm getting ahead of myself and getting off track again.

It was Friday night and as I mentioned before, the bar I was sitting in was raunchy on rails, but maybe I judged it too harshly. If they had been willing to spend some money on the place for paint, paper, new bar and tables, clean up whatever it was that had my shoe stuck to the floor, and do something about the smell the joint would have made a nice public toilet.

It was a small place and there were only half a dozen guys there, including me. Everybody sat alone except for two men in a corner booth. I sat at the bar and ordered drinks from a skinny horse-faced bartender and then stared down at my drink until I needed another one, and when I got a new one, I went back to staring. That night I drank plenty but not as much as usual. When your therapist calls you a piece of shit it's hard not to take it to heart, so I spent a lot of time thinking about it and didn't drink with my usual zeal. This went on for a while and somewhere out of the fog I heard the bartender give the last call. I left my money on the bar and stood up and headed for the door.

Normally, when a bar is closing, no one is in a big hurry to rush outside. When the lights come up everyone gets up and tries to figure out how well they can walk or if they need to find a place to puke or, in a nicer establishment, try to determine how ugly the man or woman is that they've been talking to all night with the lights down low.

Even through the alcohol fog I was aware of too much movement in the room. I could hear someone coming up behind me way too fast, and a long-haired guy at a table near the door stood up and started walking back toward me more quickly than he should have. If I hadn't been halfway in the bag I would have spotted what was happening immediately. I had seen this routine on the streets of more than one European city. It's nothing new; I'm sure it has been done for centuries. The guy coming toward you is supposed to draw your attention by bumping into you and making a big show of apologizing. The guy behind you takes advantage of that opportunity and lifts your wallet.

It sounds easy enough, but it works better with practice, and it works much better when everyone except the victim is sober. The long-haired guy coming toward me must have been wasted, because he started yelling before he actually bumped into me. It was at that moment my vodka impaired brain realized what was going on, and I got my right hand behind me quick enough to catch the wrist of the little fat man that was removing my wallet.

I forgot to mention that there is usually a third person in this crime. The third guy comes from behind the pickpocket, and the wallet is passed to him in case the victim gets hold of the thief's hand, like I had just done. In this case it appeared that the skinny bartender was supposed to get the wallet, because he was stretched across the bar, reaching for it, when I came up with the fat guys wrist and the wallet still in his hand.

I was facing the long-haired guy, holding fatso's wrist with my right hand. I balled up my left fist and backhanded longhair across the side of the head with it. He spun around and crashed across a table and chairs. I turned and got hold of fatty's wrist with my left hand, and took my wallet back. I slipped it in my back pocket and at the same time I twisted the wrist clockwise and down. He yelled and dropped to his knees as I drove my knee into the center of his face. The cartilage in his nose turned to dust and blood shot out of both nostrils. After that it got messy.

Behind me, the bartender came around the end of the bar carrying a baseball bat. I saw him coming in one of the big mirrors on the wall and turned around as he swung the bat. His arms were as skinny as the rest of him, and there was no power in the swing. I caught the thick part of the bat in mid-air with my left hand. I twisted, hard, and caught him on the side of his face with my other hand. His jaw broke and swung out sideways like a cash register drawer popping open. I could hear movement, behind me, and I spun counter-clockwise, bringing the bat with me.

The two guys from the corner booth were heading my way and doing it double-time. I'm no genius, but even I began to realize that a chunk of this place's business must have come from rolling whatever drunk was left in it at closing time. Looking back, I'm guessing that the regular drunks didn't give them too much trouble. If they had been more coordinated I would have already lost the battle, but they weren't and it gave me a fighting chance. As I swung around to meet the newcomers, I released the bat and got lucky. The two guys had come at me in a staggered formation, and I caught the closest one with a glancing blow to the side of the head. With only a fraction of a second to take everything in, I could see that my hit with the bat was more of a pop foul, and I was still going to have to deal with both of these idiots. Both men were average height, average weight, average looking and they looked a lot alike. I found out later that they were brothers. Brother Number 1, the pop-foul brother, shook his head and went fishing under his jacket for the revolver in his shoulder holster. I took a step toward him, drawing up one leg as I came forward and unleashing it, straight kicking him in the middle of the torso. His gun flew out of his hand and he went sailing backward. Brother Number 2 sidestepped and let Number 1 fly past and slam into the wall. Number 2 reached for his belt-line and got his hand around the grip of his semi-automatic just as I got to him. I wrapped my big hand around his hand, his pistol grip and his belt buckle and I squeezed real hard. The gun went off and Brother 2 screamed at the sensation of having his dick blown into his shoe.

I held onto the screaming brother for a couple of seconds, and then he passed out. I let go and he dropped onto the floor. I stared down at him for a moment, and when I raised my head I was looking at my reflection in the mirror behind the bar. I stood and looked at it for a long time. I wasn't a bad looking guy, but I had looked better. I was almost twenty-eight years old, but the guy in the mirror looked a little more haggard than that. The dark hair, that I had kept Marine regulation for ten years, looked like the shit end of a worn out mop. I needed a shave, and there was blood on my shirt and jacket. I just stood there looking at my reflection and tried to figure out how I had gotten here. A year ago I had been deployed in Afghanistan, I had been doing something that mattered, and I was good at it. Now I was looking at a piece of shit in a mirror. The doctor had called it right. I don't know how long I stood there; but somewhere through a vodka haze and the unending self-pity I began to hear sirens. I looked around and saw that the long-haired guy wasn't on the floor anymore. He must have crawled outside and called the law. I thought about my options for a moment and then I sat down at the bar and waited for the police.

CHAPTER 2

The rest of that night was a jumbled pile of images and memories, and I was never sure what things happened or in what order. The one thing that really stood out in my mind was the Police Sergeant who took my information. He was a decent enough fellow, and I got the feeling he gave a damn about what happened to me. He looked to be in his mid-fifties with thin gray hair and a pretty good middle aged paunch. He seemed like the kind of guy you could enjoy having a beer with and talk about the crap that happened at work. I was sorry that wasn't what we were doing.

"Name?" he asked.

"Kowalski, Jacob Kowalski."

"Any nicknames?"

"I go by Jake and I'm sure you know the other one."

"Ski, it is," said the Sergeant mechanically.

"Height?"

"Six feet two."

"Weight?"

"Two twenty-five...two thirty."

"Distinctive markings, birthmarks, tatoos?"

I pulled up my right shirt sleeve and held up my arm so he could see the eagle, globe and anchor tattooed a couple inches under the inside of my elbow.

The Sergeant punched away at the keyboard with his index fingers. He was an even poorer typist than the two-finger style would indicate. He pecked away at the keyboard and I alternated looking at my shoes and looking at him.

"Anything else?"

"I've got a couple of scars from some 9mm through and throughs."

"Where at?"

"Iraq."

"Why is everybody a smart ass? You know what I mean."

"One is on my left triceps," I told him; raising my sleeve so he could see it. "The other one is around my left love handle."

I started drawing up my shirttail, but the officer stopped me. "I tell you what. Let's just go with the one on your arm."

"I also have a six-inch scar at the top of the right buttock."

"You're just determined to pull your damned clothes off, aren't you?"

"You asked."

"How did you get that one?"

"Machete."

"And the cut is on your ass."

"It's just below the beltline."

"Were you running away?"

"You do know what a machete is, don't you? Of course I was running away."

"I think we have enough distinguishing marks. I don't want to take pictures of all this crap."

"Nearest living relative?"

I opened my mouth to say something and then realized I didn't know what to say. "Uhhh…shit I'm not sure."

"Your folks are gone?" asked the older man.

"Yeah, my mother died when I was twelve. My dad passed away in 2010."

"I'm sorry to hear that," said the sergeant. "My old man passed away in '97'."

"Was he a policeman?"

The Officer grinned. "Yup, he was one tough, sour-assed old bastard, but there isn't a day goes by that I don't think of him."

"Yeah, same here," I told him.

Dad had kept his troubles from me until the day the hospital called and said his heart was failing, and he wouldn't last much longer. I was in the Middle East and by the time I got home, it was too late.

After a moment of thought I said, "I guess my nearest relative is my mother's sister in Louisville, but we're not close."

"Close isn't required," replied the Sergeant softly.

He pecked at his computer keyboard, but I don't know why. The Chicago Police Department couldn't have possibly been interested in what I was telling him. I was pretty sure that no one was interested.

"What did your dad do for a living?" asked the Officer.

"Do you really need that information?" I asked him curiously.

"Nah, I'm just making conversation while I'm waiting on the computer to decide if it's going to print out what I told it to. It usually takes a couple of minutes. You don't have to tell me if you don't want to."

"It's okay," I told him. "My dad had a small farm and did construction work when the work was available."

The Sergeant's mouth turned up a little at the corner. "That was a hard-working man."

"Yeah, he was that."

A couple desks away, an old laser printer wheezed to life and started producing sheets of paper. I expected the Officer to get up and get it, but he just sat there.

"So you ended up with the farm?"

I shook my head.

The older man looked embarrassed. "It ain't my business. You don't have to tell me anything about that."

"Not much to tell. Like you said, my old man worked hard all his life, but in the end all he had to show for it was a sore back, a bad heart, and a small farm that was far enough behind on the payments the bank took it the day we put him in the ground."

"Ah shit," growled the Sergeant. "That's a damned shame."

"Yes it was."

It was hard to tell what was going on from the backside of his computer monitor but I could see his expression change when something popped up.

"Here's your military record," he said, tipping his head back to see the screen through his half-height reading glasses. "This corroborates the tattoo. It looks like you really were in the Marines," he added with a smile.

I chuckled. "Who the hell would lie about that?"

"This is a police station!" the Sergeant barked. "Everyone lies about everything."

I nodded. I had no doubt he was right.

"Marine Force Reconnaissance," the Sergeant read aloud. "That's the Marine Special Forces isn't it?"

I nodded.

"Iraq and Afghanistan," The policeman mumbled as he scanned down the screen. "Is there a war they didn't send you to?"

"No, but they did send me to a couple of places that you won't find listed there."

"Some of that Black Ops shit?"

"Something like that."

"How come you got out? You had already put in nine years."

"During my last tour I got tagged with some IED shrapnel, and now I have what the medics call a trick knee."

"Does it give you a lot of trouble?"

"It doesn't give me any trouble. I don't know what the hell they're talking about. I just know they won't let me back in."

"It doesn't look like it gave you any trouble tonight." The Sergeant took off his reading glasses and rubbed his eyes with his thumb and forefinger as he spoke. "Over the past seven years, I've answered quite a few disturbance calls to that particular establishment, but I've never seen it like it was tonight. It looked like somebody ran the place through a wood chipper."

"Are you going to take my statement about that?"

"No, I'm going to put your young ass in jail, and I'm going to take my old ass home."

"Wanna trade?"

The cop smiled, "Hang on to that sense of humor, you'll need it." The Sergeant picked up his hat and tucked it up under his arm. "Besides," he added, "you might not like the naggin' and bitchin' I have to listen to when I get home."

He motioned for me to stand up. As I did, I noticed the picture of his wife on the desk. He was right, I didn't want to trade.

My hands were cuffed behind me, and the Sergeant caught me by the arm and headed me toward the stairs that led down to the holding cells. He said, "One of the detectives will have questions for you, but, right now we are a little short-handed so you will have to wait in the lockup until they are ready for you."

He was feeling of my arm and he did it so long that I finally had to turn and give him a funny look.

"Your whole arm is rock hard," he said, "How did you get it to be like that?"

"When I was in the Corps, I worked out a lot and trained for Mixed Martial Arts competitions. More recently, I have been hauling bricks, blocks and mortar at different construction sites,"

"Maybe that's what I should have done," the old cop said as we headed down the stairs. "I've spent years in a gym, and you can't tell it by looking at me."

"I can put in a good word for you with some of the unions."

The Sergeant chuckled. "Thanks, but I'm too old to worry about it now. These days, I break a sweat when I lean over to fart. Sometimes I pull a muscle doing it."

I smiled. He was a nice guy, and he was trying to treat me decently. I had a bad feeling he felt sorry for me and that meant that I was in for it. I figured it was a good time to ask, "How are those guys from the bar doing?"

The old cop guided me down a long corridor and said, "Well, let's see. Did you know any of those guys before tonight?"

I shook my head.

"That's the same thing they told us. Let me think...the guy that called us is okay. The bartender, on the other hand, is going to have to drink his dinner through a straw for the next two months; but he should be alright. One of the guys has a shattered nose, and that's going to take some work to fix. Who else...who else...oh yeah, did you notice that two of those guys looked a lot alike."

"Yeah, I did."

"They're brothers. The one you drop kicked across the room is fine but the other one got part of his business shot off. That one's in critical condition. He may not make it through the night."

"Damn," I hissed through my teeth.

"Don't let it bother you tonight," the Sergeant advised. "Get some sleep, sober up, and see what tomorrow looks like."

He guided me to a stop in front of a cell and a second cop walked up and opened the door. The old Sergeant unlocked my handcuffs and motioned me inside. I stepped through and the door shut making that clanging noise like you hear in the movies. It's a lousy sound.

"Good night," said the Sergeant; and he turned and left before I could say anything.

The cell had four steel bunks mounted to the side walls, one over and one under on each side of the cell. I sat down on the left lower bunk next to the bars. I hadn't realized there was anyone else in the cell, and when he spoke, it scared the shit out of me.

"Rough night?" asked the voice.

The lights were out, so it was dim inside the cell, and my eyes were still adjusting. The voice was coming from the far end of the other lower bunk. I finally made out enough detail to see it was a little old man. It took me a little while to get a good look at him, but now I can give his description as five-six and scrawny except for a little pot belly. He was missing a third of his teeth and most of his hair. The gray hair that ran around the sides of his head was thin and looked like it had never seen a comb. I'm guessing the guy was in the vicinity of seventy years old. He was wearing one of those wife beater t-shirts and jeans.

"You could say that," I told him.

"That dive has always been notorious for thieves and grifters," said the old man casually.

I couldn't believe how fast news in this place traveled. "How did you hear about it," I asked.

"It's my job to know these things."

"What kind of job requires knowing about bar fights?"

"It's not my job to know about bar fights. It's my job to know when Jake Kowalski has been in a bar fight."

"How do you know my name?"

"You understand what a job is, don't you?"

Now, the old guy was starting to bug me. "I understand what a job is, but who the hell has a job keeping up with me?"

"I do," said the old guy and he made a point of showing me how serious he could make his ugly-assed face look.

"You get paid a lot for that?" I wised-off at him.

"I don't get paid anything; it's just what I do."

I stretched out on the bunk and said, "Fine, now you can punch out and go home. I'm here, and I'll keep up with me."

"You couldn't keep up with a herd of turtles if you had a rocket shoved up your ass."

I sat up quickly. My head swam when I did, and it was starting to pound. "Listen you old fart. I just want to lay here and go to sleep. Do you think you could talk to yourself or the wall or maybe not at all?"

"I would really like that," said the old man, "but I have a job to do."

"You know…" I started.

"…I'm really starting to piss you off," finished the old man.

"Something like that."

"No, that's exactly what you were going to say," growled the old guy. "Look, normally I take a few hours to do this and try to help you guys get adjusted to the idea before I do my dirty work but I'm in a hurry, you're a half-drunk jerk and I don't really give a damn what happens to you."

I lay back down and tried to keep my head from spinning around. "Adjusted to what?" I thought, but I didn't ask out loud.

There's a place for people like you," said the old man softly. "Surely, even someone as dull as you must have wondered how a guy that spent almost ten years in the Corps and was highly decorated for his bravery in multiple battles, in multiple countries no less, could end up drinking himself to death or dying in a bar fight in some asshole dive on the outskirts of Chicago?"

"How the hell does this guy know…" I started the thought, but I was fading and the old guy's voice came from farther and farther away.

"I'm taking you to a different place. It's a rough place and it will probably kill you before you can even get started; but if you manage to survive you can carve out a niche for yourself.

It is not like this place. It is where you belong."

I remember the words vividly, now. I would have forgotten the entire episode and written it off as a drunken dream, but the old guy and his speech came drifting back when I woke up in the glass box.

CHAPTER 3

The glass box had a wooden frame, and it was about 3 feet square and over 6 feet long. It was standing on one end, and I was wadded up in the bottom of it. I was trying to get untangled and get to my feet when the box started ringing. I twisted my head out from under my arm, and looking up I could see an old, really old, telephone mounted to the side of the box. The other end of the box had a light bulb mounted in the center. The phone kept ringing and I kept squirming and I was finally able to get my legs underneath me and stand up. I looked at the phone for a moment and then realized I was standing in an antique phone booth. I hadn't seen one up close, but I had seen them on television and in the movies. The phone rang again, and I answered it. I must have looked like a fool because I held it like it might bite me.

"Hello", I said in a shaky voice.

"Oh good, you're awake," the phone said back to me.

I heard a noise behind me and I turned around as the little old man, from the jail cell opened the folding door and motioned for me to step out. He had put on a red-plaid flannel shirt, but other than that, he looked the same. The booth was in the back corner of some kind of store. I looked around and asked the old man, "Where are we?"

"Jenkin's Drug Store," replied the old guy. He acted as if that was enough of an answer.

I was turning around slowly, trying to take everything in. The aisle next to us was stocked with bars of different brands of soap. They were all wrapped in paper and looked like stuff you would find in an antique store. The floor was made of well-worn wood. There were more aisles with more old stuff and scanning across the back of the store I could see something that looked like an old fashioned restaurant counter. The guy behind the counter had on a white coat and white cloth hat, just like they show on old TV shows. Two teenage girls were sitting at the counter sharing a milkshake. Their clothing and shoes looked way out of date.

I could see down the aisle and out through the front window of the store. Men and women dressed in old hats and clothes were walking by, and the cars on the street were just as old.

"This doesn't look like Chicago," I mumbled.

"It's not," replied the little old man.

"Why is everything so old?" I blurted out before what he said had registered.

The reason everything looks old to you is because this is 1947, or at least the equivalent of it.

"What...where...'47'...equivalent...," I stammered, trying to get a grip on what was happening. My head started spinning and I grabbed the side of the phone booth to keep from falling down. "What the hell is going on," I finally managed to blurt out. I should have been frantic and screaming, but for some reason I was just incredibly amazed and curious.

"You do remember being in jail, don't you?" the little guy asked.

"Yeah," I said slowly. I was trying to remember what had happened and it was coming back in bits and pieces. "You said you were taking me to a different place."

"And I did," said the old man. He nodded sharply and seemed to be proud of the accomplishment.

"What place is this?

"This," he said, throwing his arms out wide, "is New Egan."

"Where in the hell is New Egan?" I asked. "Is there an Old Egan? What happened to Chicago?"

"The original Egan is in England; it doesn't exist on your world; and there is no Chicago on this world."

"What world?" I squawked.

"This world."

"What the hell are you talking about? There's only one world."

The ugly little guy looked at me like I was a moron and said, "Since this isn't the world you have been living on, it should be obvious there is more than one."

I gave up and moved on; I had plenty of other questions. "How did I get here?"

The little man asked me, "You know anything about interspatial physics?"

"No."

"Parallel worlds?"

"No."

The old guy was starting to look really aggravated. "Quantum physics?"

"No."

"Basic physics?"

"No."

"Why am I even talking to you?"

"It's not because I like it," I growled at him.

The little guy gave me a dirty look, and since he was already butt-ugly, it was a nasty look. I had no idea what he was talking about, but I tried to meet him half-way. I didn't even get close.

"Do I need to understand inner-spatula physics to understand how I got here?"

"Interspatial and, yes, you would need to know that to understand."

I took a deep breath and sighed. "I'm never going to understand how this happened, am I?"

"Not a chance."

I hadn't had any luck with the what or the how, so I tried something else.

"If the worlds are parallel, why is everything old?"

"Some worlds run at slightly different times. This world runs a few minutes a year slower than your world, so it's only 1947 here."

That made sense but the knowledge didn't seem to help me any so I moved on to the next question. "Why am I here?"

"I believe I can explain that in a way that you can understand," said the old guy.

"That would be nice," I said through my teeth.

"Think of it like Karma."

"Oh, so it's like Karma," I said, finally understanding something.

"It's nothing like it," snapped the old guy.

I felt my eyes narrow, and I wondered how far he would fly if I kicked him between the legs. I took a deep breath, counted to ten, exhaled and said, "So I'm thinking of it like Karma."

"Very good," said the little guy happily. "A lot of people, at least the ones that believe in Karma, believe if you do good things, good things will likely happen to you, and contrarily, if you do bad things..."

"...bad things will happen to you," I finished. I thought for a moment and said, "So I beat up those guys in the bar, and now bad things are going to happen to me."

"Don't be an imbecile. Those idiots deserved everything they got."

"The law won't see it that way," I said, shaking my head back and forth.

"Not where you came from, but here it's different."

"So you're saying I did a good thing, and this is my reward?"

"Are you kidding? This place will probably kill you before the weekend." The old fart smiled like the thought made him happy.

I rubbed my forehead with my hand and said, "Tell me again how it's like Karma?"

The little guy sighed and said, "You did a lot of good things in Afghanistan, Iraq, Africa and South America when you were in the military."

"How do you know about Africa and South America?"

The old guy gave me another *you're-a-moron* look. "I just moved you from one parallel world to another. Did you really think your paperwork would thwart me?"

"Right," I rasped out slowly.

"As I was saying, those were good things."

"And that means I get to live in a new world?"

"It means that we didn't want to see you waste your life and drink yourself to death in the old world."

"Who is *we*?"

"'We is a pronoun, in this case to refer to a group of individuals you're never going to meet; and I'm never going to tell you about."

I gave the sawed-off old fart a dirty look of my own. "This world isn't starting out too hot."

The old man returned the look and said, "This world is rough as hell and will most likely kill you before the week is over."

"So it's not a better place to live?"

"Not really."

"It's just a different place to live?"

The old man's face went blank and in a deadpan tone he added, "Or a different place to die."

"This is nothing like Karma!" I barked at the old coot.

"I told you it wasn't."

I resisted the urge to see how far I could throw him, and it was then I noticed that my head was clear. I was hung-over and felt like crap but quite a bit of time had obviously gone by since I walked into that jail cell. Something had sure as hell happened

"What day is this?" I asked.

"It's Sunday evening."

"What happened in between now and yesterday morning?"

"Well, let's see…we got your paperwork in order…"

"You guys keep paperwork on your interspatial human trafficking?"

"It's not human trafficking."

"What do you call it?

"I call it saving your ass."

"Yeah, right."

"Call it whatever you like, but it's not human trafficking. There's no money in it for us and no one would want to buy you anyway."

I stood and looked at him in a way that should have conveyed that I wouldn't mind killing him. He looked back, unblinkingly; and conveyed that he was in no way afraid of me.

I gave up and asked, "What did you do besides the paperwork?"

"Well, there was the interspatial transfer, and of course, the mental conditioning."

"Mental conditioning?"

"We target centers of the brain to allow you to be more comfortable with the change."

"You brainwashed me?"

"No we didn't brainwash you. That's a crude and time consuming form of manipulation; and we are far more advanced than that."

"But you still mess with my mind to conform to what you want?

"We stimulate certain centers of your brain to allow you to be more open and amenable to the new world and changes around you as opposed to having you running down the street screaming hysterically."

That didn't sound terrible and I had to admit I was more accepting of what was happening than I would have expected to be; so maybe they had done me a favor. I found that I was actually more curious than anything else.

The old guy scratched the gray stubble on his chin and thought for a moment. Finally he said, "Let's get you something to eat."

"I'd rather have a drink," I told him.

"I'm sure you would," replied the old man, "but we are going to find some real food. If you want to crawl back in a bottle you can do it when I'm not around."

I hadn't really thought about getting rid of the old guy, but the thought gave me some hope. "Will that be any time soon?" I asked him.

He looked up at me and smiled from ear to ear. "It will be a lot sooner than you will like," he said in a way that sounded like I had a lesson coming.

I smiled back and asked, "Where are we going?"

The little guy headed for the door and motioned for me to follow. "There's a diner just around the corner. They have really good meat loaf."

Meat loaf sounded surprisingly good. I followed him into the street and squinted a little at the evening sun. There was a huge clock mounted on the corner of the building we were heading toward, and the hands said it was 6:15. It was late September or at least it was before I ended up here, so it would be dark very shortly. I couldn't help turning around and around, looking at the old cars in the street and the way people were dressed. The women all wore skirts or dresses, and they had done their hair like the black-and-white pictures on the wall at my grandfather's house. The men wore coats and ties and hats; nice hats, not some cap with a ball team logo on it. A large percentage of them were smoking cigarettes.

The cars were big and loud and fumey with chrome bumpers and fenders that stuck out from the sides of the hood and had the headlights mounted on top of them. The surrounding structures were around four and five stories but I could see tall buildings rising in the background so it looked like we were somewhere on the edge of the city. The buildings where we were walking were mostly brick and almost all of them had big windows at ground level. They were painted with all sorts of logos and store names. I was surprised to discover how much I was enjoying it. It gave me a comfortable feeling, like being with my grandfather.

I followed the old man around the corner and saw the diner he was heading for. It was one of those old restaurants made out of a railroad car, and it looked like a picture on a postcard. We went inside and looked for a seat.

The diner looked old, but it didn't feel old. The walls were paneled with dark wood, and on one long side there were small booths. On the opposite side was a counter with round swivel stools mounted in front of it. The booths were made of wood, and the cushions looked like they might even be leather. The tops of the stools were covered with the same material. The aisle between the stools and the booths was just wide enough to accommodate a guy my size. Everything was well-worn but clean.

"This is kind of nice," I said, looking around.

The old man pointed to two stools at the counter, and we sat down.

"It can be nice," he agreed. "There are good middle-class people here." He started to say something else but stopped when the waitress brought us our menus.

"The coffee's fresh," she said, giving each of us the eye. "Tonight's special is tuna surprise."

We both ordered a cup of coffee, and she headed off. I suddenly realized that I might have trouble paying for this.

I turned to the old man, but he was busy looking at the waitress's butt as she was bent over fishing around for something in a cabinet.

"Hey," I barked, trying to get the old fart's attention.

"What?" he asked, not bothering to turn and look at me.

"How do I pay for this?"

"I'll pay for this one," he said. The waitress had leaned over onto one foot and the old guy's head leaned with her.

"Is that what you meant when you said I wouldn't last the week? I don't have any money so I'm going to starve to death."

The waitress finally stood up and went over to the coffee pot. The old fart spun his seat around to face me. "No, that's not what I meant."

"Here you are," interrupted the waitress, as she set the cups down on the counter.

We both nodded, and the old man waited to see if she was going to do anything interesting. When he realized she wasn't, he turned back to me. "If you check your wallet you'll find that you have new identification and twenty dollars in cash."

"Will twenty bucks get me to Friday?" I asked.

"It will last out the month if you don't spend it on booze."

"So that sign that says this cup of coffee is a dime isn't a mistake?"

"No, it's not a mistake. You can look around if you want to, but you won't find any specialty shops where you can buy a pretentious cup of coffee for six dollars. Coffee has been a dime for a long time, and it will still be a dime for a long time to come."

"Was it that way in my world?"

"It was. Haven't you heard the expression, 'That and a dime will get you a cup of coffee?'"

"No."

"What a surprise."

I ignored him. I had always enjoyed a good cup of black coffee and getting it for a dime was a real bonus.

"Check your identification," said the old man.

I looked down to get my wallet and saw that my clothes were different. My jeans were now green corduroy and the Bears sweatshirt I had been wearing had become a t-shirt with a green-plaid flannel shirt over it. My sneakers had been replaced by a pair of worn-looking brown leather shoes. "What happened to my clothes?" I yelped. It came out louder than I wanted, and the waitress turned around to look at me. I straightened my shirt and smiled at her. She stared a moment and then went back to work.

"You couldn't wear the same clothes you had on," said the old fart. "The style of jeans you were wearing won't exist for another forty years, and there is no Chicago so there is no Chicago Bears. The football team here is the New Egan Admirals. You might be interested to know that the popular game at this time is baseball. "

"That would be the New Egan..."

"Captains," finished the old man. "Now, if you are satisfied with the local sports franchises, check your identification."

I pulled my wallet out and looked inside. The wallet was mine but everything inside was different. "Going by the sports teams and this ID, I live in New Egan, Illinois," I read aloud.

"You do now," agreed the old guy.

"My social security number is different," I told him, pulling the card out, and looking at it.

"At this time, Social Security is still a new concept. Your old number hadn't been used yet, so it had to be changed. The upside is that if you manage to grow old in this world, you will probably be able to collect the Social Security that is due you."

"This world doesn't look that bad," I said. I scanned around the room and caught sight of a dark-haired woman sitting alone in a booth. She was really gorgeous and looked like money which seemed out of place in a blue-collar diner. "Not bad at all," I said again.

"She is nice, isn't she?" said the old man. He didn't even bother to turn around and look. He just blew in his coffee and twirled a spoon in it.

"She is."

The old coot took a sip of his coffee and said, "There are a lot of good people in this world. As I was telling you, you will find a lot of good middle-class people here. That's something your old world was sadly lacking. "

"So, what's bad about this world?"

"In a nutshell: the government is corrupt, and the crime is a lot worse. Most of the time you'll find they go hand-in-hand."

"That doesn't sound like anything I can't handle."

"Oh no," said the old fart, stretching it out sarcastically. "With your command of history, the English language and your insatiable desire to drink yourself to death, this should be a breeze."

"And here I was thinking you didn't like me."

"My opinion of you has nothing to do with it. You're in a new place, and you're going to have to blend in."

The old man twirled his spoon in his coffee with his right hand and scratched his crotch with the other. "Oh yeah," I said watching him. "You blend in just fine."

"I don't have any problem," said the old fart as he switched hands and scratched with the right.

"Of course not," I said sarcastically.

"You don't believe me?"

"I believe you have all the social grace of a wet fart."

The ugly little guy didn't even look up. He said, "Do you realize that the only thing smart about you is your mouth?"

"Now you sound like my mother."

The waitress chose that moment to show up with our meatloaf. It wasn't bad. When I wasn't dodging the old man's elbow or wiping his gravy spray from the side of my face, I actually enjoyed the meal. It tasted a little like something Grandma would have made. It had been a long time since I had eaten something I enjoyed that much, and I got lost in the moment. The thought came to me that it had been a long time since I had done that.

The old guy and I managed to finish our meals without insulting each other anymore. I looked around the diner while I finished my second cup of coffee. The beautiful brunette had gotten up and gone to the restroom, so I was stuck with watching the rest of the customers. I was surprised at the number of men that were wearing jackets and ties. All of them had come in wearing a hat. That observation led me to notice that I was the scruffiest guy in the place, or at least one of the two scruffiest if you counted the old man. I don't know how, but the old coot seemed to know what I was thinking.

"There is no "business-casual" in this time period," he said without looking up from his plate.

"I was wondering about that," I said, trying not to sound surprised.

The beautiful dark-haired woman walked past us and out the door. She was wearing a

19

fire engine red blouse and a white skirt. She had on shiny, bright red pumps and stockings with seams that ran up from her high heels up to I only wish I knew where. That was worth watching, and the old coot and I didn't even bother to pretend that we weren't.

As she cleared the front door the old man suddenly got in a hurry.

"All right," he said quickly, throwing some money on the counter and pushing me towards the door. "There are a couple of things you need to know; and we don't have much time, so listen up."

"If we didn't have much time, why didn't you tell me awhile ago," I asked.

"I was eating my meatloaf." The old fart looked at me like I was being stupid.

"So I rank right under meatloaf?"

"On a good day."

I rolled my eyes and said, "I'm listening."

"The second world war ended less than two years ago. Most of the men you meet and a few of the women will have served in that war. They will assume that you probably did, too, and you will be asked about it frequently."

"So what do I say?"

"You were in the Marines so you can tell them that. You can say you served in the South Pacific, but you don't want to go into any details."

"I don't know any details."

"Don't you think that's a good reason not to go into any?" He gave me that same *you're stupid* look and I suppressed the urge to throw him through the window.

"I'm listening," I said again.

Even if you knew the history from your old world you wouldn't want to get too far into the details of it. Just like your world, this world fought a war in Europe and in the South Pacific and most of the locations and battle names are the same but some of the details of the battles are not. You don't want to get caught up in that when talking to people who were actually there."

"So what do I tell them?"

"What do you say when people ask you about what you did in Afghanistan?"

I swallowed hard. "I tell them I don't really want to talk about it."

"That will work just fine. You'll hear that phrase used a lot when people bring up the war."

"Anything else?"

"As I said, sometimes the history is identical, but not always. This also goes for geography. Overall, continents and land masses are the same, but cities and towns may not be where you left them."

"Like this New Egan place?"

"Exactly like that. We are in the same geographical location as Chicago, but that city doesn't exist here."

"Okay, I won't rely on history and geography," I told him.

"It applies to everything else. My advice to you is to not try and invest heavily in stocks and bonds that did well on your world or on sporting events where you believe you know the outcome. Sometimes they will be the same, maybe similar, but they will often be different."

"In other words I don't have any better chance of getting rich here than I did in the old world."

He didn't bother to respond, and we stepped through the front door and into the street. The cool night air felt good.

"Anything else you need to tell me," I asked.

"Yes, in this time period, a blackjack is often referred to as a *sap*."

I felt my face wad up. "Is that something I need to know?" I asked. It was just then that the screaming started.

"Oh yeah," said the old man.

I turned toward the sound and saw two guys grab the beautiful dark-haired woman. I looked back toward the old guy, but he was gone.

I took a deep breath and ran toward the screaming woman.

CHAPTER 4

The diner was set pretty far back from the street, and there was a large concrete plaza-like area between it and the road. It was probably around forty feet between the restaurant and the curb, but it seemed like a mile as I ran toward the trouble.

The two guys man-handling the brunette were big, close to my size. One was wearing a dark coat and pants and the other one wore gray. Both men wore hats but they were having trouble keeping them on. They were trying to put the brunette into the backseat of a big four-door car, and she was making them work for it. She thrashed around, screamed, scratched, kicked; and at one point, managed to bury one of those gorgeous red high heels into Gray Coat's instep. He yelled like she had broken something, and she probably had. I was hoping he wouldn't notice me running up behind him but he turned at the last minute and jumped out of the way as I swung a hard roundhouse punch. I was expecting it would take his head off; but he was too fast and all I did was fan the breeze. Before I could turn he belted me on the side of the head. I stepped back and Gray Coat dropped into a boxer's stance and began shuffling around. This guy was strong, fast, and he knew what he was doing. This wasn't going to be any fun. I moved into him and jabbed for his chin. He sidestepped me and popped me in the eye with a jab of his own. I had to end this quickly, or this guy was going to beat the shit out of me.

It was painfully obvious that the first thing I had to do was quit boxing with him. I could box, and I had done quite a bit of it, but my real fighting skills were in mixed martial arts. I decided to see if Gray Coat knew anything about Wing Chun. I moved straight at him with both hands in front of my face. I jabbed at him and he waved it aside and jabbed back. I blocked it and at the same time I drove my foot into the center of his shin. I was hoping to break it; but he wasn't leaning back enough and the edge of my shoe plowed down his shin and onto the instep that the woman had punched a hole in. I don't know if she broke any bones, but I did. I leaned into it hard and felt something crunch. He pushed me off and tried to go back to his boxing, but that wasn't going to work anymore. His footwork had turned into a hopping limp.

I moved in and jabbed at him. He was able to get out of the way, but when he tried to return the favor I drove my foot into the same shin, and that time I managed to fracture it. He howled and dropped to his knees. I stepped back and then roundhouse kicked him in the head. He pitched over sideways and lay still.

My other buddy in the dark coat wasn't having any luck with the woman. His coat was in tatters, his face was scratched on both sides, and his hat was gone. She had managed to drag him a few feet back from the car, and just as I started toward them, she kicked the car door closed. I'm pretty sure he realized he needed to do something quick or he was going to have me and her, both, to deal with. He grabbed the woman by the front of her blouse and pulled something out of his coat that looked like a thick sole from a small shoe. I didn't recognize it as a blackjack until he slapped the brunette on the side of her head with it, and she dropped toward the sidewalk with Dark Coat still hanging onto her. Her blouse ripped and she flopped roughly to the concrete.

I saw all this while I was moving. When Dark Coat looked up I saw the surprise and fear in his face as he realized I was on top of him. He reached into his coat and I grabbed his forearm and pushed it into his chest and then shoved him against the rear quarter panel, pinning his whole body to the car.

I put my nose against his and asked, "You want to try that little toy on me?"

He was a beady-eyed shit and had the mean, cowardly look of a guy that would prefer to shoot you in the back. I was sure that was true since he could have dropped the woman earlier, but he had let his buddy duke it out with me while he watched. I was going to break him in half but I glimpsed a movement just past the side of his head. It caught me completely by surprise. There was another guy in the car, the driver. I don't know why he hadn't stepped in before, but he was digging in his coat for something that I had no doubt he would try to kill me with. I grabbed Dark Coat by what was left of his lapels and smashed him in the face with my forehead. His head snapped back and bounced off the edge of the car's roof. I twisted him a little to the right and tried as hard as I could to stuff him into the open rear window of the car. That put him between me and the driver, and it was none too soon. The driver fired twice, and I could tell where the bullets had gone by the look on Dark Coat's face. As he went limp I reached into his coat and pulled his gun from the shoulder holster. I hooked my arm around, stuck the pistol through the open front window and fired blindly. The driver yelled, the motor revved, tires squealed and the car took off leaving me holding Dark Coat. I dropped him in the street, threw his gun on top of him, and went to check on the woman.

The attempted kidnapping and my little show had started to draw a crowd. People were hovering around the brunette and they moved aside as I walked over and sat down next to her, raised her head and shoulders and brushed the hair from her face. Lord she was beautiful. I could only see a faint red outline where Dark Coat had hit her, but there was a goose egg on the side of her head where she had hit the sidewalk. Her arms and hands were scratched and skinned up but, other than that, she looked okay. I put my palm against the side of her face and patted it a little, in an attempt to wake her up. She stirred for a moment but didn't wake up. It was then I heard someone shout, "Hey!"

It was a big booming voice, but I couldn't see where it was coming from.

"What the hell are you doing!" the voice shouted again, but there was no one there. The crowd parted in the direction of the voice, and we were all looking toward the end of the diner. It sounded like it might be coming from the right hand side of the building. There was a blue wall sticking out to that side, and I figured that whoever was yelling must be behind that wall. Then the wall moved. The crowd actually gasped. I'm pretty sure my eyes bugged out of my head like a character in an old cartoon. I know my mouth hung open. I couldn't believe it. The blue wall was actually a man in a blue suit. He was the biggest man I had ever seen. I've seen taller and maybe I've seen broader, but I had never seen anybody that tall that was that broad. He was six foot six, seven or better and could have used a shower rod for a coat hanger.

"What the hell are you doing with my wife!" he roared, coming toward me at a fast walk.

I'll swear I tried to dig a foxhole in the concrete with my ass.

"If she's hurt your life's over," growled the giant.

He was moving quickly, and I lowered the woman to the sidewalk. I was halfway to my feet and ready to give everyone a good show of a guy running for his life when people in the crowd came to my rescue.

"You got it wrong Mister," yelled out a tall skinny man, "He was helping that woman."

An older lady told him, "It was those other two, there in the street."

A lot more people started calling out things in my defense, and the big guy slowed his roll and walked over to where I was. I sat down next to the woman, again but I didn't pick her up so lovingly.

"Is she okay," asked the big man. There was still an edge of suspicion in his voice.

I nodded and hoped my voice wouldn't squeak when I spoke. "They were trying to push her into a car, but she gave them a hard time."

"That's my Norma," said the giant proudly.

"She should be fine. That guy in the dark coat smacked her in the head with some kind of leathery shoe-looking thing."

"He sapped her?"

"Uhhh, yeah," I said as I recalled the little old man's last words of advice.

"Was it just those two guys?" asked the big man. He jerked his head toward the street.

"Those two and the driver. He took off."

The giant looked down at the woman for a moment and then walked over and looked at the bodies. He knelt down and checked Dark Coat. "This one's dead," he called out. He said it without any emotion. He walked over and knelt down next to Gray Coat. "How bad is this one hurt," he asked.

"I'm pretty sure he's got some busted bones in his left foot and his left shin is probably fractured. When he dropped I caught him in the head with a full spinning back-kick. I don't know how much damage that did."

The big guy's face changed, and it looked like he was pleased. "That explains why the side of his head is purple." There was a little emotion in his voice that time. He seemed pleased that I had hurt this guy. I guess I had saved him the trouble.

"How about the driver?"

"I was using that guy for a shield," I said, pointing at Dark Coat. "I pulled his gun, and fired blind into the car. I think I got a piece of the driver, but not enough to count. He took off as soon I pulled the trigger."

The big man walked back and sat down on the other side of the woman. He cupped the side of her face in his left hand and reached across with the other. "Mike Manzarek," he said, offering me a hand that looked like a catcher's mitt.

"Jake Kowalski."

I shook the huge bear paw as best I could. If the old story about guys with big hands was true then Mike Manzarek was a man to be envied.

"This is Norma," said Mike softly, "Thanks for helping her out. I don't know what I'd do without her."

Norma started to come around and opened her eyes and looked up at us. She jerked for a moment and then realized that Mike was one of the people holding onto her. She relaxed and laid back down on the sidewalk.

"What happened to those guys?" she asked me.

"They're face down in the street," answered Mike. "You and Jake, here, took care of them."

"Who were they? What did they want?"

Mike and I looked at each other and shrugged. "I don't know," said Mike. "I haven't seen either of those guys before."

We were interrupted by the sounds of sirens. It was only moments before two black and white police cars slid to a stop next to Dark Coat's body. The cops jumped out and ran around checking bodies, barking questions, and generally scaring the crap out of everyone before they realized that the crisis was over and the danger had passed. They broke out their notebooks and started making reports.

Three different cops were taking statements, and they didn't seem to care who went first. There were plenty of eye witnesses and we all stood in line and waited for our turn to come up. I was enjoying watching the big guy, Mike, work the cops and the crowd. He was one of those men you automatically liked when you first saw him, one of those lucky guys that people enjoyed being around and hanging out with. He was on a first name basis with almost all the cops, and they didn't mind if he watched and listened while they were interviewing witnesses. The big man also knew a couple people in the crowd and he laughed and joked and smoked with them while we were waiting.

I noticed that everyone seemed to be smoking, at least the men. The air was one big cloud of cigarette smoke and if anybody was bothered by it, they didn't show it. I had heard people say that smoking used to be a lot more popular, but I had no idea it was this big of a deal. Some of the nearby billboards were advertising different brands of cigarettes, and it looked like you could walk up to anybody, ask for a light and expect to get it. Nobody minded where the butts went, either. People flicked them into the bushes and into the streets, and the cops didn't even blink. The middle of the twentieth-century was going to take some getting used to.

Two ambulances pulled up and four medics got out. After a moment of gathering the facts, all four of them rushed over and started tending to Norma. They fell all over each other trying to give her medical attention until one of the two cops, that was already tending to whatever Norma's legal needs might be, yelled that the gray-coated man lying in the street had been seriously injured. The medics huddled together and had a heated discussion that I couldn't hear, but I'm sure it was about who arrived first. Finally, two of the medics went back over to Gray Coat and loaded him onto a stretcher, put him into their ambulance, turned on the lights and siren and drove off.

Despite their best efforts to render more medical attention to Norma, she waved off the remaining two guys and walked toward the line of witnesses. They stood and watched her walk away; I couldn't blame them for that, and then they got back into their ambulance and left.

Mike was talking to some guy in a brown suit, so Norma crossed over to where I was standing.

"Hi sailor, new in town?" she asked with a smile that set the night on fire.

"Actually, I am," I admitted. I didn't realize my mouth was hanging open until a bug flew in it.

"Well Jake, is that right, Mike called you Jake?"

"That's right," I told her.

"Well Jake, I'm sure glad you did. I might not be here if you hadn't."

I turned my head and pretended to cough while I tried to get the bug out of my mouth. When I twisted back around I asked, "Any idea what those guys wanted?"

"Not a clue," she said, shaking her head back and forth. "It's usually Mike that has people trying do him harm. I'm his number one fan, but I try not to get too deep into the physical side of his business."

Before I could ask her what *his business* was, Mike finished talking to Brown Suit and started walking toward us. He took one last drag off his cigarette and flicked what was left into the gutter.

"How you doin' kid?" He clapped his hands against the sides of my shoulders and inspected me like a big kid looking at a stuffed toy.

"I'm okay."

"Everyone is telling the same story you told me; so just tell it again and you're in the clear."

"I will," I told him.

"Thanks again for helping Norma." He looked over at her and you could see it was a look that meant something. "I owe you one," he said; looking back at me. I could see he meant that, too.

"You don't owe me anything," I told him. "I'm just glad I could help."

At that moment, a cop standing in front of his black-and-white pointed at me and motioned that it was my turn.

I told my story just the way it had happened, and the policeman seemed satisfied. He was an older cop who reminded me a lot of the one that had locked me up the night before. He seemed like a nice guy, one of those cops who wish everyone would just behave so he wouldn't have to step in and deal with it. We were leaning over the big hood and fender of his squad car, where he was writing things down on a small notepad. "Do you have any identification, Mr. Kowalski?"

A lump jumped into my throat and then I remembered that the old toothless guy had given me new ID. I handed the sergeant my driver's license. He looked at it a moment, frowned and then turned the license toward me so I could see it.

"Is this still your address?" he asked.

The license was just a heavy piece of paper and looked old and worn. There was no plastic, no holograms, no computer printout, just some lines where someone had filled in the information with an old typewriter. I looked at it and saw that the address had been smudged, and I couldn't make anything out of it. I guess the cop couldn't either and wanted me to make something out of it for him. There was no way that was going to happen. If I hadn't been looking at the license, I wouldn't have remembered I was in New Egan, Illinois. I didn't even know the name of the street I was standing on. "No sir, I don't live there anymore," I stammered. It didn't come out as good as I hoped. It sounded like I was hiding something.

The old cop locked eyes with me and asked, "Where are you living now?"

I couldn't look him in the eye. I tried to tell him the truth as best I could. "I just got into town," I said, looking down at the car. I started to perspire, but I didn't want to wipe my forehead for fear of the cop noticing.

"Where are you coming from," he asked.

"I couldn't really say," I said nervously. I tried to think of something I could tell him, but anything I could think of would have been a shot in the dark. If I called out the name of something that didn't exist I would dig a hole I couldn't get out of. I said nothing. I was standing next to the squad car's fender, and I just kept looking down at the headlight mounted on top of it. I ran my hands nervously around the light as if it was clay and I could make something else out of it. The old cop closed his notebook and came around the front of the car until he was right next to me. I figured this was the part where he would tell me I was lying and if I wasn't going to tell him the truth he was going to take me to the police station and sweat me until I did. It never occurred to me that he had mistaken my nervousness for something else.

"There's no need to be embarrassed or ashamed," said the old guy in a soft voice.

"Ashamed…ashamed of what?" I thought, but I didn't say a word.

"A lot of vets have to go to where the work is, and they're riding the rails looking for something. It's not the same as when guys did it in the thirties, and you shouldn't be ashamed of it either way."

I was so relieved I almost laughed out loud. I bit into my cheek and tried to keep a straight face. "I appreciate your saying that," I told him.

"Do you have work here in town," he asked.

"Not yet," I answered honestly.

The sergeant fished in his pocket and pulled out a business card. He handed it to me and said, "This is an employment outfit here in the city. Sometimes they can help."

"That's nice of you," I told him, "thanks."

"Don't mention it, and don't give up," he said putting his hand on my shoulder, "something will come up."

I nodded and tried to smile my best hopeful smile. He walked off, and I finally wiped the sweat off of my forehead. I turned around and found a familiar blue wall. I tilted my head back and looked up at Mike Manzarek. He was smiling like he had just remembered the punch line to a joke.

"Why don't you throw that card away and take this one," said the big man. He held out a business card that looked like a postage stamp in his big hand. I took it and read out loud, "Manzarek Investigations, Inc., We Specialize in Discreet Information Gathering and Solutions to Difficult Problems."

"You're a private investigator?" I asked.

"I am, and a lot more," replied Mike. "I do a lot of problem solving for people."

"What kind of problems," I asked him.

"There are a lot of things in this world that need to be taken care of," said the big guy. "Taken care of by someone who can be trusted to do the right thing and keep quiet about it."

"And you want me to do that?"

"No, I want you to fetch coffee and kiss my ass while I do it," he said quickly, smiling even broader.

He really was a likable son-of-a-bitch. I looked at the ground, chuckled, and shook my head back and forth.

"On the level," said Mike, "I need somebody that I can trust; somebody with a sense of honor, somebody that I know can take care of himself. You already proved that you're all of these things."

"You got all of that out of what happened tonight?" I asked, surprised.

"That and more. There were a lot of people standing in the street, when I got here, but only one of them had put his life in danger to help a woman he didn't know."

"It sounds pretty honorable when you say it," I told him.

"How does it sound when you say it?"

"Like I'm crazy as hell."

His smile returned. "I don't think one excludes the other. Seriously, the pay is mediocre, but I can throw in room and board. I have a guest house out back of my place, and it's not a bad spot to hang your hat." He looked at me and made a face. "You do have a hat, don't you?"

"I'm between hats at the moment," I told him.

"Well, if you're interested in my offer, we can fix that in the morning. We can take it out of your first paycheck, or maybe the first couple of paychecks. Did I mention that the pay is mediocre?"

I tried but I couldn't help grinning. "Yeah, you mentioned that," I told him.

"Well?" Mike spread his arms wide and acted like I couldn't possibly say no. He was right, I couldn't.

"How could I resist such a generous offer? When do I start?"

"You already have. Consider yourself on the clock when you started tap dancing with those two goons."

I don't know when it arrived, but at some point the Coroner's wagon had pulled up and they were loading up Dark Coat. We walked past it as I walked to the car with Mike and Norma. They hadn't even asked me if I had a car, they had simply invited me to ride with them. I guessed Mike was assuming the old cop was right, that I had been bumming around, jumping on trains and going from town to town looking for work. That cop had done me a big favor. A story like that kept me from having to answer a lot of questions and made it easy to be vague about the ones I did have to answer.

Half-way down the block, Mike stopped in front of a car that was nosed into the curb. It could have easily housed a family of four. The chrome letters across the nose said, "Cadillac".

"This is my tin wheelbarrow," said Mike. He opened the door for Norma, closed it, lit a cigarette and walked around the front and got in. I walked around, the long way, opened the rear door and got in behind him.

It probably handled like river barge, but it was nice and comfortable in the back seat. I wondered if drive-in movies had been invented yet. If they had, this would be the car to go in. "This is a nice ride," I said.

"Thanks," said Mike looking at me in the rear view mirror. "It's a '46'. They started making the 46's when the last M-24 tank came off the line in August of 45. I already had my order in, and I was driving this one in November of 45."

I know they talked about this stuff in history class, but I also know I was sleeping when they did. What I remembered was that a lot of the big factories, like car factories, had stopped making the stuff they usually made and started making things they needed for the war, like tanks, ships, and airplanes.

If I understood what Mike was saying, the place where they made Cadillacs had stopped making Caddies and started making tanks during the war.

It was incredible to think about a war so big that it consumed everything; then again that's why they called it a World War. Everyone had participated, not just the guys with the rifles.

Mike flicked his ashes out the window and shifted gears with the lever on the steering column. I almost laughed out loud. I wasn't ready for a Cadillac with a manual transmission. I guess I found that I had touched on one of Mike's favorite subjects. He was really into Cadillacs.

He told me, "I didn't care that much for the 47's but I hear the 48's are hot. Word has it they used the P-38 for design inspiration. You can't beat that."

I made a mental note to get a little notebook and start writing some of this stuff down. I was going to have to look up "P-38" and find out what that was. It was easy to see that I was going to miss the internet.

We had driven away from the lights of the city, and I was just about to doze off when Mike called out, "This is it."

I looked up and was impressed to see that we were cruising down a beautiful tree lined street with huge houses on both sides. I still didn't know what kinds of problems Mike solved for people, but apparently they were expensive problems. He was doing well. The car turned into a big oxbow driveway. The house was two stories with a basement that was partially exposed on one side. The Cadillac turned off the oxbow and into the three car basement garage. There was one other car in the garage that wasn't as new or nice as the one we were in. I sat in the backseat and tried to figure out how many of my old Chicago apartments would fit inside that garage. I'm pretty sure it was three, but it might be more.

We went up the stairs from the garage, and I got an abbreviated tour of part of the first floor of the house as we walked to the back door and onto the patio. The back yard was plenty big. It not only had a guest house sitting in it, but there was enough left over space to have plenty of green grass and a tennis court.

"Norma plays tennis," said Mike, lighting a cigarette and pointing at the court with the burning match. "I can't stand it, but she has friends over to play and she says it keeps her in shape."

I just nodded. I didn't dare do anything else.

The guest house was really nice. It had good furniture, expensive furniture, and was pretty to look at. The floors were hardwood topped with rugs that felt softer than most of the beds I had ever slept in. The kitchen was full of old looking, but new, appliances.

"Towels and toiletries are in the hall cabinet," said Mike. "Sometimes people come to visit and forget to bring a razor or toothbrush, so I keep all that stuff in the cabinet. If you need something it's probably in there." He knew I didn't have any of that stuff, but he just acted like I had come with a full set of luggage. I appreciated it. It came to me that I was going to have to work hard to make this up to him.

"If you need anything, there's a buzzer over there in the kitchen. Esmerelda, the housekeeper and cook, starts at 5:30 in the morning, and she can help you with anything you need."

He started walking to the door and I said, "Mike, I really..."

"Save it," said the big man softly. He stopped without turning around. "Get some sleep. We've got a lot to do tomorrow. We have to get you a hat." He bounced his index finger off the side of his head and stepped past the door and closed it behind him.

I went to the hall closet and got everything I didn't have, which was everything. The towels were big and fluffy, and the toothpaste smelled like peppermint. The razor was one of those jobs where you screw the bottom and the top opens up like two big barn doors. The blade is loose and you set it inside and close the barn doors. The package it came in called it a Safety Razor. I didn't see anything safe about it.

The bathroom was white tile and shiny. The bathroom sink was big and clunky and just stuck out of the wall. There was no cabinet or pedestal, just the sink and some plumbing. There were two separate knobs and faucets for the hot and cold water. It took a second to figure out that I had to put a plug in the sink, a real rubber plug with a little chain on it no less, and run the hot and cold water until it mixed to the temperature I liked. I splashed the water on my face and it felt really good, especially where that guy had smacked me in the eye. In hindsight, I should have paid more attention to the water that ran down my elbows onto the floor. The tub was a big cast iron job with high sides, and it occurred to me that I couldn't remember the last time I had soaked in a hot bathtub.

It had been a long, weird-assed day and night and I was asleep on my feet. I decided it would feel good to sit in hot water and maybe sort out what had happened to me.

I stripped off my shirt, pants, and skivvies, and then sat down on the toilet to pull my socks off. I had just gotten them off and thrown them in the corner when the bathroom light chose that moment to burnout. There was a little glow of light coming in from the living room, and I stood up wondering where the hell I was going to find the spare bulbs when I stepped in one of the puddles of water I had made on the floor. My foot left the tile like I had hit black ice, and I flew sideways into the wall over the bathtub. I heard something crack as my head connected with the tiled wall, and I slid down into the tub. I lay there for a moment with my head roaring in pain and my feet sticking up over the side of the tub. After a couple of minutes my feet slid into the bathtub with the rest of me. My head hurt and swam, and I was pretty sure the warm wet feeling on the side of my face was blood.

I didn't feel like moving, I didn't feel like breathing, and for a moment I didn't feel like living. Somewhere around forty-eight hours ago, I had been drinking myself to death in a shit bar in a shit part of Chicago. I had gone from there to putting three guys in the hospital, maybe killing one of them, and after that it had gotten snakeshit weird.

I didn't know for sure where I was but it damned sure wasn't Kansas. There was no little dog, and the Wizard was a semi-toothless little fart in a wife beater t-shirt that didn't give a shit about what happened to me. I have been in some bad places and I have been scared for my life more than a few times; but I had no idea what was happening to me and after a minute or two I started to cry.

I'm embarrassed to write this down; but it's the truth. I cried and shook and called out to anyone who would help me but no one answered. I have no idea who I was calling out to, but I called. I don't know how long I laid there, sobbing like a baby, but after a while I finally stopped crying and went to sleep. I slept there; face down in the bathtub, the rest of the night.

I woke up to the sound of a woman screaming.

CHAPTER 5

My eyes snapped open, and I tried to lift my head but I couldn't. My face was stuck to the bottom of the bathtub. I tried again and felt my skin peel away from the porcelain. Judging by the looks of the bathtub I was stuck to it by my own blood.

The screaming was coming from inside the bathroom, and I raised my head to see who it was. I came up too quickly and banged the crown of my head on the damned bathtub faucet. My vision swam, and my skull felt like it caught fire. I doubled up in the bathtub and held my throbbing head. It radiated pain as if it was a huge boil. The screaming kept on going, and I managed to hook my arm on the edge of the bathtub, the sides were really high, and raise myself up. In the middle of the bathroom floor was a pretty little Latin woman. I estimated her to be in her mid-twenties, and I couldn't help thinking that she was very striking despite the fact she was sounding off like one of those steam whistles in the old factories.

I tried to say something, but even I couldn't hear it. I didn't have the ability to make a noise louder than the one she was making, so I just peeked over the top of the bathtub and looked at her. She had long, dark, wavy hair, and was wearing a cotton dress with pictures of flowers on it, that showed off a very nice shape.

Mike came bursting into the bathroom. He was in his boxer shorts and a t-shirt and holding a semi-automatic pistol. At that point my arm slipped, and I slid back into the tub.

Thank God, he was able to make a louder noise than the little Latina.

"Esmerelda!" he bellowed, in a voice so low it made the tub rumble. The little woman stopped in mid cry and turned and looked at him.

"What are you screaming about?"

She turned and pointed at the tub. I managed to pull my head up above the side of the bathtub, and she moved her finger to indicate it was me that was causing her distress.

I tried to talk and found my lips were stuck together. I tried again, and when they came apart I said, "Morning."

"What in the hell happened to you?" asked Mike. He looked at me like I had a cabbage for a head. It probably would have been an improvement.

"I slipped and fell," I told him. I banged my head and I..." I didn't want to admit that I had cried myself to sleep so I said, "...I don't remember anything after that."

"Holy shit," Mike hissed. "This floor is slick as glass when it's wet. There is supposed to be a mat...Esmerelda, donde esta la...oh," he said as Esmerelda raised the bath mat she had in her hand.

"Perdoname. No sabia que alguien estaba aqui, esta mañana," said Esmerelda.

"No es tu culpa," said Mike back to her.

"What is she saying," I asked while I tried, and failed, to get up onto the edge of the tub. Mike laid his gun on the toilet tank and moved to give me hand. "She's sorry that she didn't bring the bath mat earlier. I told her it wasn't her fault. I didn't tell her you were here until just a little while ago." He grabbed my arm from the side of the tub and pulled me up. When he did, Esmerelda started yelling and ran out of the room.

"Shit," barked Mike. "I didn't realize you didn't have any clothes on."

"I usually take a bath that way," I replied.

"Well your sense of humor is working." Mike helped me over the edge of the tub and sat me on the toilet seat.

"How bad is it," I asked.

The big man looked at me for a moment and said, "You're going to need that sense of humor." He opened the mirrored cabinet, above the sink, and passed me a hand mirror.

"Holy hell!" I hollered. "No wonder she was screaming." My face was mostly covered with dried blood, and a lot of my hair was matted with it. My right eye was black and swollen, from where Gray Coat tagged me, and there was a huge lump on the side of my head where I had banged it off the bathroom wall.

Mike grabbed a towel from the rack and threw it over my lap. He walked to the doorway and yelled, "Esmerelda!" The little woman returned and tried not to look in my direction, but she finally did and when she saw I was covered up she relaxed a little.

Mike told her, "I saw Dr. Hebert go into the Dawkin's house about twenty minutes ago. He's checking on little Billy who's got the mumps."

Esmerelda nodded and asked, "You want me to get him?"

"Yes, please. He'll try and tell you that he's too busy, but don't let him get away. Tell him it's important."

"Si," said Esmerelda, and she was gone.

The big guy turned around and grabbed a washcloth off the rack and ran water over it in the sink. "Let's see if we can get you cleaned up a little, before the doctor gets here." As he turned he looked at the wall above the tub. He stopped, and then he whistled. "You did a number on the wall," he said, pointing at a spot.

The bathroom walls were made up of three-inch square white tiles, and where he was pointing two of them were busted.

"Well, we know your head is harder than bathroom tile." He started trying to clean the blood out of my hair, and I tried to keep from yelling. I failed.

"I guess that hurts," said the big guy.

"Everything above my neck hurts," I told him.

Mike looked at me a second and then reached over the bathtub and turned the water on. He played with the hot and cold knobs for a moment, and then I heard the shower hiss. "Let's try this," he said.

He helped me into the shower, and I let the spray clean me off. I was unsteady and Mike stood outside the tub and held my arm while I rolled my head around under the shower-head. It was a little awkward to have another man holding onto me while I showered.

Mike must have known what I was thinking. He was standing there with a shit eating grin on his face, and when I turned my head to look at him he said, "Don't get any ideas. I've showered with better looking men than *you*."

I started to laugh but skyrockets started ricocheting off the inside of my skull. I grabbed my head with my free hand and yelled, "Owww shit! Don't make me laugh, you bastard."

There were a couple of spots where I couldn't even stand to have the water touch me, but after a few minutes we got my hair cleaned up and most of my face.

Mike handed me a towel, and sat me down on the toilet.

"How do I look," I asked him.

"Considering you tangled with two professional thugs and a tile wall, I guess you look alright." He thought for a moment and smiled. "You know, I never saw you until after you fought with those two guys. It's possible you always looked like shit."

I grabbed my head. It throbbed like an open wound. "You bastard, stop making me laugh."

He probably wasn't done screwing with me, but someone in the other room called out his name. "Are you here," asked the voice.

"We're in the bathroom, Dr. Hebert."

I had heard Mike send for the doctor, but I still couldn't believe it, even as I watched him walk into the bathroom -- a doctor actually doing his business at people's homes. I had heard my grandmother say that they used to do it, but I couldn't accept that I was actually seeing it. He had one of those big black leather bags like the doctors, in cartoons, carry. He was probably fifty-something, thick in the middle and his hair was running away from him. He seemed like a decent fellow, someone you felt you could trust right away.

"Hello, Mike," said the doctor, sticking out his hand.

"Doctor Hebert, thanks for coming," said Mike grabbing the doctor's hand and dragging him over to me. "This is Jake Kowalski. He's had a tough night, can you fix him up?"

"Hello," said the doctor. He reached into his coat pocket, pulled out a pair of wire-rimmed glasses and started looking me over.

He wasn't really waiting for me to say anything but I said, "Hello," back to him anyway.

He touched me on the sides of my face, moved my head back and forth, and then pulled the hair away from the place where I tagged the wall. It was on the right side where my forehead ends and my hair starts. I made a little grunting noise as he poked around the spot. He let go and reached into his bag for a little light, and used it to look into my eyes. He stuck his finger in front of my face and asked me to follow it as he moved it around. I did as he ordered, and then he put his light into the bag and went back to looking at my face. He squinted his eyes, and his mouth twisted around like he had bitten into something that tasted bad. He turned and looked at the big man. "Mike, did you do this?"

The question didn't seem to surprise the big guy. He shook his head and said, "No, Doctor Hebert, I didn't do that. Two guys were trying to run off with Norma last night. Jake took on both of them. Sometime in the middle of the night, we're not sure when, he decided to redecorate the bathroom wall with his head."

"I'm sorry," said the doctor. "I had to ask, you know. It wouldn't be the first time that you asked me to patch up one of your dance partners."

"I only do that to the criminal element," said Mike. He said it like it was just a matter of fact and didn't need any explanation. He didn't give any.

"Uh-huh," said the doctor. He turned back to me and started looking in my eyes again. He grabbed my eyelids, top and bottom, and pulled until my eyes bugged out. "Mr. Kowalski doesn't appear to have a concussion. I'm going to put a stitch or two in that gash on his head. It will probably leave a little scar, but his hair will grow back and cover it...for a few years," he added, pointing to the same spot on his head where the hair had receded back from it.

The doctor chuckled, Mike chuckled, and I just sat on the toilet half naked and watched the show. It was a little weird to sit and listen to them talk about what they were going to do, like I was Mike's kid or little brother, but it had been a weird day and night, and this was the least of it, so I just sat there and let them do it. I couldn't tell if the doctor gave me something to deaden the pain. He did at least a dozen things that felt like he was driving a needle through my skull.

"That ought to do it," the doctor said, finally. "That should heal without much of a scar. You can come to my office in 4 or 5 days, and we'll take those stitches out for you."

It suddenly occurred to me that this wasn't a military doctor that would just patch me up and send me on my way. This was a civilian doctor that was going to want to be paid, and I didn't even have medical insurance in Chicago, much less New Egan. I swallowed hard and asked, "How much do I owe you, Doctor Hebert?"

Before he could answer, Mike threw an arm around the doctor's shoulders and said, "That reminds me, I need to talk to you about something." He ushered the doctor out of the bathroom before anyone could say a word. I couldn't hear what was being said, but I was sure that the big guy was squaring my bill with the doctor. I swore then and there that I would make this up to Mike Manzarek if it took me until the 21st century.

CHAPTER 6

Mike had yelled out to finish getting ready and that breakfast would be in thirty minutes. I brushed my teeth, shaved, and put back on the same, and what I now realized were slightly smelly, clothes. I walked into the back door of the big house which went through a laundry room and then opened into a corner of the kitchen. Mike was sitting at a small table reading a newspaper. He laid the paper down and saw all the little pieces of toilet paper stuck to my face.

I had been right; there was nothing safe about that razor. I had finally gotten the hang of it but not before I had done a hack-job on my face.

"First time shaving?" asked Mike. He shook his head and went back to the paper.

"I always have trouble with a new razor," I said, giving him my prefab story.

"Uh huh...well eat up, we've got a busy day ahead of us."

He didn't have to tell me twice. I could smell the Huevos Rancheros before Esmerelda put them in front of me. As she set the plate down, she saw all the little pieces of paper and made a face. She turned and looked at Mike and he just shrugged and kept to his paper. "Why are you so mean to your face?" she asked. "You have a nice face. You should try not to hurt it so much." She smiled and I smiled back. She was a very pretty woman, around five-foot-three, with big liquid brown eyes and black wavy hair.

The meal was incredible. I ate like I had just discovered food.

Within twenty minutes I was full, Esmerelda was happy that I liked her cooking, Mike was done with the paper and we were in the car heading toward the city. It was cool outside, and we had the windows cracked, just a little, to let out Mike's cigarette smoke.

"You know," he said, acting like he was about to say something that just occurred to him, but I was pretty sure it was as prefabricated as my razor story. "When I'm looking for a new hat, I always like to get a haircut first. That way I get the perfect fit."

I was looking out of the passenger window, and I smiled. It wasn't hard to figure this was Mike's way of saying I needed a haircut. My hair wasn't really long, but it was pretty scruffy in comparison to all the other men I saw on the street. It didn't take a giant mental leap to draw the conclusion that the war had something to do with it. The night before, I had noticed that a lot of men had short, military-style cuts, and none had long hair. I was used to being in the military and having short hair, so a haircut was the least of my problems.

"That sounds like a good idea," I said.

"Do you have a barber, you like?" asked Mike.

"No, I'm between barbers," I said.

"Well, that's no problem. My barbershop is on the way."

Just a couple of miles from Mike's house, he nosed the Cadillac into a parking spot in front of a building with a long plate glass window that said Benny's Billiards.

"Where's the barbershop," I asked, as I got out of the car.

Mike pointed straight at the building and said, "Right there."

I gave him a funny look, and he added, "Well not this end. The barbershop is on the other end."

I looked down past the larger plate glass window and saw a much smaller window with the lettering, "Benny's Barbershop".

"Check this out," said Mike, pointing to our left.

On the other side of the pool hall was another window that said, "Benny's Bar and Grill."

"This guy, Benny, gets around," I said, walking toward the spinning striped pole in front of the barbershop.

"That's Benny Shapiro," Mike informed me. "He and I were in the same outfit in the Army. He swore that if he made it back home alive he would open up a combination barbershop, bar and pool hall."

"Looks like he made it."

"Yup. He said that, one way or another, this would get everybody's money. He comes in at night and tends bar."

The door next to the striped barber pole was propped open, and we went inside. The walls between the establishments had been opened, and you could walk through the pool hall and into the bar like it was one big club. There were three or four men in the barbershop and maybe seven or eight more guys shooting pool and drinking coffee next door. When they saw Mike, everybody started yelling at once.

"Hey!" yelled Mike, above the noise of the crowd. When the noise died down a little, he said, "It's not my fault you boys bet against the Yankees Saturday night. That was just the fifth game, they'll take the whole series; you watch."

The hollering started up again, but the big man wasn't paying any attention to it. There were four chairs,

but only two barbers at work. One was giving a haircut and the other a shave. Mike shouted to the one cutting hair, "Bert, can you work my friend in?"

Bert looked at me, nodded and said, "Eddie is next, but your friend can go after that."

"Eddie owes me two dollars for betting against the Yankees Saturday night," Mike informed the room.

It wasn't hard to figure out who Eddie was. He was a slim, decent looking blonde guy sitting in a chair watching two other guys shoot pool. After Mike spoke, Eddie hung his head and shook it slowly. Everyone else in the place pointed at him and yelled out their opinion of the Dodgers, of Eddie, and what they would do with an extra deuce.

"Eddie," yelled Mike, "if you let my friend go in front of you, we can forget the two bucks."

Eddie's face lit up and he made a sweeping gesture with his arm that meant the way was clear, and he was off the hook for his gambling debt.

By that time the guy getting a haircut was already out of the chair and paying. The barber snapped his sheet, and I was up.

The barber fastened the sheet around my neck and asked, "What's your pleasure?"

I was really tired of sticking out, and all I wanted to do was blend in. The barber chairs faced into the pool hall, and I scanned the crowd for a good representative. I finally jerked my nose toward a point in the mob and said, "How about you make me look like Eddie."

"Shit!" exclaimed Bert the barber. "To look that ugly, you're gonna have to beat on your face a lot more than you already have." Everyone laughed, and the room exploded again with everybody's opinion on just how ugly Eddie was.

Bert said, "I can give you a flattop like his. Will that be good enough?"

"It will," I told him.

The barber went to work, and I watched Mike start to perform the same magic that he had done the night before. Everybody wanted to ask him something, everybody wanted to tell him something, and in between, they hung on every word he said. He owned the room and was in control of everything and everyone.

"Wally," Mike called out to a man sitting in the corner. "Where have you been? I haven't seen you in weeks."

Before Wally could answer, various members of the crowd started to answer for him.

"Wally can finally leave the house now that his wife is visiting her sister in Milwaukee."

"You should let her know who wears the pants in the family, Wally."

"Wally wears pants, he just doesn't have anything to put in them."

"Word is, he got it shot off in Germany."

"That's what I heard. Some madam shot it off when he was jumping out of a whorehouse window in Dusseldorf."

I never did hear Wally say anything. I don't think he even tried. He was an owlish looking fellow with a round balding-head and wire-rimmed glasses. He seemed perfectly happy to smile good naturedly and let the foolishness follow its course. I enjoyed being there. I hadn't felt that comfortable with a group of men since leaving the Marines.

Bert turned my mop of dark brown hair into a gung ho military looking flattop. He squirted something into his hands that smelled pretty good, and rubbed it into the scrub brush that was now the top of my head.

"That ought to do it," said Bert, whipping the sheet off of me.

I stood up and looked in the mirror. It didn't look too bad. I ran my hand across the top of my head and Bert said, "I can get you a carpenter's square and a level if you want to check it."

"You better check it," yelled Eddie, "He always cuts mine lopsided."

"Yours is different," Bert retorted. "When I give you a square haircut, I follow the shape of your head."

That lit the place up, again, and everybody started yelling out blockhead jokes, but I couldn't understand any of it with everyone hollering at once.

I handed Bert a dollar and got sixty cents change. I didn't like having to do without the internet and cell phones, but dime coffee and forty-cent haircuts I could get used to.

The crowd was still squawking at Eddie when Mike and I hit the street.

Just to make conversation I asked, "Do you have any bets on the next game of the series?"

Mike shook his head. "No, the writing's on the wall about who's going to win this one. I was surprised Eddie bet against them on the fifth game. He's a pretty savvy guy and tight with his money."

"Not according to the consensus of the crowd inside," I reminded him.

"You can't pay any attention to that bunch of wise-acres. Eddie's a handy guy to know."

"That right?" I asked, just to hold up my end of the conversation.

"He drives his own taxi. He got his start running a small loan business in the Army."

"Loan Shark?"

"Nah, Eddie's rates were reasonable, not much higher than a bank's, and I don't think he had anyone's legs broken."

"But he still made good money?"

"He did. When he mustered out he came straight back here and bought his own cab and license."

"That sounds pretty savvy alright. Why do you say he's handy to know?"

The big man struck a paper match against a matchbook and lit a cigarette. "Since he drives a cab you can figure that he gets around."

"I guess he would hear a lot of stuff doing that."

"He does," he replied, waving his paper match until it went out and then flipping it toward the street.

"Plus he's got the gift of gab and people tell him all sorts of things that they should keep to themselves. That's why I say he's handy to know. I've bought quite a bit of information off of him this last year."

We jumped in the car and a short ride later we pulled up in front of a small clothing store.

"Thank God that we don't have any of that damned clothes rationing like the British were having," exclaimed Mike, as he got out of the car. "We'd have to fix you up with some of my hand-me-downs."

It was all I could do to keep from asking him what he was talking about. I made a mental note to find out about rationing right after I found out what a P-38 was. "I don't think your hand-me-downs will fit me," I said, overstating the obvious.

"We could make it work, raise the cuffs and pad the chest with newspaper."

I couldn't help myself. "Why couldn't I just do what you do and fill it up with hot air and bullshit?"

I thanked God that my new boss had a sense of humor. Mike spluttered and almost lost the cigarette he was taking a drag from. "Oh a funny man," he choked out. "I've got Milton Berle working for me now. This is really a surprise. I had no idea that wad of hair Bert cut off was the cork keeping the gas in your head."

I mentally added Milton Berle to the P-38 list.

A guy in a sharp looking suit was standing next to the door of the clothing store, and Mike called out to him, "Hey, Mickey, can you believe it? Thousands of servicemen looking for work and I had to go and hire Bob Hope here."

Mickey had on his best salesman's grin and stuck his hand out as we approached. "Corporal Mickey Crowley, Mr. Hope, it's a pleasure to meet you. I caught your show with the USO in London."

"Jake Kowalski," I said, shaking his hand.

Crowley rubbed his hands together and asked, "What can I do for you fellows?"

Mike said, "My friend Jake just got a haircut and he needs a hat to go over it."

"I can handle that," said Crowley.

"I had a feeling you could," returned Mike. "While you're at it, you might as well get him a jacket and pants to match the hat."

"Mike...," I started to protest, but he stopped me.

"I don't want to hear it. I can't have you running around looking like Lil' Abner."

If I didn't get to a pencil and paper sometime soon I was never going to be able to keep up.

"Besides," the big man added, "when you see how hard I'm going to work you, you'll realize that you got the shit-end of the stick."

"If you say so."

"I say so. Fix him up Mickey."

We went inside, and forty-five minutes later I walked out wearing a new hat, shirt, shoes, coat and one of two pairs of pants. Mickey was holding another coat with two pair of pants on layaway.

Mike caught me by the arm and started brushing something off the shoulders of my coat. "Now you look like a working man."

"What did I look like before?"

Mike chuckled. "Shit, first you were a comedian, now you're a straight man. Pick a career and stay with it."

I could see my reflection in the store window, and I checked out my new look. I had gotten used to not giving a shit about what I was wearing. In the Marines, we were expected to keep our uniforms perfect and squared away. I had always taken pride in that, but for the past year I had completely ignored my clothes. As long as my dingus wasn't hanging out and I wasn't cold, I figured my clothes were good to go. It felt good to look sharp again, even if I was 70 years out of style. My coat was a dark blue, my pants were tan and my shirt was white, with the collar open. The hat matched what I was wearing and looked much better than I thought it would. I looked into the window and my grandfather looked back at me. I was suddenly very sorry that he couldn't see me, that he couldn't be here to enjoy the things he used to talk about. I was sorry, and getting sorrier by the minute, that I hadn't paid closer attention to his stories and asked him more questions about the things he did as a young man. It sure would come in handy to know what he knew. I was also sure he would know about Milton Berle and Lil' Abner.

Mike looked at his wristwatch. "It's time to call in."

"You have to check in?"

"I don't have to, but in this business it's a good idea. I call the house every couple of hours and let them know I'm okay and pickup any messages." He tapped a new cigarette out of a pack, lit it, and flipped the match into the gutter.

"You'll need to get used to doing that too. Do you still have the card I gave you?"

I nodded.

"Good, that's the work line. If we're not together, make sure you call in every two or three hours or Norma will send the First Infantry and the Tenth Armor out looking for you."

I nodded again. I was going to miss cell phones even more than I thought I would, but it was nice to know that somebody was watching out for me.

"Now that I'm thinking about it," said Mike, "you should call in now. I'll grab another phone and call some people I know to see if I can get a line on who tried to grab Norma last night."

We walked to a drugstore on the corner and went inside. It was very similar to the drugstore I had found myself in the evening before, except that this one had tile floors. When I thought about it, I couldn't believe I hadn't even been in this world for twenty-four hours. A lot of things had happened and were still happening.

There were three phone booths in the back. One of them was occupied, so Mike and I grabbed the others. I closed the door behind me, took the phone off of its little prong hook and then realized I was going to have to read the instructions to figure out how to use the silly thing. In my own world, I had seen payphones, here and there, but I had never used one or even taken the time to look at one closely. According to the information on the front of the phone, it cost a nickel to make a local call. That seemed fair considering how much trouble I had to go through just to make a call. There were round openings at the top of the phone labeled five, ten, and twenty-five cents. The size of each opening corresponded to the size of the coin you wanted to stick in it so you wouldn't screw it up. I stuck a nickel in the opening and when I did the phone came to life and gave me a dial-tone. I dialed the number on the card, and Esmerelda answered on the third ring.

"Hi Esmerelda," I said. "Mike says it's time for us to call in."

Her voice was as cute as she was and seemed to brighten up when she realized that it was me. "You listen to Mr. Manzerek. He will keep you safe."

"I will. Are there any messages for us?

"Si, Lieutenant Briggs called and said that the man you sent to the hospital is awake. The police are questioning him now. He said Mr. Manzerek can talk to him later this afternoon."

That caught me by surprise. "The police are going to let Mike question that guy?"

"Mr. Manzerek can do many things in this town. He is an important man."

"You don't have to convince me. If he's running for office, I'll vote for him."

There was a sharp rapping noise on the door of the booth, and then it opened. Mike stuck his head in and said, "Tell them I'm going to drop you off in about thirty minutes."

"I thought I was going with you."

"Change of plans, I'll tell you about it in a minute."

To the phone, I said, "Mike says he's dropping me off at the house in about thirty minutes."

It might have been my imagination, but Esmerelda seemed to brighten up even more. "That will be nice. You can have lunch with us."

"I'm looking forward to it."

I hung up and stepped out. Mike was thumbing through a small notebook and mumbling to himself as he wrote something down. When he finally looked up he said,

"What took you so long? I made two calls and took a piss while you were in there."

"I was reading the instructions on the phone."

"That's cute, but I know what you were doing. You were sweet talking Esmerelda, weren't you?"

"Are you talking about the screaming woman that woke me up this morning?"

"That's the one. You be nice to her, she's family."

I smiled. I'm nice to everybody."

"Yeah, there's a guy in the hospital that thinks you're a real sweetheart."

"Oh, shit," I said. That was the message Esmerelda gave me. "The guy I kicked in the head is awake, and the police are questioning him. A lieutenant...what's his name...?"

"Briggs?"

"That's it. He called and said you could talk to the guy later this afternoon."

"Perfect, that fits right in with my plans."

"Are you sure you don't want me to go with you?"

"Very sure, I have something important that I want you to do. Let's get going, I'll tell you on the way."

The big guy set a fast pace, and I had to hustle to keep up. As we walked he fired up a cigarette, and I started to wonder if everybody smoked as much as he did. One glance at the street told me they did. The sidewalk and gutter were littered with butts and matchsticks. The middle of the twentieth century was a very strange place to be.

As we got into the Cadillac Mike said, "I want you to watch Norma this afternoon."

"Shit!" I barked. "I can't believe I didn't even think about it. We shouldn't have left her alone at the house."

"We didn't. I had a buddy of mine keep an eye out. He's been sitting in front of the house since we were having breakfast, this morning."

"I'm glad one of us was thinking."

He grinned. "Don't beat yourself up. You'll get the hang of it."

"I know a few guys with their finger on the pulse of the criminal elements in this town. I'm going to visit a couple of them and see if they can tell me who tried to put the grab on Norma, and why."

"Do you want me to go with you when you talk to the guy at the hospital?"

"That would probably be a good idea. It would give us a psychological edge to have the guy that put him in the hospital standing there." He took a slow drag and blew the smoke out the window. "Let's play it by ear though. Keeping Norma safe will always be the top priority."

"Works   for   me,"   I   told   him.

CHAPTER 7

As we approached the house Mike pointed at a shiny, light blue, two door car parked just down the street from the house and on the opposite side. "There's Callahan's car."

Mike pulled up next to the car, so that my window was next to Callahan's. He looked like he was reading the paper and not paying attention to anything else.

"Are you sure this guy is keeping an eye on things," I asked.

"That's just the way he does it," replied Mike. "Anytime you see him he's reading the sports section, or going over a racing form, or shooting the breeze with somebody. You would swear he's just cheating you out of your money, but when you ask him what's been going on he can give you a detailed report, to the minute, including license plate numbers and descriptions."

"Was he in the army with you, like Benny?"

"No, Callahan was 4F. He has asthma real bad and couldn't pass the physical. His brother and I served together."

"What does his brother do?"

"He lies under a granite stone near a little town in Italy that I can never remember the damned name of."

"I'm sorry."

"Me too, he was a good guy. Roll down your window."

I did, and Mike yelled out through it. "Is that what I pay you for, to sit around and read the funny papers?"

Callahan lowered the page a little and looked at us across the top of it as if he had just noticed we were there. "Are you kidding? Judging by checks you give me I can't actually prove I'm getting paid. I had to get a magnifying glass to see the number on the last one, and the bank charged me to cash it."

Mike grinned and shook his head. "Anything going on around here?"

Callahan folded his paper, and the amusement left his face. You could actually see him replaying the morning's events in his head. "You live on a really quiet street. How much detail do you want? The trash truck went through at 8:12. At 8:43 a station wagon went by with a little old lady driving it. I can give you the license number, but I'm pretty sure she came out of the red brick house on the corner."

"That would be Mrs. Wilson," said Mike. "That's probably a little too much detail. Did you see anything that looked suspicious?"

"Nope, everything I saw came out of or went into a driveway on this street."

"Okay, that's good news. By the way, this is Jake Kowalski, he's your relief. Jake that's John Callahan. "

John and I nodded and exchanged pleasantries and Mike asked, "John, have you left anything out of your report?"

Callahan thought for second, and shook his head when he didn't come up with anything. "Like what?"

"Like who the hell's car is parked in my driveway?"

"Well that just pisses me off," growled Callahan. "According to Mrs. Manzerek, that belongs to a guy you had an appointment with this morning at 10:00"

"Damn, I forgot all about that," said the big man.

"That's what pisses me off. I bet your old lady two bits that you hadn't forgotten."

"I warned you about betting against her," said Mike. He checked his watch and asked, "It's eleven; do you want us to relieve you now?"

Callahan shook his head. "I don't have to be anywhere until mid-afternoon. Why don't you guys get some lunch and then relieve me around one."

"And you can get paid for another two hours," added Mike.

"With the extra time I should be able to afford the whole cup of coffee."

"Yeah, yeah, Jake, here, is a comedian too. I've got to go, but he's going to eat with Norma and Esmerelda. He'll be out to relieve you at one."

Callahan made a face like he was trying to remember something and then went back to his newspaper.

As we headed up the driveway Mike said, "Can you believe him? He's the cheapest guy I know, but he's got money to burn. His parents died in a car accident about eight years ago. His old man left John and his brother a fortune and John *sits* there and cries about wanting extra hours and losing twenty-five cents on a bet."

My new boss skirted around the big Buick belonging to the ten o'clock appointment, and let me out at the front steps.

"Take your time. When you're ready you can take John's place. Ask Esmerelda to fix him a sandwich and a soda."

"Will do."

The corner of Mike's mouth went up on one side. "Do you need a newspaper to keep watch?"

"No, I do things the old fashioned way. I'll sit on the front porch, and then alternate doing a walk-through with a walk-around every thirty minutes."

"That should do just fine. I'll be back as soon as I can."

Mike drove away, and I went up the steps to the front door; but as I reached for the knob, a man opened the door and walked out of it.

Norma was right behind him. "Jake, I'm glad you're here. Let me introduce you to Paul Cantrell. He's a new client of ours."

Cantrell was a nice looking guy, early thirties, dark hair and a gray suit that I was sure my new yearly salary wouldn't buy.

I said, "Hello," and shook his hand. He did the same, but he didn't look me in the eye. He knew I was just the hired help, and he was happy to treat me that way. He put his hat on and headed towards his car.

As Cantrell drove away, Norma asked, "Did you meet John Callahan?"

"I did. He said he owes you a quarter."

The beautiful woman chuckled softly. "I knew Mike had forgotten."

We stepped into the house and she asked, "Are you hungry?"

"I wasn't until just now." I breathed deeply. "What is that smell?"

"Esmerelda's homemade chicken soup, you're in for a treat."

The front door led into an open foyer, just to the side of a huge living room. I asked, "Where can I wash my hands?"

There were two doorways on the right hand side of the room and she pointed to the second one. "It's down that hallway, first door on the left. Are you going to keep your new hat on in the house?"

I had already taken a few steps and I turned around and walked back toward her, snatched the hat off of my head, and tried not to look as foolish as I felt. I hadn't worn a head cover since the Marines, and it was going to take some getting used to. She pointed to a hat rack, and I gently hung the hat on it. The rack was actually for more than just hats and had big wooden hangers on it. I decided I would take advantage of that and hung my coat on it, as well.

I went to the bathroom, washed my hands, and went back across the living room. There was only one doorway on that side of the big room, and it led into the kitchen. The aroma was fantastic. Esmerelda saw me come through the door and her face clouded over, for just a second; and then she brightened up.

"Jake! I almost didn't recognize you." The kitchen was big. In addition to having lots of cabinets and the table where Mike and I had breakfast; it had one of those islands for the cook to work on. Esmerelda came from behind the island, put her hands on her hips, and nodded her head in approval."

"You look good," she said. "Those clothes look nice on you.

"Thanks," I said. "Mike dressed me."

"He might as well. You already shower together."

I wadded up my face and turned red while Esmerelda giggled hysterically. She motioned for me to have a seat, and she continued to giggle as she went back to cooking.

I suddenly remembered Callahan. "When you're finished laughing at me, Mike asked for you to make a sandwich for Callahan, the guy outside."

The pretty woman bobbed her head up and down, but she didn't stop giggling.

I took a seat at the same kitchen table where I had eaten breakfast. There was a big dining room that ran parallel to the living room and joined the kitchen. I could see the long dining table through a double-door sized opening in the side of the kitchen. I guessed that the formal dining room was only used for company and special occasions. I have always been a pretty simple guy and eating in the kitchen suited me just fine.

"That smells good," said Norma, coming in from the living room. "What's so funny?"

Esmerelda tried to stifle her giggling and ended up snorting, which made her giggle even harder. She ended up pointing at me and saying, "He takes showers with Mike."

45

Now it was Norma's turn to laugh. She looked at me and asked, "Is there something I should know?"

I'm pretty sure I turned redder. I put my face down on the table and crossed my arms over the top of my head.

"If it makes you feel any better," said Norma, "I've also showered with Mike, and I liked it."

"That doesn't really help," I said into the table.

"Heads up," commanded Norma, "Your soup is ready."

I sat up, and Esmerelda put a steaming bowl in front of me. She put her hand on my new flattop and rubbed it back and forth. She nodded and winked, with the whole side of her face, to let me know I had chosen well. She walked back to the island to get another bowl, and I watched her do it. Even with her apron on and a rag holding her hair out of her face, it was worth watching.

Norma interrupted my train of thought. "I have a job for you, Jake."

"That's great," I said. "What do I need to do?"

"The gentleman I introduced you to at the door, wants us to watch his wife for a few days."

"Why does he want her watched? Is somebody after her?"

"Somebody may be after her, but not in a harmful way. Pass the crackers."

"Ohhh," I said. "It's one of those things."

"That's what Mr. Cantrell thinks. He and his wife have had a falling out. She has left the house and taken an apartment."

"What caused the falling out?"

"Mr. Cantrell didn't really want to say, but it appears they had a disagreement about how many girlfriends he should have."

"They couldn't come to terms?"

"They were too far apart. He thought he should have lots of girlfriends and she thought she should put all his clothes on the lawn and set them on fire."

"A woman of action," I said between spoonfuls. "You have to admire that."

"Maybe you'll get a chance to admire her in action. Mr. Cantrell is hearing rumors that she is receiving gentleman callers and doing two shows a night in front of the big window in her new apartment."

"Ouch! That's got to hurt," I said sympathetically.

Esmerelda caught my attention and raised a ladle from the soup pot. I nodded, and she took my bowl, touched it up a little and returned it.

"Why does he want *us* to watch her?" I asked. "He could just go over and look for himself."

"I asked Mr. Cantrell the same thing. He claims, despite his infidelity, that he still cares for her and couldn't stand to see it if the rumors are true."

"Do you believe him?"

Norma nodded. "I'm not sure. He has the morals of an alley cat, but he appears to really love her and doesn't want their marriage to end."

"In that case, should we advise him not to go looking for trouble?"

"I'm not sure what you mean."

"It might be a good idea to forget about what may have been going on. If he loves her, he can contact her and try to work things out. If we find out that she's..." I tried to think of a polite euphemism for having sex that they might use in 1947, but I didn't know what to call it so I said, "...that she's doing what he heard she's been doing, then they might not be able to reconcile."

Norma seemed surprised. "Jake! You're a romantic."

That caught me off-guard. "That's the first time I have been accused of that."

"He sounds like a romantic to me," chimed in Esmerelda. "You better keep an eye on your husband, especially when he's showering."

I looked at Norma. "She's not going to let that go, is she?"

"It doesn't look like it." She made a face that said she was thinking, so I concentrated on finishing my soup while I waited.

"I like your idea," she said finally, "But I think the best course is to go ahead and do the surveillance. When we are finished we can offer him the option of reporting what we find or not."

She must have noticed the curious look on my face, because she added, "That way, even if he wants to opt out, we can still charge him for the service."

I smiled and bobbed my head up and down. "That's a great idea."

"You didn't think Mike was the brains of this outfit, did you?"

"I can honestly say that never occurred to me."

"It shouldn't be a problem, Mr. Cantrell can certainly afford it."

I broke a handful of fresh crackers in my soup and asked, "What does he do for a living?"

"He's a gangster," said Norma, matter-of-factly.

I inhaled my mouthful of soup and broke into a coughing fit. Esmerelda ran over and started smacking me, feverishly, on the back with her small hand. Judging by the look on Norma's face, it was probably as funny looking as it felt.

"I'm guessing you're not used to working with gangsters," said Norma.

"No," I rasped out, reaching for my glass of iced tea, "I'm not."

"You should probably start getting used to that. We work both sides of the fence."

"When you say we work both sides..."

Norma held up her palms and waved them back and forth. "We don't engage in any criminal activity or do anything illegal."

"So when you say 'we work both sides...'"

"We work for the criminal element the same as we work for the law-abiding. We shadow their wives and husbands, we find their runaway children and long lost relatives and any other service or investigative work they need. "

"But we don't do anything illegal?" I asked, looking for a second confirmation.

She smiled reassuringly. "We don't do anything illegal. We turn down quite a bit of questionable work every year."

That made me feel better but it seemed odd. "How did you wind up doing that?" I asked. "Working for criminals, I mean."

"That was the easy part. Mike used to be one."

The coughing erupted again and Esmerelda ran over and started flailing madly against my back. This time Norma laughed out loud.

"I beg your pardon," I managed to choke out.

"Mike used to be a criminal," she said slowly and firmly.

"Would you care to elaborate on that?"

"During prohibition Mike ran illegal liquor from Cuba to Key West and Miami."

I tried to remember what I could about prohibition. I knew that the U.S. Government outlawed making and selling liquor sometime in the early part of the twentieth century and then later they overturned that law and made it legal again. I couldn't remember exactly when it was, and I was racking my brain to try and remember how long the law was in effect."

Norma was looking at me with her eyes narrowed and her eyebrows pushed closer together. "I know what you're thinking."

"*I really doubt that*," I thought.

"You're thinking Mike must have been really young to have been able to do that."

I forced the corners of my mouth to go up and nodded like she had me pegged.

"He was. He was nineteen when he started rum running in 1929, and he did it until sometime in 1931."

Esmerelda started clearing our dishes away. "Get Mr. Manzerek to tell you about the time his boat broke down and he had to paddle out to the three mile limit. It's hilarious."

It was official. If I hadn't figured it out before, I was now sure that Mike Manzerek was one of those larger than life characters whose biography would be titled "Audacious". I couldn't imagine going out on my own and taking on the world at nineteen, much less running around the Caribbean smuggling anything. "How long have you been married," I asked.

We just had our seven-year anniversary. We met in 1939."

"So you were apart during the entire war?" I asked.

"Most of it. Mike signed up in June of '42'."

"Wow, that's rough. What did you do during the war?"

"I was working as a secretary to Congressman Nelson. One of the few times I was able to see Mike was when he came to Nelson's office to petition the Medal of Honor for one of the men from his unit."

"The CMH? Did they give it to the guy?"

Norma shifted in her chair and looked at the wall for a moment before she answered. "No, Mike's request ended up being one of many requests that Congress was forced to turn down."

I was suddenly conscious of having spent a lot of time in therapy when I said, "It looks like that bothered you."

"They all bothered me. I read all the requests for medal nominees as they came across the Congressman's desk. There were so many of them. It wasn't hard to find a hero in Europe or the South Pacific. They were all wearing American uniforms." It was obvious the subject made her sad, so I tried to change it. "What did Mike do between running illegal liquor and the war?

Esmerelda brought us both a cup of coffee and took our bowls away. Norma started spooning sugar into her cup. "He started working for a private investigation firm. He said he wanted to try something on the legal side for a while."

"So that's where he learned about criminal investigation?"

"Not right away. His original position was as a bounty hunter."

"Oh this keeps getting better and better."

Esmerelda brought a wrapped sandwich and laid it in front of me. "You said you wanted a sandwich for John Callahan."

"Oh that's right. Thanks for remembering."

"No problem. There are sodas in the refrigerator." She pointed at the big appliance opposite the stove. "If no one needs anything, I'm going upstairs to clean the bathrooms."

Norma and I both shook our heads, and the cute Latina headed upstairs.

"So..." Norma said in a way that let me know that she was making a hard change in the subject. "Tell me about Jake Kowalski. Where does he come from and what does he like to do when he's not saving damsels in distress?"

The way she said it caught me a little by surprise. "You make it sound noble."

"It is noble. How do you think of it?"

"To be honest, I don't think of it. Something inside tells me to do something, and I do it."

The beautiful lady chuckled silently and then took a sip of her coffee. "And you don't see any nobility in that?"

"No ma'am, I really don't," I told her truthfully.

The look on her face changed and was actually a little sad. "You may be the noblest of us all."

"There's nothing special about me. I just do what I do. Lots of guys would do the same thing and probably do it better."

The sad look on her face remained, but her eyes changed focus and they looked at something very far away. "I just told you about the men who we turned down for the Congressional Medal of Honor, but sometimes, and it was one of the things I enjoyed the most, we got to participate in awarding the CMH."

"Yes!" I barked, a little too loud. "Those are the noble guys you're talking about. They're the real heroes."

She forced a smile into the sad look on her face and her eyes misted over. "No matter who we gave it to, the winners all told us the same thing. Do you know what that was?"

I shook my head.

They told us, "I didn't do anything special. Lots of guys would do the same thing and probably do it better."

I couldn't think of anything to say, so I didn't say anything. I wasn't used to being called noble and being compared to CMH winners. I was used to waking up between a dumpster and a port-a-crapper and trying to determine which of the three of us smelled the worst. I didn't see anything noble in that, and I doubted the beautiful wife of my new boss would think so either.

I finished my coffee, and I was grateful when Norma broke the silence.

"I hate to admit it, but there's a soap opera I like to listen to at this time every day." She stood up and headed toward the living room. "Would you care to join me?"

I stood up as she walked out. "No, thank you" I said, "I should take over for Callahan.

I'm going to go tell him he's relieved, and I'll be on watch until Mike gets back."

"You make it sound so official," said Norma from the other room.

"Hey, it's my new job. I want to make a good impression on the boss or I won't get the mediocre salary he promised."

I walked into the large living room and then remembered the sandwich Esmerelda had made. I turned and started to go back into the kitchen when I saw the door to the laundry room swinging open. I pulled back into the living room and flattened against the wall on the side of the opening. I looked around quickly, to see what I had to work with. The back wall of the house was a few feet to my left. The front wall of the house was twenty-something feet to my right. The living room was all one big open area with only a couple of support columns. There was a large sofa, two or three recliners, and a baby-grand piano. Closer to the front wall, near the big bay window, was a small sofa that sat in front of what looked like an old fashioned TV without a screen. I assumed that was the radio where Norma would listen to her soap opera. There were doors and openings, on the wall opposite me, that lead to other rooms. I didn't see Norma anywhere.

The wall directly across from where I was standing was covered with big framed pictures of family and friends, and I was able to see the reflection of the laundry room door in the glass of a big black and white picture of some ancient couple. The image wasn't great, and I was trying to look across eighteen feet to make it out; but it looked like a guy with a pistol coming toward the doorway on my right side. I stood completely still. I didn't want him to catch any movement in the same reflection that I was using. As he got closer I was able to see more details about him. It looked like he had on a blue coat and pants, but it was hard to tell in the reflection. Judging from my height, in the same glass, he was a touch shorter than average, maybe five-six or seven. He had blondish hair with a crew cut. He was broad across the shoulders and carrying the gun in his left hand. He moved very cautiously as he got to the doorway. In the reflection I could see him crane his neck and scan right and left of the opening. He stepped closer and a piece of the semi-automatic pistol came into my peripheral view. If he leaned to each side and looked, as he had just done, he would see me. He leaned to his left and tried to see as much to the right as he could. As he leaned to his right, I reached across and grabbed the pistol with my left hand. I pulled hard and he yelled as the rest of him came through the opening. I drove my right elbow into his temple, and he dropped to his knees. He and I both still had hold of the gun, and I drew back with the intent of taking his head off. Norma chose that moment to run into the living room. She came in from a door toward the end of the big room and was standing in front of the huge bay window that overlooked the front lawn.

"What was that noise...Oh dear Lord!" she exclaimed as she caught sight of Shorty.

At the same moment something else came into the edge of my vision. I turned my head to see a tall skinny man, with dark slicked-back hair, coming through the laundry room door. He was carrying a Browning Automatic Rifle. He saw me and started to bring up the BAR as he ran toward me. I cut across the opening, and clipped Shorty in the side of the head with my knee, as I did. Skinny decided it would be a good idea to use that other opening in the kitchen and shoot through the dining room wall.

It *was* a good idea. The BAR started cutting into the wall and pieces of wood, nails, and drywall filled the living room. I ran straight at Norma with 30-06 rounds angling across the room, just behind me. In my peripheral vision I could see them striking the wall on my left. My options were limited, and I took the only one I had. I never slowed down, and Norma screamed as I ran full-tilt into her. I wrapped both arms around her, crushed her to my chest, spun around and pitched backwards out of the bay window. The glass and frame burst with the impact, and we flew into space.

The basement was partially exposed on the big house. At any given point the first floor was anywhere from one foot to eight feet above the ground. As we came through the window, I looked up into the sky through the branches of a big oak tree and hoped I had picked a short spot. Six feet down I slammed into the earth with Norma on top of me. The impact knocked all of the wind and some of the piss out of me. The back of my head bounced off the ground, and the pain felt like someone had connected a set of jumper cables to my ears. In at least a half dozen places, I knew I had landed on pieces of glass that sliced into my back and legs. I tried to breath and couldn't. Norma was still on top of me shouting, "Jake, are you all right?" I couldn't breathe and could barely move; but we didn't have much time to save ourselves. If Skinny stopped to help up Shorty, then we had, maybe, four or five seconds. If he didn't; we had one. I shoved her off of me and pointed toward the tree and shrub thicket next to the neighbor's house. I forced the air in my throat to make a sound and croaked, "Run."

I could see in her face that she didn't like it, but I'm sure she could see in mine that we didn't have a choice. She did as she was told and scrambled into the bushes. It wasn't a moment too soon. Skinny and Shorty stepped into the opening above me, where the bay window used to be. I couldn't do anything but lay there and look up at them. It occurred to me that the ugly-assed, toothless old man had been right. I wasn't going to last the week.

"Do you think maybe you can shoot him now?" asked Skinny in a voice that was as nasty as he looked.

"Yeah, yeah." growled Shorty as he raised his pistol and pointed it at me.

Something suddenly turned loose inside me, and I was able to suck in air. I drew a deep, noisy, gasping breath and tried to enjoy it since I didn't figure I'd ever do it again.

"Hijo de la chingada!" a small female voice yelled from somewhere in the house.

Esmerelda's cursing barely caught the attention of the two men standing in the window opening. They turned and looked at each other and Skinny said, "Aw hell, we forgot all about the maid."

He said it, matter-of-fact fashion, the way someone might mention their sandwich needed mustard. The other sound got a completely different reaction. It was the sound of someone cycling the slide on a pump shotgun.

"Pinches mamones pendejos!" screamed Esmerelda as Skinny and Shorty came flying out of the window at the same time. She dropped the hammer on the 12 gauge and, in midair, the left side of Shorty's coattail burst into a cloud of dust. That side of his body twisted forward, and his left arm whipped out in front of him. They both cleared where I was lying by a good yard. Skinny hit and rolled and the BAR went sliding across the lawn. Shorty just hit and stayed there.

"C'mon," yelled Skinny, grabbing Shorty by his uninjured arm and pulling him up. I twisted my head back so I would be able see them, and Skinny looked back at me. I could see a thought cross his mind, but he changed it at the sound of the slide going back and

51

forth on Esmerelda's 12 gauge. She was standing in the open window, still wearing her apron and head scarf. She let go another blast with the big gun and blew away the dirt where Skinny had just been standing. He was half-carrying half-dragging Shorty across the yard as fast as he could make it happen. They disappeared into the trees and high shrubbery on the side of the yard. A few seconds later I heard a car fire up and the sound of tires squealing.

I tried to get up, but my head swam and I dropped back onto the grass. It felt like a liquid blackness was rising around me, trying to swallow me whole. I fought it, how long I don't know, but after a while I heard sirens in the distance. A moment later the blackness covered me up.

CHAPTER 8

The liquid blackness became thinner, and the light started to shine through. I opened my eyes and looked into the face of Dr. Hebert.

The doctor was holding a syringe, and I assumed that was what woke me up. He knelt down in front of me and yelled, "He's awake!" I was lying on my side, and his face was about six inches from mine. Still, it wasn't me he was speaking to. The face disappeared, and Mike squatted down in front of me. He had a big smile on his face, so I was pretty sure everything was alright. I asked anyway. "Is Norma okay?"

"She's fine." His grin got bigger. "I'm going to take that bay window out of your salary."

I tried to smile and realized it hurt; laughing was totally out of the question. "How much could it cost," I managed to wheeze out. "It's a cheap piece of shit. Two people can jump right through it without a problem." I tried to roll onto my back, and Mike and the doctor started yelling at the same time. Mike caught me by the shoulder and held me in position.

"You probably don't want to lie on your back just yet," said Dr. Hebert. I've stitched you up in five different places, one near your right shoulder blade, two just above your belt, on each side, and two on the upper part of your left leg."

"Thanks, Doctor. I'm pretty sure I know where they are," I told him.

"I'm sure you do," said Hebert. "Considering the amount of glass you landed on, it could have been a lot worse. You have twenty-eight stitches altogether, and in addition to the sutured areas, you have at least a dozen smaller cuts on your back and legs. I have already given you a shot of penicillin. Do you know what that is?"

I thought it was an odd question. Then it dawned on me that somewhere I had read that penicillin was developed during the Second World War, so it made sense for him to ask. From his vantage point the stuff was cutting edge. That thought brought on a second one. He hadn't even asked me if I was allergic to it before injecting me. Fortunately, I was not.

He fumbled in his bag and pulled out a little glass bottle. "I'll leave you a little something for the pain. We should be able to take these stitches out in about a week." He picked up his bag and headed toward the door. Mike motioned to me that he would be right back and stepped out behind the doctor.

I looked around and found that I was in my bedroom in the guest house. The alarm clock on the nightstand claimed it was three o'clock, and since it looked like the mid-afternoon sun coming into the bedroom window, I figured the clock must be right.

I became aware that I could hear the voices of Dr. Hebert and Mike just outside the doorway.

"Are you sure it's okay to have him here," asked Dr. Hebert.

"He's been pretty helpful, so far," replied Mike.

53

"You don't know anything about him; and you can tell he's dealing with some kind of internal problems."

"Doctor, I understand your concern. I don't know much about him and it's obvious that he has been out of touch. He hasn't heard of a lot of things everyone else has and he isn't up on the latest..."

His voice trailed off where I couldn't hear it, but what I had heard was kind of a letdown. I had thought I was covering my ignorance better than that.

"That's exactly what I'm saying," said the Doctor. "It's quite possible he has been institutionalized."

"You know what?" replied Mike, "He might have been. I don't know, but what I do know is that he has stopped two attempts to kidnap or harm Norma, and he's done it with his bare hands against armed men. He's earned my trust."

"I see what you're saying," said Hebert, "But I do hope you will keep an eye on him, and be careful."

You could hear the smile in Mike's voice when he said, "Watching him will be easy. He's working for me now; and believe me, we're always careful."

I heard the front door open and close and a thought popped into my head so quickly that I yelled out just as Mike walked back into the room, "Callahan! Is he..."

Mike held up his hands to stop me. "Callahan's fine. Your friends sapped him good and hard ,but he's okay."

There was that word again. They had incapacitated Callahan with a blackjack the same way they had Norma.

Mike sat in a chair in front of me. "Callahan said a guy came walking down the street, stopped at the car, and asked for a light. He leaned in and got the light, but his real purpose was to get Callahan's attention and block his side view mirror so the other guy could come up from behind and turn out the lights."

"Skinny, dark haired, greasy guy and a short, broad-shouldered guy?" I asked.

"He said the guy was pretty non-descript -- medium height, medium weight, brown hair, brown coat and pants, but he never saw the other one.

"That doesn't fit the description of either of my playmates. It sounds like there might have been a third guy." I lay there for a moment and then realized I had forgotten something. "Hey, did you go talk to that guy in the hospital?"

"The guy's gone," said Mike with an edge in his voice.

"Gone? How did he get gone?"

"He was resting nicely in a hospital bed, according to the policeman that was supposed to be guarding him, when an orderly showed up with a lunch tray. The cop leaned in to check it out, and somebody blackjacked him from behind. The cop woke up in the hospital bed he had been guarding."

"And our buddy's gone."

"Like snot through a two year old. Nobody has seen him."

"Shit. Did the police get anything out of him before he took off?"

"Other than asking for his phone call and a lawyer, he didn't say a word."

"Double-shit. What do we do now?"

"*We* don't do anything. I'm going to beat the bushes and see if anyone knows anything.

You stay where you are and try to rest. Somebody will check on you every hour or so."

"Check on *me*? Who's watching Norma?"

"I know a number of cops that will do security and legwork for me, when they are off-duty. Two of them are keeping an eye on the house now. Esmerelda's got her shotgun and Norma's got my .38 Smith and Wesson. The police said they would make an extra trip or two and check on us during the night."

"That should do it," I said without much enthusiasm.

"You don't sound real sincere when you say that."

"I guess what I'm trying to say is, 'That should do it for any regular problems.'"

Mikes eyes narrowed. "You don't think we have regular problems."

"Do you? Two guys attacked Norma, in public, last night. Today, two more guys came after her at her own home, in broad daylight, with automatic weapons."

Mike's face clouded over. I could see that he was starting to think what I was thinking.

I continued, "The guys that were here, today were really at ease. They were semi-professional and they were taking their time.

"Why do you say 'semi-professional'?"

"The short guy that Callahn didn't see -- he was careful and entered a room like a policeman would; but he let his gun barrel lead him a little too far. That's how I got a piece of him."

"And the other one?"

"The way you said they took out Callahan was professional. They did it in the open, they did it quietly, and nobody noticed. The tall skinny guy knew what he should be doing, but for some reason, he stopped doing it when he got to the house. He should have been helping the short guy check the area, and there was no need to cut loose with a BAR just because he had one."

Mike said, "I know what you're talking about. He's one of those guys that know what's right and what's not, but he's a psycho wildcard that may or may not do it."

"That's what it looked like."

"I saw guys like that in the Army, but we didn't let them stay around long. Who would have a guy like that on their payroll?"

"The only reason I know is that his boss hangs onto him, because he will do the nasty kind of things that no one else will do."

"Or whoever hired them isn't too particular."

"I guess that's possible."

"I don't like where this is going. Last night I thought they were trying to make off with Norma, but If they sent out a guy like this skinny psycho, that means..."

"They don't care what happens to her," I finished.

"I agree with you. This isn't a normal problem and that reminds me, I talked to my friends today."

"These are the friends that keep up with the criminal goings-on in the city."

"The same."

"Well, what did they tell you."

"Nothing, they didn't know who was after Norma or me, and they hadn't heard a thing."

"You sure they were being straight with you."

"They know better than to do anything else."

The way he said it, I was sure he was right. I wouldn't want to be on the bad side of Mike Manzarek.

"Okay then," said the big guy, "first things first. You need to rest up and get better. Dr. Hebert said you can only have sponge baths for the next couple of days. You'll probably need a little help with that, at least tonight. I'll have Esmerelda give you a hand."

"That sounds good to me, but it's a lousy job for her."

"She deserves it. She's been running around the house giving me the gas about you and me showering together."

"Yeah, she worked me over with that at lunch." I didn't move my head, but I rolled my eyes to the side to look at Mike. "She saved my life. She probably saved Norma's too."

"According to Norma, it took both of you." He paused for moment, then added, "All kidding aside, I'm grateful."

"Hey, it's my job," I said softly. I was starting to fade. I could feel the liquid blackness rising again.

He asked, "Do you need anything before I go...water...radio...magazine...?"

"I don't need any of that, but to be perfectly honest, I'd kiss your ass for a gun."

His mouth curled up on both ends. "I thought you might say that." He reached down to the floor and brought up a brown paper bag. He opened the bag and took out a leather shoulder holster with a big semi-automatic in it.

"It's my old army pistol," said Mike. He hung it on the bedpost nearest to me. "Do I still get my ass kissed?"

I tried to think of something cute to say but the liquid blackness washed me out to sea again.

The tide went out on the blackness, for the second time, and the light started to creep in. This time it wasn't sunlight. The light by the bed was on and shining on the side of my face. I raised my head a little to look out the window at the head of the bed, but it was too dark to see outside. The clock by the bed said 7:00. I heard something make a bumping noise just outside my bedroom door. It startled me, and then I remembered that Mike had said someone would check on me every so often. I looked toward the door and realized that whoever made the noise was carrying a 12 gauge pump shotgun, because I could see the barrel of it pointed down toward the floor sticking into the doorway.

I kept my eyes on the doorway as I reached over to the holster hanging on the bedpost and slid the pistol out. I glanced at the gun. It was a Colt M1911 .45 caliber semi-automatic, standard military issue during the Second World War. It was in good shape and judging from the smell of gun oil, it was freshly cleaned. I touched the magazine release and slid the magazine out far enough to feel the weight and know that it was loaded. I slid it back in and got ready to make my move. I needed to move fast, and I knew it was going to hurt, but I willed myself to do it. It turned out to be a righteous mistake.

I thumbed off the safety, jerked back the slide on the pistol and chambered a round as I jumped from the bed. As my feet struck the floor my head swam and the room spun violently. At the same time it felt like someone threw flaming gasoline across my back and legs. I yelled in pain and pitched forward on the wooden floor. The pistol came out of my hand and slid across the floor and through the open doorway. I tried to catch myself with my hands, but my arms doubled up under me and I ended up on my knees with the side of my face against the floor and my ass sticking up in the air. I was more or less facing toward the doorway, and I could still see the barrel of the shotgun sticking through it. The barrel started to move, and more and more of it came into view. I couldn't see all of the attacker, but I could see the skirt and apron she was wearing.

"Shit," I said into the floor. It sounded sloppy, and I realized I was slobbering.

"Estupido!" barked Esmerelda. "What are you doing?"

"I saw the shotgun barrel sticking out in the doorway and thought someone was sneaking in."

"Yeah, it's a good thing you were able to get to your gun and throw it at me. Otherwise, I might have finished setting the time on that clock next to the door."

"Why were you setting the time?

"It runs fast. Why did you throw your gun away?"

"It slipped out of my hand when I fell on my face." I was still face down on the floor. It hurt too much to move. "Why do you have the shotgun with you?"

"I have the shotgun in case some pendejo tries to shoot me. Why did you fall on your face?"

"I thought I could stand up and defend myself. I was wrong."

Esmerelda laid her shotgun on the bed and bent down to help me up. Between the two of us, I was able seat myself on the edge of a wooden chair, next to the bed. At that moment, it came to my attention that I was only wearing my boxer shorts and a t-shirt.

"I should probably put something on," I said.

"That will make it hard for me to give you a bath."

"Oh crap, I forgot about that."

"Let me see what we need to do," she said lifting my t-shirt in the back. She raised it and stopped, then raised it further and stopped again.

"A Dios mio," she said softly. It must have looked as bad as it felt. "You're not going to like me very much."

"Don't worry. I'll direct all my anger at that asshole that made me jump through the window."

She started toward the bathroom and I asked, "Would you please go pick up the pistol? Be careful it's cocked and the safety's off."

"Oh, that's good. Maybe I shouldn't give it back to you. You might hurt yourself."

"C'mon, be a sport. I may need to throw it at someone else."

She retrieved the gun, lowered the hammer, switched on the safety and put it back in the holster.

Once that was taken care of she went into the bathroom and got a sponge, some soap, a big pan of warm water and brought it out where I was sitting. She put the pan next to the chair and then finished taking off my shirt. She stood looking at my back for a while before I noticed that if I twisted my head a little, I could see her in the mirror over the dresser. She was staring at my back, and the pain in her face reflected what I felt.

"Just go for it," I said. "I'll take it like a man." My voice had no strength in it and was none too reassuring for either of us.

"Are you sure?"

"Yeah, I'll wait until you're gone to scream and cry like a little girl."

I almost didn't make it. Esmerelda went to work. She was kind, patient, and gentle; but before she was done, I had almost passed out twice. My eyes ran water and my jaw hurt from clamping my teeth together.

"That's all of it," she said finally. "I put the ointment like the Doctor said, and I put new bandages on."

I was straddling the chair backwards, hugging the back of it with both arms, and I didn't have the ability to raise my head; so I rested my cheek on the top of the chair. "Thank you," I said weakly.

She helped me back to bed, and I lay over on my side. I could feel her gently pushing pillows up against my back to keep me from rolling on it.

"Esmerelda."

"Yes."

"Thank you for saving my life. If you hadn't jumped in, I wouldn't be here."

I'm sure she said something sweet and pleasant but I couldn't hear her over the sound of the   black   tide   coming   in.

CHAPTER 9

The next day turned out to be rather mild after the first full day's excitement. I managed to wake up around 6:30 and get out of bed without any drama. A new pair of pants and a shirt were lying on the wooden chair next to the bed. They were duplicates of the clothes I was wearing when I went out Mike's front window. I had no idea what happened to the originals, but if they looked anything like my back and legs; I would guess they were in the trash. The note pinned to them said, "This is coming out of your salary."

I couldn't help smiling. I had the feeling that, not only was he not going to take any money out of my check, he probably wouldn't let me pay back the money I actually did owe him. I got my teeth brushed and found that I could master the Safety Razor well enough to only need a couple pieces of toilet paper stuck to my face. I washed my hair in the sink and replaced the bandage on my scalp-line. It took a while, but I managed to get dressed. I thought I was going to have trouble with the shoulder holster Mike had left me, but that turned out okay. It was an expensive looking, old-style leather rig and had a nice feel to it. As it turned out, the straps bypassed most of the bad spots. Tying my shoes was the worst of it. Between the stitches on the back of my thigh and the bruising on my chest and ribs, where Norma had landed on me; I thought I was going to lose consciousness before I finally got my left shoe tied.

I was going to go up to the big house, but before I could, Esmerelda brought me breakfast. She fussed at me for having gotten out of bed, but she didn't seem serious about it. She came in with a tray of eggs, sausage, juice, milk, toast, coffee and a newspaper. She had a paper bag in the other hand and a Browning Automatic Rifle slung over her shoulder. It was almost as big as she was, and I had to chew on my lip to keep from laughing at her.

"That rifle doesn't go with that dress," I told her.

"Callate chistoso, Mike told me to bring you this."

I helped her unsling the rifle and took it from her. "Is that the same one that shot up the house?"

"Si."

"I thought the police took it."

Esmerelda spread her hands and shrugged her shoulders. "They must have missed it."

"Oh yeah, a twenty pound, four foot rifle would be easy to overlook. It probably rolled up under the refrigerator."

I inspected it from end to end. It was pretty dirty and needed a good going over. The skinny guy hadn't taken good care of it, even before he slid it across the yard. "Is Mike expecting more trouble?" I asked, flicking some mud from the front edge of the barrel.

"He didn't say. He just told me to give it to you and that you would know what to do with it." At that point she stuck a finger under my chin and made sure she had eye contact when she told me, "Mike said to make sure you understand that you are only supposed to do this when you feel better."

"Yes, ma'am," I squeezed out against the pressure of her finger.

She took it away be waved it in my face while she gave me a stern look to show she meant business.

Thinking aloud I said, "I'm sure Mike has a gun cleaning kit somewhere. If I can find it, I can give this thing a good scrubbing and…" My voice trailed off when Esmerelda held up a paper bag. It contained everything I needed to clean the rifle, as well as two more magazines and two new boxes of cartridges.

"Do you need anything else?" Esmerelda asked, with a smug look on her face.

"Yeah what does 'Callate chistoso' mean?"

"Chistoso is like a…a…joker."

"What's 'callate'?"

"It sort of means 'be quiet'."

"What do you mean 'sort of'?"

"It's a little more forceful than that."

"More like 'shut up' than 'be quiet'?"

She started giggling and left quickly.

I ate breakfast and spent the rest of the morning reading the newspaper. My grandfather had always taken a newspaper, a couple of them actually, and he seemed to spend a lot of time reading them, but I had never been much of a newspaper man. This paper was a little different than the ones I was used to. It was thicker and seemed to have more information in it. I guessed that was probably because, other than the radio, the paper was the only source of news and information. There wasn't any internet to compete with, and I thought there weren't any televisions until I read the paper. According to the New Egan Sentinel, dated October 7, 1947, an estimated 3.9 million people had watched the opening game of the World Series on September 30. It was the first time a World Series had been telecast, so the paper had a lot of related information. It said that an estimated 32,719 televisions had been produced in September, bringing the year-to-date total to 101,398. It was amazing to think about.

In the 21st century there were medium sized towns that had that many televisions.

There was an article citing different people's opinions of the future of television. A couple of them actually thought it was a fad and would fade away. I hoped they weren't betting their life savings on it.

The comics section was two full pages of comics, and some of them were pretty funny. I was happy to find out that Lil' Abner was a satirical comic strip about a family of screwball hillbillies. It was funny and Lil' Abner was a tall, muscular, good looking guy. I had been compared to worse. On the other hand, he was a simpleton that dressed in rags and worked at the Little Wonder Privy Company cutting the crescent moons in outhouse doors. Maybe the comparison wasn't so hot.

After I finished with the paper I started breaking down the Browning. In the Marines, part of my job was to know about a lot of different weapons and be able to use them; however, the BAR was not one of those weapons. Fortunately for me, while I was in the Corps I was friendly with quite a few guys who collected guns, including old military and antique firearms, and no matter where I was stationed I was always a card carrying member of the local gun club. Thanks to these associations, I had fired a BAR on a couple of different occasions.

The rifle I was holding was marked M1918A2 so this model wasn't very old, relatively speaking. It was classified as a light machine gun and had two rates of automatic fire, 350 and 550 rounds per minute. It didn't have a single shot selection, but I had been told that I could fire a single shot if I got my finger off the trigger quick enough. I had never tried it. It was too much fun to set the selector on *sprinkle* and go for broke.

It took me a little bit to see how it all went together but I finally got it torn down. It was dirty, inside and out, and I was surprised that it had even fired. I gave it a really good cleaning, until it looked like a rifle should look; then I oiled it up and fitted it back together. It would be ready to go if we needed it.

Around eleven o'clock, I went outside and took a slow walk around the house. A crew of carpenters was out front working on the bay window. There were three of them, and they were making good progress. Four additional guys were running in and out of the front door and working to repair the damage to the lathe and plaster walls in the dining and living room. I watched them for a little bit, then I walked out to where Callahan's car was parked and I asked him how his head was. He asked me how I was doing and then we ran out of stuff to talk about, so I walked back to the house and went in for lunch.

As I walked in I noticed that the door nearest the big bay window was open. It had been closed every time I had seen it before. My original intention was just to peek in and move on; but once I saw it, I stepped inside without further thought.

The room was magnificent. It was an antique collector's dream, only in this world, nothing was antique yet. The floor was polished hardwood and it matched the bookcases that were built into the walls around the room. It also complemented the big leather wing-back chairs that surrounded a massive coffee table. It looked good with a huge mahogany desk that sat near the big window at the end of the room. There was a polished wooden stand with a huge dictionary on it standing near the door, and I ran my hand across the smooth dark wood.

"What do you think?" asked a female voice behind me.

I spun around so fast it scared Norma almost as bad as she had scared me. "Ahh crap! You scared the life out me." I exclaimed as I tried to smile.

Her beautiful eyes widened, and she looked at me while I tried to get my heart rate below 200.

"Are you okay?"

"Yes," I said. "I'm fine. You just surprised me." I thought for a second, and then it dawned on me that possibly I shouldn't be in that room. "I didn't mean to snoop around, but the door was open and this room was so pretty I couldn't resist looking at it. My mother loved wood. I'm sorry she isn't here to see this."

"She's not still living?"

"No she passed away in two thousand...ahhhh...a few years ago." I tried not to look like I was hiding something, and I'm sure I failed.

Norma's eyebrows went together in a way that said what I had started to say puzzled her, but she let it drop. "I'm sorry; it's really hard to lose your mother, especially at a young age."

I nodded and desperately tried to think of something to say that was worth hearing. The best I could come up with was, "Is this like a library or office or something?"

The beautiful woman nodded, "That's pretty much what it is. I designed and decorated it to be a library, but Mike uses it for his office."

I scanned the shelves around the walls and said, "You must read a lot,"

"No, I read a little. Most of these books are Mike's."

I turned and looked at her and she smiled a wide smile. "You didn't think that big gorilla had ever read a book in his life, did you?"

I turned away a little and said, "Well I figured he must..."

Norma leaned her head over until her eyes found mine again. I stopped talking and came to the realization that the day would never come when I would be able to tell her a lie.

"I assumed he didn't know how to read," I finished.

She laughed, just a little, way back in her throat. "That's the stereotype, but believe it or not, that big bull reads a ton of things. These are just the books he keeps for reference; for all his other reading material he makes a trip to the library a couple times a week.

"*The library*," I thought. It wouldn't be as good as the internet, but that's where I could get a lot of the information I needed. It would beat trying to learn everything from random articles in newspapers. That thought gave way to another one. "I'm going kind of stir crazy," I said, "Would you mind if I came in here and read a little this afternoon?"

"I don't mind, but you should rest a little. Yesterday would have been a tough day for anyone."

"I guess, but I would rather be doing something. I'm not very good at resting."

"I didn't figure you were. You and Mike seem to have a lot in common, and he can't sit still for more than two minutes at a time. Unless Mike is using this room you are free to use it at any time."

"Thank you."

"You are more than welcome. You came to my rescue for the second time, yesterday, and I'm very grateful."

"I was happy to help. I'm sorry my methods weren't more elegant, but I'm glad it worked."

"I don't think you're giving yourself enough credit."

"I don't think I can take much credit. Don't forget the part about the little Mexican woman having to save the day at the last minute."

"Jake, yesterday when I said you were noble, you said, 'Lots of guys would do the same thing and probably do it better.'"

"Uh-huh," I said fearfully. I knew I was about to be strung up by my own words or deeds.

"There are not a lot of guys who could do what you did, and no one could have done it better."

She strung me up good. I tried desperately, but I couldn't think of anything to say.

Norma sensed my discomfort and let me off the hook. "I said you can use the library, but you will have to hide out from Esmerelda. She thinks you are in bed. If she finds you out walking around, you're in trouble." She checked her watch. "Speaking of which, she's getting your lunch ready to take over to the guest house. If she finds you AWOL, I don't know you."

"I understand," I told her as I headed for the front door. I still couldn't move fast, but I shuffled as quickly as I could to the guest house and went inside without getting caught. I tried to tidy the place up a little. I attempted to make the bed but it was a poor attempt. I finally just pulled the sheets and covers up until it was presentable. It came to me that I couldn't remember the last time I had made up a bed. It felt good. It reminded me of how I used to feel when I was in the Marines. Other than the nagging pain on the back side of my body, the day was going pretty well.

I went into the living room and tried to turn the radio on. It was the size of a three-drawer filing cabinet and looked more like furniture than a radio. It was made out of mahogany and kind of pretty in a really old way. I had turned it on but, other than lighting up the dial, nothing had happened. I turned the volume knob and spun the tuning dial, but that didn't help either. I was looking to see if it was really plugged in when Esmerelda walked in with lunch.

She had a tray loaded with grilled ham and cheese sandwiches in one hand and two soda bottles in the other.

"Is something wrong with the radio," she asked, setting the tray on the coffee table.

"I can't get it to come on."

"How long has it been warming up?"

I'm sure I had a stupid look on my face when I said, "Has it been what?"

At that moment the radio hummed and came to life. I couldn't believe it. It was like a hot glue gun; it actually had to warm up before it would work. It was way too loud, and I fumbled around trying to turn it back down. I finally got it quieted down, and I tried not to look sheepish when I turned to face Esmerelda. "I guess I didn't let it...warm up...long enough."

"I guess not." She giggled. "Sometimes you act like you come from another world."

"You mean a world where radios don't have to warm up."

"Yes, that world."

"Maybe I do," I said playfully as I sat down on the sofa. "Maybe I come from a world where people carry wireless telephones in their pockets and fly in spaceships that go to the moon."

"And the men shower together."

"Well, actually..." I began.

"I don't want to hear it. Your world sounds too strange with people calling on their telephones from the moon."

"Oh yeah, this world is a lot better. In this world, women with shotguns give men sponge baths."

"In your world, do men jump out of windows with other men's wives?"

"Yes, but they usually leave the other man's wife behind when they jump out of the window."

"Oh, then that's the same as this world." She giggled again and sat down next to me. She handed me a sandwich, pulled a bottle opener from her apron, popped the top on a soda and handed me that as well.

"This is nice of you," I told her. "I could have gone up to the big house and eaten at the table like a big boy."

"You should be lying in bed, resting, and not making beds and fighting with radios."

"I'm not very good about sitting around doing nothing."

"I can see that, but you need to get better at it. You also need to get better about sneaking around the side of the house if you don't want me to see you doing it."

"I don't know what you're talking about," I told her.

"Mentiroso, you don't even lie well." She shook her head disapprovingly. "I don't think you're going to make it in this world."

"I had that same thought yesterday," I said in a more serious tone.

"So did I. I was afraid I was too late."

There was a lot of sadness in her voice, and I tried to take things somewhere else. "This sandwich is fantastic," I said with as much enthusiasm as I could muster.

"Stop changing the subject. I was afraid you were going to get killed."

"*You* were afraid," I exclaimed. I started chuckling, and she tried to look stern, but she began giggling, and then we both laughed for a long time as if something were really funny. It felt good and, afterward, we ate our sandwiches and drank our sodas and forgot that the rest of the world could be cruel and insane.

We finished lunch, and we both leaned back on the sofa. She didn't have anything more to say than I did, but it appeared that neither of us wanted to leave. I enjoyed her company and her sense of humor. She was one of those "what you see is what you get" people. There wasn't any game to her. She would tell you what she was thinking or feeling; you didn't have to guess. I really liked that.

She turned and looked at me, and I looked back. Even after half a day's work and with a rag holding her hair back she was very pretty. Her eyes were a shimmering liquid brown, and I knew a man could be lost forever in eyes like that. She leaned her head a little to the side, and I could see she was surveying the damage from my first night on this world where radios needed to warm up. She put her hand on the side of my face, and with her thumb; she softly stroked the area where my eye was still black and blue.

"This is healing nicely," she said softly.

I could barely hear her. Her touch was electric. I'm sure she thought it was nothing, but it was setting off a fire that I knew would engulf me in seconds.

Something chose that moment to slam into the front door. I didn't know what it was, but it was something big and it crashed into the door three times in rapid succession. I jerked the .45 out of the shoulder holster as I came off the sofa. I managed to get between the door and Esmerelda before the door started to open.

I was surprised the door was still on its hinges but it swung open slowly and I stood frozen, waiting for whatever it was to make the next move. I kept the pistol pointed at the door, and I reached down and put my left hand on Esmerelda's shoulder so I could guide her when the shit hit the fan. The door continued to inch open and a voice said, "Jake, are you in there?"

"Mike!" I shouted in a voice that was half relieved and still half scared.

Mike Manzarek opened the door, stepped inside, and saw me standing with the gun in my hand, still holding Esmerelda's shoulder. "What are you folks doing in here?"

"We *were* having lunch," I told him as I holstered the 45.

A smile split his face. "What are you doing now?"

"Shaking out my skivvies. You scared the living daylights out of us."

"I knocked."

"With what, a schoolbus?"

He looked puzzled for a moment and then he realized what had happened. "I'm sorry. Sometimes I get involved in something and don't pay any attention to what I'm doing, and I even forget my own strength."

"What's going on?" I asked him.

"Give me a sec and I'll fill you in." He turned and motioned to someone in the yard, then he stepped inside the guest house followed by two uniformed policemen. "Jake, this is Lieutenant Briggs and Sergeant Faustino. "

I shook hands with the two men, and both of them spoke to Esmerelda, who they apparently already knew.

Mike continued, "I have been talking to these guys all morning, and they've convinced me that we need to change what we are doing and get Norma to a safer place than here."

I started to agree with that idea, but before I could, the Lieutenant started talking.

"We think that whoever wants to hurt Norma has only failed because they ran into something they weren't expecting."

"That would be you," said Mike, pointing at me.

The Lieutenant went on, "Whoever tried to kidnap her night before last wasn't expecting someone to jump out of the crowd and take them down. I'm sure that whoever is behind this simply chalked that attempt up to bad luck and sent another couple of guys out to finish the job yesterday afternoon. They wouldn't have had any idea that you had gone home with the Manzareks, and you ended up surprising them again."

"Me and a little woman with a 12 gauge shotgun," I told him. I turned and winked at Esmerelda, and she winked back.

The Lieutenant nodded at Esmerelda," That's what Mike told us. What is worrying us now is that we are out of surprises. We don't think these people are going to continue making frontal assaults in the hope of getting through."

"What do you think they'll do?" I asked.

"I can't be sure, but I suspect that their next attempt will be a lot more forceful, something along the lines of dynamite under the house or throwing a hand grenade into an open car window."

Mike jumped in, "If they come at us like that..."

"...we won't be able to keep her alive," I finished.

"I've got a couple of handpicked men with me," said Briggs. He gestured toward the Sergeant and said, "There are two more on the way, and Patrolman Owens is with Norma now."

I started to say something, but Mike must have known what I was about to ask.

"I've known Lieutenant Briggs since he was young Bobby Briggs. He and I go way back, long before The War. We can trust him, and that means we can trust Faustino and Owens and whoever else he says."

"That's good enough for me," I said. "What's the plan?"

"We have an idea for a couple of safe places," said Briggs. "We would like to move Norma to one of them as soon as possible."

"That sounds good, too," I said, "but for how long?"

Mike's voice was flat and without emotion when he answered, "Until we find out who's after her and deal with them."

After that, the house was a storm of activity. Esmerelda ran out to help Norma with whatever she needed, Mike conferred with the police officers, and I stood like a lump and watched it all. I didn't have any idea how I could be of help so I just tried to stay out of the way. I hated not being able to contribute to the effort, and it occurred to me that a large part of what I had enjoyed the last couple of days was that I had been able to help. It had made me feel like I was back in the Corps. I enjoyed the feeling of being able to help, to make a difference. The hope of being able to continue making a difference made it bearable to grit my teeth and watch everybody else work and make things happen.

At a certain point the officers wouldn't allow anymore assistance from Mike or Esmerelda. They backed a squad car into the garage and closed the door. They loaded all the baggage themselves and led Norma to the car. Her face was wet from crying, and her eyes were puffy and red. I'm sure she felt as helpless as I did, and she had to leave her home and husband on top of that. I would have cried too. Now that I look back upon that moment, I remember that I did.

Mike was finally allowed to approach and say his goodbyes. The big man engulfed her in his arms and kissed her like he meant it. Esmerelda stood and wrung her hands and watched. The tears streamed down her face in a torrent. I should probably have tried to comfort her, but I wasn't sure if we were on friendly enough terms to try, so I stood, watched, felt useless and wondered where I might get a drink.

Mike whispered something to Norma, and then released her to the Police. She got into the back of the squad car, waved goodbye to the rest of us, and one of the officers closed the door. Mike hit the button on the wall and the garage door opened up to show two more cars waiting outside. The remaining police officers got into the two cars and when one of the two cars pulled out, the squad car, with Norma pulled out behind it. The other car fell in behind and the procession left the driveway and drove away.

We watched them until they were out of sight, and then hit the button on the wall again. As the door came down Mike walked toward me. I looked up at him with the tears still on my face. My father had taught me that if I needed to cry then I should cry, but "Don't," he told me, "be ashamed of it." His philosophy was that if you were ashamed of crying, you shouldn't do it. Mike's father must have gone to the same school. His face was as wet as mine, and he didn't bother to wipe it off or lower his gaze.

"I'm going to find whoever's doing this and murder them," he said in a low solemn voice.

I nodded and asked, "When do we start?"

"You've done your share. You need to rest up and heal."

"Don't ask me to sit this out," I growled.

"You're in no shape to go where I'm going."

"Maybe not, but I'd rather take a bullet than be forced to sit and do nothing."

"You're not very good at judging your own limits."

I scoffed. "When it comes to that, I'm probably twice as good as you are."

Mike snorted softly through his nose. "You may be right about that."

I could feel my new lease on life slipping away, and I made the quick decision to go all in and put all my cards on the table. "Mike, I've spent most of the last year sucking on the end of a bottle and feeling like a useless piece of shit. It seems like forever since I was useful to anyone, but the last two days have made me feel like I have earned the right to breathe the air and walk on the ground. Don't take that away from me."

I could see he was thinking about it, but I knew he wasn't convinced. "Look, if you need to go into a situation that requires more physical ability than me and that BAR can deliver, then by all means, call someone to give us a hand, but don't bench me completely."

"I feel like I'm signing your death warrant, and I don't want that on my conscience."

"You can do this with a clean conscience. I'll swear, I'd rather be dead than sitting this out."

He took his big right hand and kneaded the lower half of his face like it was bread dough. Finally, he said, "Alright, it's your funeral. This afternoon, I'm going to beat the bushes for some information, and it would be better if I do that alone." He took a deep breath and let it out slowly. "If you don't hear anything else from me, be at breakfast at six sharp. We'll start then."

"Thank you. You won't regret it."

"We'll see. Will you at least get some rest today?"

"Are you kidding? I thought we had a job watching some guy's wife screw the population."

"What?" exclaimed Esmerelda from the corner of the garage.

Mike grinned, and I turned red. "I'm sorry," I said, "I forgot you were there."

"Cochinos!" she barked out as she stomped her way across the garage and back into the house.

Mike translated, "She thinks we're pigs."

I nodded. She was probably right.

CHAPTER 10

The afternoon went by slowly. Callahan had staked out Cantrell's wife's apartment the night before and told Mike that he hadn't seen anything. She had closed the curtains around 9:30pm, and no one showed up at her place before or after. He had said there was no reason to go over until after dark, so I spent the afternoon taking advantage of Norma's offer to use Mike's office.

There was a lot of noise coming from the carpenters and sheet rock crew in the living room; but after a few minutes of sitting in Mike's library, I was able to shut out everything else and concentrate on my reading. I tried to learn everything I needed to know to keep up. Thanks to a pile of Time magazines that I found stacked in the corner, I discovered that a P-38 was an airplane used during the war. It was a pretty cool looking plane with twin props and twin booms on each side of the fuselage. Mike had said they were using it as inspiration for the 1948 Cadillac. Looking at a picture of a P-38, I thought it was a good idea.

I also found some articles on the rationing that Mike had mentioned. According to the magazines, a lot of things were in short supply during the war. Since the guys doing the fighting overseas got priority on whatever food and equipment there was available, a lot of people stateside had to do with less or without. The items in short supply looked like stuff people would be unhappy to do without. Some of the things were sugar, cheese, gasoline, meats, canned fish, fuel oil, kerosene, butter, bicycles, tires, nylons, coffee, typewriters and shoes. I'm still unsure as to why bicycles and typewriters were rationed, but after reading the articles the other stuff made sense. Britain had rationing, as well, and that included the clothes rationing that Mike had mentioned.

The government passed out war rationing books. In the magazine pictures they were just little wallet looking things made of thick paper. They contained a handful of little pages of stamps called ration stamps. Later in the war they came out with little colored cardboard tokens that allowed people to get change for their ration stamps. It was incredible this worked at all and even more amazing to think of people having to deal with rationing sugar and coffee, but it really got bizarre when it came to gasoline. People had to put stickers on their car windshields to show how much gas they could buy each week. I didn't study it hard, but it seemed like the more important you were to the war effort, the more gas you could buy each week. It looked like a lot of people had car pooled, taken public transportation, or walked to work during the war.

It was amazing to imagine the whole country putting in that much effort to help out the military. The magazines were full of ads with supportive slogans for the troops. For a moment in time, everyone was pulling together and working toward the same goal. I was so engrossed I didn't notice how late it had gotten. I jumped when Mike stuck his head in the library and called me to dinner.

"What have you been doing in here, all afternoon?"

That was a harder question to answer than I would have thought. I couldn't tell him that I was trying to figure out what people had been talking about for the past two days. I held up one of the Time magazines and said, "I was just looking through some of these and reading any of the articles that looked interesting."

"Did you find anything," Mike asked looking very doubtful.

"I found out that during rationing, Doctor's and Preachers could put a red 'C' gas rationing sticker on their car windshields."

Mike made a face like he wasn't sure what to do with me.

"You're easy to entertain, I'll give you that. Esmerelda said dinner will be ready in a couple of minutes."

"That sounds a lot more interesting than rationing. I'll be right there."

I stacked up the magazines as I had found them, washed up and headed into the kitchen. Esmerelda had our plates ready with fried chicken, mashed potatoes and green beans. It was fantastic. I was glad that Mike didn't know I would have taken this job just for the food.

Esmerelda was still put out with us from earlier in the day. She stood with her hands on her hips and proclaimed, "I should feed you the garbage. That's what pigs are supposed to eat. "

Mike was no help. "Esmerelda, don't be mad at Jake. It's not his fault that someone offered to give him money to peep through a bedroom window and watch another man's wife doing filthy things with strange men."

"You're both dirty cochinos," barked the pretty Latina. She spun on her heel and went back to the stove.

After a couple of plateful, Mike and I allowed Esmerelda to take our plates and pour us a cup of coffee. As Mike waited on his cup to cool, he said, "Callahan is going over to watch Cantrell's wife around 7:30. If you're still feeling up to it, you can ride with him."

"That's great," I told him, "I'll be ready."

"You should really stay here and rest."

"I probably should, but I'd rather do that."

"Pig!" shouted Esmerelda from behind the stove.

"I meant I'd rather be working," I shouted back.

She made a horse noise with her lips. "You should meet my Uncle Jorge. He sits in front of the radio with a beer in his hand and calls that work, too."

I looked over at Mike. "I'm not going to win this, am I?"

"Are you kidding? If I were you, I'd wait for Callahan out on the curb."

I was saved by the bell, literally, when the front doorbell chimed.

Esmerelda started in that direction but Mike motioned for her to keep doing what she was doing, and he went into the living room and made his way toward the front door. I could hear him banging into the saw horses and toolboxes that the workmen had left when their day ended at 4:30. I heard the front door open, and I could just barely hear Mike speaking with someone; but I couldn't make any of it out. A minute later I could hear Mike bringing his guest back through the maze in the living room. He walked into the kitchen with Lieutenant Briggs behind him.

Mike motioned for him to sit down and said, "Jake, Bob has some good news for us. Bob, do you want something to eat or a cup of coffee?"

"Coffee sounds good," said Briggs, taking a seat at the table next to me.

Mike looked around for Esmerelda and saw that she was already filling a cup. He took it from her and sat down on the other side of the lieutenant.

"Thanks," said Briggs, taking a swallow from the cup. He winked at Mike and said, "You know she makes the best coffee." He said it to Mike, but he said it so Esmerelda could hear it. I heard her giggle from over Briggs' shoulder. I was suddenly aware that this bothered me a little. I looked at Briggs' hand and saw that there wasn't a wedding ring on it. I also noticed for the first time that he was a good looking guy. That bothered me a little, too. I had spent the last couple of days in the small environment of the house and had forgotten there was a whole new world out there. Considering how pretty Esmerelda was, it should have occurred to me that a big chunk of this new world would be interested in her. I had been thinking that I might have a shot with her; but if good looking, career-oriented guys like this Police Lieutenant were chasing after her, an out of town bum living in Mike Manzarek's guest house probably didn't have a real chance.

I snapped out of my pity session when I heard Mike say, "Tell Jake what you were telling me."

The lieutenant took a black and white picture out of his pocket, and it crossed my mind that I was starting to miss colored photographs.

"I came by to let you guys know we got an ID on this guy from the hospital."

"That was fast," I said.

"Yes, it was," agreed Briggs. "We sent the photo over to the local FBI offices and asked them to send it on to their headquarters in Washington. "

"It got back and forth to Washington that fast?" I asked. That would have been hard to do in the 21st century with email and digital photos. I couldn't imagine they could make it happen in 1947.

"No, it never made it out of town. One of the guys in the local FBI office has seen your boy before. "

"That's a real stroke of luck," said Mike.

"It's a *major* stroke of luck," said Briggs. "The agent couldn't remember your man's name, but he said the fellow works in Security for Republic Aviation."

I assumed it was for my benefit when Mike said, "That's a big government contractor. "

Brigg's head went up and down. "Right, that's how the FBI agent knew him. His assignment before New Egan was in Washington D.C., working on a project with Congressman Nelson."

Mike's face drew up tight. "That's the Congressman that Norma worked with during the war."

Briggs continued nodding. "I remember." He took a sip of his coffee and continued. "Anyway, the president of Republic Aviation visited the Congressman's office a couple of times during the war, and at least one of those times, your friend came along as some kind of lackey."

"He's no friend of mine," snarled Mike, turning toward me.

"Don't look at me," I said. "I don't think he would be my friend. I kicked him in the head."

Briggs picked up the picture and looked at it again. "I wondered why the side of his face was so dark. "

"That's the reason," Mike affirmed. "It was a really nice shade of purple the last time I saw it." The big man wadded up his face and massaged his chin. "It looks like we have our link, but what kind of link is it."

Briggs said, "You're thinking that maybe the Senator and Republic had some under the table shenanigans going on."

"That's possible," replied Mike. "I have nothing against Nelson, and I never heard of or saw him doing anything shady; but he's a politician and I have built-in distrust of politicians."

"Who doesn't?" asked Briggs.

I saw Mike's face light up and he looked at me and said, "Hey, you know who might be able to help us... Callahan?"

The lieutenant's face clouded over. "Are you talking about John Callahan?"

"Yeah, why? You have problems with Callahan?"

"He's always seemed a little squirrelly to me."

Mike frowned. "I was in the Army with his brother, Charlie. How do you know him?"

"He does a lot of private dick work."

For the first time in my life, I tried to stifle a full-blown belly laugh. I twisted my head to the side and clamped my teeth and lips together. The pressure was too much and shot violently out of my nose as a loud snort.

"Gesundheit," said Mike.

I raised my hand and wiggled my head up and down to acknowledge the gesture, but I kept my face twisted to the side as if I was afraid I might I do it again. My eyes watered and I bit down on my lip and feverishly tried not to laugh out loud.

Mike continued. "Charlie told me that he and John had been doing freelance private eye work before the war. It was mostly surveillance stuff. I still call John when I have any overflow work. He's been helping us watch over Norma."

If I was interpreting things right, the folks in 1947 could use the terms Private Investigator and Private Dick interchangeably. This was going to take some getting used to. I grabbed a paper napkin from the table and wiped at my nose as if I had really sneezed.

"That's how I know him," said Briggs. "He's been called to give testimony on a couple of cases we were working on.

"That shouldn't have been a problem. He's got a memory like a movie camera."

"He does," agreed Briggs, "but he always came off as some kind of eccentric genius."

Mike smiled. "Oh, that kind of squirrelly, yeah, he's definitely that."

Briggs added, "We got the convictions. His ability to recall detail is extraordinary." Briggs squeezed his lips together as he thought for a moment, and then asked, "What did he do during the war?"

"He was 4-F. He ended up working in Security for Republic Aviation during the war."

Briggs made one of those well-what-do-you-know looks and said, "You're right, he might be able to help us."

4-F was a term I hadn't heard very often. Mike had used it earlier that day and it was the first time I had heard it in quite a while. The designation was used more for selective services than anywhere else and it applied to anyone that the military saw as physically or mentally incapable of being in the armed forces. There were tons of other classifications but 4-F and its complete opposite, the 1-A designation, were the ones that popped up the most. It wasn't any different in the 21st century. Anyone with medical or mental issues wouldn't be inducted into the armed forces.

According to my afternoon's reading; during the second world war, when the vast majority of men of a certain age either volunteered or were drafted to serve, a lot of the ones who had been classified 4-F were pretty bitter about not being able to take a direct part in the fight. From what I read, calling someone 4-F, whether they were or not, could be taken badly and could easily start a fight.

"Callahan will be here later to pick up Jake for a job. We can ask him then," said Mike.

Briggs nodded and said, "Oh I almost forgot why I came over in the first place. Norma asked me to give you a couple of messages." He turned and looked at me like he was unsure if he should continue talking. Mike opened his mouth to say something, but I let him off the hook.

"I'm going to head out back. I have to wash up a little before Callahan gets here."

I didn't wait for a response; I just headed for the back door. Mike was putting on a brave face; but I knew he was worried about Norma, and I didn't want to get in the way of any personal communication she might be sending.

I went to the guest house and decided I had enough time to do what I had said I was going to do, so I stripped down and went to work on cleaning myself up. I changed out the bandage on my scalp and noticed that the coloring around my eye had gone from purple to yellow. It was getting better, but it wasn't a good look for me. It took a little contortion work, but I managed to remove the bandages from my back and leg. The wounds on my leg were easy enough to reach, but the ones on my back were a different story altogether. I finally wet a towel, rolled it up and, as softly as possible, dragged it back and forth across my back. It was nowhere near the fine work Esmerelda had done the night before, but it got the job done. I ran water in the tub and sat on the edge of it and finished washing everything else.

It took a little while, but when I was done; I was clean and presentable. The only problem I had at that point was putting new bandages over the stitches. I searched around the house and discovered a wooden backscratcher with "Thank You for Visiting Niagara Falls" stamped on it. Between that and a pair of barbecue tongs I found in the kitchen I was able to get the bandages in place. Again, it wasn't a pretty job like the one Esmerelda had done, but it would do.

It was almost 7:30; so I got dressed, slid on the shoulder holster with the .45, grabbed my hat, and headed back to the main house. Mike and the Lieutenant were still sitting at the table in whispered conversation. I didn't want to disturb them and was trying to think of an excuse to be somewhere else when I was saved by the bell. The front doorbell chimed and Mike said, "Jake would you get that? It's Esmerelda's night off, and that's probably Roberto."

I nodded and headed into the living room. I walked past all the stuff the workmen had left and peeped out the window next to the front door where I could see a Latin man standing under the porch light. He was medium height, looked to be in his late twenties, wearing a nice suit, highly polished shoes, and carrying a handful of flowers. He was a good looking guy, and it didn't take a lot of effort to figure out why he was here. If this was the "Roberto" that Mike had mentioned, then this guy had been around before. I opened the door and said, "Hello." He looked surprised for a moment, and actually looked around to see if he was at the right place.

In another place and another time I might have been able to be angry with this guy, but I was too busy feeling like a piece of shit. I couldn't help thinking that it had actually crossed my mind to go looking for Esmerelda to see if she would put the new bandages on my back, and now this guy had shown up with no hair unshaven or uncombed and a fistful of beautiful flowers. He was bear hunting with a Howitzer, and I didn't even a have a pea shooter.

"I'm Roberto," he said, finally, "I am looking for Esmerelda."

"Mike said it might be you at the door," I told him, stepping aside and motioning for him to come in. "I'm Jake, "I told him, extending my hand. He accepted the hand and shook it firmly while he looked me square in the eye. Under different circumstances I could see liking this guy.

He looked puzzled and unsure of what to say so I cut him some slack.

"I work with Mike. He hired me last Sunday."

That was enough to make Roberto's night. The puzzled look went away and was replaced with a big flawless smile.

I reached for the knob to close the door and found Callahan standing in the doorway.

"Evening," I said as he stepped inside. He nodded and said, "Hey, Roberto! How are you doing?"

It looked like this night was just going to keep on giving. I think I would have preferred armed men sneaking in the back door.

"I'm guessing you know each other," I said as cheerfully as I could manage.

Callahan removed his hat as he said, "Yeah, Roberto and I worked together for a few months before he was drafted into the Army."

I had forgotten all about the afternoon's conversation until that moment.

"Was that at Republic Aviation?" I asked.

Now it was Callahan's turn to look surprised. "Yeah, how do you know about that?"

"Mike was talking about it earlier. We're hoping you can help with something." As a matter of fact," I said, turning to Roberto, "you both might be able to help."

I motioned for them to follow me, and I headed toward the kitchen. The lieutenant was still sitting at the table. Mike was at the sink pouring another cup of coffee.

"I found some guys that can help us," I announced, walking into the kitchen.

Mike waved them in. "Hey, John, Roberto, come on in. Anybody want coffee?"

Mike introduced Briggs to Roberto and got Callahan a cup of coffee. The four of them sat around the little table, and I leaned against the island counter and looked over Briggs' shoulder.

Mike pushed the picture between Roberto and Callahan. "We have it on good authority that this guy has worked for Republic Aviation; do either of you guys know him?"

"He doesn't look familiar," said Callahan.

"That's Max," said Roberto, "Max Winston." He turned to Callahan. "You remember him. He always had that sour look on his face, just like in this picture."

"Are you sure," asked Callahan, picking up the photo. He studied it for a moment and said, "That's not him. It looks a little like Max, but I don't think it's him."

"I'm positive it's him," assured the Latino.

"Does this guy, Max, still work for Republic," asked Briggs.

"I don't think so," replied Roberto. "He was there a long time before John and I worked for Republic, and he was there when I left, but the last time I saw one of the guys we used to work with he said Max wasn't around anymore." He thought for a moment and added, "Did you know that just before he came to Republic he was making his way up as a prize fighter."

This caught everyone but me by surprise. He boxed way better than average, and my head was a living testament to that fact.

Briggs whistled. "That's new information."

Mike looked over at me and gave me a look that let me know I had come up a little in his esteem.

"What took him away from prize fighting?" asked Briggs.

"Trouble with his knees," said John.

"Been there," I thought.

Mike was smiling and his face was lit up like a beacon. It was easy to see that he was happy to have something to work with, even if it was doubtful. He asked, "How do we find this guy? Is there anybody at Republic that we can talk to?"

"Oh sure," offered Roberto, "You can talk to Henry Gallagher. He's the head of Security."

"Do you think he's there now?" asked Mike excitedly.

The young Latino looked at Mike like he was insane. "No, there's no chance of that. All the higher-ups are gone by this time. Republic doesn't even run a second shift anymore. The only guys you are going to find out there now are the night watchmen and the janitors."

"Shit," grumbled Mike, "what time do they open up in the morning?"

"The plant opens at 6:00," volunteered Callahan, "but Gallagher never shows up before 8:00."

"Shit," Mike repeated. He looked at me and added, "Tomorrow's going to get busy. Be ready to roll out of here at 7:00."

I nodded. "I'll be ready."

"We'll be ready too," said Briggs firmly.

Mike's head swiveled to face the Lieutenant. "You're not going to cut me out, are you?"

Briggs put his hand on Mike's shoulder. "No, you can tag along, but don't forget this is a police matter. You follow my lead, you let me do the talking, and you let me ask the questions."

Mike's look soured, "What am I supposed to do, just stand around and look stupid."

Briggs smiled, "It's always a good idea to go with your strengths."

"You bastard!" bellowed Mike as he began laughing. He pointed at the officer, then me. "Between you and the hired help, I'm stuck working with Hope and Crosby."

I had seen enough old late-night movies to know about "Bob Hope and Bing Crosby," and I was pleased with myself that I had finally gotten a reference.

A female voice interrupted my thought. "Why is everyone in here?"

We all stopped talking and turned to look. It was worth the effort. For a moment I didn't know what I was looking at. The woman standing framed in the doorway of the kitchen was incredible.

Shining black-blue hair cascaded past the fur wrap around her shoulders and framed a face of mocha skin, scarlet lips and liquid brown eyes that shimmered when the light struck them. She was wearing a pastel purple, no, lilac dress that knew just where to hang on and where to let it go. The neckline went deep and showed off a beautiful gold necklace and more. Where the dress stopped, gorgeous brown legs ran down into high-heeled matching pumps.

"Esmerelda, que linda eres," bellowed Mike.

"He is right," agreed Roberto, "you are beautiful."

"I always hate to agree with Mike but this time he's right," said Briggs.

I tried desperately to say something; anything, but I couldn't seem to find the bottom half of my mouth. It was absolutely possible that I was standing on it. I finally managed to say, "Wow."

Esmerelda giggled and said thank you to everyone. Roberto walked over to her and offered his arm. She turned and took it and waved goodbye to us over her shoulder, as they walked toward the front door.

Briggs whistled soft and low. "Mike, somebody just set off a bombshell in your kitchen."

"You're not kidding," the big man agreed. "If I was ten years younger and single, Roberto wouldn't have gotten out of here with her so easily. I'd have given him a hell of a run for his money. Of course, I would have had to come up with a smoother line than Jake here." He looked at me and grinned. "How does that go again...'wow'?"

For the second time, in two minutes, I tried to think of something clever to say and failed. I threw up my hands, and then hung my head.

"Better luck next time, champ," said Mike, "you and John better hit the road."

He didn't need to tell me twice. Any excuse to escape was a good one. I followed Callahan through the living room, grabbed my hat off the rack, and locked the door behind me.

Tracy E Johnson

CHAPTER 11

It was nice to get out of the house. Whatever traffic there might have been had thinned out, and we cruised easily toward the tall part of the city that we could see in the distance. The air was chilly, but the car was hot inside; so it worked out well for John Callahan to crack his window and let out his cigarette smoke.

According to John we were riding in a 1938 Studebaker coupe. It didn't feel as nice as Mike's Cadillac and I didn't think it was half as nice to look at; but I would have ridden a jackass to get out of the house and see a little of the city.

We headed toward the big skyline, but before we got there Callahan turned off. He put the big part of the city to our left and headed to what he described as, "The part of town where the rich-assed people live."

Way out on the right I could see Lake Michigan, at least I assumed it was still Lake Michigan; and that meant we were headed north. I tried to take in as much as I could in case I had to go out on my own. I knew almost nothing about the city, and I also knew there wasn't going to be a smart phone with GPS in my near future. I looked at the lights of the city through Callahan's window, and I tried to find any similarities between New Egan and Chicago. Other than the big lake to the east of us, I didn't see any matching architecture or landmarks. The city skyline had an old Gothic look to it. That isn't to say that it didn't look good; but at the same time, it was a little sinister. It was sort of like looking at a tiger in the zoo. It's pretty, but only as long as you aren't standing next to it. We ended up keeping our distance as Callahan drove to the rich-assed part of town. I made the assumption that rich-assed correlated to lake-adjacent property, and I ended up being right. After about twenty minutes of driving we turned toward the water, and not too far from the shore, the Studebaker pulled up to an apartment complex. It appeared to be new, so I assumed it would be considered modern in 1947. I had seen places similar to it in Chicago. It was one of those places modeled after the open air style buildings of Los Angeles. The apartments all had big windows and open breezeways and stairwells. It was in an expensive neighborhood where innovations like these were common and money was more plentiful than common sense. Young upwardly mobile couples, well-to-do young single men, and the mistresses of older rich men are instantly moved in as quickly as the vacancy sign goes up. Then the seasons change, and they realize that they don't live in Los Angeles, and they are freezing their asses off walking to and from their apartments and up and down the stairs. They also find out their heating bill is sky high because the big windows, especially in 1947, leak heat so easily they might as well be screen doors.

If Mr. Cantrell had been correct, Mrs. Cantrell didn't choose these accommodations because she wanted to look uptown or trendy. She chose it because she wanted to show everyone who would stop and watch, what Mr. Cantrell had been stupid enough to lose.

The apartment building was one of five matching apartment buildings situated at eight, ten, twelve, two and four o'clock around a huge cul-de-sac. Sidewalks came out from between each of the buildings and connected with the sidewalk that ran in a circle in front of all the apartments. There was a bus stop on one side of the cul-de-sac about the three o'clock position, and John pulled into the curb just behind it.

The lawns swelled up from the edge of the street and rose a few feet as they approached the apartments. This put the apartments up on a knoll and gave onlookers a real drive-in movie experience. I was wondering if that might be where the idea came from. From our vantage point we could see all of the left hand side of the complex and especially into the large window at the 10 o'clock position straight off the left side of the car. John pointed at it and said, "That's our bird."

The buildings were all two stories and since there was only one big window on each floor, I assumed that there was only one apartment on each floor. It looked like there were more apartments being constructed on the other side of knoll, but I couldn't tell how many from where I was sitting.

"We showed up right on time," said Callahan, pointing out the front window of the Studebaker. A woman had come around from the back side of the building and was headed across the front walkway with a big bag of groceries. It was hard to get a total picture of her as she was wrapped up neck-to-knees in what John said was mink. She had a pretty face. I guessed the rest of her matched it because her attitude said she was a pretty woman and that she knew it. I figured she would need an attitude like that if she was going to show off in front of that big window. I said as much to Callahan.

"Oh yeah, Evelyn Cantrell's got looks, attitude, and then some." He punched in the cigarette lighter on the dashboard and cracked his window a little more. The lighter popped out and he lit up. I took the opportunity to crack my window a little more as well.

"She was a burlesque dancer," continued John. "Cantrell found her taking her clothes off at some night club over in New York. She was billed as <u>Evelyn from Heaven</u>. "

He tilted his head back and blew smoke at the space above the window. I thought he was about as effective at clearing the air as I would be if I tried farting through the same opening.

The lights went on in the apartment, and the big window came to life. John pointed out the driver's window and said, "It's just like going to the movies isn't it?"

I agreed and started to mention that it reminded me of the drive-in, but I decided I had better keep that to myself. I had no idea when drive-in movies were invented, and I had enough problems without spouting off about something that might be off into the future. I looked around at the other apartment buildings but other than a light or two there wasn't anything going on. I looked out the passenger side of the car at the big window directly across from Evelyn Cantrell's. The curtains were closed, but at the moment I glanced there was some commotion with them. Whoever was in there had been quick, but not quick enough to keep me from seeing the end of a telescope.

"What are you looking at?" asked John.

"Somebody in there had a telescope sticking out through the curtains," I told him.

John chuckled, "I'll bet they did. The guy that told me the story said that Mrs. C. drew a small crowd four nights out of five last week. He claimed they called the cops all four times, to come out here and make her close the curtains." He craned his head to look at the big window on my side of the car. "If I had a ringside seat like that, I'd get a telescope too."

He was probably right, but something about the moment bothered me. I turned my attention back to the job at hand and looked toward the big window off the port side of the car. Evelyn Cantrell had a nice living room. The paneling was walnut in color, and there were a couple of pretty paintings on the wall opposite the window. I could see the back edge of the couch against the window. I assumed that was where she put on her show, if she actually did. I was beginning to have my doubts. We hadn't seen anyone else go into the apartment, and no one had greeted her at the door. "Do you think Cantrell was wrong about her," I asked Callahan. "I don't see anybody else in there."

"I don't think so," said John slowly. "Too many people are talking about last week for nothing to have happened. Then again," he offered, scratching his chin, "she left the curtains open last night, but there was nothing to see. Nobody showed up, and she didn't do anything but read a book and listen to the radio."

He looked at his watch and said, "Speaking of which, Milton Berle is on." He grabbed the volume knob on the car radio and snapped it on. The light came on, but it didn't make any sound. It was amusing to see that it was just like the radio in the house; it had to warm up. He waited a moment and then twisted the tuning knob until an announcer came on and informed everyone that, "If every smoker knew what all Phillip Morris smokers knew, then they would all change to Philip Morris." I was waiting for the announcer to tell me what these other smokers knew, but instead some little kid got on the microphone and squalled, "Call for Philip Mawreese," at the top of his lungs. I had trouble not laughing out loud. Was this really what passed for advertising in 1947? I found it impossible to believe that this ridiculous racket would entice a smoker to switch brands. I could see how it might make a radio listener switch stations, but would this kind of advertising really sell anything? I looked over at the cigarette pack that Callahan had lain on the seat and saw that it was, sure enough, Philip Morris cigarettes. It looked like the advertisers in 1947 were as good for their time as the ones in the 21st century were going to be for theirs.

I had at least found out who Milton Berle was, and commercials aside, I enjoyed the program. Berle and his announcer, some fellow named Gallup, did a lot of back and forth joking that was pretty funny. Then Berle did some skit where he played a Girl Scout leader. Callahan and I sat and stared at the radio and laughed like idiots. For half-an-hour I forgot that I needed a video screen to be entertained. I forgot about television, the internet and streaming video and enjoyed listening to a brand new seventy year old radio show.

A guy named Red Skelton had a program right after Milton Berle's, and he was funny as hell, too. I started to wonder why anyone had bothered to invent television. I laughed, shot the breeze with Callahan and watched Mrs. Cantrell read a book.

When the news came on, at 9:00, Callahan turned the radio off. I hated that, because I was hoping to learn something by listening to the news, but I didn't want to make anything out of it, so I said nothing. To make things even worse, he didn't say anything. He just sat there, smoking a cigarette, and stared at Evelyn Cantrell's window, and watched her read. I scanned the area, but it was quiet. Everyone else was either not at home or had pulled the drapes. I checked out the big window on my right again, but I didn't see any movement or any strange lenses sticking out between the drapes. It looked like someone was still in there, because I could see a dim light around the edge of the window but nothing more.

I was trying to think of something clever to start a conversation, but it was John who finally broke the silence.

"How do you like working for Mike?"

I chuckled and told him, "I like Mike well enough, but it's been a little rough so far."

The corner of Callahan's mouth turned up in a wry grin. "When you jump out of a window you're supposed to leave the other man's wife behind."

" Esmerelda said the same thing. Maybe next time I'll get it right."

"How many stitches did you end up with?"

"Couple dozen."

"They bother you?"

"Only if I'm standing or sitting."

"Shit," said John, stuffing a cigarette into his smile. He punched the lighter into the dash and talked around the cigarette as he waited for it to heat up. "Getting stitches reminds me of the time Charlie and I were pushing over outhouses."

"You were doing what?"

The lighter popped out and John lit up. "Pushing over outhouses, don't tell me you haven't done it."

"Well I…"

"It was Halloween in…shit it must have been '32…Charlie and I had started out egging houses but we ran out of eggs."

"Been there," I said sympathetically.

"So we started pushing over outhouses."

"I'm not sure I understand the appeal in this."

John's face twisted up. "Hey, we were kids. Don't tell me you haven't done it." He flicked ashes out the window and said, "Anyway, we had pushed over a couple when we got to this one farmhouse. We go out back and there's a nice new outhouse just ripe for turning over."

"You couldn't pass that up," I said as if I knew what the hell he was talking about.

"Course not. Anyway, we do the deed and discover the damned farmer was sitting in it reading the Sears and Roebuck, just waiting on a couple young fools like us to push it over. "

"Are you kidding?"

"I am not. He's got a double-barrel, rabbit-ear 12 gauge, and fires one barrel into the air. The he starts screaming that he's going to kill us."

"I'm guessing you ran."

"Like Jesse Owens with his ass on fire. The old man was just trying to scare us and have some fun but we didn't know it then. Charlie took off in one direction and I took off in another."

Callahan took a hit from his cigarette, then tilted his head to the side and blew smoke at the window opening from the corner of his mouth.

"Charlie was running at top speed, but he kept looking behind him to see if that old farmer was about to shoot him. He ran full tilt into the wall of the farmer's barn and knocked himself out cold."

"What happened to you?"

"I tried to jump a barbed wire fence and didn't make it. "

"Ouch."

Callahan leaned over, took his finger and ran it down the back of his pants as if he was lighting a match. "I plowed a groove in the cheek of my ass that took nine stitches."

"I can feel your pain," I said, raising my leg and rubbing the back of it. "What happened to Charlie?"

"I kept heading toward the house; but when I realized Charlie wasn't meeting up with me, I turned around and went back."

I laughed softly. "I think you're braver than I am," I told him.

"Hey, he's my brother. What else could I do?" Callahan shrugged and blew smoke at the opening above the window. "Anyway, I get back to the farmer's house and he and Charlie are sitting on a bench, laughing about how funny it had been when Charlie took off and ran into the barn wall, and how hysterical it had been to see the look on our faces when we turned that outhouse over and saw the old man sitting there with that shotgun."

I laughed, "It's only funny if you're the one with the shotgun."

"That's the damned gospel!" Callahan hooted in agreement.

"Your brother sounds like he was a great guy," I said. "Mike says he really liked him."

"Oh yeah, everybody liked Charlie," said Callahan softly. "He was just one of those people." He picked up his cigarette pack and jiggled it, but nothing came out. He upended the little pack and looked into the hole as if the package were a telescope. "Shit! I'm out of smokes," he barked. He looked over at me; but before he could ask, I held my palms up and shrugged.

He wadded up the cigarette pack and flipped it out of the window. "Oh well, we probably won't be out here much longer. I'll grab a pack on the way home."

Littering seemed to be prevalent in 1947, but I didn't think it was something I could ever get used to.

John slid down in the seat a little, put his hands into his pockets and rested his chin on his chest. "Did Mike tell you how Charlie died?" he asked.

"No," I told him. "He just said it happened in Italy, near some town he couldn't remember the name of."

"I don't know the name of it either. Nobody seems to remember. "

He didn't say anything for a little bit and I thought he wasn't going any further, when he said, "It was pretty bad. Mike still can't bring himself to talk about it."

"That's rough," I told him, as sympathetically as I could. "Did you ever find out what happened to him?"

"Yeah, a guy named Benny Dunbar, one of the guys in the same outfit as Mike and Charlie, stopped by to see me a few months ago. He had been in town visiting Mike and was on his way to the bus station when he dropped by and told me about some of the shit he and Charlie had gotten into when they were in Europe. He didn't want to tell me how Charlie died either, but I begged him. I'm kind of sorry I did; it was pretty awful."

"I'm really sorry," I said softly. I meant it. I had seen enough death and carnage in my lifetime that I wasn't curious about the details of his brother's death. I was hoping he would stop there, and I was grateful when he did.

"Let's talk about something a little more pleasant," he said finally. He straightened up in the seat and started telling me how happy he was that we were watching someone pretty like Evelyn Cantrell and not a fat, hairy Italian guy like the fellow he had been watching the week before.

It turned out that the Italian also liked to parade in front of windows without his clothes, but no one wanted to watch. John went from there to talking about some woman he was dating, but my attention drifted away. I started wondering how Esmerelda and Roberto were doing. I wondered how many times they had been out already and that made me wonder if the "third date rule" was in effect in 1947. Callahan brought my attention back to the present.

"Well that's it", he said sitting up straight in the seat and pointing out the window.

I looked up at where he was pointing, and saw Mrs. Cantrell hanging up the phone.

"When she does that, it's all over. After this, she pulls the curtains together, turns out the lights, and goes to bed…alone."

On cue the pretty woman walked to the window and started drawing the curtains closed.

Who was she calling? I asked.

Callahan flicked his ashes out the window. "No idea. She could be letting her Mom or Dad know she's alright, or maybe it's the guy that isn't here. Who knows? By this time I'm usually half way up the street."

It took another couple of minutes for the lights to go out, but just before they did a couple of guys came out of the apartment on my side of the car. They both wore trench coats with the collars turned up and carried large leather briefcases. They had their hats pulled down low but there was plenty of light from the street lamps and I could see their faces. They both had dark hair and were clean shaven, but I couldn't see much more.

"What are the G-Men doing here?" John asked in a voice that wasn't very curious.

"What are G-Men," I asked back.

"Are you kidding me? Don't you ever listen to the news or go to the movies?"

I should have thought before asking but it was too late, so I just continued looking at him, waiting for an answer.

"Melvin Purvis?" he prompted and gestured with his hands as if he was trying to toss the name to me.

I kept staring at him, and he returned it with a disgusted look as he said, "Government Men; they're FBI."

That made sense but the understanding only brought new questions. "How can you tell just by looking?"

"Trust me. If you've seen one; you've seen them all."

They did share a type of look, whatever it was; so I figured he was probably telling me right. "Do you think they were the ones in that apartment watching Mrs. Cantrell?"

"That would be a good thing for them to do. They might just be off duty and waiting for the show like us."

"Then why would they be in that apartment?"

"First of all, you don't know that those guys were in that apartment, and second; do I look like J. Edgar Hoover to you? How would I know what they're doing here?"

I shrugged and looked back at the two men standing on the sidewalk talking to each other. They both looked in our direction, but didn't seem to care that we were sitting there. They turned away and then walked to the same place where Evelyn Cantrell had originally come from between the structures. It was becoming apparent that the parking for these apartments was on the other side. The two men disappeared between the buildings.

"There is a lot of stray skirt running around here," Callahan mused aloud. "Those boys might be after some of that."

I shrugged again, but didn't say anything.

My stakeout partner suddenly seemed in a big hurry. He touched me on the arm and said, "Hey, speaking of stray skirt, do you mind catching the bus back? There's a lady that might be available if I can get over to her place quick enough. I drop in on her every now and then, and I think this would be a good night to go over and see her."

"Booty call?" I asked him, without thinking.

"What?"

"I said...duty calls." It was lame, but serviceable. "You have to do what you have to do, right?"

"You got it," said John, twisting the key and starting the car. "Do you have change for the bus?"

I didn't know how much change I needed but I had some, so I figured I could make it work. I didn't want to show that I was ignorant of how much bus fare was so I told him, "I'm good," and got out of the car.

"Take care," Callahan yelled out the window. He wheeled the Studebaker around in as tight an arc as he could manage and headed away.

I watched him drive away and then walked over to the bus bench and sat down. My first thought had been that I didn't know the bus schedule, and I was going to have a hard time figuring out which bus to catch. As I pondered that, it dawned on me that this might be the least of my problems. I didn't know Mike's address or what part of town he lived in. I thought hard for a minute or two and then I looked toward heaven and reached into the pocket of my coat. At the bottom of the pocket I could feel a piece of paper, the receipt for the clothes Mike and I had bought. Half my prayer was answered. If the receipt had Mike's address on it, I had a fighting chance of getting home. I took it out slowly and kept my eyes closed while I unfolded it. I cracked one eye open, just a little bit, and for a moment couldn't figure out what the receipt had written on it. That guy Crowley apparently wrote with his feet. I opened the other eye and studied the receipt a little harder. Sure enough, next to the word 'address' was a bunch of Chinese looking characters that I finally deciphered enough to read, "332 Charles Ave." I breathed deep, looked up and said silent thanks. That was only the first hurdle. Now I had to figure out which bus went to this address. I looked around the bus bench, but there was only a sign post with a lot of numbers on it, showing which buses came to this stop. It didn't say where they went. The only thing I could think to do was wait for a bus to pull up and ask the driver if they knew where my address was and what bus went to it.

I didn't have to wait too long for a bus to come by. I found out later that the major thoroughfare which we had turned off of dead-ended about a quarter of a mile north so the bus routes used this big cul-de-sac to load-up, drop-off and turn around. I stepped up on the first bus that came by and asked the driver, "Do you go by 332 Charles Ave?"

The driver was a big fat guy with a cigar stub sticking out of his mouth. He made a fork with the first and second fingers of his left hand, snagged the cigar out of his mouth with them and asked, "What part of town is that in?"

It was a fair question, but I couldn't have told him if he put a gun against my head.

"I don't know; I only have the address."

"What is it again?"

I told him and he shook his head. "If it was a main road I might be able to help you, but you'll need more than that." Gesturing with his cigar butt, he added, "You need to get a map and find out where that street is. Then you can check the bus schedules and find out which bus you need."

I knew the answer, but I asked anyway, "You wouldn't happen to have a map would you?"

"Hey, I'm just a bus driver, not a gas station. I can give you some bus schedules." He fished in a bin mounted on the dash and handed me a bundle of folded pamphlets."

"Thanks," I told him as I backed down the bus steps.

He waved his cigar at me, stuck it back in his mouth and roared off.

I sat on the bench and tried to decipher the bus schedules, but the driver was right. Without a street map, I didn't have a chance of figuring out which bus I needed. I tried the next two buses that pulled up, but they weren't able to help me anymore than the first bus. As the temperature dropped, I became painfully aware that I was close to the lake. It was getting pretty cold, and the coat I was wearing wasn't up to the task of keeping me warm. On top of that, the stitches in my leg weren't getting along with the bench I was sitting on. I kept trying to bunch myself up to keep warm, but that hurt my leg and I had to lean over and stretch out which was making me colder. I would have given a lot for a smart phone at that moment. I resolved that I would ask the next bus driver if he was going anywhere near a telephone. I still had the number to the house and I could call and ask what I needed to know and, besides that, the bus would be warm.

"It's cold as shit out here," said a voice next to me.

The sound scared the daylights out of me, and I yelled and jumped sideways on the bench. This hurt the stitches in my leg, and I yelled again. I rubbed the side of my leg and stared in total disbelief at the semi-toothless little old man that had brought me to this world. He was wearing a fur lined denim jacket and had on a hunter's cap like the one Elmer Fudd wears.

"You scared the shit out of me!" I barked at him.

The old coot smiled with one side of his mouth and asked, "Why do you have to overstate the obvious? Everybody within hearing distance knows you were scared."

"How did you get here?"

"The same way I get everywhere," replied the old fart.

I let that one go by. I didn't feel like playing games with an ugly, toothless little Sphinx.

"What are you doing here?"

"I came to check on you?"

"Is that part of the job?"

"It is. How are you doing?"

"I'm stuck here. I don't know how to get back, and I'm freezing."

"Is there anything else? Do you want to tell me about the bandage on your face or the cuts on your back and legs?"

"It sounds like you already know all those things. "

"I do. I just want you to feel that you're part of the process and that I'm listening and helping to meet your needs."

"That sounds like a lot of useless business-speak."

"You caught me, that's where I got it."

"If my needs were being met, I would have an overcoat and a cell phone."

"You caught me, again. I'm not that interested in your needs."

I glared at the old coot while I took a deep breath and exhaled slowly. The light wind from the lake carried the fog of my breath away even as it bit through my shirt and pants. I managed not to shiver by a pure act of will.

"Let me get this straight," I said slowly. "Your job is to watch me and keep track of me."

"Right," said the old guy proudly.

"But you don't give a shit what happens to me."

"Right again."

"Then why are you watching me?

The old guy looked indignant. He stuck his chest out and said, "It's my job." He shook his head and looked at me like I was a moron.

I wondered how much heat he would produce if I killed him and set fire to him. I don't know why, but I decided against it and asked, "What's the point? I thought the idea was to strand me here and leave. "

The old guy's head swiveled hard and he glared at me. "What are you talking about? You don't have to stay here if you don't want to. We're simply trying to offer you an alternative. We're not kidnappers."

"Alternative? Alternative to what?"

The old man scoffed as if it were a stupid question and said, "To a destructive lifestyle that would most likely lead to an early grave."

"And you think my lifestyle is destructive?"

"You shot a man in the balls during a drunken bar fight."

"I wasn't arguing with you," I muttered, looking away. "I was just clarifying,"

"We don't make anyone stay against their will," said the old man.

"Have there been lots of others?"

"There have only been a few. We can't move people around willy-nilly. Certain criteria have to be met."

"What   criteria?"

"Well, for starters, we can't move someone to a world where they already exist."

"Does that violate some law of nature or physics?"

"No, it's just a pain in the ass if they happen to run into each other."

"But I will exist in about 40 years, right?"

"No, the man that would have been your Grandfathers' father was killed in the Meuse-Argonne Offensive in 1918."

"My great grandfather was a hero in WWI. He was awarded the Army Distinguished

Service Cross. "

"Not in this world."

"So I will never exist here."

"You will if you want to. That's the point I was trying to make. You can call this your home anytime you say. If not, you go back."

"How many people, before me, have decided to stay?"

"I guess it's around fifty percent. This world is a little tough, and some folks can't live without color television or the internet."

"I do miss those things. I'd kill for a smartphone right now."

"It's up to you."

"If I'm not stranded here how do I go about getting back? Do I just click the heels of my ruby slippers together?"

"How can you be so ignorant?" snapped the little man.

"I've always been ignorant about things I don't know," I snarled at him. "I'm funny that way."

"I don't know how you're going to survive here," he growled back at me.

I gritted my teeth and stuck my face in his. "You keep saying that, but I'm still here."

He turned away and looked toward the apartment building. "Yes, I guess you are."

"So I'm really not stranded here?" I asked, still not able to believe what I was hearing.

"You can go back if you want."

This was certainly news to me, and it was a real game changer. For a moment, I forgot all about being cold as a torrent of things ran through my mind.

"What would I need to do to go back?" I asked.

"Just say you want to go back."

"And you'll take me?"

"Yup"

"I guess I would have to go back and face charges for those guys I beat up in the bar. Hey! Did that guy, the one that got shot, did he make it?"

The old man nodded. "He did. He'll be alright…with just one testicle."

"I guess they'll be mad, because I escaped from jail."

"No one's mad about anything and no one's looking for you."

"How did you manage that?"

"It's no big deal. It was pretty obvious that those guys were out to rob you; and as far as the guy with one testicle goes, his gun went off in his pants. It's hard to press charges for that."

"What about escaping from jail?"

"The dayshift officers that went to release you thought the nightshift had already let you go. Since the paperwork was good, nobody cared."

"I guess you handled that."

"I did."

I smiled and said, "It looks like you really are watching out for me."

"What have I been saying? You must have a head like a rock."

I looked at the ground and thought for a couple of minutes. I finally asked, "How long do I have to give you an answer about staying here or not. "

"You can have until the end of the week. If you survive, and if you want to go back; you can tell me then. If you want to stay here I'll leave you alone and you can get on with your life."

I looked down the road leading out of the cul-de-sac. The surprise had worn off, and the cold had returned. I was shivering and wondering if it would be warmer on my old world. I had only been on this world for two days, but in that time I had fought with two different sets of armed men, gotten cut up jumping through a window, and spent a night sleeping face down in a bloody bathtub. I would have thought these things would add up to a screaming vote of "Get me the hell out of here!" But somehow they didn't. Other than being terribly cold, I wasn't unhappy with what was going on. I was glad he was going to give me time to think about it.

At the far end of the street I saw a bus turn in and decided I would get on that one and ask the driver to let me out at the nearest payphone.

"How do I get in touch with you?" I asked, with my eyes still on the bus.

When I didn't receive an answer, I turned around to look; but I already knew the old man was gone.

The bus pulled up and I got on and put ten cents in the box. When the driver closed the door, I knew I had guessed right. I asked him about the phone. He nodded and said there was a good spot about a mile away. I thanked him, sat down and wondered, what in the world I should do and which world I should do it on.

CHAPTER 12

The part of town where the bus driver let me off wasn't nearly as lavish as the part where Mrs. Cantrell lived, but it looked like a decent middle-class area and that suited me fine. On the corner near the bus stop, I saw a neon sign that said, "Billy Gray's All Night Diner," so I headed in that direction. It was a decent looking place with a long Formica counter on one side and booths lining the windows on the other side. In the back were two phone booths, and I used one to give Mike a call.

It caught me by surprise when Lieutenant Briggs answered the phone.

I stammered for a second and then said, "Hello Lieutenant, I didn't expect you to still be there."

I don't know how, but I could tell Briggs was turning his head and looking over his shoulder as he spoke into the phone. "Mike was really down, so I hung out and had a couple of beers and played some Gin Rummy."

"That was nice of you. I know he's missing Norma."

"Yeah, and I don't blame him. I assume that's who you need to speak to."

"You know, now that I think of it, you might be able to help me better than he can." I explained my predicament and asked if he was familiar with the bus routes and could he direct me.

"Let me think a minute. The 52 runs near where you're calling from but I can't remember if it's on that street or if it's two streets over on Perkins. I know the 73 runs near that diner, but I can't remember if it goes north or south. You know what, the hell with this shit. Talk to Mike while I get a map."

Before I could say anything, Mike's voice was on the phone asking, "What's going on?"

"Not much," I told him. I gave a quick synopsis of the evening and told about Callahan's booty call using John's terminology and not mine.

"You gotta be shittin' me," Mike bellowed into the phone. "If he wants to go over to the Town Pump that's fine, but he should have given you a ride home first. I'll have a talk with him."

"You don't have to do anything on my account," I told him.

"It's not just about you…wait a sec, here's Bob."

The Lieutenant's voice said, "Screw these damned maps; stay where you are and somebody will come get you in a few minutes. "

"Uh, okay," I managed to say before the phone went dead.

I really didn't want anybody going out of their way for me; but if he wanted to come get me, I would gladly sit and wait for him.

I sat down at the counter next to a big glass dome that covered what looked like an apple pie. The guy behind the counter walked over to where I was. He was fortyish, and his brown hair was so curly it played the devil with the little white cloth hat he was wearing. He flipped a dishrag over his shoulder and asked me what I wanted.

"Is that apple?" I asked.

"It is."

"Let me have a slice of that and a cup of coffee."

He nodded and made it happen. The pie was pretty good, and so was the coffee. I was really enjoying the moment and it fascinated me that I would get so much pleasure from such simple things.

I started thinking about what the little old man had said. I had already consigned myself to the fact that I was stuck here and would have to make the best of it. Now, I found out that I wasn't stuck anywhere. Going back to the 21st century wouldn't be a bad thing. I missed my Smartphone, and I missed being able to watch streaming video when I was stuck waiting somewhere. It hadn't taken me long to discover that I didn't like public pay phones at all. I still hadn't gotten the hang of 1947. I figured it was going to be a long time before I actually blended in, before people didn't look at me funny because I was ignorant of something that everyone else in the world knew. On the other hand, I hadn't been doing such a hot job living in the future. It had been embarrassing earlier that morning when I had confessed to Mike that I had spent a good part of the last year drunk. It surprised me; because I had admitted it to him and myself at the same time.

A lot of things had changed in forty-eight hours. That little old man had brought me here and within minutes I mattered again. I had saved a woman's life and been offered a decent job for doing it. Of course, the cost of being able to matter had been high. I had taken a number of shocks in the last two days. I was living in an impossible place; I had taken a couple of beatings, and I had dealt out a couple. I had been knocked around, shot at, and cut up; but I was still moving. If I had to admit it, I was proud of myself. It felt as if my eyes were opening, and I could see things as they actually were. I was starting to see that it wasn't Mike Manzarek, or the little old man, or even this world that made the difference. It was me. It pissed me off to realize it had always been me. Instead of doing menial grunt work and feeling sorry for myself, I could have been doing the same things in the 21st century that I was doing here. I could have gotten work as a bodyguard or applied at any of the Detective Agencies. I could have been a bounty hunter like Mike had been. Hell, it was possible that some of the small town police departments might not be so picky about my knee problems. I should have at least looked around and maybe given something a try.

The little bell hanging above the door tinkled, and I turned to see a uniformed policeman enter. I guessed he had come in for a slice of that good pie, so I turned around and finished mine. I could hear the officer's heavy footsteps on the tile floor, and it became ominously apparent that he was standing directly behind me. I looked up at the counter guy who looked back at me and then over my shoulder at the cop. He had a scared look on his face, and I'm sure he was wondering if the cop was going to ask me if the pie was any good or if he was going to arrest me for some heinous crime. If he had asked, I wouldn't have been able to tell him.

"Are you Jake Kerwaski?" asked the cop.

I turned around to face the officer. He was about my height and weight with dark hair and the squarest jaw I had ever seen on a man. "I'm Jake *Kowalski*," I told him.

The policeman rubbed his square chin with his thumb. "Oh, that's what the dispatcher was saying. Well, whatever your name is, I'm supposed to pick you up."

"For what?" I asked. I was feverishly trying to figure out what I had done to get the attention of New Egan's finest. I was wondering if Mrs. Cantrell had spotted us and called the law to have us arrested for being window-peeking perverts. I had, for the moment, forgotten that her show was open to the public.

"Don't you need a lift over to Mike Manzarek's place?"

My mouth fell open. When Briggs had said somebody would come and get me, I thought he meant himself or Mike.

"Yes, yes I do," I confirmed.

"Let's go then," he said, waving his thumb at the door. "I can't wait long."

I drained the last of my coffee as I stood up and reached into my pocket. If I was reading the check right, and I couldn't believe I was; the quarter I flipped onto the counter should cover everything, including the tip. The counter guy winked and smiled, letting me know I had been correct. I still couldn't believe it.

The officer's squad car was parked at the curb, in front of the diner, and I hopped in. It was interesting to ride in an old police car, but it wasn't pleasant. I tried a couple of times to make some small talk, but the officer wasn't interested, so I rode along quietly. I don't know what fat assed cop had been riding shotgun in that thing, but he had made one hell of a dent in the seat. I never did find a comfortable position. The car smelled like sweat, vomit, cigarettes, and cigars.

I have no idea how the officer understood the police radio. When a call came in, it made a thick scratching sound like an old car bumper being dragged across asphalt. The officer seemed to have no problem with it; then again, he had misheard my name. Every now and then he would pick up the microphone and say something into it. The radio would reply with the scratchy, grinding noise; and then it would be quiet for a while.

We made good time and in about twenty minutes we were headed up the street toward Mike's house. As we went by the neighbor's, a couple houses down from Mike's, I noticed a car parked on my side of the street. It looked familiar, and as we got even with the vehicle I could see two people struggling in the front seat. As we passed it turned out that they weren't struggling, at least not in a bad way. It was Roberto's car, and it looked like he and Esmerelda were trying to get their tongues untied before he took her back home. I had the incongruous thought that I would have killed Roberto for a nickel or given a million dollars to trade places with him. Nobody offered me the nickel, and I didn't have a million dollars so I just made a face like I was sucking a lemon and lumped it.

If the crappy little clock on the dash of the squad car was correct, it was 11:35 when we pulled up in front of Mike's house, and the officer unceremoniously motioned for me to get out. I hopped out, closed the door and yelled thanks through the window. The policeman touched his finger to the visor of his hat and sped off.

I walked up the driveway and as I reached the front door, Mike and Lieutenant Briggs stepped out onto the porch.

"It looks like Patrolman Conley got you here in one piece," said Briggs.

"He did. Thanks for sending him; I thought I was going to have to walk back."

Mike shook his head, "I can't believe Callahan booted you out so he could run over to see the Town Punchboard."

Briggs busted out laughing. "That's where he went?"

"Yeah," barked Mike indignantly. "Can you believe that? He gets all hot and bothered watching Cantrell's old lady through her front window and then he kicks Jake out to go ride the Town Bicycle."

I started laughing, too, but I really wasn't sure why.

"I told you he was squirrely," laughed the Lieutenant.

"Yeah, but we're all squirrely like that," Mike replied.

Briggs spoke loudly over his shoulder as headed toward his car. "That we are, my friend, that we are." He got in and drove off, waving out the window as he headed down the driveway and out into the street.

"Nice fellow," I said, waving back.

"He's the best," agreed Mike.

The lights from the Lieutenant's car had no sooner faded than Roberto's headlights played down the road. He turned into the driveway and stopped in front of the porch.

"Do we need to give them some privacy," I asked.

"I don't know," said Mike thoughtfully. "When you came up was Roberto parked down the street trying to see how much of Esmerelda's face he could get in his mouth?"

"Well they were parked next door, but I figured they had lost something and were looking for it," I lied.

Mike smacked me on the upper arm with the back of his hand. "If it was Esmerelda's tonsils; I'll bet he found them. You do realize you don't lie worth a shit, don't you?"

"Yeah, I never have been any good at that," I confessed.

Roberto got out of the car and walked around to open the door for Esmerelda. He had a big happy look on his face, for which I couldn't blame him; but I sure could hate him for it.

"Are you waiting up for us?" he asked, opening the door and smiling even more.

"No," said Mike nonchalantly. "Briggs just left, and Jake just got here."

Roberto took Esmerelda's arm and brought her back the way he had taken her. Her hair was mussed up, and I guess Roberto had swallowed most of her makeup; but she was still gorgeous.

It was easy to hear the sympathy in her voice when she asked Mike, "How are you doing? Have you heard anything from Norma?"

"I'm okay. Bob said Norma was doing fine. She asked us to send some books and magazines. I have the list."

"I'll work on that first thing in the morning," said Esmerelda. "What time do you want breakfast? "

"Jake and I should probably roll out of here around 7:00"

"Then I'll have breakfast ready at 6:30."

She turned to me and asked, "Did you have a nice time watching the burlesque show?"

"Not as nice a time as Roberto had," I thought to myself. Aloud I said, "There was no show this evening. She just read a book and then closed the curtains."

"How sad for you that you didn't get to see her do all those dirty things you heard about."

"Maybe tomorrow night," I said.

"You're going back?" she exclaimed. She did it so loud and so quickly, I jumped.

"We've been hired to watch her," said Mike.

"Qué cochinos son ustedes! What pigs you are!"

She stomped up the steps and into the house, and the three of us happily watched her do it.

"Being a pig is hard work," said Mike, "I think it's time I went to bed."

"I should go too," agreed Roberto. "Goodnight," he said, getting into his car.

Mike and I watched him drive away and after a moment Mike said, "That was big of you not to say anything when you had the chance. I assume you noticed the same thing I did."

"That Esmerelda's dress was on inside out?"

"Uh-huh."

"I didn't notice," I said.

"You really need to learn to lie better."

CHAPTER 13

I was at breakfast promptly at 6:30. The boss was already at the table, sitting behind a newspaper, drinking a cup of coffee. I exchanged greetings with Esmerelda, who motioned me to sit down, and with Mike, who never lowered his paper. Esmerelda put a plate in front of me as I sat down and one in front of the boss. The smell of country ham, eggs, and biscuits caused a stir behind the paper, and he folded it up and tossed it aside.

Mike dug in, and Esmerelda poured my mug full of coffee. Mike asked, "So there was nothing going on last night?"

"No, we just watched Evelyn Cantrell read a book and then go to bed."

"That should put her old man's mind at ease."

"I think so…hey, there was one thing that was interesting; but I don't know if it had anything to do with her."

Mike's eyebrows went up to let me know he was listening and I told him, "It looked like a couple of other guys were also watching Mrs. Cantrell. I caught a quick glimpse of a telescope sticking out through the drapes; and later when she went to bed, two guys came out of that group of apartments and left."

The Big Man blew on his coffee for a moment, and then asked, "Could you tell if they came out of the same apartment where you saw the telescope?"

"No, there was no way to be sure of that without asking them."

"But you think it was?"

"To be honest yes, I do. I can't prove it, but I have a feeling about it."

The Boss sampled his coffee and thought for a moment before asking, "Do you think they were just watching the show?"

"Callahan said they might have been. He also said they were FBI."

"FBI, are you sure?"

"That's what John told me."

"He's got the eye for that sort of thing."

"Yeah, he claimed it was easy to tell. He called them, what was it?"

"G-Men?"

"That's it."

Mike's head wagged up and down. "Well now we know why Paul Cantrell didn't want to come over and look for himself. I wonder why the FBI has the place staked out."

I assumed that was rhetorical, so I started eating. I had barely put a forkful 1 in my mouth when the doorbell rang, and Esmerelda hustled out to answer it.

"That should be John Callahan," said Mike, with a mouthful.

"What's going on with him?"

"I don't know. He called at 6:00 this morning and said he had something important to tell me."

Esmerelda came in with John behind her, and it took me a second to identify him as the same person I had been with the night before. His left eye was black and the cheek just under it was a harsh shade of purple. His upper lip was cut on the left side, his lower lip was cut on the right and both of them were swollen. His right eyebrow appeared to have been cut open just a little bit, right in the middle. He walked like he was in pain and the look on his face confirmed it.

Mike shoved a chair out for him and said, "John, what the hell happened to you?"

John sounded like crap, speaking through his swollen lips, but he was understandable. "Last night when I left Jake, I went to see a woman I know."

"So I heard," said Mike, with an edge in his voice.

"I probably shouldn't have done that, but can we worry about it later?"

"Yeah," said Mike, "Go on."

"When I got to this woman's house there were two guys coming up the walkway at the same time I was. They were both around 6 feet, two hundred pounds. One of them stopped me and said I had no business there and told me to get lost. I told him to go shit in his hat. One thing led to another and I woke up in the alley outside the lady's apartment building."

Mike said, "Damn, John, you must have wanted it pretty bad to take on two big guys."

John nodded. "It wasn't one of the smartest things I've ever done, but that isn't the real news."

Mike rubbed his forehead and looked like he was afraid to ask, "You didn't try and go see another girl, did you?"

"No, I went home laid on the sofa."

Mike looked relieved.

"I had only been home a few minutes when I heard a knock on my door. It was a guy my brother Charlie and I used to do business with before the war."

"What kind of business?" asked Mike.

"This guy sells information. He's pretty much a street rat, and every now and then he hears things and goes around to different people he knows to see if the information is worth some money. "

"This is starting to sound like real news," said Mike.

"It is. He said he had some information about a gang that had tried to kidnap a woman last Sunday night and again on Monday."

Mike was pleased, but he wasn't jumping in with both feet. "Who is this guy? Is his information good?"

"Yeah, everything he ever brought to us was on the level. I can't tell you who it is. It was part of our deal that I would never tell. By the way, this information cost twenty dollars; can I put that on my expense account."

"We'll square that later. Stop being a mercenary and tell me what he said."

"He said that it was some guys in Jules Epstein's organization that were trying to put the grab on Norma."

The look on Mike's face soured into disbelief. "What the hell?" he barked. "This doesn't sound like real news anymore. I know Jules Epstein. Why the hell would he try to run off with Norma?"

"That's what I asked the guy, but he didn't know. He claimed he had made a few discreet inquiries, but he couldn't come up with anything more. That was all he had."

Mike pulled twenty dollars out of his wallet and laid it on the table in front of John. "Tell him there's plenty more where that came from. We'll pay good money for any information he can bring us."

"I already did. He said he would do some digging and try and get back with me tonight or tomorrow."

Mike's gaze went blank as he scratched at his chin with his thumbnail and ran things by in his head. I took the opportunity to ask, "Who is Jules Epstein?"

Callahan gave me one of those, "where have you been" looks and said, more than asked, "You're not from New Egan, are you?"

"Nope," I said flatly.

"Jules Epstein is the last of the big gangsters. He made his money running booze, dope, gambling and prostitution during prohibition and has managed to keep his business alive and thriving ever since. The cops have never been able to touch him."

"This doesn't sound like someone we want to piss off," I said.

"It's not," agreed Mike. I know Jules socially, and I have no idea why he would want to do anything to me or Norma."

"Socially?" I asked.

Mike's head bobbed slowly. "Yeah, I've played golf with him, made small talk at a few charity and political fundraisers. He sees himself as just another businessman and technically he is. He has legal and illegal business ventures, and they are all well-run and profitable."

"And he gives to charity?"

"Lavishly…during the depression, he opened the first soup kitchen in New Egan."

"How do we find out if he's behind this," I asked.

"I'm thinking we should go and ask him," replied Mike.

Esmerelda walked over and put a breakfast plate in front of Callahan. It reminded me that my own breakfast was getting cold, and I turned my attention back to my plate.

John asked, "Are you sure that's a good idea? Epstein's the kind of guy you don't want to mess with."

Mike said, "You're right about that, but I think I know him well enough to tell him I've heard something and ask him if there's anything to it. I also don't think there is anything to this information. Jules is way up high on the food chain, so he is not afraid of me. If he wanted to do anything to me or Norma, he would just do it."

Callahan mumbled around a mouthful of eggs and ham. "So, you really don't think he was involved?"

Mike stood up, wiping his mouth with his napkin. "I don't think so, or as I mentioned, it would have happened. I'm wondering if some of his boys have gone freelance and are doing some work on the side. That's the question I want to put to Jules." He tossed the napkin on the table and headed toward his office. "I'm going to make a couple of phone calls. I'll be right back."

Esmerelda caught my eye and motioned that there was more, but I waved my hands and shook my head. "No thank you. This is all I can handle."

"I still think Mike is asking for trouble," said John. "Epstein is big time bad news."

I raised my hands and spread them apart. "I just do as I'm told. He's the boss."

"I think your boss is going to get you killed."

I shrugged, finished off my plate, and watched Callahan stuff his face for a while.

Mike's booming voice re-entered the kitchen before he did. "Epstein isn't in his office, but I got hold of his secretary. We have an appointment to see him at 5:00 o'clock this afternoon."

"He has a secretary?" I asked.

Mike looked at me as though I was being obtuse. "Who do you think schedules his tee times, Eisenhower?"

"Well I didn't really think…" I began.

Mike chuckled and explained. "Epstein's name means big business, both legal and illegal and he runs them by the rules of each." He sat down and toyed with his coffee cup. "His legal businesses have factories, laborers, secretaries, executives and board members. His illegal businesses have lieutenants, enforcers and henchmen."

"That still sounds weird," I told him.

"Maybe," acquiesced Mike, "but that's the way it works. If you were to cross him on one of his legal ventures you would find out that he has multiple high-level law firms on retainer and a full battalion of Ivy League attorneys standing by to come down from their ivory towers, take you down to the courthouse and kick your ass over the moon."

"And if someone crossed him on an illegal venture?"

"Do I really need to tell you? In that case, a couple of guys named Izzy 'Icepick' Goldberg and Abe 'The Axe' Weinfarb, will take you down to the docks and kick your ass into Lake MIchigan."

"Are you making those names up?"

"I am not."

"Oh shit!" barked Callahan, blowing toast crumbs across the table. "I almost forgot." He fished a piece of paper from his shirt pocket and handed it to Mike.

"After my friend left last night, I was having a nightcap, for the pain you know."

Mike rolled his eyes. "Oh, yeah," he indulged, "I can understand that."

"Well I was having my drink and I get a call from an old friend of mine at Republic Aviation. We spent about half an hour shooting the breeze and talking about old times at Republic."

Mike turned the paper, so I could see it. It looked like an address.

"Is this your friend's address?" asked Mike.

"No, that's Max Winston's address."

Mike shouted with excitement. "The guy Jake kicked in the head?"

"I still don't think it's the same guy as in the picture, but my buddy from Republic said that he went out to Max's house sometime last year, and that's the address.

"This address is in farm country," said Mike.

"Yeah, Max lived somewhere in the city when he worked for Republic, but after they let him go he went back to live at his family's old place."

Mike drained his coffee cup, looked at me and barked, "Let's roll out. Grab your hat."

I stood up, said, "Thank you" to Esmerelda, grabbed my hat off the back of the chair and fell in behind the boss as he headed for garage.

Yelling back over his shoulder, Mike told Callahan, "I really appreciate this information. I'll put a little something extra in your check."

"It's about time I was appreciated for my stellar contributions," John eulogized loudly.

As we got farther away from the kitchen Mike's voice got louder to cover the distance. "Don't sit around here patting yourself on the back, eating up my food, and annoying Esmerelda. Hit the streets and see if you can find out anything more."

I couldn't hear a reply. My guess was that Callahan was still eating.

As we started down the steps to the garage, Mike stopped and turned to look at me. "Are you heeled?"

"What?" I asked, praying to God that he wouldn't simply repeat it. I had no idea what it meant.

"Do you have a gun on you?"

I pulled my coat aside to show him I had on the shoulder holster with the .45 in it.

Mike's massive right hand massaged the lower half of his face as he thought for a moment. "Did you clean that BAR?"

"Uh-huh. It's cleaned, oiled, and ready to go. I couldn't test fire it, of course."

Mike didn't respond. He was obviously running something through his head.

"Are you're thinking we might need a light machine gun sometime today?" I asked.

"I can think of a couple of times in the last few days when we could have used one."

"Good point."

Mike smiled and asked, "Do you ever have one of those nagging little feelings that goes off like a little alarm and tries to warn you or tell you something?"

"You have a feeling that is telling you we need a BAR?"

"Unless you have a Sherman Tank you can lay your hands on."

"I'll get the BAR."

Mike smiled and said, "I'm kidding. I was thinking we could take the rifle to a gunsmith I know and have him check it out. It bounced across the lawn, and it's no good to us unless it's accurate."

"Now, who can't tell a lie," I said evenly, "That feeling is really going off, isn't it?"

"You think I'm nuts, don't you?"

"No, I don't think you're nuts. I've learned to listen to that little alarm."

"Has yours been going off too?"

"For the last three days."

Mike nodded. "You get the rifle, and I'll make a call to Briggs and give him this address, so he will know what's going on."

I turned around and headed toward the guest house. "I'll meet you out front," I called back. I retrieved the weapon and the ammunition and met Mike as he rolled in front of the house. I stuck the rifle in the back seat and jumped in the front.

"What did Briggs say?" I asked.

"He wasn't in. I left a message with the dispatcher."

We headed away from the city, and it didn't take very long for suburbia to become Illinois farmland. It was unseasonably warm outside, and the fields and trees were still green. It was pleasant to look out over pastures full of cows, sheep or goats. We passed quite a few chicken farms and a couple dairies. It had been a long time since I had been outside the city, and it dawned on me that I should do it more often. We had the windows down and the nice grass and hay smell managed to get through Mike's cigarette smoke from time to time. I lay back in the seat and enjoyed it.

I didn't realize that I had dozed off until Mike's booming voice woke me. "You know, I still can't figure out how any of this pieces together."

"Which part," I asked, hoping I sounded interested and not sleepy.

"All of it." Mike punched the lighter on the dash and fished his cigarettes from his pocket. "Somebody is trying to run off with Norma, but they don't seem to be real concerned if they run off with her in one piece or not. The only lead we have is this Winston guy that Callahan says isn't the guy."

"You think Callahan's right," I asked.

"He's got a memory like a camera. He's squirrely, like Briggs says, but he isn't usually wrong."

The lighter on the dash popped out and he snatched it out and lit his cigarette. "Assuming he is wrong, the only connection between Norma and Republic Aviation is Congressman Nelson."

"Maybe Norma saw the Congressman out in the moonlight burying a body," I offered.

"With a politician that's always possible, but I just can't picture Nelson being that kind of guy." He took a drag off his cigarette and exhaled slowly as his thoughts whirled around. "I can easily believe he would take a little extra if it was offered to him, and if he was on the fence he could probably be persuaded to vote a certain way."

"Sounds like standard political stuff."

"Yeah, just business as usual up on Capitol Hill, but I can't see him doing anything that would require kidnapping or killing people to cover his trail. Shit, I can't see him being stupid enough to even leave a trail. He's a sharp guy, and the riff-raff you've been dealing with is a cross between Murder Incorporated and the Keystone Cops. "

"Well I don't know about that…" I started, but Mike was simply thinking out loud and wasn't listening.

"The information about Jules Epstein, that Callahan brought in this morning, makes even less sense."

"You're sure Epstein wouldn't do this?"

"Oh, he might do it, but he would need a reason. Epstein is a smart guy and he doesn't do anything without a reason. "

"Have you ever crossed him in any way?"

"Are you kidding? Nobody crosses Jules without being killed or forced to live the rest of his life hiding in a Tibetan monastery." He rubbed his chin and added, "That's the weird part."

"That you're not living in Tibetan monastery."

"No, that Norma or I could run afoul of Jules and not know it. He doesn't keep things bottled up or spend any time turning the other cheek. If you piss him off his vengeance is swift, merciless, and *loud*. He wants everyone to know you're in pain."

"You're saying that since he's not yelling you must not be standing on his foot."

"That's the way I see it."

"Seems a little thin to base anything on," I told him.

"It is. That's the reason we're meeting with him this afternoon. I'll just ask him if he has anything against me, and we'll take it from there."

"You really think he'll tell you the truth?"

"Oh yeah, he's known for that."

This new world was getting more confusing all the time, and I'm sure the confusion showed in my voice.

"This particular gangster is known for telling the truth?" I asked.

"That's been his reputation from the start. The word of Jules Epstein is gospel. You can bank on it."

"I don't think I'm ever going to get used to this."

Mike didn't say anything else, and I dozed off again. When I woke up we were on a tar and gravel road that ran to the horizon. There was only farmland on both sides of the road as far as I could see, and a lot of the fields were full of corn. It was just about harvesting time and the green color was very pretty. Some of the fields had other crops or had been harvested, and through them I could see a lot of fences and barns and every so often, way back from the road, I could see a farmhouse. A couple of times I noticed a much smaller shack between thirty and forty yards from the backside of the farmhouse.

"Is that a tool shed," I asked, pointing at one.

Mike looked where I was pointing. "I guess it could be if the guy put his tools in the shithouse."

An outhouse, how could I have missed that? I know I turned red, and without turning my head I knew Mike was giving me one of those "How can you not know that?" looks.

Mike must have seen my discomfort and decided to have fun with it. "Are you even from this planet?"

"Well actually…"

"Shit! Is that Route 2?" he yelled, hitting the brakes.

I put my hands against the dash to keep from being thrown forward. The big car slid to a stop and Mike threw it in reverse and backed up next to a gang of mailboxes mounted on a big wooden railing on my side of the road. Most of them had red lettering that was now pink or brown from having been out in the weather for a few seasons.

"Is that Route 2?" asked Mike again, pointing at one of the mailboxes that appeared to have been nearly pried off the rail.

I squinted at the box. "It says RR2."

"Rural Route 2 it is," boomed Mike. He spun the wheel and turned onto a dirt road beside the boxes.

Including the other side of the road there were at least three more dirt or gravel roads that radiated out from the cluster of mailboxes, and I asked, "How do you know the house is on this road?"

"I don't," said Mike. He stuck his cigarette through opening at the top of his window and flicked his ashes into the wind. "This just looked like the nicest of all the roads at that junction."

"What if this isn't the right road?"

"Oh, it's probably not," said Mike, "but I don't think we'll have any problem as there is usually...here we go."

There was a young, blonde, high-school-age girl, wearing a blue cotton dress walking down the road swinging an empty bucket. Mike stopped the car and lowered his window.

"Good Morning dear, I'm sorry to bother you, but would you happen to know where the Winston house is located?"

"Yes, sir," said the girl, pointing back the way we had come. "You just go back out to the road and go straight across. It's about a quarter mile on the left."

"That's wonderful," said Mike. He stuck a dollar bill out the window. "Thank you very much. You go get yourself something to put in that bucket."

The girl thanked him and took the dollar. Mike made a three-point-turn and drove back toward the road. We crossed the road and stopped. The road continued and swept around a small house about fifty yards away from where we were sitting. The house and a stand of trees, another fifty yards behind it blocked our view of where the road went. On our right was a cornfield with tall corn ready for harvesting.

Mike pulled a .45 caliber revolver out of his shoulder holster and flipped the cylinder out. It was fully loaded except under the hammer. He said, "I don't know how well that little girl can judge distance, so I'm thinking we might want to walk from here." He closed the cylinder and slipped the pistol back into the holster. "I want to make sure we surprise this guy."

Mike started talking about the tactics he wanted to use, but I was distracted by the house in front of us. I could see that someone, years ago, had taken some pride in the place. Unfortunately, that someone was obviously long gone. The house was white clapboard and could have used a coat of paint and trim work. The tin roof was rusting and curled up at a couple of spots. It would need a little mending if you wanted to be sure the rain wouldn't come in. Something else caught my eye, and I realized that it was something very important.

He was still in full cry about how he wanted to sneak up on Winston's house when I interrupted him. "Mike..."

"What?"

"I don't think that little girl was any judge of distance."

"Why do you say that?"

"Because," I told him, pointing at a sign next to the house's front porch that said, "Winston est. 1897, "That *is* the Winston house."

CHAPTER 14

"Shit, so much for surprising that asshole!" yelled the big man, throwing the car into gear and letting out the clutch. "If I had known, we could have snuck up through that corn field. I can't believe I did something that stupid."

"Norma did say you weren't the brains of the outfit," I offered the boss.

"Can that shit and grab that BAR!" he shouted back.

It didn't sound like it was the first time he had used that phrase. I did as he ordered as fast as I could, as well as stuffing an extra magazine into my pocket and flipping the strap open on my shoulder holster

Mike slid the Caddy to a stop next to the house's small front porch and bellowed, "We've lost any hope of surprise; let's make a show of it!" He jumped out of the car with his gun drawn, using the car door for cover. He pointed to the right side of the house and ordered, "Run around the side and cover the back. Make sure no one tries to leave. I'll meet you inside."

I trotted around the side, keeping low against the house to make it hard for anyone to get at me through a window. I stopped at the back corner and did a quick peek-around. There was still no sign of life.

Mike's big booming voice carried to where I was standing. "Winston, we're not the cops. We just want some information."

Around the corner of the house I could see an even smaller porch than the one on the front. It was screened-in and a couple of wooden steps led up to it. I covered the distance and was on it in just a few seconds. I put my back to the wall of the house and scanned the area. There was a good-sized space that might have been a nice back yard at one time, but now it was overgrown and weed infested. Behind that was a row of trees that was hard to see past, and out to the right of the trees was a pasture. From this location I could see that the road continued, following the edge of the pasture.

The little screened-in porch covered the back door and one window. I peeked over the bottom edge of the window to see if I could see anything. I guessed it was the kitchen window since it was covered with greasy film that made it hard to see through.

The big rifle was heavy, and I needed one of my hands free. I slung it over my shoulder and drew out the .45. I still had my back against the house and I reached over with my left hand to try the knob on the door. My hand was almost on it when Mike's voice exploded in my ear. "Jake don't touch the door!"

I jerked my hand back as if I had been bitten. "What's going on?" I yelled back.

"Winston won't give us any trouble," said Mike with less volume. Come back around to the front.

I walked back to the front and found the door standing open. I stepped into what looked like the main room. It wasn't a huge room, maybe twelve by fourteen. The floor was cheap linoleum, and it was a bloody mess. There wasn't much furniture, just a couple of easy chairs and a table holding up a breadbox sized radio. The light hanging from the ceiling was a lone bulb with a thin metal dish over the top of it.

The walls were bare except for a couple of old posters from Winston's boxing days. They showed him in his boxing shorts and gloves under the heading 'Max the Marauder' Winston. The posters advertised real prize fights, so Max must have been pretty good in his prime.

There was an overturned wooden chair in front of the table. It was lying on top of a dirty, and bloody rug that looked like it had been kicked around the floor. Mike was standing next to the wall opposite the door and looking down at a man lying on the floor with part of his back propped up against the wall. Judging from the blood smear on the peeling and faded flowery wallpaper, his last act had been to slide down into that position. He was wearing a sleeveless undershirt and corduroy pants with the leg slit open to accommodate the walk-around cast on his left foot.

"This looks like your friend," said Mike, kneeling next to the body. "Somebody rammed a knife into him, real close to his heart."

"Yeah, that's him," I confirmed. I could still see the bruising from where I had made contact with my heel. "Why did I have to walk around," I asked Mike. "Why couldn't I just come in the back door?"

"I don't want either of us to touch anything more than we already have. Briggs and the cops shouldn't be that far behind us, and if there are any fingerprints or clues; I want them to be able to find them."

"The knob on the back door would be a good place to look for some," I agreed. "What do you figure happened here?"

"I don't know," said the big man. He patted at his own pockets looking for something. "Do you have a light on you?"

"No," I told him looking around. I walked over to see if there was anything on the table. "There's a soup can here, that he was using for an ashtray, but I don't see any matches or a lighter."

Mike dug through Max Winston's pockets and came up with a wallet, keys, and change, but nothing else. "He doesn't have a light either," he said, putting everything back. He looked up at me and said, "There's a matchbook over the visor on my side of the car." I nodded and went out and got the matches. When I returned, Mike was walking around the room with the unlit cigarette still in his mouth. He had his arm extended and was pointing at the blood smears on the floor as if he was tracing them. He moved around the room a couple times, then stopped. When he looked at me, I tossed him the matches. As he lit up, I wondered how modern forensic people would feel about someone smoking in the middle of their crime scene. For all I knew, the folks in 1947 might not like it either.

Mike took a drag and pointed to the table with his chin. "Do you see anything funny about that soup can ashtray?"

I looked at it for a moment and told him, "The only things in here are ashes and a half-dozen butts. Somebody has dumped a pretty good bit of unburned tobacco on top of them."

"I find that tobacco interesting. Whoever was here field-stripped their cigarettes and took the filter and papers with them."

It had been awhile since I had heard the term "field stripped" used for cigarettes. It was a technique smoker were taught in the military. As anyone who has ever been on a military base can tell you, the Armed Forces are very intolerant of litter. If you were smoking in a place that didn't have an available trash can, like the middle of a field or obstacle course, you were expected to peel the paper off the cigarette, scatter the biodegradable tobacco to the wind, and wad up the paper and filter to put in your pocket for disposal later.

"Why the hell would they do that? I asked.

"That's a real good question, "Mike replied.

"How do you know it wasn't this guy?" I asked pointing at the man in the floor.

"No matches or smokes on the body or in the general vicinity and no real ashtrays. This guy didn't smoke."

I ran my hand back and forth across my new flattop and tried to think things out. "So, two guys came here," I began.

"Three," corrected Mike.

I shook my head to clear it. "How do you know there were three?"

"There are six butts in the can. "

"Yeah," I agreed, but they look like they are all the same brand.

"They are," said Mike. "They're Luckies, same brand I smoke."

I had seen Mike's cigarette packs enough to know that "Luckies" must be short for Lucky Strike.

I still couldn't see what he was seeing, so I asked, "Why do you think there were three people smoking?"

The big man took a pencil from his pocket as he stepped over to the makeshift ashtray.

"See this butt?" prompted Mike pointing at it with the pencil.

"Uh huh."

"It has been smoked down to the center of the label."

"Okay, "I acknowledged, "but what does that mean?"

"It means that it looks exactly like two of the others, "responded Mike, poking at the matching pair.

What was clear to Mike was suddenly very clear to me. "I see what you're saying. These other three were only smoked to the edge of the label, and it looks like they've been crushed out differently."

Mike nodded and smiled his approval. "You've got a good eye. Judging from the way they are twisted, there's a good chance the second smoker was left handed and he definitely chewed the filters."

"So, three people came here and killed Winston?" I wondered aloud.

"No, the two guys smoking the Luckies were gone before the third guy showed up.

"How can you tell that by looking at an ashtray?"

"All the unburned tobacco is on top of the butts. The guy field stripping his cigarettes came later; otherwise everything would be mixed together. "

"That brings us back to the original question, 'Why would this guy field strip his cigarettes?'"

"I'm thinking he didn't want anybody to know he was here, or at the very least, he didn't want them to know what brand he smoked."

I looked at the soup can for a moment and then at Mike. "If that's the case, then whoever it was, came here with the intention of killing Winston. "

Mike's big head bobbed up and down. "That's what I'm thinking."

"But it looks like there is enough tobacco here to have come from three or four cigarette butts. Why would anyone stand around that long, talking to this guy, if their real intention was to murder him?"

"I can only guess at that," said the big man, "but I do have a guess."

He stuck his cigarette in his mouth and twisted his lips as he stared at the table, but he didn't say anything.

"And your guess would be…," I finally prompted.

A big finger pointed at a place on the table, next to the soup can, and I bent down to look at it closer. It looked like a watermark that a wet glass might leave, but it was a funny shape. Instead of a round outline, this one resembled a small hotdog.

"Does that look like anything you've seen before?"

I didn't really know but I started saying what I was thinking aloud, "It looks like the bottom of a really skinny or warped canteen...hey, wait a minute, that's the bottom of a hip flask!"

Mike nodded, "Well done. What was in it?"

"Some kind of booze, I assume."

"You don't have to assume. Check the finish on the table."

I ran my fingers over the outline and said, "That thing really cut into the finish."

The boss took a hit from his cigarette, turned his head to the side, and blew the smoke toward the ceiling; all the while continuing to stare at the table. "Thirty years ago, this was a nice piece of furniture with a French Polish finish." He ran his hand over the top of the table -- touching all the dents, scratches and chipped places in the surface before his fingers came to rest on the flask print.

"Now it's just a neglected piece of shit, but the fact that our friend's flask cut into the shellac finish tells us that it contained alcohol; because as everyone knows, alcohol dissolves shellac."

I wanted to say that I didn't think everyone knew that since I certainly didn't, but I was sure that I was already over my ignorance quota for the day. Besides I was more interested as to what Mike's theory was.

"So, what's your guess? Why would anyone stand around so long, talking to Winston, if their real intention was to murder him?"

"I think whoever was here was trying to work up the courage to do the foul deed."

That sounded thin to me, so I asked, "Winston was a tough guy, but he had been kicked in the head and his leg was in a cast. Why not just walk in, pop him, and walk out?"

Mike smiled and nodded. "That's what you or I would do, but I don't think our unknown friend had the brass to pull it off. He knew that Winston was a loose end known to the cops, and he needed to be taken care of; but I think he needed to work up to it, and that included a few braces from his portable drinking equipment."

"If he was skittish why didn't he use a gun? A knife is pretty personal."

"I'm guessing it was for the same reason." The boss frowned and rubbed his jaw. "Everything about this guy says he was afraid of being caught, and I'm thinking he didn't want anyone to hear a gun go off and come looking for the reason.

I wasn't totally embracing what Mike was saying but I kept quiet. He turned and pointed at one of the easy chairs with his foot. "There's a beer bottle and a small puddle of beer under that chair. I'm guessing Max here was drinking a beer while our killer talked and smoked."

"Max didn't offer the killer a beer? That seems odd."

"I think he probably did but our murderer refused the offer. I checked the refrigerator; there are five more beers in there."

"Why didn't our killer just drink what Winston had? Why did he bring his own?"

"I think there are a couple of answers to that. First, he needed something a lot stronger than a beer to get up the courage to do Winston in and, second, our cautious killer wouldn't risk leaving any evidence that he didn't have to. If he was conscientious enough to field strip his cigarettes he sure wouldn't want to worry about cleaning up any glass bottles that might have his fingerprints on them."

I nodded. The little pieces all made sense to me, but I still didn't see a big picture. "Did you see the knife anywhere?"

"Nope, it's not on the floor or in the cushions of these chairs and there isn't anything obvious missing from the kitchen."

Mike had stopped moving and was just staring at the bloody swirls on the linoleum.

"Can you make heads or tails out of that?" I asked.

"That puzzle is much harder to put together," said Mike. He pointed at the blood as he had done before and started moving around the room and then he raised his arm to point at me. "It looks like the trouble started about where you're standing, next to the table. I don't think it I'm going too far out on a limb in speculating that Mr. Winston wasn't expecting our killer to shove a knife into him." He turned, almost 180 degrees and pointed to the body. "It caught him near the heart but not close enough to kill him quickly."

"He should have used a gun," I reiterated.

Mike's head bobbed up and down slowly. "Since our killer isn't proficient with a knife it would have been a better choice. "

"We're pretty secluded out here," I pointed out.

"Yeah…you can get away with firing a gun in an area like this much easier than you can inside the city but you still risk someone hearing it and coming to see what all the shooting's about."

Mike looked out the front window. You can see those mailboxes from here so I'm staying with the theory he used the knife because he was worried someone might hear the gunshot."

"Then what?"

Mike reached out, with both hands, and grasped me by the shoulders. "The killer was right here when he knifed Winston. Judging by that dent in the wall, behind you, and the plaster dust on the floor, Winston either shoved the killer away or struck him and drove him into the wall."

I turned around and checked out the wall. There was a circular dent in it almost the size of a compact disc. I made a mental note to try and find something besides a CD to use as a reference and not say that out loud. The center of the dent was between three and four inches below my eye level.

I told Mike, "If that's the back of the guy's head then he's around five feet eight or five feet nine."

"Very good," Mike replied. "I'm guessing Winston stepped back at this point. Maybe he pulled the knife out maybe the killer still had hold of it. I don't know."

I turned away from the wall and faced Mike. If I'm the killer and Winston has moved away from me then I can make a break for the door. It's only a few feet to my left."

"I think he tried but your friend Winston had probably only backed up a step. When the killer made a break for It, Max caught him by the arm and swung him into the middle of the room. "

"How can you be sure?" I asked.

"I can't be. There is a lot of turning and swirling going on here and it wasn't all made by Winston. He definitely danced with someone. "

Mike stood still for a moment, stared at the floor and massaged his jaw. "This would be hard enough to piece together if it was intact but judging by the blood on the rug and some of these smears on the floor our killer used the damned thing to wipe away some of the blood."

"What was the purpose of that?"

"He might have been removing some footprints in the blood. He didn't actually wipe it up, he just smeared it around."

I bobbed my head up and down in agreement. "That would make sense. He was pretty meticulous about everything else. He sure wouldn't want to leave his footprints."

"Yeah, if you're going to leave your tracks in wet blood you might as well just show up at the police station with a noose around your neck.

I looked at the swirls of red in the floor and tried to make a story out of it, but I couldn't read the signs as well as Mike. "Okay, so he grabbed Max and danced around the floor with him. What then?"

"Good question. We know that our killer was smaller than Winston. We also know that Winston had been a professional boxer and punched like a freight train."

I touched the corner of my eye and said, "I can attest to that."

"I'm going to go out on a limb, but I'm guessing the killer still had the knife in his hand. If Max had the knife then his size and strength should have put him in control, and that would have made for a lot less foot painting in the middle of the room."

"I see what you're saying. The killer still has the knife, so Winston has hold of him with one hand and is beating the hell out of him with the other hand to keep from getting stabbed again."

"And all the while they are going around and round like a little boy getting switched by his mama."

"Okay, I don't have any trouble buying into this scenario, but how did the killer stop the fight?"

"I don't think he did. Judging by the prints it looks like Max took a couple of steps backward, hit the wall, slid down into the floor and stayed there. "

"I think I'm with you. There are no other footprints or smears following him to the wall so he had let go of the killer by then."

"Uh-huh, I think he bled out enough that the fighting was making him tired and dizzy. He let go, stumbled back, and expired."

"The killer takes the rug, smears whatever footprints he created and takes off."

"That's the story I'm telling, but it took a lot of guesswork to get there." He looked toward me and asked, "What do you think?"

I took a moment and considered the question and the answer very cautiously before I told him, "I'm not with you on this one." I watched closely for his reaction. I hadn't done much disagreeing with this new guy that would someday sign my paycheck, and I wasn't sure how far I could go.

Mike's eyebrows went up as he said, "You have a different theory?"

"Only slightly," I said quickly. "I think you're right about this guy being scared and jumpy. I picture him as being very afraid of what he was doing, and that's why he brought a gun…and a knife." The Boss went to rubbing his chin, so I could tell that he was at least thinking about it. "I also think our man is left handed," I finished.

The Boss's eyes lit up as he latched onto my train of thought, and he smiled as he started laying out the scenario.

"So," he began, "we both believe that just before he was stabbed Winston was about here." He squared himself directly in front of me and announced, "I'm Winston."

I was still standing next to the table with my back against the wall. "That makes me the killer, and I'm in the right place too."

"So, you pull a gun on me with your left hand," said Mike.

I raised my left hand with the index finger pointed. "Or I already pulled it and threatened you with it, but I'm such a wimp that you don't believe me and approach anyway."

The big man's eyes narrowed. "If I'm this close then I'm going to grab the hand with the gun,"

"I think you did," I told him.

Mike caught me by the wrist and used my whole arm to point my finger away from him.

"Okay," I said looking at my finger gun. "I didn't have the guts to pull the trigger on the gun until it was too late, but now my life is in danger."

"So, you pull a knife?" asked Mike, showing the foolishness of the idea on his face.

"My life is on the line and my adrenaline is running. Then again, maybe I'm such a coward I already had my hand on it when you crossed the room."

"So, you whip it out and stab me with it," Mike offered.

"But it's my off-hand, so I don't hit the mark I want."

Mike nodded. "At this point I have a bad knife wound, and I have one hand occupied restraining the gun."

"But that doesn't keep you from wailing on me with your free hand, and since I'm a coward I probably won't pull the knife out or let it go so you're the one doing all the slugging."

The boss let go of my wrist and stood quiet for a moment before saying, "You're scenario plays a little better than mine. I like it." He turned and surveyed the wall and ceiling behind him for a couple of minutes before he added, "I was hoping that maybe the gun went off. If we could find a bullet hole in the ceiling or wall your supposition would carry a lot more weight but I don't see anything."

"I'm long on guesses, and short on facts," I agreed.

"That makes two of us."

We both continued looking around the room for other clues or telltale signs; but Mike didn't say anything more, and nothing jumped out at me either.

I was curious about when he had been killed, so I asked Mike, "How long do you think he has been dead?"

"Good question," he answered. He walked over and started manipulating, or at least trying to manipulate the arms, hands and legs.

Mike tried to move the corpse's feet, and then he squeezed at the ends of his shoes.

"Hmm…Rigor Mortis starts stiffening at the head and neck, and then starts to move down the body. Full Rigor takes about twelve hours to fully set in and then…"

"Starts to dissipate." I finished.

"Knowing that, we can manipulate the limbs and see if everything is stiff."

"Is it?"

"I think I can move his toes a little. I could be sure if I pulled his shoes off, but I'm just not that curious." He turned to me. "If you are…"

"No, I'm good."

"A body starts to smell around the twenty-four hour period, so we know it hasn't been that long."

I knew that temperature mattered, so I suggested, "It was a little on the cold side, last night; but it has been pretty warm this morning."

"It was cold, where you were, out by the lake."

"I forgot about the lake. That would make a difference. So out here in the farmlands it was warm last night and this morning."

"Unseasonably so," Mike agreed, "and since temperature has a hell of a lot to do with the speed at which a body decomposes we are pretty much just guessing."

Mike looked at the body and rubbed his chin. "Going more on my experience with dead bodies and not so much on science, I'm thinking he was killed between 8 and 10 hours ago."

Mike looked over at me. "What do you think?"

"I was thinking 8 hours or less, but my experience with dead bodies has mostly been in super-hot areas, and I think that is throwing me off. Let's go with your guess."

Mike made a disparaging noise in the back of his throat before he said, "A lot of my experience has been in the snow, so mine may be off too." He wiped his forehead with the back of his hand. "I sure could use something cold to drink. There's a little country store about three miles back down that tar and gravel road. Let's head that way and get a soda and wait for Briggs to show up."

"That suits me," I told him. "I just need to hit the head first." I stepped to the side of the room and looked down the hallway. Mike began chuckling.

"If you're looking for the latrine you'll need to go out back to the tool shed."

"Oh yeah, I forgot," I said, trying to sound like Mike had only reminded and not educated me.

Mike knelt next to the corpse on the floor. "I'll hang out with your friend Max here."

I still had the BAR slung over my shoulder, so I unslung it and laid it across the arms of one of the easy chairs. I threw my coat and hat on top of it, and went left, out the front door and then around the side to the back of the house. Even though it was in line with that side of the house, it took me a moment to find the outhouse as it was partially hidden behind the line of trees I had seen earlier. I hiked back to the little shack thinking it was odd that it was so far away. It must have been between fifty and sixty yards from the house and that seemed excessive until I got closer to it. A few yards to the rear of the little shack was a stack of hay bales which had mostly gone to rot. I wasn't sure why Max Winston was living on a farm because he certainly wasn't interested in doing any farming. As I got closer I could see what was left of an old rusted car just off to my left. Apparently automotive maintenance or cleaning up his yard wasn't interesting to him either. I had thought the distance to the bathroom excessive, but that thought only lasted until I got near it. The little shack was terribly unpleasant. It was made of old, dark, weathered boards with gaps between them, some of them so wide you could slide your flattened hand through. The seat inside was simply a wooden platform to sit on, with a large hole cut into it. Despite the late date in the season, there was a pretty good number of flies swarming around. In lieu of paper there was a very old yellowed catalog from Union Hardware and Electric Supply Company. I stood in the doorway staring at it and thinking that the twenty-first century was starting to look really good. I was sorry the little old man hadn't left a way for me to get in touch with him. I went inside, closed the door and took a seat.

I made the best of things, while I was sitting there, by thumbing through the catalog and looking at all the old tools. I noticed that the pages with the farm and garden tools had been mostly torn out. That seemed to confirm my suspicions about Mr. Winston not having any affinity for farming or yard work. There were only a couple pages of the garden tools left so, in memoriam, I tore out and used the rest of them.

As I reached down to pull up my pants, from behind the shack I heard the way too familiar sound of a pump shotgun racking a shell.

CHAPTER 15

I let go of my pants, twisted off the seat to my left and flattened myself against the side wall of the outhouse. The shotgun blast blew a hole, the size of a basketball, right behind where I had been sitting. The shot went straight through, and tore the door from its hinges. Dust and wood bits swirled in the air, and the smell of cordite mixed with the rest of the stink. I didn't have time to waste on any of it. I heard the shotgun cycle again as I jerked the .45 from its holster and spun around. I fired, half-blind, through the hole the big gun had made and tried to get a bead on the shooter through the cracks in the wall.

I fired three rounds, and didn't hit him but I got close enough to make him run for cover behind the stacks of hay bales. He fired again, but he was busy moving and didn't even hit the outhouse.

I knew an opportunity when I saw one. I squatted down, grabbed my pants and fired two more shots through the hole. I stood up, pulling my pants up with my left hand and held onto them as I bolted into the open. Running from the doorway the hay bales were about five yards to my rear and to the right. In the opposite direction, about the same distance, was a big tree stump with a big pile of chopped wood sitting to the right of it. I sprinted for the woodpile as hard as my legs would make it happen. It wasn't going to be close; the distance was too far. I just hoped his aim was bad. I went into a flat dive over the top of the woodpile. I still held the .45 in my right hand with my arm stretched out in front of me and I held my pants up with the other. The shotgun roared again, and the heel on my left shoe tore away. I felt a flash of heat run up the side of my left calf and something tore open my pants leg.

I landed on my side and slid a few feet across the grass. As if bouncing on the ground wasn't bad enough, the wounds on my back started burning to let me know they were still there. It made my eyes water, but I would have to deal with it later if I still had that luxury. I twisted around in the grass and wriggled back to the stump.

I hadn't gotten a good look at the guy shooting at me, and I wasn't even sure it was just one guy. If there were two of them, I was most likely screwed. There wasn't anything behind me, but open space. To my right was the line of trees, and thirty to forty yards past that was the house. The trees would have made good cover, but the closest one was twelve yards away, and I had no idea where my shotgun toting friend was. The tree might as well have been in Idaho.

Off to my left, past the woodpile, was the old rusted out car I had seen when I first came down the hill. I heard the sound of rocks and gravel coming from that direction, and realized my new pal was sneaking around that way using the old car for cover. I squirmed around and put my right side against the stump and put the wood pile between me and the car. I took a second to finally fasten my pants and then crawled closer to the woodpile. My elbow banged into something heavy and metallic. It was a shovel head that had been broken off the handle. In front of me, leaning against the woodpile, was the broken handle. I grabbed it with my left hand and used it to steady myself as I rose up on my knees, very slowly, and tried to get a peek at my attempted murderer between some of the chopped wood on top of the pile. If I could see him I had a fighting chance. I finally got into a position where there were some openings in the woodpile, and I searched desperately for my would-be killer.

I finally saw him…out of the corner of my right eye. I was doing a good job of hiding behind the woodpile, but that wasn't going to help since it wasn't between him and me. He must have thrown some gravel under the old car and then ducked into the outhouse. While I was fastening my pants, he was getting into position to murder me. None of this went through my mind at that moment. There wasn't time. My only thought was, *"I'm dead,"* and then all hell broke loose.

There was a roar of machine-gun fire, and 30.06 rounds began chewing into the outhouse. I spun to my right and crouched lower behind the stump. Between the trees, I caught a glimpse of Mike Manzarek standing on the back porch holding a raging BAR. My pal with the shotgun dove from the doorway of the outhouse and landed spread-eagle into the dirt. He lost his grip on the twelve-gauge and it clattered up next to the stump I was kneeling behind

I didn't need a better invitation than that. I came across the top of the stump with the .45 in one hand and the shovel handle in the other. The man on the ground was close to my size with broad shoulders and a big head. He knew an ass-whipping when he saw one coming, and he rolled over onto his hands and knees and scurried on all fours like a trapped rat as he tried to turn around and get his feet under him to run. Inspiration struck me and I holstered the .45 and grabbed the shovel handle with both hands. He was facing away from me with his ass in the air when I caught him between the legs with a golf club swing that would have impressed the crowds in Augusta. When I connected he made a sick wet sound like he was trying to throw up something way too big to get through his throat. He grabbed himself with both hands and pitched, face first, into the dirt. He rolled over onto his back, still holding his crotch and making a gurgling noise. He drew his legs up, and I brought the handle down across his shins. He wailed pitifully, but I didn't have any mercy to give him. I reached down and grabbed him by the collar. My only thought or intention was to hold him with one hand and punch his big head until I got tired of doing it, but it suddenly dawned on me that I didn't hear or see Mike anymore. He wasn't coming down the hill to help me, and there was no sign of him outside the house.

Now it was my turn to feel sick to my stomach. I had been a diversion. This guy had been sent to kill two birds with one shotgun blast. He would blow me off the toilet, which would cause Mike to go to the back of the house and that would allow an unknown number of assailants to go in through the front door and sneak up on him.

I looked back down at Big Head. I was still holding onto his collar and he was still holding onto himself. His face was just a wad of fear.

"How many are with you?" I growled at him.

His eyes got wide and he started to shake, but he didn't say anything.

I drove my fist into his face. His expression didn't change, but his eyes watered and a stream of blood ran from his nose. I did it again, but he was still silent. I didn't have time to deal with him. I looked up toward the house, and even though I could see it between the trees, I knew Big Head and I would be nearly invisible from there. The outhouse was the only thing that you could see well from the house. I was pretty sure that was the reason Mike had targeted it with the BAR. I stared at the back of the house and felt my luck and time bleeding away. I needed a way to get back up that slope without letting anyone know I was coming. I jerked the .45 out of its holster and backhanded Big Head against his temple with the butt of the gun. He went limp, and I dragged him to the far side of the outhouse. His coat was a darker blue than my trousers, but it was close enough, and while my shirt was white, his had a light purplish pastel color to it. I stripped to the waist and then did the same for him. The shirt sleeves were just a little short, but that wouldn't be a problem. I buttoned the shirt, put on the coat and then went looking for Big Head's hat and shotgun. They were only a couple feet from each other. I grabbed them both and threw the hat on my head. It dropped down over my eyes and almost covered my nose. I was mad at myself because I should have seen that coming. I grabbed a woodchip from the ground and wedged it between the hatband and my head. It wouldn't pass a close inspection but I wasn't trying to.

I pointed the shotgun at the woodpile and fired off one more shell for good measure; then I walked past the trees and up the slope toward the house. It wasn't a moment too soon.

"Did you finally get him Ernest?" yelled a voice from the side of the house. I was pretty sure that whoever owned that voice was also leaning out the side window while they were yelling, but I didn't dare raise my head to look. I kept the brim of the hat pointed toward the ground and I raised the shotgun in a victory gesture.

"It's about damned time," said the same voice. This time the sound receded at the end, and I hoped that meant that whoever was talking had pulled their head back inside the house.

While I was changing clothes I had noticed that one of the pockets of Big Head's coat was full of twelve-gauge shells. As I walked toward the house I began reloading the weapon.

At that point I had a decision to make -- should I go in the front door or the back? I had no idea how many there were or how they were situated throughout the house or what the hell they were doing. It was possible there was only one guy in the house, but I doubted it. My best guess was two guys. If there had been more, I would have expected two guys to come down and shoot me off the crapper. I flipped a mental coin and went to the left around the side of the house and toward the front. I didn't dare look up or peek into the window, but I could hear voices as I passed by.

The one I had heard before said, "Just stay calm. When Ernest gets here we'll all go for a little ride."

A different voice asked, "You want me to go get the car?"

"No," said the first. "We'll send Ernest. You and I can keep an eye on our amigo here."

That answered my questions. There were two of them, and they were in the main room where we had found Max Winston. The ground on the side of the house was cut away more than in the front, so much so that I was walking by the windows with only my hat in view. The front was higher so my shoulders and head were in full view. I figured that my thin disguise wasn't going to get me much farther than the threshold of the front door so I played it for all it was worth. I kept the brim of the hat pointed down and put the shotgun over my right shoulder, to help hide my face, and I didn't stop or slow down as I went past the front window and walked up the steps of the front porch.

The door was wide open. I stepped across the threshold and raised my head. Mike was straight across from me with his hands raised above his shoulders. There was a man standing on either side of him, and both of them had their backs to me. The one on my left was a big man, about the size of the guy I had left next to the outhouse. He was wearing a dark blue pinstripe suit and dark hat. He was pointing a .38 revolver at Mike.

It was easy to recognize the other one from the day I jumped out of Mike's front window. It was my old pal Shorty. He had his left arm in a sling and a .45 automatic in his right hand.

Mike was facing the front door so he saw me first when I lowered the gun and raised my head. He didn't give anything away, but Shorty turned to say something to the man he thought was someone else.

"Ernest, run get the...shit!" he yelled as he saw me and brought his gun around.

The shotgun thundered in the little room and the blast folded Shorty in half. He slammed into the wall and landed on top of Max Winston. I swiveled to the left hoping to get the other man before he got me, but I needn't have worried. Mike wadded up his fist and slammed it down across the side of Pinstripe's head. Pinstripe's body slammed into the linoleum and slid into the hallway. I wouldn't have given better than even odds that he was still alive.

Mike watched him for a moment and when he had finally decided the guy wasn't moving he turned his head toward me. The woodchip that I had wedged in my hatband chose that moment to fall out. The hat dropped over half my head and Mike laughed out loud.

It was a nervous laugh that showed his relief. "I sure am glad to see you alive," he cackled. "I thought that guy had gotten you."

I took the hat off and tossed it on the little table. "If you hadn't interrupted him with that BAR, he would have."

Mike gestured to the men on the floor. "I was going to come down to help you, but Mutt and Jeff, here caught me on the back porch."

"I figured something like that had happened. That's when I changed clothes with that guy at the outhouse."

"Is he still alive," asked Mike.

"He should be, but I didn't have time to make sure."

Mike walked over to Shorty and bent over to check him. "I don't think this one is still with us. Check the other one."

I went over and put my fingers to Pinstripe's neck. .

"He alive?" asked Mike.

"Yeah, I had to hunt for it, but he has a pulse."

"Outstanding," said Mike. He fished a set of handcuffs from his coat pocket and threw them to me. "Cuff his hands behind his back, and then we'll go down to the outhouse and get Ernest."

The boss stood up and looked thoughtfully down at Shorty. "It looks like you finished the job Esmerelda started; he's gone". He lifted his hat and dabbed at the sweat on his forehead with a handkerchief. "Now all we have to do is fetch Ernest and sit around to wait for Briggs to show up."

On cue, a big four door car turned off the main road and pulled down into the driveway.

Mike and I walked outside and he asked, "Why are you limping?"

I hadn't realized I was doing it until he mentioned it. I told him, "That bubble-headed jackass blew the heel off my shoe with this shotgun." I bent down and pulled up my tattered left pants leg. The shoe looked like hell. "I don't think they're going to be able to fix that," I said.

"Probably not," agreed Mike, "but better the shoe than your foot." His eyes narrowed and he asked, "What's that on the back of your leg?"

I twisted my leg around and could see a shallow red gouge, almost the diameter of a soda straw that ran three inches up the back of my calf.

"That," I said slowly, "is a lot closer to getting my leg blown off than I care to think about."

"You were lucky," said Mike. He paused for a moment and added, "We both were."

Briggs rolled his car up next to Mike's Cadillac. He and two other men, one older officer and one very young, got out. They were each holding a bottle of Coca Cola.

"Well, hell!" bellowed Mike. "You stopped for Cokes and didn't bring us one."

"Oh we brought you one," said Briggs dramatically. There's a little girl, about half a mile up the road selling them out of a bucket for ten cents apiece."

Mike smiled, "Blonde girl, high school age?"

"That's her. She said a big handsome man in a Cadillac gave her a dollar to tell him where the Winston house was."

"It's all true, Officer," Mike told him.

"I'm sure it is," affirmed Briggs sarcastically. "The same information cost me a dollar, but at least I got five sodas for my money."

"You're a shrewd businessman," said Mike.

"Oh yeah, I'm so shrewd I got hustled by a little girl," griped Briggs, reaching through the window of his car and coming out with two more bottles. Mike took them and walked toward his own car.

Briggs pointed the neck of his bottle at the house and asked, "What did you find here?"

"Max Winston's dead," Mike told him. "We're guessing he was knifed sometime during the night." As he spoke he opened the passenger door of his Cadillac. He took one of the Coke bottles and stuck the end of it in the door's latching mechanism and pushed it down. I heard the sound of gas escaping and then the sound of the little metal top bouncing off the bottom edge of the door opening. He did the same for the second bottle and handed it to me. I tried to pretend that none of this was new and interesting.

Briggs caught the attention of the other two policemen and motioned them inside with a jerk of his head. "Did you touch anything?" he asked us.

"Hold up!" Mike commanded the two officers. They stopped on the porch and looked back at Briggs.

"We didn't touch anything…at first," said Mike slowly.

Brigg's eyes narrowed to slits and he asked, "What does that mean?"

The Big Man raised his palms toward Briggs. "First things first -- there's a half-naked guy down by the outhouse that we should probably bring up here before you get started."

"Is he alive or dead?" asked the older officer from the porch.

Mike looked at me and I opened my mouth to say something; but I wasn't positive so I just spread my hands apart and shrugged.

Briggs looked at me and asked, "Would you mind showing Officer Muldoon where this guy is located?"

It was nice of him to phrase it as a question, but it wasn't. I nodded quickly and the older officer stepped off the porch and motioned for me to lead the way.

"Before you go," asked the Lieutenant, "would either of you mind telling me *why* there's a half-naked guy by the outhouse?"

"Jake took his clothes," replied Mike.

"Why?"

"So he could masquerade as the guy who tried to back-shoot him while he was on the toilet."

Briggs made a face like his antacid wasn't working and said to Mike, "Why don't we let Mr. Kowalski and Officer Muldoon go fetch the gentleman by the outhouse. You and I and Officer Jones can go inside, and you can start this story from the beginning." He motioned for us to go and asked Mike, "Did you mess up my crime scene?"

Mike told him, "We walked into the crime scene before we realized it was one. We only went in through the front door and we didn't touch anything after we realized Winston was dead in there."

"That sounds fine," acknowledged Briggs, as he and Mike joined Officer Jones on the porch.

Muldoon and I headed around the corner of the house as the boss said, "You would think so, but then we ran into some trouble."

As we passed by the side windows we heard Jones shout, "Holy shit! What the hell happened in here?"

CHAPTER 16

While we walked down the slope to the outhouse, I gave Officer Muldoon the abbreviated version of what we had found when we arrived and what had taken place afterwards. Muldoon was just under six feet tall and big around the waist. He listened to my story and grunted every now and then.

We found Ernest where I had left him. He was face down in the dirt and his nose bleed had stopped, but he had managed to slobber a pretty good sized puddle. The right side of his face was covered with dirt and mud. We rolled him onto his back and I shook him to see if I could wake him, but it didn't have any effect.

"Let me try," said Muldoon. He stuck a big ham hand into his back pocket and came out with the largest hip flask I had ever seen.

"A little Irish Whiskey will bring him around," he said, reaching down and opening Ernest's mouth. He had poured about a shot worth into the open hole when Ernest coughed a little and opened his eyes. Muldoon saluted me with the flask and then took a stiff hit and offered it to me. I waved it off and grabbed Ernest by the arm and pulled him to his feet. I took off his coat and shirt and handed them to him. I picked my own shirt up off the ground where I had left it. As I started to put it on, I wondered why I had bothered changing back. The shirt was smeared with dirt and grass stains from where I had slid near the stump. It looked like crap, but I went ahead and put it on.

"You should have kept the clothes you had," offered Muldoon. "That looks like a bad trade."

"I think you're right," I agreed, "But his stuff didn't fit me right."

"It couldn't have been that bad," replied the Officer.

Muldoon cuffed Ernest's hands behind his back, and the Officer and I walked back with Big Head between us. Ernest was making a show of walking slowly with his legs spread apart and Muldoon finally asked him, "Why are you walking like that?"

Ernest motioned at me with his big head and told him, "He hit me in the nuts."

"Oh, that's right", replied Muldoon, "I had forgotten about that part."

"I think he messed me up down there," groused the big headed man.

"Really?" asked Muldoon, feigning concern. "I think it sounds like a cheap price to pay for trying to back-shoot a man." He took a big meaty hand and prodded Ernest in the back with it. "If you had done that to me your cods wouldn't be sore…they'd be in my pocket."

Big Head didn't say anything. He was in a bad position, and he had enough sense to keep quiet.

When we got to the house, we found Lieutenant Briggs leaning against the front of his police car smoking a cigarette. I could hear the voices of Mike and Officer Jones coming from inside the house as they tried to untangle the mess we had made of the crime scene. Briggs didn't seem to mind simply standing outside and listening. When he saw us he came over and helped Muldoon take our prisoner to the car. They talked for a couple of minutes and then Muldoon got behind the wheel and drove off. Briggs shoved Ernest over in front of Mike's car, leaned him back against the hood and then put his foot on the bumper, just to the side of the big headed man, and resumed his smoking.

I walked over and put my foot on the bumper, on the other side of Ernest, and asked, "Where's Muldoon going?"

"He went to find a phone. You boys have plowed up more criminals and dead bodies than we can handle."

I thought of how much Briggs would like 21st century police radios or even a regular cell phone, but since I couldn't say *that* I said, "I see what you mean."

We stood there quietly for another minute or two and the Lieutenant finally flipped his cigarette butt out into the driveway and said, "Well, let's get started." He leaned in close to Big Head's big face and asked, "Ernest Who?"

Ernest just looked at him without saying anything.

Briggs looked over at me. "Oh dear," he said in nice even voice, "I didn't know Mr. Lightbulb Head was a tough guy. " He put his fingertips together and twiddled them against each other. "He's way too tough for me." He smiled a wicked smile and to me he asked, "Would you please go get that shovel handle Officer Muldoon mentioned?"

"Okay," I said, turning around and heading back the way I had come.

"Thanks," Briggs called out after me. "Once you've batted Mr. What's-his-name's balls into that cornfield, I'm sure he won't mind telling us his name."

I was almost to the corner of the house when Big Head growled, "It's Dulay."

The Lieutenant made a show of taking out a small notebook and asked, "I'm sorry, what was that again?"

"It's Dulay gahtdamnit. My name is Ernest Dulay."

The Officer nodded and smiled. "That's very helpful. Thank you Mr. Dulay." He leaned in close and put his face next to Big Head's and asked, "What brought you out here, today, Mr. Dulay?"

Ernest just looked at him.

"Well, Mr. Kowalski," Briggs said to me, leaning back from the car, "It looks like we will need that handle after all."

I was walking back toward the car, and I was only about two long steps from Ernest. I tried to put an aggravated look on my face and I snarled, "Damnit Briggs, why the hell do I have to walk down to that outhouse and bring back a shovel handle just so you can jerk this guy around. Ernest turned to look at me. I cleared the distance between us in two quick strides. I cupped my right hand and drove it up between Big Head's legs grabbing everything my hand could hold and, as I mentioned before, I have a big hand.

In fractions of a second, Ernest's face went through a range of emotions, but the one it settled on was terror.

"Why don't I just take his toys with me and beat them against that woodcutting stump when I get there." I squeezed down and twisted my hand for emphasis.

Ernest came up on his toes, snot and blood shot out of both nostrils and in one long sentence with no breaks and no spaces between the words he said, "We came down here because Shorty said he had work for us all we had to do was take out one guy and tie up another and then take that guy back to Shorty's house and wait for more instructions."

"You call him Shorty?" I asked, surprised.

Ernest was near tears, "Yes," he whined, "I don't know his real name."

That made sense to me since I called him Shorty for the exact same reason. Briggs jotted something in his notebook and said, "This is interesting Mr. Dulay; we appreciate your cooperation."

"Screw you, you mother…owww," wailed Ernest as I clamped down harder on his equipment.

I put my lips next to Ernest's ear. "Now…who are you working for?"

"I don't know who the big guy is," spluttered Ernest. "Shorty told me and Skeevers that he didn't know either, but we didn't believe him."

Briggs leaned in from the other side and asked, "If nobody knows who the big boss is, how do you get your instructions?"

"Shorty claimed he got a phone call this morning. The guy on the phone told him Max was dead and that Shorty was in charge now. He told Shorty to find as many people as he needed, and he would pay us a thousand dollars apiece to capture Big Mike Manzarek. "

"What about me?" I asked.

"He said that there might be a guy with Big Mike, the one Shorty saw when he tried to grab Mike's old lady. He said that we could do what we wanted with him."

"And you chose back-shooting?" I asked, twisting my wrist a quarter of a turn.

"I'm sorry," wailed the big headed man. "It was Shorty's idea. He said he didn't know much about you, but you had already caused him trouble so he didn't want to take any chances."

"How did you know Mike was going to be here this morning?" asked Briggs.

"We didn't," blubbered Ernest. "The guy on the phone said he would probably be out here sometime today, so we waited in the cornfield. " He cut his eyes in my direction. "When you two separated we made our plan to catch him by using you for a diversion."

"Where were you supposed to take Mike?" asked Briggs.

"To Shorty's house, the guy on the phone said he would call later and if we had the big man we would setup an exchange for our money."

"Where's Shorty's house?" asked Briggs.

"I don't know," whimpered Big Head.

Briggs snarled, "Yank this idiot's nuts off."

"I don't know," squealed Ernest, at the top of lungs. "I've never known where he lived. He only calls when he has a job and we pick him up and drop him off at a bus bench downtown. He never wanted us to know his real name or where he lived."

"Whose car did you come in?" I asked.

"Mine, it's parked on the other side of the cornfield."

"Ask Shorty," pleaded Ernest. "He'll tell you what you want to know."

"We can't ask him," said Briggs, "Mr. Kowalski here, blew a hole in him with your shotgun."

I wouldn't have believed it possible, but Ernest turned a shade paler. "Is Skeevers still alive? He'll tell you the same as me.

Briggs made a motion with his head, and I removed my interrogation aid from Ernest Dulay's crotch. The officer walked him to the front porch and sat him on the middle step. He returned to the car and his original posture with his foot on the bumper. He put a cigarette in his mouth and snapped open a metal lighter. Putting the lighter to the tobacco he still managed to say, "Muldoon says you did a damned good job down there," from one side of his mouth. He removed the cigarette and used it to point down the slope toward the outhouse.

"He's just being nice," I said.

Briggs started coughing and smoke puffed out of his nose and mouth. "You were around Muldoon for about twenty minutes. Did you actually discover anything nice about him?"

"I see your point," I conceded. I wanted to change the subject, so I pointed at the house and asked, "Is your man having any luck in there?"

"Officer Jones is one of our rising young stars. He's a country boy, and a born hunter. He can track men through the woods or through the streets, and he's the second best crime scene investigator I've ever seen. I'm pretty sure he could get a fingerprint off of a wet fish."

"If he's second best, who's first?" I asked.

"The man in there with him."

I chuckled softly and shook my head.

"Does that surprise you," asked Briggs.

"No, I think I'm done being surprised at the things Mike can do."

The Lieutenant blew a smoke ring and watched it dissipate. "Don't bet on it," he said softly.

"Well this might still work out," I offered.

"How so?"

"Mike has a working theory about what happened here."

"Is this before or after you cut a man in half over the top of my crime scene?"

"That would be... before."

Briggs stubbed his cigarette out on the heel of his shoe and thumped the butt into the driveway. "Well, if Officer Jones concurs then maybe we have ourselves a horse race."

I wasn't exactly sure what that meant, but I took it as, "We'll see."

We waited while the Lieutenant smoked another two cigarettes. At that point I heard the sound of a car turning off the main road and onto the dirt driveway. It was Muldoon. He parked the car where it had been before and got out.

"I called the dispatcher. They're sending the Coroner out to pick up the bodies."

"What about the live ones," asked Briggs.

"They're going to send another black and white out with the Coroner's wagon."

"I take it you couldn't find a phone nearby," said the Lieutenant.

"What's that supposed to mean," growled Muldoon.

"It means you took a long time to make a phone call so you must have gone looking for a phone in a bar, and there wasn't one near here."

Muldoon's face brightened up. "Oh yeah, that's exactly right. The nearest joint is almost seven miles up the road."

Briggs rolled his eyes and shook his head back and forth but didn't say anything. Muldoon came over and bummed a cigarette from him and just as Muldoon flipped his butt into the driveway Mike and Officer Jones stepped onto the front porch.

They both appeared pleased, so I figured they had come to the same conclusions. Jones told the story of Winston's murder pretty much the way the boss had sussed it out, and Mike gave his firsthand account of Shorty's demise. I said nothing. I only nodded my head every now and then when Briggs looked over at me.

Briggs jotted down things in his little notebook and then told Jones, "Let's talk to that guy in the pinstripes."

"We don't need to," said Officer Jones trying to stifle a laugh.

Mike was wearing a smile that said he was happy with himself, and he just stood there watching Jones laugh.

"Would anybody like to fill me in?" growled the Lieutenant.

Mike proceeded to tell the story of how Pinstripe, Skeevers, had regained consciousness as he and Jones were sorting out the crime scene. When Mike heard Ernest spilling his guts to us he had gone to the window to see what we were doing. When he saw what was happening he dragged Skeevers over to the window, just for a moment, so he could watch me threaten Ernest's family tree. After that, every time Ernest yelled or squealed out loud, Mike embellished on what was going on and how badly we were torturing him. It only took a couple of times before Skeevers was singing harmony to Ernest's lead. As it turned out, Ernest had been telling the truth. The man in the pinstripes confirmed everything he told us.

"So what's your next move," Briggs asked Mike.

"I have an appointment with Jules Epstein."

"Hell of a time to go running off and fraternizing with gangsters, isn't it?"

"Yeah, it is, but Callahan got word from one of his people on the street that Epstein's people were the ones trying to run off with Norma."

"Whaaaat?" asked Briggs, drawing out the word in disbelief.

"He said a guy that has always given good information is claiming that our trouble is coming from Epstein."

"That doesn't play," said the Lieutenant. "If Epstein wanted you dead, you would be."

"I know," said Mike. "I told Callahan the same thing."

"Until today, the guys you've been dealing with have all been two-bit thugs." He pointed to the porch and added, "Excluding the newly deceased, these new boys are better than the idiots that went after Norma at the house, but even these guys aren't in the same league as Epstein's people." He jerked his chin up towards Ernest. "Any of Epstein's people would know to have a shell chambered in the shotgun before sneaking up on somebody." Briggs looked at me. "Today would have gone much differently if he had. Am

I right?"

I nodded. He was right. It would have.

Mike cleared his throat and asked, "How did it go at Republic Aviation?"

My head snapped up at the question. I had completely forgotten that visiting Republic had been our number one priority when I woke up that morning.

"It didn't," replied Briggs.

Mike's eyes narrowed. "You didn't go?"

"We went, but the Security Director extended his out of town business trip and he won't be back until tomorrow morning."

"That's a little suspicious," said Mike softly.

Briggs' chin went up and down. "Yes, it is."

Mike started doing that thing with his hand and the bottom part of his face which I had come to understand meant he was thinking. He asked, "Can't we talk to someone else?"

The Lieutenant shook his head. "I talked to a number of people, but all of them told me I would have to speak to the Director of Security. No one else was interested and no one else offered."

"Shit," snarled Mike, "Can we get a warrant and go in?"

"A warrant to go in and get what?" queried Briggs. "The only thing we know is that we found a murdered guy that used to be employed there."

"The same guy that tried to kidnap Mike's wife night before last," I offered.

"That means diddly-squat. We could get a warrant for a lot of things, but not to storm Republic Aviation. We don't have anything that ties this jerk's crimes to his work."

"So we wait," groused Mike.

"Yup."

"What if they shine us on tomorrow?" asked Mike.

The officer smiled, "Then we can tear into their asses for obstructing an investigation."

The sound of tires on dirt drew our attention toward the main road as a black and white station wagon and a black and white cruiser pulled up to where we were standing.

The Lieutenant walked over and started talking to the driver of the station wagon, and Muldoon began waving his arms and giving orders to Officer Jones and the young officer in the cruiser. The two junior policemen gathered up Ernest and Pinstripe and put them in the back of the cruiser. Jones got in with the other young officer, and with a wave to everyone else, they backed out and headed down the road.

We watched them leave, and then I realized that Mike was staring at me.

"What?" I asked, a little too loudly.

Mike raised his arm and made a twirling motion with his hand and finger that meant I should turn around. I only got halfway around when the boss's big hand stopped me.

"You've got blood back here," he said in a low voice.

"I was afraid of that," I told him, stripping off the shirt so he could get a better look. "How bad is it?"

"Hmmm…I think the bleeding has stopped. You opened the corners of a couple of these wounds, but it looks like the stitches are still holding. "

"Well that's good news," I said as I put the shirt back on.

"Yeah, we need to find a phone and call the house to let Esmerelda know what's happening. When we stop, make sure you have your coat on or you'll scare the crap out of some unsuspecting soul."

I nodded and went in the house to get my coat. Then we got into Mike's Cadillac and headed out.

CHAPTER 17

It seemed like weeks had passed since breakfast but the little clock on the dash said it was just before noon. The adrenaline that had sustained me while we questioned Ernest was long gone and I just wanted to lie down and go to sleep. I didn't get the chance. As soon as we pulled onto the road The Boss punched in the lighter on the dash and as it popped out he started thinking out loud.

"Now," Mike rumbled slowly as he lit his cigarette. Then waving the car lighter as if he were cooling a match, "help me figure out what the hell happened today."

"You're asking me?"

"You were there."

"I'm lucky I'm not still there," I barked.

"That makes two of us," agreed Mike, "and that's the problem." He took a long drag from his cigarette and then tapped his ashes in the car's ashtray. I had forgotten that cars had those things.

"We should be dead or at least at the mercy of those assholes," Mike continued. "They knew we were coming, and I want to know how."

"Shit, that's right, they did know."

"Uh huh, and that can only mean that the guy that gave Callahan Max Winston's address told them we would be coming."

"Or someone told him to give Callahan the address."

"Or one of those guys is the one that called Callahan."

"That would be a good possibility," I said.

Mike's big right hand squeegeed the lower half of his face. "That call was pretty convenient, don't you think."

"You figure the killer did his business and then had one of his cronies at Republic give Callahan a call and set us up."

Mike's gaze was fixed out into the distance and he bobbed his head slowly. "That is the theory that makes the most sense."

I thought for a moment and asked, "Is it possible the killer *is* the guy that called Callahan?"

"That's another possibility. Either way we need to find out who that guy is and pay him a visit." He motioned toward the windshield with his jaw and said, "Hey, that's just what we need, up there on the left."

About two hundred yards away, on the left hand side of the road, was a market of some sort. It took up about as much space as a mobile home and wasn't much more than a tin roof with supporting poles. Plywood had been nailed along the backside of it and the rest was tables and bins of fruits and vegetables. The only other thing was a phone booth, about two car lengths from the front of the structure, at the edge of the road.

"That's what we need?" I asked skeptically.

Mike spun the wheel on the big car and pulled into the dirt parking lot and angled up to the market.

"This is exactly what we need. Esmerelda said to buy fresh corn and snap beans if I saw any, and I believe I see some. Plus," he added, pointing at the phone booth, "we need to call her and check in. We're overdue."

The construction might have been shoddy but the merchandise was wonderful. There was bin after bin of corn, broccoli, beans, cabbage and dozens of other fresh vegetables and a few fruits. Mike grabbed a paper sack and started loading up. The only other person in the place was a large, round, middle-aged woman wearing a tent dress. She was sitting in a folding wooden chair that looked like it wasn't going to last the day.

Mike stuck a paper bag under my nose and pointed at a bin full of snap beans in the rear of the market. I headed over and started stuffing the bag. While I was doing that, I noticed something interesting on the other side of the bin from where I was standing. There was what appeared to be a large shiny metal pitcher, like a tall teapot, sitting on a table. On top of the pot was a little glass bubble and something dark was boiling inside of it. I wanted to ask what it was, but I was afraid to for fear of being embarrassed. I was right not to ask. Just as I filled the sack a large arm came over my shoulder and pointed at the shiny pot.

Mike called out to the woman in the chair, "Sweetheart, is the coffee for sale?"

The woman didn't get up, but called back, "Honey, the coffee's free to paying customers; but I'd let a good looking fellow like you have a cup anytime."

"I'm telling Norma," I whispered from the corner of my mouth.

"Can that shit and go get our free coffee," ordered the Boss.

Mike took my sack and headed to the front to let the woman weigh everything. I went around the bin and found a stack of paper cups sitting near what I now knew to be a coffee pot. I poured two cups, but there was no picking them up. I really missed polystyrene foam cups, or at least those nice cardboard sleeves that go around a paper cup and keep you from burning your fingers. I pulled a handful of napkins from a dispenser on the table and wrapped a few around each of the cups.

I carried them to the front of the store where the woman was weighing the bags that Mike had taken to her. She did some calculations on the side of one of the bags and then folded her arms over the top of her big stomach and announced, "That'll be a dollar fifteen."

Mike fished a bill from his pocket and asked her, "I'm sorry but all I have is a twenty, do you have change?"

The woman let out a big snorting laugh and informed him, "Handsome, just because I look like Ava Gardner doesn't mean I have her bank account.

I made a mental note to write, "Ava Gardner" on my paper when Mike wasn't looking.

The big woman got up, and I was sure I heard the wooden chair take a breath. She waddled out behind the back of the market and called out, "I'll be right back."

We could hear a car door open and in a moment we heard the car fire up and drive off.

I handed Mike his coffee and asked, "Did she just rob us?"

Mike was inspecting a head of cabbage and said, "I don't think so. I'm pretty sure she is running up the road to get change." He smiled and added, "At least that's what I hope she's doing."

I watched her drive, casually, to a farmhouse about three eighths of a mile down the road. She pulled off the road and then plodded up to the house and went inside. I had mostly forgotten the stories my Grandfather told me about a time when people didn't bother to lock their cars or their houses, a time when a fellow could hitchhike from one place to another and not worry too much about being robbed or murdered. I touched the bandage on my head and realized I could be the poster boy for the meanness and cruelty in this new world, but it was obvious there was a lot of good in this place.

Mike interrupted my thoughts. "Have you got change on you?"

"What?"

"Change…for the phone. We need to call Esmerelda."

"Oh, yeah," I said, jingling the change in my pocket.

"Give her a call and tell her that we should be back before one o'clock and to hold lunch for us."

I nodded and headed toward the lone phone booth next to the road.

The phone booth was made of glass and wood like the one I had found myself in when I arrived in this world. Everything inside the booth was dusty, but it looked functional. I put my nickel in and dialed the number and was surprised when a woman came on the line and asked me to deposit another fifteen cents for three minutes. "*A telephone operator,*" I thought. That was another thing that my grandfather told me about and I had pretty much forgotten. The operator was intervening, because even though we weren't that far away from New Egan; it was considered long distance and in 1947-money a long distance call was obviously pretty pricey. I put in the extra change and after a couple rings Esmerelda answered. Suddenly, I wasn't tired anymore. The sound of her voice turned a really weird and scary morning into a hopeful afternoon. Even when she was fussing at me I enjoyed listening to her.

"Why are you taking so long? If you don't come and eat I'm going to feed your tacos and frijoles to the neighbor's dog."

"Don't do that," I implored in complete honesty. Tacos and frijoles sounded really good at that moment. "We ran into a little problem that we had to clean up, but we're on our way back. We should be there before one o'clock."

"Tell Mike to hurry or I will eat your tacos and feed the two of you to the neighbor's dog."

"Yes ma'am," I said sharply, "We're on our way."

I hung up and returned to the market just as the lady waddled back to Mike with the change. She gave her thanks and went back to shortening the life of the folding chair. Mike and I loaded our produce into the trunk and started for home. I was hoping to catch a little nap on the way back, but Mike was still trying to work things out.

"We need to get into Republic Aviation and find out what their connection is."

"Uh-huh," I grunted. I wanted to sound involved so I asked, "What about Norma's connection with the Senator?"

"I don't know," replied Mike. "When it was just Norma they were after that angle might have made some sense, but since they seem interested in taking me too, I don't see the connection anymore."

I didn't see it either and I didn't have any good ideas, so I let my mind wander and noticed that the back of my leg was itching where the shot had grazed it. I reached down to try and give it some relief. It was easy to get to the back of my calf since the pants leg had been torn open.

"Is that giving you trouble?" asked Mike.

"It itches," I replied as I probed around the area.

"Don't scratch that thing," Mike warned, "you'll get it infected."

"I'm not, but I want to at least scratch around it and see if that helps."

It didn't fix the problem, but it did help a little. Once that started to feel better I noticed that a couple of the wounds on my back felt like they were burning. Scratching wasn't going to help, so I tried to think about something else and remembered Callahan's story of how he got his stitches.

"At least I'll have something new to show John the next time I see him," I told the boss.

Mike punched in the dash lighter. "Are you guys having measuring contests when you're supposed to be watching Cantrell's old lady?"

"She wasn't putting on much of a show the other night, so John was telling me about how he got hurt when he and his brother were pushing over an outhouse. " I paused for a moment and added, "I never did figure out why they were pushing over outhouses."

Mike snorted, "Yeah, like you haven't done it."

"Well actually…" I began.

"Did he tell you that they pushed over one with a big burly farmer sitting inside with a gun?"

"Double-barrel rabbit-ear shotgun."

The lighter popped out and Mike lit a cigarette and shoved the lighter back in the dash. I tried to remember if I had ever seen anyone in the 21st century use the car lighter for a lighter, or if they just took it out like I did so they could plug in their phones and computers.

Mike blew a plume of smoke out his window and said, "The farmer and the gun get bigger every time he tells that story."

"If it wasn't a big angry man with a double-barrel shotgun, what was it?"

"A sixteen year old kid glad handing it to a copy of Spicy Stories magazine."

I started to laugh and said, "That kid must have had some tool on him to scare John into jumping a barbed wire fence and running away."

"John has never been the brave one in the family," Mike replied, and after a moment he added, "He's no paragon of courage today, but when he was young you could scare him with a loud fart."

"I'm guessing his brother Charlie was different."

Mike nodded and exhaled a slow cloud of smoke. "They were as different as night and day," he confirmed. "Charlie had more brass than a whorehouse cuspidor. "

I slipped my piece of paper and pencil out of my pocket and started to write down a reminder to look up the word cuspidor when Mike said, "It's a spittoon."

Up until that moment I had thought I was getting away with these things, but my ignorance was apparently more obvious than I had hoped.

"Thanks," I said softly, putting the pencil and paper back in my pocket.

I was afraid the boss was going to begin an interrogation as to why I was an unending vacuum of knowledge but what he said was, "I've heard a lot of people say that we left the best of this country lying on the beaches of Europe and the South Pacific." He had to stop clear his throat before he continued. "In Charlie's case that was true, except it wasn't a beach."

"You said he died near a little town in Italy," I prompted.

"He's buried near it." He paused for a moment with a faraway look on his face and then started speaking again. "I can never remember the name of that place, but Charlie's buried near it. He died on one the town streets."

"During   the   fighting?"

"No, there was no fighting in that little town. Charlie died badly. I don't like talking about it, but I can tell you he wasn't killed by the war. He was a great guy; he had a wonderful life and was killed for a man's enjoyment."

"That's terrible," I said softly.

"More than you could know. Every couple of months I dream I'm back in that damned little town. I always think that I can save Charlie, but I still wake up yelling out his name and then crying myself to sleep. Norma's had to put up with way too much of that."

"I'm sorry."

"Don't be. We all brought shit home from that damned war and we all have to deal with it."

I wondered just how badly Charlie died if the big man was willing to tell me the story he had just told, but not the other one. I didn't say anything else and we drove along in silence for awhile. After a few minutes I reached down to scratch around my leg wound again, and the torn pants leg reminded me of my busted shoe, and that reminded me of the ruined shirt. I looked down at my ratty clothes and asked Mike, "Is there a laundromat anywhere near the house?"

It surprised me when Mike asked; "A what?" and I figured I might have just asked for something that didn't exist yet.

I didn't repeat it. "Is there a place near the house where I can wash my clothes?"

Mike's mouth reared up on one side and he scoffed through his nose. "You're actually going to try and wash that?"

"It's a brand new shirt. I hate to throw it away without at least trying to wash it."

"I suppose you're right, but I wouldn't get my hopes up."

The Boss stubbed his cigarette out in the ashtray and informed me, "I already talked to Esmerelda about this. If you pay her fifty cents a week, she said she would wash your shirts, socks and unmentionables and iron the shirts."

"That sounds like a sweet deal."

"It is a sweet deal, but I wouldn't show her *that* shirt. She'll beat the grass stains out of it with your ass."

"I don't doubt that," I conceded.

Mike didn't say any more after that, and I didn't realize I had dozed off until I woke up as he was turning the car into his driveway. I tried to ease up straight in the seat and pretend like I had been awake, but I was drooling from one side of my mouth and my neck was stiff. The wounds on my back were burning, and I could tell that my left side was going to be sore where I had landed on it "Feeling better?" asked Mike. He pulled into the garage and shoved the gearshift on the steering column straight up. When I wasn't sleeping, I had been watching him shift the car and if I was guessing right, he had just put it in reverse to park it.

"Yeah, I'm sorry I must have dozed off."

"Don't be sorry. You've taken a pretty good beating in the last few days, and you had a rough morning. I would need some rest too."

We got the produce from the trunk and headed for the kitchen. The smell of carne asada and frijoles wafted through the house and got stronger as we got closer to the kitchen. It was wonderful.

Esmerelda was stirring something in a big pot, so her back was turned to us as we entered. "Esmerelda, buenos tardes," bellowed Mike, as we entered the kitchen. "That smells fantastic. I hope you made a lot because we are starving."

"Si, hay mucho…A Dios mio, que paso?" she cried as she turned and looked at me.

I tried to think of something clever to say, but I just stood there with my mouth hanging open. She pulled back the lapels of my coat and then surveyed the damage to my pants leg.

"What is it with you and your clothes?" she demanded.

"We ran into a little trouble," I finally croaked out.

"Is it just your clothes or are you hurt?"

"It's just the clothes," I tried to say with conviction.

"Mentiroso, show me your leg."

Mike had been right; I really needed to learn to lie better. I tried to make light of things and raise my good pants leg, but she whacked me on the arm with a big wooden spoon and yelled, "The other leg, *payaso*."

"Clown," the boss translated before I was forced to ask.

I raised the tattered pant leg and she stepped around where she could see my calf wound and my heel-less shoe. "A Dios mio!" she cried out as she crossed herself.

At that point she took a wider stance, put one hand on her hip and threatened our lives with the wooden spoon in the other if we didn't tell her the truth about what had happened.

We told the story as quickly and gently as we could. Every now and then she would stop us to call out to God or threaten to send one of us to him. She finally decided she knew enough and motioned with the spoon for us to sit down at the table.

Callahan must have been in Mike's office, because as we sat down I heard him yelling to us as he came through the living room toward the kitchen.

"Well it sounds like you guys had an interesting morning," he said loudly, popping into the kitchen with a big smile splitting his face. "I just got off the phone with a friend of mine down at the precinct. "

Mike had picked up his paper but stopped opening it to ask, "What did he have to say?"

John pointed at Mike. "He said you got into a gunfight in a farmhouse and had to shoot it out with three guys, one of which didn't make it."

Mike gave me a quizzical look and I returned it. "What did he say about me," I asked.

"Oh yeah, he said you shot up an outhouse and then ran out with your pants down and grabbed some guy by the crotch."

"Ay, cochino!" exclaimed Esmerelda. She smacked me on the shoulder with her open hand and then went back to the stove.

Suddenly my whole head seemed warm, and I had no doubt my face was red. Mike and I had left the interrogation part out of the story we told Esmerelda.

The boss chuckled. "Looks like you're already making a name for yourself in this town,"

I shook my head slowly. "I don't think this is the kind of reputation I want."

Mike saved me further embarrassment by changing the subject.

"Are you hungry, John," he asked Callahan as he pointed to a chair at the table.

Callahan sat down immediately. "Well, now that you mention it."

The meal was fantastic. Esmerelda served carne asada tacos with spicy refried beans, and everything was handmade from the salsa to the tortillas. I hadn't realized how hungry I was until I started eating.

Mike didn't seem as interested in food as I was and started reading the morning paper while I was still eating. Of course, that didn't stop him from making fun of me. He saw me chasing the last of the frijoles with a wadded up tortilla and called out, ""Esmerelda, will you get this guy some more beans before he wears a hole in his plate with that damned tortilla."

"I'm good," I said with my mouth full.

Esmerelda was already standing next to me with the pot from the stove. "Are you sure," she asked waving the wooden spoon at my head when she spoke.

"This food is wonderful," I said, dodging the spoon, "but I can't eat another bite."

Callahan pushed his plate away and announced that he was done too.

Mike had obviously been waiting for him to finish his lunch before he asked the question he had been waiting to ask since they had left Max Winston's house. "John, I need to know the name of your informant."

Callahan looked down at the table and exhaled a long breath. "Yeah, after talking to my buddy down at the police station, I figured you would want to know that." His lips mashed into thin lines and it looked like he was fighting an internal battle. "I hate to go back on my word," he said, finally, "but I understand why you need it."

"We don't have a choice," prompted Mike.

Callahan kept looking down at the table and running his index finger back and forth under his nose. "I know you don't." After a moment he looked up and said, "The guy's name is Elmo Hickock."

Mike took out a little notebook and started writing.

John leaned his head to one side and looked thoughtful. "He's a well-built guy but not very tall, maybe five-six."

Mike's head snapped up, and I suddenly felt very cold.

I could tell from the look on the boss's face that he was hoping that he had heard wrong when he asked, "Did you say five-six?"

"Yeah," replied John, nodding slowly. "He doesn't go by his given name. Everyone calls him Shorty."

Mike flipped his little notebook shut and stared at it. I closed my eyes and hoped tears didn't run out of them.

"What's wrong?" asked Esmerelda and Callahan, at the same time.

Mike took a breath and let it out before he said, "I'm pretty sure that's the guy Jake cut in half with a shotgun this morning at Max Winston's place."

For a moment, John just sat with a blank look on his face and then said, "That doesn't make any sense. Why would Shorty give us the inside scoop and then work the other side?"

"I don't know that he gave us the inside scoop," replied Mike. "We're going over to Epstein's later to check out the tip, but I don't believe he's part of this. I'm thinking your friend was feeding us bad dope to get us chasing after shadows."

Callahan raised his hands in front of him. "Whoa, how did he get to be my friend?"

"I thought you said he was a buddy of yours and Charlie's?"

"I said we knew him and that his information had always been good before."

Mike suddenly became all business. He looked at his watch and then stood up and tossed his paper on the table.

"I need to make some calls," he announced, as he stood up. He pointed at Callahan and said, "Get down to the morgue and verify whether that guy is your informant or not."

Callahan stood up and grabbed his hat from the table. "Will do"

"Are you boys still on for tonight?" asked the Big Man.

"If you're paying, I'm watching," said Callahan.

"Yeah," grunted Mike, "You wouldn't want to watch a burlesque dancer take her clothes off without being well compensated for it."

"A guy's gotta make a living," countered Callahan as he headed for the door.

"Yeah, you rich boys have it rough," Mike retorted. Before you go making a living, be sure to get me the information on that guy at the morgue and let me know as soon as possible."

The boss turned to me and said, "You've done plenty today and we still have to go meet with Julius Epstein around 5:00, so you don't have to go with him and watch Mrs. Cantrell, tonight, unless you want to."

"I'm willing to watch for nothing," I replied cheerfully.

"Cochinos," yelled Esmerelda.

Mike ignored her and added, "Be here and ready to go at 4:30. I'm going to go make those calls."

He headed toward his office as Esmerelda called to him from behind the stove," Mike, don't forget this is my afternoon to go to the beauty parlor."

I wondered why the pretty woman needed to go to a beauty parlor, but I wasn't going to dwell on it. My grandfather told me that women would always be a mystery to me, and I have never had reason to doubt that he was right.

"Ah shit," growled the boss, "I completely forgot about that."

"Do you need me for something or is it okay to go?" asked Esmerelda.

Mike shook his head. "No, I don't need anything, but you can't go alone." He turned to me. "Go with her."

"What do I need him for," asked the Latina.

My self-esteem dipped a little, but I didn't say anything and tried not to show that it bothered me.

"He's for your protection. We have people watching the house, but if you go anywhere Jake or I need to go with you."

"I can protect myself," huffed Esmerelda, putting her foot to the floor.

"That's what I thought this morning until a couple of guys snuck up on me and stuck a pistol in my ribs. If Jake hadn't been *there* I wouldn't be *here*."

"Fine," agreed Esmerelda grumpily, "I will take him."

My self-esteem didn't exactly spike, but I felt a little better. Mike left the room and as he did the pretty woman looked at me, and then wagged her finger as she spoke. "My appointment is at 3:00 so go cleanup and be ready at 2:30."

"Yes, ma'am, as soon as I help you with the dishes."

She laughed, put both hands on her hips and said, "You do understand that I get paid to cook and clean around here. It's my job."

I stood up and put my hands on my hips, even though it didn't look as good as when she did it, and said, "Well my job is to…"

"Yes?"

I felt my face bunch up as I tried to figure out what the hell it was I was paid to do. "I think my job is to follow Mike around and try to keep anyone, including me, from getting shot or kidnapped."

"There you go," said the pretty Latina. "That's your job. Do you still want to help me with mine?"

"I think I'd prefer it," I replied honestly.

I hung my coat on the back of my chair and started picking up the lunch dishes from the table. When I turned my back to Esmerelda she cried out, "A Dios mio, por que hay sangre en tu camisa?"

I didn't understand a word she was saying, but it was easy to tell she was upset about something.

"What's wrong?"

"Why is there blood on your shirt? You said your leg was the only place you got hurt."

"Oh crap, I forgot all about that," I told her as I started to put my coat back on.

She grabbed my arm and looked up at me. Slowly and calmly she asked again, "Why is there blood on your shirt?"

Her liquid brown eyes shimmered and I was glad I could tell her the truth, because I couldn't have looked into those eyes and lied. "It's okay, honest. Some of the wounds on my back opened up a little when I was working with Mike."

She seemed satisfied with the answer and released my arm. After a moment she smiled and asked, "By *working* do you mean running out of an outhouse with a gun in one hand and holding up your pants with the other?"

I'm sure I turned red. "Well it just sounds silly when you say it."

She took my coat and said, "Leave the shirt here and go clean up. I will come and get you when I'm ready to go." She pointed her finger again. "Be ready."

"Yes ma'am."

I went back to the guest house and went through my bathing ritual of sitting on the edge of the tub and washing everything I could and then gingerly running a wet towel back and forth across my back. I dried off and put on my skivvies and trousers. I was going to finish getting dressed and then I noticed the .45 in the holster where I had hung it from the bedpost.

I usually cleaned my guns right after firing them even though the ammunition I was accustomed to using in the 21st century allowed shooters to leave their guns un-cleaned even after multiple trips to the range. Mid-twentieth century ammunition, on the other hand, was considered corrosive and a weapon needed to be cleaned every time it was fired. I broke out the cleaning kit that Mike had put in the bag with the gun, spread a newspaper over the little kitchen table and went to work on it.

I got lost in what I was doing and I was even humming to myself when a voice behind me asked, "Are you clean and ready to go?"

The sound scared the daylights out of me and I yelled as I tried to twist around in the chair. I caught the edge of my kneecap on the table leg. "Mother…," I blurted out before the pain shot up my leg and straight out the top of my head. I must have hit a nerve because for a couple of seconds I saw wavy lines in front of my eyes and I think I generated my own electricity.

I stood up and hobbled around in a circle massaging my leg and trying to keep my eyes from watering in front of an attractive woman.

"Do you have to hurt yourself every time you move?" asked Esmerelda.

"Apparently," I said through clenched teeth. "You scared the crap out of me."

"You forgot I was coming?"

She actually looked hurt. It was easy to figure that she wasn't used to people forgetting about her.

"No, I hadn't forgotten. I got caught up in what I was doing and wasn't paying attention."

"Well, are you ready to go? Are you clean?"

"I was before you scared me."

I looked at the clock on the wall and saw that it was only 2:15.

"I thought you said to be ready at 2:30."

The Latina grinned. "I did, but I thought you might be wasting time and not getting ready."

At that point, she made an odd face, as if something was bothering her. She was looking at me and then she narrowed her eyes and made a twirling motion with her index finger. "Turn around," she said softly.

I turned around and as I did she stepped closer and surveyed my back.

"Does everything look okay," I asked, hopefully.

"It looks a little red and poofy where you were bleeding."

She motioned to the chair and ordered, "Sit the way you did the other night, and I will put the ointment."

I did as I was told and straddled the chair and folded my arms across the back of it.

"I want to wash my hands first," she said heading towards the bathroom. She pointed back over her shoulder toward the table with the pistol on it. "You know a lot about cleaning guns. Did you learn that in the Army?"

"Marines," I corrected. "Yeah, I got most of my training in the Corps. Weapons and fighting are the two things I know the best."

From the bathroom she asked, "You don't know anything else?" Her voice sounded surprised and maybe a little sad, but that might have been my imagination.

"I never needed to know anything else until I couldn't stay in the Corps," I told her. Now it was my voice that sounded a little sad.

"Since you are not in the…Marines any more, are you going to be able to get a job that doesn't involve shooting and fighting?"

"I'm not sure. There seems a lot of shooting and fighting in the job I have."

"I guess that is true," she said, walking out of the bathroom with the ointment.

"Is it always like this?" I asked her.

She thought for a moment and said, "I'm not sure how to tell you what it is usually like around here. A couple of times Mike has been hurt and a few times he has been forced to shoot at people, but it has never been this bad."

"Maybe in the future this job won't be all about shooting and fighting," I offered.

"Are you hoping it will be all about naked women getting sexed in front of a big window?"

"Are you still on that? I haven't seen any naked women. I've only watched one fully clothed woman read a book, and while I did that I had to listen to Callahan tell me big windy stories that were mostly crap."

Esmerelda's face lit up with inspiration. "That's it," she said firmly, "*That* is what it is usually like around here."

I dropped my forehead onto the back of the chair, not sure whether to laugh or cry out loud.

"Raise up," ordered the pretty woman, "and hold still while I put the ointment."

I did as she ordered, and it went a lot better than it had the first time. My eyes watered a little when the ointment hit the spots where the wounds had reopened but, other than that, it actually felt nice. Afterwards she applied new bandages. It was over in no time. I stood up, put on my shirt, and slipped a magazine into the .45. I holstered it while Esmerelda finished washing the ointment off her hands.

The pretty woman walked toward the door, and as she did she raised her hand next to her ear and gestured for me to follow by curling her finger. I grabbed my hat and jacket and fell in step behind her with the thought that Roberto was the luckiest man in the world.

CHAPTER 18

When we got to the garage Esmerelda walked toward the old Chevrolet, so I did the same. I hadn't thought about it before then, but I guessed the old car was for *the help* and that was us. I didn't have any problem taking the older ride. The problem occurred when we both walked to the driver's side of the old Chevrolet.

"What are you doing?" I asked Esmerelda, as we both reached for the handle on the driver's door.

"I don't think you should be driving," she stated firmly.

"Why is that?" I asked cautiously.

"Because you won't be able to change gears with your leg wound," she replied, trying to look sincere and concerned.

It took everything I owned not to laugh, but I didn't.

I told her, "If you want to drive why not just say so?"

She smiled up at me and said, "I want to drive."

I smiled back, headed around the car and tried not to show how relieved I was that I didn't have to drive. I knew how to drive a manual transmission and had done so many times, but I was accustomed to a floor shifter. That shifter on the column, just as if it were an automatic shifter, was new to me. I had been watching Mike, and I thought I had it worked out. I was pretty sure that if I took the handle, while it was in the center position, and pulled it toward me and then straight down, that should be first gear. If I pushed it back up to center and then pushed it away from me and then straight up, that should be second. If I was right about the other two gears and pulled the handle straight down from second that would be third. I had never seen Mike do anything else so I assumed there was no fourth gear or overdrive. I was still glad I didn't have to put all this to the test in front of Esmerelda. I happily went around the car and got in the passenger's side.

There's no way I could ever call a '39' Chevy cool or sexy, but the old car had character. It was a black two-door loaded with chrome and body details. It didn't have much in common with the cars of the 21st century. In the magazines I had been reading two days earlier, there had been a lot of articles and illustrations about what cars in the 21st century would look like. Most of the articles predicted that the cars would fly and would resemble some type of space ship. I wondered if anyone would have been so interested in the cars of the future if they had known they wouldn't fly and the body styles all resembled used bars of soap.

Esmerelda pushed and pulled some knobs under the radio, twisted the key, revved the engine a couple of times, and then took off. Our particular '39 was underpowered, but it still had personality and I liked that. The closest thing it had to a modern feature was the radio, which was only AM; and it took half a minute to warm up. In spite of the lack of an automatic transmission, power steering and power brakes Esmerelda handled the old tub like a pro, and in a couple minutes we were out of the subdivision and sailing down the road with the windows down and the radio playing songs by what the announcer called the Harry James Orchestra. I remember my grandfather listening to music like this, and I remembered not caring for it when he did; but for some reason, it sounded good at that moment. I wondered if I enjoyed the music because I was acclimating to being in 1947 or if it was because being around Esmerelda made everything seem better. Either way, that guy James blew a pretty mean trumpet, and I drummed my fingers on the top edge of the door while a song called Ciribiribin played through a speaker that sounded like it belonged in a fast-food drive-through. I wondered how long it was going to be before FM stereo would catch on, and then I wondered how soon fast-food drive-throughs would come along.

I tried to start up a conversation by asking the pretty woman if there was any special reason for going to the beauty shop or if this was just a regular visit. She told me that she wanted to have her hair done because she had a date with Roberto Thursday night. I was sorry I had asked, but fortunately for me the trip was pretty short.

Before I could think of something else to get a different conversation started, Esmerelda turned down a street and nosed the old car into the curb. She smiled at me and hopped out of the car. I did the same and as I looked down the sidewalk, I realized that The Cut and Curl Beauty shop was in a familiar place. About halfway down the block I could see the barber pole in front of Benny's Barber Shop where I had gotten my haircut. It seemed like that had happened weeks ago instead of the previous Monday.

I tried to follow Esmerelda into the beauty parlor, but at the door she turned and looked at me like I had lost my mind. "Where are you going?"

"I was going inside with you."

"Are you going to get your hair styled?" She tilted her head side-to-side and said, "I don't think you have enough to style."

"I'm supposed to be watching you."

The pretty woman pointed down the street, "You can watch from there."

I wasn't sure where she was pointing, but I got the impression that it really didn't matter as long as I wasn't with her.

"Why can't I go with you?"

"We don't want any men sitting around listening to all our chismes."

"Listening to your what?"

"Our…como se dice?…gossip. We don't want you listening to our gossip."

"I don't think I want to be listening to that either," I said honestly.

"Good, come back in an hour." She spun around and went inside and I tried to figure out where to hang out until then.

I looked around for a spot that would give me a decent view of the front door of the beauty shop and spotted the wrought iron and wood bench sitting under Benny's Barber Pole. It was a little farther away than I liked, but it looked as if I would be able to see who entered and left the beauty parlor, so I headed that way. I sat down on the bench and took in the surroundings. It was coming up on three o'clock and not much was going on. We were on the outskirts of the city and the street resembled something more like you would see in a small rural town than in a big city. The tallest building in view was three stories high and most of them were only two. A lot of the store fronts had awnings that came out over the sidewalks and were painted bright colors, many with stripes, and most of them had the store names and logos on them. The majority of the windows had signs painted on them, and a lot of the doors were propped open. There was a small movie theater directly across the street. If I was reading its posters correctly, it was so small it only showed one movie. The marquee sign read <u>Singapore</u>, and showed that it starred, "Fred MacMurray and Ava Gardner." The posters for the movie were mounted on the walls facing the street and after studying them I finally understood the humor in the woman at the vegetable market comparing herself to Ava Gardner. I made a mental note to go over and get a better look before I left.

There was very little traffic on the street and not too many people on the sidewalk. It was very pleasant and even peaceful. The barber shop I was sitting in front of had the door open, and I could hear the banter from inside.

"Who do you think had it worse, Patton's tenth armor or the First Division?" a faceless male voice asked.

"What do you mean worse?" asked a second male voice.

"Which one had the roughest go of it?"

"Does catching the clap count?"

"What the hell has that got to do with anything?" yelled the first voice.

"A bunch of us caught the clap from a women's church choir in Palermo. That was pretty rough."

"I'm talking about the war."

"Do you think we'd have screwed that bunch of snake charmers if there wasn't a war on?"

That lit the place up as five or six new male voices began shouting out their opinion of what they thought the second guy would screw, war or not.

A new male voice finally broke through the clamor, "I was with the First Division. The Big Red One had it pretty bad, but I don't know that we had it any worse than anybody else. If you were in Europe you caught hell. It was that simple."

Another voice from farther away said, "Bill was with Patton's Tenth Armor. Ask him what he thinks."

Bill must have been in the pool hall, because the questioner had to yell, "Bill, what did you think of being with Patton during the war."

Bill yelled back, "I wish I'd shoveled shit in Louisiana."

It went on like that for a while. It was all crap, but it was comfortable crap. The kind of ridiculous and useless banter that men in the military kick around when there's downtime. What I found amazing was there was so much of it. So many men had gone to war at the same time, fought in the same regions, the same battles, and that shared experience seemed to bring huge segments of people together. I had noticed it everywhere. Everyone seemed to be on the same page and speak the same language.

I had known lots of men that had trouble dealing with the battles they fought in Iraq and Afghanistan. It was common to hear them say, "No one understands what happened over there. They don't understand what I've been through."

What they said was true. Most people didn't understand but in this world, it was different. Vast numbers of young men had entered the military and gone to war. They all had their individual stories, but the stories came from places that everyone had heard about even if they hadn't actually been there. I had a feeling that this would have made a big difference to some of the guys in the 21st century. I thought that a few of them might have been able to deal with their problems a lot easier if they knew everyone else went through the same hell. This wasn't my time and it wasn't my war; but I found myself feeling more at home and more comfortable than I had in a long time, longer than I could remember.

I was mulling this over and looking down the street at the beauty shop when a voice next to me asked, "That's a fine haircut you have young man. Who cuts your hair?"

I turned and looked up at Bert the Barber.

"Hi, Bert, don't tease me about my haircut. The fellow did the best he could."

The barber cringed and clutched at his heart as if he'd been shot, but then he smiled and after studying my face a moment he said, "Your eye has a normal color to it, and it looks like you have a smaller bandage on your head, so I'm guessing you're doing better than when I first saw you.

I smiled back and didn't bother to mention the other injuries that I had picked up when I replied, "Yes sir, I am, thank you." Bert continued to stand in the same spot and I asked, "Are you taking a break?"

"Yeah, I don't have any real clients at the moment and there's only so much of that ridiculous palaver that I can stand.

I figured *palaver* was a synonym for bullshit, but I made a mental note to look it up. I started to say something but before I could, Bert asked, "Is that hand bothering you?"

I looked down and realized I was rubbing the knuckles on my right hand. They were all skinned, and the two in the center were discolored a little. It took me a moment to remember that I had punched Bubble Head, Ernest Dulay, in the face pretty damned hard.

"I guess I banged it up a little this morning," I told him. "I didn't even realize it."

I was sitting with most of my body weight on the leg without the stitches in it; but in spite of that they still burned and itched. It was no wonder I hadn't noticed my hand was a little bruised but I didn't mention any of that to Bert.

"Looks like Mike is leading you into trouble," said the Barber. He reached over and lifted my hand and inspected it like it was something he was about to put on the grill. "I've got something that will help that. I'll be right back."

While he went inside I surveyed the street to make sure nothing was happening to Esmerelda. It was still as quiet as it had been when I sat down.

The Barber came back out with what appeared to be a whiskey bottle, half full of pale yellow liquid, and a fistful of cotton. He uncorked the bottle and said, "This is a little concoction I learned to make when I was in the Marines."

"I knew there was something I liked about you," I told him.

"You a jarhead?"

"For 10 years."

"I hope the other six of them were good. I can't imagine what it must have been like for you boys over in the Pacific."

Bert hadn't even asked if I had been in the war, and I'm sure he would have been surprised if I told him that I hadn't; but of course I couldn't say that so I tried to shift the topic. Bert looked to be in his mid-sixties and I asked, "You didn't serve in the war?"

"Not the last war, the one before it."

"You were in World War One?" I exclaimed, realizing, too late, that I shouldn't have let my excitement show, but I had never had the chance to speak to a WWI veteran.

"Don't act so surprised," said Bert. "I know they call it the Lost Generation, but there are a few of us still around." He poured some of the yellow liquid on the cotton and reached toward my hand with it.

I pulled back and asked, "This won't hurt will it?"

"Are you kidding?" asked Bert, looking at me as if I had lost my mind, "You can wade ashore at Guadalcanal or Tarawa, but you're afraid to let me rub this on your boo-boo?"

I could have told him that I hadn't done either of those things, but he still had a point so I grudgingly put my hand back on top of my leg and he dabbed some of the liquid across my knuckles.

The liquid was cooling and pulled the skin a little tight, but it felt good and soothed the raw skin a little.

"What's in there?" I asked him.

"Oh shit," Bert exclaimed. "I forgot to ask, 'You're not allergic to Armadillo urine are you?'"

"What?" I shouted, yanking my hand away.

The older man chuckled. "I'm just kidding. Stick it back out there."

I did, and he went back to swabbing at the knuckles.

"How long have you been doing this?" I asked him.

"Barbering or administering medical services?"

"According to the guys inside, the two would need to go together," I said, trying to get even for the Armadillo gag.

"Well you can't pay much attention to that gossiping bunch of Hedda Hopper wannabes. They need to be up at the Cut and Curl cackling with the other old hens and not standing around in my shop disguised as young non-paying male customers."

I made another mental note to look up Hedda Hopper while I was looking up palaver. Then I asked again, "So how long have you been barbering?"

"I started when I retired from the Marine Corps in 1920," replied Bert.

I tried not to look amazed and wondered if I would ever get used to having conversations with people that could say things like that.

"How long were you in the Corps," I asked.

"I just did my twenty and got out."

"What made you want to join the Marines?" It was the stock question I asked most Jarheads I met.

"I always wanted to be a Marine," replied Bert proudly. Out of nowhere he surprised me by asking, "Did you know that John Philip Sousa was a Marine?"

The question came out of left field, and I chuckled and told him, "No, I didn't know that."

"I saw him lead the Marine Corps Band at the Olympic Theater when I was…let's see…that was 1892, so I would have been ten years old."

I hadn't done the math when Bert had said he retired in 1920 after twenty years of service, but this time I ran the numbers. My barber was eighteen years old when the century changed in 1900. It took an incredible act of will to keep my mouth from hanging open.

Bert looked off into the distance as he reminisced about that time in the late nineteenth century. "I had always wanted to be a Marine, but when I heard the Marine Corps Band play the Marine Corps Hymn, with John Philip Sousa himself leading them, I was never able to consider anything else."

He turned toward me and asked, "So why did you decide to join the Corps?"

My eyes must have been the size of Compact Discs. I tried to say something, but it was as if my mind couldn't get any mental traction. I felt my mouth go up and down, but nothing came out. I may not have been breathing.

"Are you okay," asked the older man. "Is that a painful memory for you?"

The memory wasn't painful, I just didn't want to try and follow a story like that. In addition, there was no way I could tell him the truth.

"A recruiter came by the school and talked me into it," I lied to him.

"Why did you get out after ten years," asked Bert. "You were halfway there."

"I planned on staying until they kicked me out, but my knee tangled with a piece of shrapnel from an IE…from a land mine."

"Shit, I'm sorry to hear that," said Bert, sympathetically.

"It's not that bad. It doesn't bother me but the doctors said I couldn't stay in the Corps."

"That's a shame," said the Barber, "I'll bet you were a good Marine."

I smiled and told him, "There are a couple of lieutenants that might disagree with that, but a lot of other people thought I was pretty good."

"How about you," I asked, "Why didn't you stay for thirty?"

"The war was part of it," said Bert. "I didn't want any more of that."

"Were you worried there would be another one?"

"Shit no!" exclaimed the older man. He looked at the ground and took a deep breath before he spoke again. "We didn't think there would ever be another war. I still can't believe there was."

What he said caught me off guard, but it shouldn't have. I had forgotten that The First World War was called "The Great War" and "The war to end all wars." Even if I had been at liberty to say something, I wouldn't have had the heart to tell Bert that this wouldn't be the last war either. In another three years the United States would be neck deep in a police action that would later be known as The Korean War. My grandfather's younger brother served with the First Marine Division and fought his way out of a frozen hell called the Chosin Reservoir. When I was young, my great-uncle told me a few of the stories about being in Korea but I was little and he tried to keep the stories light by telling me about silly things he and his friends had done, or how he learned to process machine gun coolant for drinking.

When I was older, my grandfather filled in the gaps and told me about the fighting that went on. I'm sure the men that were there didn't care much for it, but they were heroes; and I was inspired by what they accomplished. That was what made me want to join the Corps.

"You said the war was part of the reason you retired. What was the other part?" I asked Bert.

"I wanted to cut hair," he said simply.

"It was that easy?" I asked him.

"Pretty much," Bert confirmed as he nodded his head. "In my case it was very easy. I knew that I enjoyed cutting hair, and I did quite a bit of it during the war. One of the guys in our group was a barber, and he gave me my first barbering lesson in a foxhole near Verdun."

"That doesn't sound like a fun way to learn anything."

"It's not, but I really enjoyed learning how to do it. After that first lesson, I practiced on all my friends. We were far away from home and we looked rough anyway, so nobody gave a shit if their appearances took a turn for the worse."

"Did they?"

"Oh, hell yes! What I did to their scalps was criminal, needless to say, I didn't have the best barbering tools available. I'm lucky I didn't give someone tetanus, but after a while I started to get better at it. After that, our group was always well groomed and shaved thanks to my practicing."

I chuckled. "So the secret to being happy is cutting hair?"

Bert laughed softly. "No, the secret to being happy is to be aware of when you *are* happy."

I smiled broadly and said, "Your philosophic advice doesn't run very deep there Bert."

"Comes across a little simplistic doesn't it."

"To say the least."

"Let's see how simple it is," said the barber crossing his legs and clasping his hands just below the knee of the one on top. He looked at me, grinned and asked, "What makes you happy?"

My mouth opened to answer and that's where it stopped. My mind was in full gear and as it raced to give Bert an answer, it quickly dawned on me that I didn't know. I sat there with my mouth hanging open for what seemed like hours.

I expected the barber to laugh at me, but his smile diminished a little as he said, "It isn't that easy, is it."

I shook my head and sat there for a moment still trying to think of something. I finally asked, "Does screwing or getting drunk count?"

"Sure, but unless you can make a living doing one of those things, you won't have long to be happy."

"That makes sense," I said, more for the sake of conversation than having anything to offer. I was still trying to figure out if anything made me happy.

"It does," affirmed the older man. "A guy might enjoy playing with himself, but there's no money it."

"And that's a damned shame," I said with a straight face.

"It truly is," agreed Bert, solemnly.

I glanced down the street to make sure no one was sneaking up on the Cut and Curl or doing a drive-by or something else I hadn't thought of. I just knew that I needed to make sure no one bothered Esmerelda.

"What are you looking for?" asked Bert.

"I'm watching out for Mike's housekeeper. She's getting her hair done, and Mike wanted me to keep an eye on her."

Bert coughed and informed me, "Oh, I've known Esmerelda for years." One side of his mouth swept up in a wide arc as he continued, "Let me get this straight. You're being paid to sit here and watch that Latin bombshell Mike has for a housekeeper?"

"You make it sound a little better than it actually is."

"The hell you say. Why am I lecturing you about being happy? You're a good looking young man that has a job watching a beautiful woman. I should be taking lessons from you."

"I don't have anything to teach anybody," I said sincerely.

"You're not happy doing what you're doing?" asked the barber.

"I don't know. I sort of fell into this job, and I haven't thought much about it."

"You might want to stop and think about it." He smiled even broader and added, "Hell, it makes *me* happy thinking about it."

"Well, maybe someday I'll be like you and realize I'm happy. Is that how it works?"

"That's how it worked for me. It was late September in 1918, and I was in the Argonne Forest. It was a day or so before the Meuse-Argonne Offensive began in earnest."

"That doesn't sound like a place to be happy."

Bert turned his head to make sure he was looking me in the eye. "That's the whole point," he said. "It's as good as any."

"It was around eleven o'clock in the morning, and a buddy of mine was sitting on what was left of a stone wall that stretched out across a pretty green field. There had been a lot of fighting the day before and, as it turned out, there was a lot of fighting that afternoon; but at that moment there was only the sound of artillery off in the distance. A nice cool breeze was blowing and I was stropping my razor so I could give my pal, Will, a shave. I had heated some water in my helmet, and he was relaxing and enjoying the hot towel. I finished sharpening the razor and when I stood up the breeze blew across my face and I leaned my head back and watched the clouds move in the sky. The forest was very pretty and I thought, 'I like being here…at this place…at this moment'."

"You were standing on a battlefield in the middle of a war," I pointed out.

"Yup, and the war was awful and so was the battle."

"And you were happy."

"For that moment, yes I was. I wasn't happy later that day when they shelled the living shit out of our position, and I wasn't happy the next morning when we mounted an offensive against the Germans, but at that moment, I was happy."

"And that's the trick?" I asked.

"That's the trick."

I sat for a moment and it occurred to me that I wasn't *unhappy* sitting there, but I wasn't sure I could say I was happy either. The stitches on my ass itched, I was wearing way too many items of clothing, and the internet was half a century away. I wasn't sure that 1947 and being happy were ever going to be synonymous.

Bert saw a guy coming down the street and said, "There's one of my regulars, I gotta go." He stood up and put his hand on my shoulder. "If you need help watching Esmerelda give me a call."

I returned his smile and assured him I would do that, and he went inside.

I checked the Beauty Parlor and didn't see anyone coming or going, but when I leaned back against the bench and looked directly across the street I recognized a familiar face.

Roberto was coming out of the movie theater, still holding a box of popcorn, and putting his hat on with the other. It struck me as pretty silly to go to the movies alone when he had such an incredible woman to go with him.

"To each his own," I thought.

It was at that moment, a nice leggy blonde walked out of the theater and strutted toward the street. She was much prettier than Roberto, so I watched her walk. Then I watched her put her arm through Roberto's arm, and I watched them walk together, talking and laughing about something. They only walked a short distance before ducking into the doorway of a shoe store. The door was closed and the wooden sign above the door read, "Olsen's Shoes" and had what looked like a big bumper sticker pasted across it that read, "Out of Business". Roberto and the blonde were out of sight from most of the people on the street and they got down to business in that doorway. My blood got real hot watching them.

I stood up and headed for the curb. There wasn't much traffic, so I jaywalked across the street and pointed my nose toward the doorway of the shoe store.

Before I got there, the blonde stepped out of the doorway and walked towards me. I tried not to pay any attention to her, and she went on by. As I reached the shoe store Roberto stepped out of the doorway and was going to head in the opposite direction of his lady friend until he caught sight of me.

My presence startled him, but he recovered quickly. He was a much better liar than I was.

"Hey Jake, what are you doing here?"

"I was talking to Bert the Barber."

"Oh yeah, I forgot there was a barber shop next to the pool hall. I get my hair cut across town," he said raising his hat and running his hand through his dark hair.

"Who was that woman?" I asked him. I managed to say it soft and without anger. I really wanted this not to be what it looked like.

"Oh, she's a friend from work," said Roberto. He put way too much effort into it and he watched my face way too closely, wanting to see if I bought what he was saying.

"You may know her from work, but I think you are more than just friends," I said in the same soft voice.

"I'll swear to you, we're just friends."

"You always stick your tongue in your friends' ears?" I asked less softly.

Roberto realized things weren't working and he went on the defensive. "Look," he said pointing his finger at my chest. "What I do is none of your business."

It ran through my mind that earlier I had stood outside an outhouse and punched the face of a man that had tried to back-shoot me while I was sitting on the toilet. It was sad to think that experience wasn't nearly as unpleasant as the conversation I was having with Roberto.

Once I knew there was no chance things weren't what they looked like I gave up on any ideas of diplomacy and decided to finish this as quickly as possible. I reached out slowly and took hold of the lapels of his coat. I curled my hands and brought him in close, shirt button to shirt button, and then I curled over forward a little which forced him to curl over backwards a little. I pushed my face toward his but even curled over I wasn't quite nose to nose to with him so I twisted even harder on his lapels. The muscles in my shoulders bunched up around my neck and my elbows went past Roberto's body on either side and the muscles in them swelled as I lifted the Latino onto his toes.

That put us nose to nose and the fear radiated from Roberto's wide eyes.

"You're lucky it's me and not Mike," I said softly. "Mike thinks of Esmerelda as family and he wouldn't be happy if he found out what you're doing to his family."

"Wh…wh…what are you going to do?" stammered Roberto as he strained to lean his face back from mine and failed.

"I'm going to tell you that you need to make a choice. You can break it off with Esmerelda or you can break it off with the blonde but you can't have them both."

"It will take a little time," said Roberto.

"You have a date with Esmerelda tomorrow evening…right?"

He tried to nod but I had him so wadded up he could barely make it happen.

"You have until then. If you don't have everything all taken care of, I'm going to tell Esmerelda myself. Then I'm going to stomp a mud hole in your ass for making me be the bad guy that had to tell her she has a cheating asshole for a boyfriend. After that, I'm going to give what's left of you to Mike and tell him what you've been doing."

"Okay…okay," said Roberto in a trembling, breathless voice. "I'll break it off with the Susan."

"Susan, pretty name, pretty woman," I thought. I wondered how a guy like Roberto could juggle two gorgeous women while I was spending my time cleaning guns, reading old magazines and looking up words like palaver.

"*There's no justice*," I thought as I lowered the smaller man to the ground. I uncoiled my hands at the same time and pushed him back a couple of steps.

"I'm taking you at your word Roberto. If I find out your playing me, you won't like it."

"Everything will be okay," replied the Latino in the same frightened and breathless voice. "I'll break up with Susan. I'll do it right now."

He headed past me, down the street, at a fast walk and tried to straighten his coat and tie as he went. I watched him until he reached the next cross street where he disappeared around the corner. I hoped he was telling me the truth. I didn't want to see Esmerelda hurt.

The beautiful Esmerelda chose that moment to step out of the beauty parlor. It was easy to tell they did a lot more in that place than gossip. The sun flashed off her shiny dark hair as she turned toward me. She looked fantastic.

I waved to catch her attention and then made my way toward the car.

CHAPTER 19

The ride home was pretty quiet. I complimented Esmerelda on how nice she looked and I tried to start a conversation by asking her if she heard any good rumors at the beauty shop, but she barely answered me. She was nearly silent, and I had a bad feeling that she had seen Roberto and his lady friend on the sidewalk, but there was no way I could ask her about that, so after a few minutes I stayed quiet as well.

It was almost 4:30 when we arrived back at the house, and Mike was ready to go as soon as we pulled up. I hopped out and waved goodbye to Esmerelda, who ignored me. I jumped into Mike's Cadillac and we headed into New Egan. It was the first time I had seen the city in full daylight. I kept looking for similarities to Chicago, but there weren't any. This city was its own entity and something about it gave off a gritty toughness. The skyline was unique, but not necessarily attractive. There was something slightly dark and not just a little bit filthy about it. Between these observations and my wounds, it was easy to understand why the little old man had claimed this place would most likely kill me before the week was out. The thought reminded me that it was only Wednesday. New Egan still had plenty of time to do me in.

I watched the big buildings get closer and crowds on the streets get thicker. The weather had changed as much as the scenery. The proximity of the big lake made a difference. It had been a lot warmer that morning at the farmhouse. Now it was chilly with a stiff breeze blowing, and the men and women stooped into the wind holding their coats tight with one hand and anchoring their hats with the other.

"Where does this guy, Epstein, live?" I asked. I was guessing he had a mansion in one of the nicer areas of the city, and I told Mike so.

"That's a good guess; and he does have one," replied Mike, "but he also has a penthouse on top of the Gifford Palace Hotel. That's normally where he stays."

"Then why does he have the mansion?"

Mike chuckled, "His wife has to live somewhere."

"I'm guessing he doesn't care for her company?"

"Or she doesn't care for his." He shrugged. "I haven't asked, and I'm probably never going to."

We drove on for another twenty minutes and went right into the heart of the city.

The skyscrapers grew up around us, and I found myself gawking up at them like a tourist. When I wasn't looking up I was looking down the street. Between the old cars and the old clothes, it was easy to feel that I was watching a movie or a play; that I wasn't part of what was going on around me.

The brakes on Mike's car reminded me that I really was part of the action and not just a spectator. "Here we are," said Mike, sliding the big car up next to the curb on my side.

Mike slid his revolver from its holster and said, "Pop open the glove compartment and put your gun in it."

I wasn't too thrilled with the order, but I did as I was told. I didn't have to ask why. I figured that one of the ways Julius Epstein had managed to stay alive this long was by not allowing people with guns to get too near him.

Before I could open the car door, someone did it for me.

"Welcome back Mr. Manzarek," shouted a skinny kid in a red uniform. Another uniformed skinny kid on the other side hauled Mike's door open and mimicked the first kid.

The kid that opened my door had curly blond hair and the other one had curly black hair. They both looked to be about seventeen, but other than the hair I couldn't tell them apart.

"Jimmy, Tobey," bellowed Mike in a voice loud enough to be heard above the traffic, or a truck horn. "How are you boys doing? You're not getting into any trouble are you?"

"No, sir," said the blonde one. "We don't associate with those kinds of boys." He said it with a straight face and he seemed sincere enough until Mike asked him, "So you boys wouldn't have any idea where a fellow could find a good dice game?"

"Yes, sir," replied the dark haired one with a big toothy smile, "We do associate with *those* kinds of boys. There's a High Roller's game on the twelfth floor, and a big money poker game up on nine, but word has it there's better money to be made playing Five Card Stud over at the Winslow."

He said it, without emphasis, as if he was telling us where to get a good hamburger. Then the blonde one chipped in, "We can also get you good odds on a couple of Saturday's games, Notre Dame against Purdue or Georgia Tech against VMI."

Mike laughed and stuck a bill in each of their shirt pockets. "If I want to throw my money away, I'll just give it to you boys."

"Thank you, Mr. Manzarek," they crowed in unison.

They jumped into the Cadillac and headed away from the curb. There was no doubt they would guard it well.

Large steel letters fastened to the face of the building let everyone know it was the Gifford Palace Hotel. I estimated it to be about thirty stories tall and whoever had put the letters there seemed rather proud of the place.

If anyone had asked me I would have told them that I spent every waking minute extremely cognizant of the fact that I was living in the past, but walking into the lobby of the hotel was a forceful reminder that this wasn't my world or my time.

The huge open lobby of the hotel was lit with a large chandelier in the center of the room. The sofas and chairs were all light brown leather, and even though I've never been that interested in furniture or architecture, I knew Art Deco when I was looking at it. All the furniture had round corners and there were subtle neon-lit accents in different parts of the room. Venetian blinds were on all the windows, and they were framed by huge heavy drapes. I could see the wooden cabinets of two huge radios in different parts of the room that stayed with the Art Deco theme. The carpet ran wall to wall and had a wide border around the entire perimeter.

Mike said, "Good afternoon," to the doorman, the janitor, three men in suits, and two couples walking toward the door. He tipped his hat to the ladies as he spoke. I tried to do the same by grabbing my hat by the brim, but all I managed to do was fold the brim and put my thumb in my eye. I wondered if Esmerelda was right, that maybe I did hurt myself every time I moved. The boss called everyone he met by name and they did the same.

We stopped in front of a stand where two black men were shining shoes. I had seen shoeshine stands overseas, but this was a little flashier. The men working were making a big show of whipping long thin rags back and forth on the tops of shoes to bring them to a high gloss shine. They popped the rags in time to a tune they were whistling in harmony; and danced back and forth as they exchanged customers. They were fun to watch and I was hoping Mike was going to stop for a shoeshine, but he headed straight for the elevator, so I did too.

We stepped in and I turned to punch the button, but instead of a panel of buttons there was a black man in a red uniform standing in front of a big lever.

"Good afternoon, Mr. Manzarek," said the guy, "Where to?"

"Good afternoon, Johnny," replied Mike. "The penthouse, if you please."

The uniformed man grabbed a handle on the side of the open doorway and unfolded a heavy wooden lattice across the opening. He latched it, then stepped back to his station. He slid the lever to the side and the elevator started up. Mike made a little small talk with Johnny, and I tried not to appear surprised or fascinated by everything that was going on.

Johnny moved the big lever, and the elevator came to a stop. "Penthouse," he announced proudly.

Mike thanked him, and we stepped into what looked like a large foyer. There were two men waiting there. One of them called out, "That'll be all Johnny."

I could hear the door close behind us and as the sound of the elevator going down diminished, I took stock of the two men. Neither of them wore a jacket or tie, and they both appeared to be in their late twenties. One was pretty good sized, with a dark complexion and dark oily hair that he slicked straight back from his face. He was around six-four and looked like he knew what the inside of a gym looked like. The other one was around five-ten, balding, and looked like he didn't know anything. I was wrong, because when the elevator doors closed he showed us that he knew how to pull a revolver out of a shoulder   holster.

CHAPTER 20

We raised our hands as Mike said, "I believe there has been a mistake."

The big one with the slick hair stepped next to me, clapped a big hand on my left shoulder and pushed down to force me onto my knees. I might have been able to stay on my feet, but at the same time he unknowingly drove his fingertips into the stitched wound next to my shoulder blade. I didn't dare fight back while his friend pointed a gun at Mike's stomach. Something the big guy was doing caused my hat to fall off and it rolled around in a circle on the floor in front of me. My teeth ground together, and I made a growling sound that I didn't know I could make as he forced my knees onto the floor.

Mike tried to keep his voice from sounding angry as he told them, "You boys must be new. I'm sure if you will get Julius, or even Abe, we can straighten out any problems."

Bald Guy waved his pistol and said, "You're the one that needs to get things straight. Nobody comes in here and tries to take a shot at Mr. Epstein. If they try, they leave on a slab." He pointed to the floor with the gun barrel, "Now get on your knees like your friend."

"What the hell are you talking about? We're not even heeled, and we have an appointment with Julius."

"You can stop trying to peddle that shit. We know what you came here for. We know about the hit."

Now Mike was furious. "What kind of horseshit talk is that?" he bellowed.

Bald Guy smiled. "I thought that would surprise you. One of your friends dropped a dime on your ass."

The boss' voice rose in volume. "What the hell are you talking about?"

"He didn't leave his name, but he gave us all the details."

"You idiots!" roared Mike, "you're being played. Call Julius so he can set this straight."

"Oh, sure I'll just go get the guy you came to kill and bring him in here." He prodded Mike in the stomach with the end of the pistol. "We'll call him as soon as we've finished asking you and your friend a few questions." He prodded him again, "Didn't I tell you to get   on   your   knees?"

The pain in my shoulder was crippling and that would have been bad enough, but inside was where it really hurt. Mike had been worried that I wouldn't be able to hold up my end because of my injuries, and here I was on my knees with water running out of my eyes because of exactly that.

I twisted my head so that I could see The boss' face out of the corner of my eye, and he looked down at me. I expected him to look at me with pity or disappointment, but he did neither. His eyes narrowed and turned hard. I didn't know what was up, but I returned the look.

"Hey!" snapped Bald Guy, "I'm not going to tell you again!" He jabbed at Mike's midsection with the gun, but this time Mike's big left hand engulfed the smaller man's hand -- gun and all. I could hear something crunching, and I took it for granted that it was Bald Guy's fingers. He started to squeal but the Boss's big right hand shot out like a jackhammer and drove the little man's head into the wall. His head smashed completely through the lathe and plaster. When Mike drew his fist back, the bald guy was still hanging from the wall by his head.

At the moment that happened, Slick grunted. I had been planning on grabbing the arm that held me down and seeing what kind of damage I could do to it; but when he grunted, I realized that he was stooped over with his head just above mine. I reached up with both hands and I can only assume that Slick was busy staring at his friend hanging from the wall, because I was able to grab both his ears and some of the oily hair around them.

He yelled and tried to stand up, but I yanked down and smashed his face against the top of my head. Something bit into my scalp. I didn't know if it was his teeth or the cartilage in his nose, but it didn't matter. He tried to push away, but his hand slipped off my shoulder and I slammed his face down twice more. I tried to do it again, but the oil in his hair let him slip out of my grip. He staggered away holding his face with one hand and reaching for his shoulder holster with the other. I jumped to my feet and went after him. He was having trouble, because his face was covered in blood and he couldn't see. He was sideways to me and I kicked down on his knee. It made a wicked cracking noise. Slick made a wet blubbering sound. He began to fall to his knees, but I caught him with a sleeper hold as he dropped and choked him out. When he went limp I pulled his Colt 1911 from the holster and threw him, face forward, onto the floor.

A couple seconds after he struck the tile, someone started yelling from outside the foyer. It was obvious the shouter was coming towards us at a fast pace.

"Oscar, Lenny, where the hell are you guys? If you're giving Big Mike any trouble I'm going to fry your asses in the same oil that Lenny uses in his hair."

I bent over and snatched my hat from the floor and then thumbed the hammer back on the automatic. Mike put his hand out and motioned for me to stop.

"Lay it on the floor," he hissed.

This seemed to be a day for getting orders that I didn't like, but I put the hammer back down and did as I was told.

The yelling man entered the room, still in full cry. "Why the hell don't you answer...holy shit what the hell happened in here?"

That was the second time, in the same day, that I'd heard that phrase. I was beginning to think it would be our slogan.

"Hello, Abe," said Mike.

Abe looked to be in his early forties. He had a large nose and short, dark, curly hair that was starting to thin at the corners. He was around five-nine or ten and was a little soft around the middle. He was still in his dress pants and shoes, but he had stripped his shirt off and was wearing a sleeveless t-shirt. He looked more like a guy that I would see selling cars than a guy Mike had called, "Abe 'The Axe'."

"I'm sorry about the mess, Abe," Mike told him. He actually sounded apologetic.

Abe sounded the same way. "Mike, this isn't your fault. I just now heard about that damned phone call and tried to get here before these young Turks hurt anybody...or got hurt."

"They said that someone called and claimed we were coming to kill Julius?"

Abe stared at the guy hanging from the hole in the wall and nodded his head. "Mr. Epstein's secretary, Wendy, answered the call. The guy claimed that you and some shooter had an appointment with Mr. Epstein, but that your real play was to kill him. At that point, she went nuts and set up such a squawk that Oscar," he turned and pointed at the bald guy, "took the phone and started giving the guy the third degree."

Mike snapped open his lighter and lit a cigarette. What else did the guy say?"

Abe shook his head back and forth. "I don't know. The little bit I just told you I got from Wendy a couple minutes ago." He looked back and forth from the man stuck in the wall to the one on the floor and asked, "Do these guys need an ambulance...or a wagon?"

Mike and I looked at each other, shrugged, and then started checking our attackers for signs of life. I rolled Slick over onto his side and checked his pulse and breathing. He had both, so I gave Abe the thumbs up and watched him and Mike slide Bald Guy's head out of the wall. They laid him down, and Mike made the same checks I did. The top of my head was burning, so I reached up and started fishing around in my hair.

"This one's alive," announced Mike, "but some of the bones in his jaw and face are broken."

"This one is too," I informed them. I looked at the little white pieces I had just pulled out of my scalp and added, "But he'll need some dental work."

"Serves them right," snarled Abe. "They should have checked with me or Izzy before running off half-cocked, trying to make their bones."

Mike caught my attention and tossed me his handkerchief. He pointed at the left side of his face so I swiped at the same side of mine with the handkerchief. It came away bloody. It wasn't hard to figure out that it was trickling down from the top of my head. I mopped the side of my face and up into my hair. I had a feeling that I wasn't going to enjoy shampooing that evening.

Abe saw me cleaning up and asked, "I'm sorry guys; I should have asked already. Are you two okay?"

"I'm okay," replied Mike.

My head was hurting, my scalp was bleeding, and I was pretty sure the wound on my back was open again; but when Mike looked over at me I was proud to say, "I'm good."

"Alright then, follow me," said Abe heading for the doorway. "I'll have some people clean this mess up. I don't think these guys will be working for us anymore." He stopped, swiveled his head around and smiled a funny smile. "They're too high strung. You can't be in this business if you're wound too tight." He chuckled a little and motioned for us to continue following him. He led us into a large living room. It was furnished a lot like the lobby except that the furniture looked even more expensive. Large walnut bookcases wrapped around the walls and centered on a big marble fireplace. Next to the fireplace was a bucket full of coal. It suddenly became obvious where some of the darkness and filthiness of the city was coming from.

The bookcases complemented the thick dark paneling and big heavy molding, the size of a street curb, that wrapped around the room. Huge, heavy leather wingback chairs bracketed the fireplace, and a ridiculously big leather sofa and equally ridiculous coffee table faced all of it.

Abe motioned for us to have a seat. I couldn't help but wonder what it cost to live in the penthouse of the Gifford Palace Hotel. I had a feeling my yearly salary wouldn't even be able to buy the big sofa I sat down on.

"Can I take your hats or coats?" Abe offered.

We declined and he said, "Make yourselves comfortable, I'll let the boss know you're here."

Mike nodded, and Abe headed out through one of a number of doorways that opened into the big room.

Mike didn't take a seat. He held his hat in one hand and smoked his cigarette with the other.

I held my hat in one hand, as well, and tried the handkerchief against the side of my face again. It came away with nothing on it, so at least my head had quit bleeding. The wound on my shoulder blade was throbbing and I was hoping it had quit also.

After a couple of minutes, Abe returned with a woman following him.

"This is Wendy, Mr. Epstein's secretary. She wanted to know if you guys would like something to drink. It doesn't matter what it is; we have it."

"*This is definitely the middle of the twentieth century,*" I thought. I couldn't imagine the Executive Assistants of the twenty-first century schlepping cocktails for the boss' company. She was a pretty woman and wearing a pinstriped coat and skirt that I was fairly positive was silk, so it crossed my mind that she was most likely well-compensated for whatever work she did. It also crossed my mind that it would be hard to compensate an employee to take phone calls from people claiming that someone was coming over to kill their boss. That train of thought brought on the realization that I had to actually prevent people from killing *my* boss, and that I probably couldn't afford a silk suit. At that point my head started to throb in earnest, and I gave up thinking about anything for a while.

Mike asked Wendy for a cup of coffee, and I did the same. She left the room, and when she came back a few minutes later, an older gray-haired man was with her. He looked a lot like Abe and could have passed for his father. He was wearing a suit that made Wendy's look like a rag. I assumed I was looking at Julius Epstein.

Mike started to motion me to my feet, but I was already moving toward him.

"Mike, how are you?" asked the older gentleman extending his hand. "I just heard about what happened at the elevator. I am so sorry. Are you alright?"

"We're fine," said Mike, grasping the older man's hand. "I'm afraid we made a mess in your foyer, and we hurt those boys pretty bad."

"Please don't think twice about it," said Epstein.

I had never had reason to use the word surreal before that afternoon, but talking about two guys with broken teeth and bones as if they were a rug we had spilled wine on was surely a way to define the word.

"I'm just glad you weren't hurt," he continued. "I was afraid those boys would be trouble. I hired them on as favors to their fathers, but it was easy to see that their fathers should have done the boys a favor by raising them better."

I began to wonder how a father should raise a boy to work for an organized crime kingpin, but the throbbing in my head turned to pounding so I stopped thinking about it.

Mike pointed at me and said, "Jules, this is my new associate, Jake Kowalski. Jake this is Julius Epstein."

Mike called him Jules but it hadn't escaped me that Abe had called him, "Mr. Epstein," so I did the same when I shook his hand and told him I was happy to meet him.

The older man sat in one of the wingback chairs and waved Mike into the other one. It took me a second to come to the understanding that I was being treated as the hired help, so I went back and resumed my position on the sofa. Wendy came around from behind me and offered a large mug full of coffee and a big smile. She was an attractive woman with light brown hair. I smiled back at her. The silk suit fit her well, and I figured it must been specially tailored to fit her that closely. It was money well spent. I wondered if the smile was for me or if she was just showing her appreciation for us not killing her boss.

The room was big, and the two bosses spoke softly enough that it was hard to hear them, so I didn't try. I found that if I sipped my coffee slowly and didn't try to think, my head didn't hurt much, so that's what I did. After a few minutes had gone by, Abe came back into the room and sat down next to me on the sofa.

He seemed genuinely concerned when he asked, "How are you doing?"

"I'm okay," I told him.

"What you did was pretty impressive. I've seen Lenny whip three grown men in a bar fight, and you took him apart with pretty minimal damage."

"I'm sure I'll feel it in the morning," I said, touching the top of my head.

"I didn't realize who you were when Mike introduced you."

I had no idea what he was talking about, and I guess the look on my face told him as much.

"You're the guy who saved Mike's wife in front of the diner a few nights ago and then again at Mike's house."

"I didn't realize that kind of news got around," I replied.

"People that travel in certain circles pick up on these things." He looked at me for a second and said, "If you ever decide you don't like working for Mike, you give me a call. I can use a guy with your skills, and I'll fix you right up."

I couldn't imagine working for a gangster; but a week before I couldn't have imagined living in 1947, so I didn't completely dismiss the idea.

"Thanks," I told him, "but Mike's been really good to me and..."

"Say no more, nobody appreciates loyalty more than I do; but if anything changes, don't forget me."

I couldn't imagine that happening either, so I assured him that I wouldn't.

Wendy slipped in behind both of us and handed Abe a Highball. He thanked her; she smiled at me and left. Abe didn't miss the exchange, but he didn't say anything about it. He had other things on his mind.

"What brings you and Mike over here tonight?"

I wasn't sure what I should and shouldn't say, but I was feeling too banged up to try and dance around the truth so I didn't.

"We got the same kind of information that you did. Someone claimed that it was part of Mr. Epstein's crew that was trying to make off with Norma."

"No shit?" Abe murmured into his Highball as he took a sip. He gestured with the glass toward the bosses. "Mike doesn't buy any of that, does he?"

"No, he said…" I began and then hesitated.

"He said what?" asked Abe.

Abe had a strange look on his face, and it wasn't until that moment I could see the guy Mike had called, "The Axe." It was a weird psychotic look that let me know this guy would murder me as the punch line to a joke and never think about it again. I didn't want to get on his bad side, but I figured I had started with the raw truth and I had better stick to it. I took a deep breath and told him, "He said that if Mr. Epstein wanted Norma gone she'd be gone, and if he wanted us dead we'd be dead."

The strange look on Abe's face lingered for a couple of seconds, and then in an instant it was gone.

"Yeah, that's true," he said in matter-of-fact fashion.

We watched the bosses talk for a couple of minutes and then he asked, "Any idea who's after Norma?"

"No, and we're not sure it's just Norma."

"Because they went after Mike, this morning?"

"You guys really are connected," I blurted out.

Abe looked a little like he was hurt. "I thought that was understood."

"It is now," I told him. "Yeah, when those guys went after Mike all of our working theories went out the window."

"You don't have any leads, nothin'?"

"Nothing. Do any of your connections know anything?"

"Not really. We know that a few of these boys used to work for Republic Aviation, but I think you guys were already aware of that."

"Yeah, a couple of people that used to work there put us onto it."

Abe took a sip of his Highball and thought for a moment before he spoke. "We spent no small amount of time asking around about this; but we haven't found anything, and that's unusual." He looked over at the bosses and satisfied himself that they didn't need anything before he continued. "We have our hands in a lot of pies. Not much happens in this town that we don't know about."

"But this hasn't shown up on anybody's radar?" I asked before I stopped to try and remember when radar was invented. I was thinking it was around the Second World War, but I wasn't sure. It seemed like forever until Abe spoke and let me off the hook.

"Not a thing and that's odd. When that happens it usually means that some newcomer has started something and slipped in where we aren't used to looking."

"Whoever's after Mike and Norma seems to be very smart. Up to this point, he's been way ahead of us," I offered.

"If he's so smart, how come he hires a bunch of stumblebums to pull off his jobs?"

Abe asked it in simple, offhanded fashion, but I thought it was pretty ironic since we had been forced to beat the shit out of his hired help just to get in the door. I didn't want to see that strange look again so I said, "That's a good question. Captain Briggs noticed that, too."

Wendy had returned to the room and was speaking with Mike and Julius about the call she had received earlier. She was speaking softly, so I wasn't having any better luck hearing her than I was the bosses.

It was becoming painfully obvious that Julius Epstein's organization was a very well-run machine, and that made it less likely that any of his people had gone rogue and were trying to do anything to Mike or Norma. I told Abe what I was thinking and asked what he thought.

He sat with his upper lip hanging over the top of his glass for a while and finally said, "We do keep pretty close tabs on our *associates* but nothing's impossible." He turned to me and smiled. "That little altercation that you and Mike had at the elevator forces me to confess that we can't be one hundred percent sure of what's happening every minute of every day."

"But?" I asked, feeling that there was one coming.

"*But*, incidents like these are usually short and quickly discovered, just like that one."

I nodded in agreement. "That and the fact that somebody tried to sell you the same information they tried to sell us, makes me pretty sure this is a dead end."

"It doesn't mean we aren't going to check into it," said Abe reassuringly.

"Thanks, we appreciate that."

A movement at the corner of the room caught our attention. A guy in a gray suit came through the doorway removing his hat as he did. He had thick, dark, curly hair and heavy dark eyebrows. He was in his late thirties, around five-ten and very slim. His face was narrow, and it caused his large nose and lips to show more prominently. He glanced over at the bosses, and then saw Abe and me sitting on the sofa and headed our way.

Wendy caught him halfway between the sofa and the door, handed him a highball, and took his hat and coat. I couldn't hear what she said to him, but it was something that definitely got his attention. It looked like he wanted to know more but she kept moving and so did he.

As the newcomer approached us, Abe motioned toward me and said, "Iz, this is Big Mike's new associate, Jake Kowalski." He motioned in the other direction and added, "Jake this is Isaiah Goldfarb."

I stood up, and a smiling Isaiah grabbed my hand, pumped it furiously and said, "My friends call me Izzy, so that means *you* call me Izzy."

"It's good to meet you…Izzy," I said, not sure of how I had made such a fast friend of the man Mike had called, "Izzy 'The Ice Pick'"

Izzy let go of my hand and used his to gesture for me to sit down.

Abe was on my left and Izzy seated himself on my right. He asked Abe, "What happened to Lenny and Oscar? Wendy just said they got into some trouble."

Abe grinned from ear to ear. "Somebody called her on the main line and claimed that

Mike Manzarek and his associate…" he cuts his eyes toward me and then raised his highball and pointed at Mr. Epstein, "…were coming to put down the boss."

"And she believed that shit?" asked Izzy.

"I don't know what *she* believed, but Oscar got hold of the phone, and swallowed it hook, line, and sinker. The next thing I know, they've both gone running to the elevator."

"Oh hell, I told you neither of those two idiots have the sense of a goat."

"Everybody knows that. The Boss only hired them on as family favors."

"Wendy said they were hurt pretty bad. I guess Lenny didn't feel like such a big man after he tangled with Big Mike."

Abe grinned, "Jake took out Lenny," he said, raising his highball and taking a sip.

Izzy turned toward me and his face lit up like he was the birthday boy at a surprise party. "Holy shit, that's right, you're the guy that cleaned up at Max Winston's place this morning. That was some serious work."

I had no idea how to reply to that properly. "It…it was…serious," I finally agreed.

"Look," said Izzy leaning in close, "we could use a guy like you…"

"I already asked him," interrupted Abe.

Izzy leaned around in front of me to talk directly to Abe. "What did he say?"

"He said he's loyal to Big Mike."

Izzy nodded understandingly, but he turned to me and added, "Nobody appreciates loyalty more than we do, but if…"

"I already told him," Abe interrupted.

Izzy raised his hands, lowered his head in surrender, and then sat all the way back in his seat.

Abe leaned back and spoke to Izzy behind my head. "What did you find out?"

"Oh, shit!" barked Izzy in a low voice. "I almost forgot. That tip we got was dead on."

Abe bent forward so he could see Izzy across the front of me. He had a serious look on his face and he flicked a finger at me and said, "This is something you may want to hear."

He took a minute to tell Izzy why Mike and I were there in the first place, and Izzy turned to look at me. "Yeah, he's right; you're going to want to hear this." He took a swig from his glass and in a conspiratorial voice told us, "There's some serious firepower moving in from Detroit."

Abe's face grew real dark. "Whose is it?"

"Everything I'm getting is secondhand, but it looks like they're all freelance," Izzy replied.

"How many people are we talking about," asked Abe.

The Icepick wadded up his face and thought for a moment before he finally came up with, "Between eight and ten."

Abe growled low, way back in his throat. "That's a lot of damned heat," he rasped.

"What does this have to do with us?" I prompted.

Abe looked thoughtful. "Maybe nothing," he replied, "but this information came from outside our network."

"Just like what's been happening to Mike and Norma?"

Abe nodded, "They don't appear to be related, but I have a problem with coincidences."

"And these things showed up awfully close together," I offered.

Abe nodded. "That's the way I'm seeing it."

I still wasn't' hearing everything I wanted to hear, so I prompted again, "You're thinking somebody in Detroit is trying to pull something?"

"Nah," growled Izzy into his drink, "These guys are mostly freelance. Besides, we have a working arrangement with all the big names in Detroit. We would know about this kind of movement if it had anything to do with us or it was doing any real business in New Egan."

It sounded a little vague so I asked, "By real business you mean…"

"…money", finished Abe.

Izzy and Abe seemed to be on the same page; but I wasn't, so I threw out the question, "What kind of business are these guys doing?"

"We don't know," replied Izzy. "This came in under the radar just like the shit that's been happening to Big Mike and his old lady. Somebody's spreading some money around and pulling some strings, but they don't show up on our tote board like everybody else does."

The information was still too thin for me to process. I didn't understand Abe's definition of business, and I couldn't figure out how they knew what they knew without knowing more. When I added that to the trouble Mike and I had found when we walked in, it made me wonder if John's informant might have been more reliable than we expected. I mulled this over for a second and finally blurted out, "I'm not sure I understand."

Izzy grinned and said, "It's like this. If Artie Shaw and his band come to town and they're playing at one of the big theaters, everybody in town hears about it."

"And a lot of people gear up to catch some of that action," added Abe. "There's parking, concessions, and right off the bat there's liquor to consider. There may also be an increase in peripheral activities, like local gaming."

"Okay," I said slowly, assuming that Artie Shaw was a 1947 version of a rock star. "So that would be the *business* you were talking about."

"Exactly," confirmed Abe. "You can imagine how upset we would be if something like that came to town with the intention of cutting us out."

He said it in a business-like manner as if he was talking about selling cars or insurance. He also seemed very comfortable talking about such things openly, and I got the feeling that meant he trusted me. Truth be told, it made me feel a little better.

"But," continued Izzy, "If somebody…with some serious coin…pays Artie and his boys to play at a private party, then there isn't any outside business to be had, very few people hear about it, and if you actually happen to see him in town you don't even know why he's there."

"So," interrupted Abe, "We found out that someone has hired a lot professional muscle and gun for a private party, but we don't know who's throwing the party or what they're throwing it for."

"But you're sure it isn't for *business*?" I asked.

Abe shook his head. "I don't see how it could be, but we damned sure need to find out. " He looked at the floor for a moment, and then he turned to Izzy. "Is there any chance we can catch any of these guys at the train station and find out what they're doing here?"

"They're already here," Izzy told him. "The guy that told us only found out about it when he saw a couple of them together down at the docks."

"Damn, we are really sucking hind teat on this one. We need to send Ollie, Earl, and Benny out to scour some of the hotels and bars near the docks and see if they can spot any of these guys."

The thin man nodded, "They're already on it."

The two men near the fireplace chose that moment to stand up, and the three of us did the same and waited for cues as to our next move.

The Bosses shook hands and said their goodbyes. Mr. Epstein turned and headed out the same way he had entered. Izzy shook my hand and told me, "It's been a pleasure. We don't know if these Detroit boys have anything to do with you or Mike, but if we hear anything more you'll be the first to know." He moved quickly to follow his boss. Abe stepped to the doorway where Mike and I had entered and ushered us out the same way we had come in.

When we got to the foyer I was surprised to find it empty and the floor mopped and spotless. A tall skinny table had been added and a vase on top of it covered the hole in the wall.

I stood there looking at the table thinking, "*Wow, these guys are really efficient, at least when it comes to these types of dealings.*"

"It was good to meet you," said Abe, extending his hand.

"Likewise," I said, trying to appear nonchalant, as if this was the way I spent most afternoons.

Abe cocked his head back to look at Mike and said, "If you get tired of this guy, send him our way. I already told him we'd be glad to have him."

The boss pretended to look perturbed. "Damn it Abe, don't run off with my help. It's hard to find guys that work as cheap as Jake does."

"Aw hell, you're not gonna try and peddle that crap with me are you? Everybody knows that Big Mike Manzarek pays well. I'll bet there are two kids downstairs guarding your Cadillac with their lives."

"There are," I confirmed.

"Of course, they're making book at the same time," added Mike.

Abe spread his hands and cocked his head to one side. "That goes without saying, and that reminds me…" He fished in his pocket and came out with a couple of wadded up bills. "Give this to Tobey, and tell him I'll take VMI."

Mike took the money and laughed. "Why don't I just throw it out of the car window on the way home? The spread isn't big enough to cover what Georgia Tech's going to do to them."

Abe snorted indignantly. "I'll throw it away in my own fashion, thank you. Just give that to Tobey."

"All aboard," called a voice behind me and I turned around to see Johnny opening the elevator doors and smiling at us. I smiled back and followed Mike aboard.

CHAPTER 21

Tobey and Jimmy returned the Cadillac with the windows cleaned and the tire pressure checked. Mike gave Abe's money to Tobey and told him to put it on VMI. Tobey made a face like he smelled something bad, but it didn't stop him from taking a little notebook out of his pocket and putting Abe's bet down.

Jimmy handed Mike his keys, and we got in and headed home. As we pulled away from the curb The Boss stabbed the dash lighter with his finger and I figured that meant he was about to start thinking out loud, so I waited for it.

"Julius said that today was the first he had heard of any rumor about his people coming after me or Norma."

"Do you believe him," I asked, already knowing the answer.

"Yeah, I do. I didn't think he had anything to do with it when we went over there, and I'm even surer of it now."

The lighter made a noise that sounded like "snick" as it popped out. Mike lit up and blew his smoke out through the crack at the top of his window...or most of it anyway. He gestured at me with his lit cigarette. "You and Abe and Izzy were getting pretty cozy. Did you find out anything?"

"Izzy says there are...what did he call them...freelancers arriving from Detroit."

"Shit," Mike hissed around his cigarette. "How many are there?"

"Eight, maybe ten, he wasn't sure."

"Are they all muscle and gun?"

"That was one of the things he and Abe called them."

I watched Mike blow smoke out the side of his mouth at the open top of the window, and I asked, "Do you think this has something to do with us?"

"I don't know, but I'm not a big believer in coincidences."

"Abe was thinking the same thing."

"Did he say they would find out what these guys are doing?"

"They already have people working on it."

"That's good; you can bet your paycheck they'll find out. They have one hell of a network."

"You're telling me? They already knew about what went on this morning at Max

157

Winston's farmhouse."

"That doesn't surprise me, but I *was* surprised to hear they didn't have any information on whoever's after Norma. Julius didn't know anything."

"I got the same from Abe."

Mike nodded and blew smoke at the window. "I noticed you were doing a lot of looking in Wendy's direction."

"I liked that silk suit she had on," I managed to say with a straight face.

"Don't get any ideas. It would take two months of your pay to buy what she was wearing." He turned towards me and grinned. "It would take you two years to pay for the one Julius was sporting."

"I'm guessing there's not a silk suit in my future."

"Are you kidding? The way you go through clothes we should just wrap your ass in butcher paper." He blew smoke from his nostrils and added, "I hope that isn't the only thing you noticed about Wendy."

"Her shoes looked nice, too," I offered, stifling a smile.

"Shit," growled Mike, "Remind me not to shower with *you* anymore."

We spent the rest of the trip in relative quiet. Mike smoked and muttered a little to himself, and I tried to make sense of what was going on. I was having enough trouble trying to figure out how to get around in 1947 without the problem being compounded by people trying to kill me or run off with my boss or his wife. Due to the pounding in my head, I couldn't put much thought into it, and that was probably a good thing. I was stuck in a completely different world about which I was embarrassingly ignorant, and if I thought about it too much, I was more likely to cry than anything else.

When we got to the house Mike nosed into the driveway, and I could see one of the off-duty policemen move to the railing on the front porch to see who was pulling in. As he did, another one walked around from the back of the house to do the same thing. It wasn't hard to guess that Mike was paying a pretty good penny to have guards around the clock, but these guys made it look like the money was well spent.

We parked the car and headed straight for the kitchen. I was only halfway there when I started to pick up the smell of fried pork chops.

As we entered the kitchen Esmerelda looked up from the stove. She motioned us toward the table; but before I could turn and go she pointed at me and then curled her finger for me to come to her. As I moved in that direction Mike went to the table, and I heard him say, "Oh good, the evening paper is here."

Somewhere in the cobwebs of my memory, I thought I remembered my Grandfather talking about different morning, afternoon, and evening editions of newspapers; but I couldn't remember having ever seen one. I didn't have time to give it much thought. As I approached Esmerelda, she squinted and stared intently at my hair. I wasn't sure how she knew something had happened to the top of my head, but she *did* know. When I walked up to her she still didn't speak. She just started pulling on my tie and the lapels of my coat so she could drag my head down to her level to inspect it.

"A Dios mio," she hissed softly as I bent over where she could see the top of my head.

I tried to think of a gentle explanation as to why some wannabe gangster had been teething on my scalp, but nothing was coming to mind.

It didn't matter because she didn't ask. She turned away and went to the refrigerator while I just stood there and watched her.

She opened the freezer and took out a rectangular metal tray and set it on the counter. She turned and motioned for me to come to her.

I walked over to her and she pointed down to the metal tray like I should know what to do with it. It took me a moment to identify it. It was an ice tray.

It wasn't anything like the old plastic ones I had seen. This thing had moving parts or would have had moving parts if they hadn't been locked in ice. This tray had metal louvers like venetian blinds. I stood there looking at it, and Esmerelda stood there looking at me. After a while, she made a face and used both hands to gesture impatiently at it. I was guessing that this type of ice tray was the frozen equivalent of the lid on a pickle jar and I was expected to use my strength to get the ice out of the tray. I was pretty sure I was strong enough to get the ice out but it was the very real possibility of not being smart enough that worried me.

There was a handle attached to the metal louvers and it laid flat on top of them. The ice came almost up to the handle. I could only get part of my fingers under the handle, but I realized the whole tray was going to come up if I didn't hold it down. I had no idea what I was doing but I knew I needed to do something. I put my left hand on top of the ice and louvers just in front of the handle and then I hauled up on the handle with my right hand. For a moment nothing happened, and I was coming to the conclusion that I wasn't doing it right when the ice smashed loose with a loud "crack" and tiny bits of ice sprayed up on my face and across the backs of my hands.

Esmerelda grabbed the tray and started pulling out the cubes. She gave me a funny look and I couldn't tell if she felt sorry for me and or was just tired of fooling with me. She fanned the back of her hand at me and motioned me toward the table. I went and sat down as obediently as I had done everything else. It was obvious something was wrong, and it didn't take a rocket scientist to figure it was Roberto. I felt bad for her and wanted to say something, but I couldn't figure out what it should be. So I just sat and watched Mike read his paper.

The pretty, but silent Latina brought two plates, and we dove into pork chops that had been pan fried in green salsa, mashed potatoes, and the rest of the refried beans from lunch. There was no way I would ever be able to fault 1947 for the cooking. I started cutting into my pork chop, and Esmerelda came back with a dish towel tied up into a bag. It made a clunking sound as she dropped it on the table next to my plate, and she turned and walked away before I could ask her what it was for. I picked it up and discovered it was cold. She had made an ad hoc ice bag from the ice cubes I had liberated. I picked up the bundle and called out my thanks, but she didn't acknowledge it.

It bothered me that she wasn't happy. I had only known her a couple of days, but to me she was wonderful, and I didn't enjoy the thought of her being upset and spending her evening upstairs crying over a cheating boyfriend.

The ice bag did feel good, and I sat there with it on my head and ate the wonderful food

As he dug into his second pork chop, Mike said, "I got the 'okay' to see Norma tonight, so I'm heading that way in just a little bit, and I won't be back until late."

Mike hadn't said much about it, but I knew that being away from his wife must be eating at him. Hell, I barely knew the woman and even I missed her. I didn't have any trouble understanding his motivation, but I thought safe houses were supposed to be off limits for everyone. I didn't want to sound curious, but I was so I asked, "How does that work?"

"How does what work?"

"Going to see someone at a safe house. I didn't think they let people know the whereabouts or come by for visits."

"Normally, they don't, but they made an exception for me. "

"Briggs?"

Mike tried to look offended. "I've got more than one friend."

"With that kind of pull?" I asked skeptically.

"Okay…it was Briggs," Mike admitted.

"Is it a lot of trouble?" I asked, still curious.

I don't really know any of the details, but apparently it is pretty complicated. The police have to do a whole bunch of maneuvering to get me to the safe house without being followed. I have a feeling it involves me riding in the trunk of somebody's squad car.

"If it makes you feel any better, I've ridden in the front of one, and I don't think the trunk would be any worse."

"I've ridden in a couple and I believe you're right. While I'm thinking of it, I need to tell you that I won't be able to call you or vice versa while I'm there."

"No problem," I told him. "I'll be watching Mrs. Cantrell with John."

"I wish you good hunting," said Mike as he stood up and patted his pockets to make sure he had everything. "Do you need anything from me?"

"That's a good question. If you aren't here, I won't have anyone to call if I need another ride home."

"That's true and that reminds me, you can tell John that if he strands you again he'll be sporting a stylish new hat that used to be his ass." He stopped and scratched his chin as he thought for a moment. "Having said that, things do happen; so I want to make sure you have whatever you need before I get out of here.

I started to say something but before I could, Mike lowered his voice and spoke in a whisper that only I was able to hear. "If anyone asks, I'm at a bar somewhere. You're the only one who knows where I've really gone, and you're the only one who needs to."

I nodded, mostly because I couldn't speak. What I could have done was cry. If I had thought about it, I might have been able to say that I had earned all the faith that Mike had just placed in me, but it had been a long time since anyone had done that, and the emotion was almost overwhelming.

I tried to act like I was rubbing my forehead and thinking, but I was really rubbing my eyes to make sure they didn't water. As I did so a thought struck me. I gave my eyes one last rub and said, "I could use a map. I have the pamphlets the bus driver gave me, but I don't know where all the roads are. I need to cross reference everything to find out what buses I would need to take."

"There's a stack of city maps and a couple of state atlases in the office," Mike replied. "I'll grab one for you."

Esmerelda grabbed a handful of dishtowels and rags and went into the laundry room. I took advantage of the opportunity and asked, "Will she be okay?"

Mike looked toward the laundry room and said, "I would think so. There should be two guys on patrol all night. Check and make sure they are both here before you leave the house. If one of them doesn't show up for some reason, stay here with Esmerelda and let John go by himself." Mike thought for a moment and added, "Make sure they aren't both sitting on the front porch shooting the shit or pulling on a flask. At least one of them should be patrolling around the house at any given time."

"I'll make sure," I told him.

Mike started to turn away and then a thought struck him and he turned back.

"Find out what Callahan learned at the morgue. If it turns out that our Shorty is his Shorty, and I'm pretty sure it is, then grill John for whatever he knows about that guy. If we could get an inkling of who hired him or at least who was paying him, we would have a trail to follow."

"I will," I replied

Mike headed into the other room and I finished working on my dinner.

He had left his paper on the table, and I thumbed through it hoping to find something that would augment my knowledge of 1947.

Esmerelda noticed my empty plate and took it away without a word. I watched her walk away. I would have done so even if she was talking to me, but this time there was no pleasure in it.

She washed the dish then took her apron off and left the kitchen without speaking.

I was turning the pages of the newspaper trying to figure out if there was something that I could do to help her, and I didn't realize that I had dozed off until I heard someone ask, "Who's been chewing on the top of your head?"

I jerked awake and spun toward the voice which connected the side of my left knee with a big wooden knob on one of the table legs.

"Son of a..." I rasped through my clenched teeth before the pain shot down my leg and I lost the will to speak.

"Are you okay?" asked Callahan. "I didn't mean to scare you."

I stood up and hobbled around in a poor attempt to walk it off. John watched me limp around in a circle and added, "This morning Esmerelda said she didn't think you could move without hurting yourself. I thought she was joking but..."

"Yeah, yeah," I growled.

"What happened to the top of your head?"

"I beat a guy's face against it."

"What the hell for?"

"He startled me and woke me up," I growled.

I took a deep breath and then gave an abbreviated version of what had happened at Julius Epstein's penthouse while I got my leg to bend properly again.

Callahan actually sounded sympathetic when he said, "You've had a hell of a day."

"I've had easier ones," I agreed.

"Are you sure you want to go watch a woman take her clothes of?"

"Is this a trick question?"

"In that case, are you ready to go?"

Mike was already gone and Esmerelda wouldn't want to talk to me, so I didn't need to tell her goodbye. All that was left to do was make sure the cops watching the house were doing as Mike had instructed.

"I guess I am," I said grabbing my coat from the back of the chair.

CHAPTER 22

John pulled out of the driveway and headed out to Mrs. Cantrell's apartment. He lit up a cigarette; and at my insistence, he started talking about his trip to the morgue.

He had his window rolled down, and we had to speak louder to be heard above the wind noise. "Holy shit!, You made a mess of that guy at the morgue," he squawked. At the same time we rolled up to a Stop sign and he stuck his arm straight out of the open window. The gesture struck me as odd, and it took a moment to figure out that he was signaling for a left turn.

I let his commentary pass and asked, "Was it your informant?"

Callahan eased away from the intersection and shifted into second gear. "He looked a hell of a lot better the last time I saw him in person, but yeah, that was him."

"Shit," I hissed through clenched teeth. "What else do you know about the guy, John? Did you ever know anybody that he worked for or maybe some people he hung out with?"

John exhaled cigarette smoke through his nostrils, and the smoke vanished quickly out of the open window. He stared straight ahead, thinking for a moment.

"I don't recall ever seeing him with anyone else or hearing him mention anyone that he was friendly with. What can I tell you? He was a street rat."

I could feel my face wad up when I asked, "Are you sure?"

"Yeah, I've seen the guy, on and off, for years, why?"

"I only saw him a couple of times; but he was scrubbed, pressed, and shaved -- way too clean for a street rat."

John's eyes were still discolored from the fight he had been in and the dark patches under them bunched up as he thought about it. "That's weird. He's usually pretty scruffy and smells of stale beer." He took another drag from his cigarette and let the smoke trickle out through his mouth and nose. "You said they were being paid big money for snatching Mike. Maybe Shorty used a little of it to clean up."

I shrugged. "Anything's possible. None of this makes sense, so Shorty's grooming habits are the least of our worries."

I sat and stewed for a moment and then asked, "So the only times you've ever had contact with him was when he came to you?"

"Yeah, and that's what happened the other day; he just showed up. I don't remember ever meeting him anywhere or even running across him on the street by accident."

"How about a wife or a girlfriend?"

"Same story. I never saw him with a woman and he never mentioned one."

"You don't know where he was living?"

"Haven't a clue."

I sat there trying to think if there was anything I was missing or if there were any angles I was overlooking. After a minute or two I became aware that I was hunched forward in the seat with my eyes closed and my fists and teeth clenched. The frustration had definitely gotten the best of me. I willed my hands to open and my jaw to relax; then sat back in the seat and watched the scenery go by.

It was dusk, and the lights of the city were coming on. The trip to the Gifford Palace Hotel had made me more sensitive to the Art Deco style and against the bluish-gray dying light that framed the skyline I picked out a couple of buildings with rounded corners and roof edges. As I watched, the accent lights flickered and came to life on one of the buildings framing its lines in pale neon red.

The city looked even dirtier in that light and took on a far more sinister character than it did in the daylight; but if I was forced to admit it, I would have said I liked the way it looked.

After a few minutes of silence, John asked, "Well, other than beating a guy's face in, how did it go at Epstein's?"

I told him everything Mike and I had learned, but he was mostly interested in how well Wendy's suit fit. It seemed to bug him when I told him that she was really friendly to me and smiled a lot, so I played that up as much as I could.

Callahan finally got tired of me busting his chops and stopped asking about her. He reached over and slid another cigarette out of the pack lying next to him on the bench seat. He produced a wooden match from his shirt pocket, ignited it with his thumbnail and lit up. When he got the cigarette burning he extinguished the match by wagging his hand back and forth, then threw the matchstick out the window.

I knew the United States had cleaned up a lot in the second half of the twentieth century, but I'm pretty sure the obituary for the first half read, "They threw a lot of trash in the street."

"What did you think about Abe and Izzy," John asked.

I shrugged slightly. "They're interesting."

"They're nuttier than squirrel shit is what they are. I hear stuff on the street, and it isn't pretty. Those guys have done things that would chase a veteran Priest out of a confessional."

I didn't have any trouble believing that, and I told him so.

"So…" John said slowly, "Those guys said they didn't know anything about the information we got off the street?"

"No, and it makes sense now that we know the information was no good."

Callahan tilted his head to the side and slowly exhaled a cloud of smoke. He was obviously musing about something and he finally said, "You're assuming the information is no good because the informant tried to kidnap Mike after he sent his buddy to shoot you off the toilet."

"That was my thinking, yeah," I replied in my best *no shit* tone of voice.

"I realize our friend at the morgue is running low on credibility, but are you totally convinced the information was no good? Ol' Shorty might have been playing both sides, taking my money for a small piece of information while he's taking Epstein's money to run off with Mike and ruin your afternoon siesta."

I wondered if there was anybody that could actually use an outhouse for a siesta, but what I said aloud was, "I hadn't thought about it, but I guess that could be a possibility." I considered it for a moment and something else occurred to me. "Now that I *am* thinking about it, it doesn't make sense."

"No?"

"No, Dulay said they were offered a thousand dollars apiece for the job. Why would Shorty play the other side for a couple of twenty dollar bills?"

John's darkened eyes squeezed together again. "Yeah, you're right; that doesn't wash."

"If I had to call it right this minute, I would have to say that I believe Abe and Izzy were being straight with us."

"What makes you so sure? Those lunatics would run their grandmothers through a bandsaw if the urge struck them."

"That's the impression I got," I replied quickly. "If they wanted to do something, I think they would just do it. I don't believe they would hire a bunch halfwits to do their work for them."

"What about the halfwits that met you at the elevator?"

"Well, you've got a point there; and that's gone through my mind more than once. They explained it away pretty well, but it does cut into the plausibility of their story."

"They might be on the up-and-up, but don't let your guard down around those two," John muttered around his cigarette. His right arm was busy with the steering wheel and his left arm was stuck out the window again but this time it was bent at the elbow with his hand sticking straight up in the air. He was signaling for a right turn. I wondered if there was any particular reason he was doing that instead of using the turn signal. I finally decided he was used to using the hand signals and just used whichever method he felt like using at the moment. I had noticed quite a few of the other drivers using their arms to signal. I could have questioned him about it but I was afraid of looking more ignorant than I already did, so I didn't ask.

John turned the old Studebaker down Mrs. Cantrell's street. It looked just the way it had a couple of nights earlier. We parked in the same place, and I tried to make myself comfortable. My head wasn't throbbing anymore, but it was itching and so were the stitches on my back and legs. I tried to ignore it, but I couldn't stop squirming. I had rolled up the maps Mike had left, and I was using them to scratch around a row of stitches when John asked, "What are those for?"

"I told Mike that I had the bus route pamphlets, but I needed real maps to find out how to get from one place to another."

"Like from here to Mike's house?"

"That would be a good example," I said sarcastically, but John didn't seem to notice.

He replied, "You catch the local number 4, and take it to the Crescent Hills station; that's near the diner where you went when I left the other night. After that, change to the New Egan Metro 120 and get off when you get to the end of Mike's street. You'll have to walk to the house from there."

I was impressed. "You must ride the bus a lot."

"I've never ridden the bus."

"Then how in the hell…?"

"You remember I told you an old friend of Charlie's, one of his Army buddies, came to town a few months ago?"

"Yeah, it was a Benny something."

"Benny Dunbar, that's right. He spent a couple days with me before he left town. On his last day here I took him to the bus station, and while we waited on his bus I looked at the routes and maps mounted on the wall."

I was no longer impressed; I was astounded. "You can just look at something and remember it like that?"

John shrugged his shoulders. "It's what I do." He looked thoughtful and in a saddened voice he added, "It's probably the only thing I could do better than Charlie. He was pretty much a wizard at everything he turned his mind to."

I tried to think of something cheery and uplifting to say, but before I could come up with anything John asked, "Where is Mike anyway?"

"He said he was going to a bar somewhere."

"He didn't say where?"

"He did, but my memory is not like yours."

John shrugged and then looked at his watch. "Oh good, it's almost time for my program."

The radio was already on, but it was turned down so low we couldn't hear it. John turned it up and fidgeted with the knob until he found the station he was looking for.

I was expecting a comedy show like the one we had listened to on Tuesday night, but an announcer talking over what sounded like an old horror movie soundtrack claimed the show was called, Suspense. It came across as corny as the backing music and I was trying to figure out if I could make some excuse and walk to a bathroom or a phone somewhere when John asked me if I listened to the show.

"No, I don't usually," I confessed. I was hoping that would make him change the station, but I didn't have any luck.

"Are you kidding? This show is fantastic! Some weeks it's a horror or fantasy story, and some weeks it's a mystery, but it's always good. I never miss it."

It looked like I wasn't going to be able to leave without using a gun or somehow making Callahan understand that the shows I never missed were in high definition video.

This particular week the show turned out to be a murder mystery. After it started I thought that between it and the itching of my wounds, I would go insane.

It was just about that time that Mrs. Cantrell showed up looking much the same as she had when we had seen her the first time. She came around from the back side of the building and was headed across the front walkway with her arms full of shopping bags. She was wrapped up in fur, but it looked different from the mink we had seen her wearing before. I mentioned it to John.

"Oh yeah, she's got different furs for each day of the week and then some. That mink and sable number she's wearing tonight must have set her old man back some serious coin."

The well-dressed object of our stakeout went inside, and after she laid her packages down she removed her furs and revealed a low-cut dress that made our trip worthwhile.

"Now, that's a dress," said John in a throaty voice.

She went through the same routine we had seen before. She fixed herself a drink, then sat on the sofa and started reading a book. Even with the hot dress, it didn't take long for that to become as excruciatingly boring as it had the first time.

I don't know how much later it was when I realized I had forgotten about the itching, and I was even able to tolerate watching Mrs. Cantrell sit and read a book while I listened to the radio show that had captured my complete attention. Callahan was right, it was a good show. I was really surprised that I could enjoy something so outdated.

When the show ended John spun the dial as quickly as he could and tuned in a show about a married couple named George Burns and Gracie Allen. I never did figure out how a married couple got away with having different last names in 1947, but the show was funny as hell so I didn't care.

The show went to a commercial and it was just as over the top as the show itself. John took the opportunity to light up and said, "It looks like your girlfriend isn't going to take her clothes off tonight, either."

"*My* girlfriend? If it was my girlfriend, I'd like to think she would, at least, take off her clothes for *me*."

Callahan smiled and blew smoke out of the upturned corner of his mouth. "Just for you? Some pal you are. I'll bet you'd close the curtains, too."

"That's a safe bet. I don't do peep shows."

John made a scoffing sound and said, "Then I'm glad she has the boyfriend she's got. If he ever shows up, we'll all have a good time."

"Have you gotten any word on who it might be?"

"That's *all* I'm hearing. Everybody's got an opinion on who it might be, and they are all pitching it as the gospel truth."

"Does any of it sound better than the rest?"

"Nah, that's the problem. There's so much of it there's no way to tell if any of it has merit."

"That makes sense."

" Callahan took a drag and exhaled through his nostrils as he continued. "The only thing we know for sure is that he's out of town."

"If you don't know who he is, how do you know that?"

"That part's easy," he said gesturing toward Mrs. Cantrell's window with his cigarette. "There's a Burlesque dancer sitting in that apartment that will put it to him right across the back of that sofa if he'll just show up." He turned and smiled at me for emphasis. "There's no way in hell he's in town."

I grinned and raised my hands in surrender to let him know I found his logic flawless. As juvenile as it was, I was sure he was right.

As if on cue, a man came from the back of the dwellings and headed for the apartment we were watching. The guy was slim, about average height, and had on a long overcoat with the collar turned up. He had his hat pulled down low. It was hard to tell, but he looked to have dark hair and features.

None of the man's precautions fooled John. "What the hell?" he exclaimed whipping the cigarette from his mouth and throwing it out the driver's window. "That's Jackie Banks!"

That meant nothing to me, but I didn't say anything. We watched the guy walk up to the apartment, open it with a key and walk right in.

Evelyn stood up. They embraced for a moment and then exited the room. They were out of sight for a few seconds and then I could see Evelyn Cantrell's hand reach around the corner and hit the light switch. The room went dark.

Callahan's shrieking would have waked the dead. "Are you kidding me?" he howled.

I tried not to laugh, but the look on John's face was priceless. Between that and the release of nervous anticipation I curled up in the seat and brayed like a jackass.

John gave me a dirty look. "Screw you, this ain't funny." I just kept laughing, and after a few moments he started to smile despite himself. "I can't believe we have been sitting out here just to have that bitch go in the bedroom and turn the light out."

I felt the same way but there were a lot of things I didn't know and I started asking questions.

"Who's Jackie Banks?"

"Jackie is the head of a large gang based on the north side of the city."

I let that roll around in my head for a moment and said, "That doesn't sound good."

"It's not. He's stepped on Cantrell's toes more than once."

"Is his outfit the same size as Cantrell's," I asked.

"No, Banks' army is a lot bigger."

"As big as Julius Epstein's?"

"Shit no! Both of those gangs together don't hold a light to Epstein's syndicate. Banks and Cantrell are local. Epstein does business from Washington D.C. to Hollywood."

"So," I mused, "if Jackie Banks is a bigger man about town than Cantrell, then what's Cantrell going to do about Jackie sleeping with his wife?"

"That's a good question. Cantrell has the balls to take on Banks, but he doesn't have the brains or the guns to accomplish anything other than getting slaughtered."

"Well, Cantrell did say that he was afraid she was doing this stuff just to hurt him."

The side of John's mouth curled up. "This ought to do it," he replied.

He continued to watch the dark window and mumble about how he couldn't believe this was happening, but since there wasn't anything to see I looked out the passenger window and noticed that there was a flurry of activity in the same apartment that had caught my attention on our previous visit. This time it was quite obvious that people in that apartment were interested in the goings-on at Evelyn Cantrell's. The slats in the venetian blinds had been pulled apart, and someone had stuck the end of a telescope into the opening.

I nudged Callahan and motioned toward the window.

"Shit, I don't blame them," he snorted. "If I had that apartment I'd charge a nickel a peek and sell popcorn and refreshments."

"Now what?" I asked.

"Good question," replied John. He fished another cigarette out of the pack and lit up. "The bedroom window is on the end of the apartment, and the curtains are already drawn. I could see them when we drove up."

"Is there any way to peek in that window?"

"Not without somebody seeing us doing it and calling the cops." He took a drag from his cigarette and exhaled through his open window. "Sitting in a car on the side of a cul-de-sac just makes us ordinary citizens enjoying a cool New Egan evening; but peeking in one of those windows makes us perverts, and the cops would have a field day with us."

I didn't know if he was telling it straight up or if he was just afraid to take what looked like a minimal risk. I remembered what Mike had said about him being scared of his own shadow.

"So what do you want to do," I asked.

"Let's hang around a little bit and see what happens. Maybe they'll come back out and do something."

I flipped my palms up and shrugged as a "why not" gesture.

"We can listen to the radio until there's nothing good playing, and if they still haven't come out we'll give it up."

That's what he said, but just a couple minutes later he slid down in the seat, asleep, with his hat over his face.

I was glad to have the virtual solitude and time to think as I sat and listened to Burns and Allen on the radio and to John snoring lightly into his hat. I certainly had a lot to think about, and I owed the little old man an answer about staying here or going back to my world. It wasn't much of a choice; I really missed television, computers, and not having to deal with cigarette smoke. If this had been the 21st century, I could have passed the time streaming movies on my smart phone.

I didn't think there was a good argument for staying, but a little voice in my head created one anyway, and it wasn't bad. The argument was a simple one. I was doing a lot better here than I had been doing in my time. I had a good job, and it was nice to be needed and appreciated. For the first time since I had left the Corps, I had a purpose in the world even if it wasn't my world. I had to confess to the little voice that it felt good and was worth the bruising and stitches it had taken to be able to feel that way.

Still, if I went back, I could put what I had learned on this world to good use. I didn't have to sit around drinking and wishing I was back in the Corps. I could probably get a job with a security company or maybe even a rural police department that wasn't too picky about knee injuries.

Something caught my attention, and I noticed a guy pretending that he was strolling casually around the inside of the cul-de-sac as if he was just out for a walk. He was a big guy, about six feet tall, with a broad chest, broad shoulders and a thick neck. He had on dark colored coat and pants and a pink pastel shirt with a big collar that he pulled over the collar of the coat. A gorilla wearing the same suit wouldn't have stuck out any more than this guy, especially considering that they wouldn't have been far apart in size. He came around the curve of the road and began walking straight toward the front of the car with the same *nonchalant purpose*.

I continued to look straight forward as if there was nothing wrong and without moving my mouth very much I said, "We've got company."

Callahan raised his hat a little without raising his head and replied, "There's another one coming up behind us."

I cut my eyes over to look in the side mirror and there wasn't one there.

"Where's the side mirror?" I asked.

In a voice that suggested I was a moron John asked, "Why the hell would there be a mirror over there?"

He lowered his hat and said, "Don't say anything. Let me do all the talking."

Truth be told, I didn't have much faith in my companion to get us out of a jam; but I didn't have any good options, so I said, "Suits me."

The guy coming from behind got to the car first and used his big fist to rap on Callahan's window. Judging by the noise it created, I assumed he was more interested in smashing the glass than getting our attention. I was surprised when it didn't break.

Callahan lazily lifted his hat off his face and looked at the big face in the window. "Lester is that you?" He took the window crank and rolled down the window as he asked, "What the hell are you doing out here?"

The big man with his head stuck in John's window was a mirror image of the man I had been looking at. Callahan was acting like everything was fine, but I still didn't have a good feeling about his ability to get us out of any trouble. Nevertheless I went ahead and rolled my window down as the other guy reached my side of the car. He slapped his big hands down on the top of the door and stuck his head in the opening. He smiled as if he didn't mind being so far into my personal space, and I tried to act as if I didn't either.

Callahan turned to the new face. "I was just about to ask where Larry was. How're you doing Larry?"

Larry just kept smiling and didn't say anything.

Callahan went on as if nothing was awkward. "Jake, this is Lester and Larry Delgado. They're twins in case you hadn't noticed, and the best muscle in New Egan."

Neither of them extended a hand, so I just nodded at each them.

"What are you doing out here Callahan?" asked Lester.

"Probably the same thing you guys are doing. " He motioned toward Evelyn Cantrell's apartment. "We heard the woman in that apartment was getting naked and mattress dancing with her boyfriend in front of that big window."

"Do you know who lives in that apartment?" asked Lester. Apparently he was the spokesman for the pair. Larry just continued smiling at me.

"You're damned right I do. That's Evelyn Cantrell's apartment."

"You boys drove out here just for that?"

"Are you shitting me? I got word that she was out here last week doing a couple of shows a night, so me and Jake jumped in the car and drove over."

"What does your friend do for a living?" Lester asked pointing his chin at me.

"Jake just started working for Mike Manzarek."

The smile left Larry's face and Lester asked, "Jake...*Kowalski*?"

I had already eased my hand around the door handle. I tried to brace myself in the hope that, if trouble started, I would be able to drive the car door open against the gorilla leaning on it.

"That's right," I told him as calmly as I could manage.

Larry flipped the back of his big hand across my chest and asked, "You're the guy that took out Max Winston last Sunday night."

"*Oh great, friends of Max's,*" I thought. "Yeah, that's me," I said aloud, tightening my grip on the door handle.

"This is a real stroke of luck running into you," said Lester. "Larry and I saw Winston fight at the Emporium a few years ago."

I tensed for it and Lester added, "He was a brawling son of a bitch. Anybody that can handle him is tops in our book."

Larry stuck his other big hand in the window, and it took an act of will to remove mine from the door handle to shake it. "Thanks," I offered lamely as Larry grabbed my hand and wagged my whole arm with it.

Lester said, "You know we could use a guy like you."

At that John piped up, "C'mon guys, you're not gonna poach Mike's people are you?"

"Quiet Callahan," said Lester flatly, "we're talking to your friend. Good talent is hard to find."

John put his fingertips to his chest. "What am I chopped liver?"

Lester shook his head still not looking at John, "No, I got a use for chopped liver."

Callahan looked at me and feigned offense, "You can see how I'm appreciated in this town."

Fortunately for me I had already practiced this interchange. "Thanks guys, but Mike's been really good to me and…"

Lester stopped me, "Say no more. Nobody appreciates loyalty more than we do, but if anything changes don't forget us."

"I won't, thanks."

Lester pushed back from John's window, and looked toward Mrs. Cantrell's apartment. "So have you seen anything this evening?"

Callahan mashed his lips together and took a moment before he said, "Some guy went in about thirty minutes ago, but he went straight to the bedroom and she turned out the lights and went after him."

Lester tried to act disinterested, but he was no better at it than his brother was. "Could you see who it was?"

"Nah, the guy had his collar pulled up and his hat pulled down. It could've been Clark Gable for all I know."

"Are you boys going to stay out here much longer?" He tried to make it sound like a question, but there was no mistaking that we were being told to leave.

Callahan fished around in the seat for his cigarettes. "I don't think so. We were going to finish listening to Burns and Allen and then hit the road."

Lester bobbed his head to indicate that plan of action agreed with him, but before he could say anything John asked, "You never did say what you guys were doing out here."

Lester grinned. "We're just getting some exercise."

Callahan had found his cigarettes and used an unlit one to gesture at each of the brothers when he squawked, "Exercise, are you kidding? Look at the shoulders on you boys. You need to go get a ballpark hotdog and a beer and sit in front of the radio more often. You two are making the rest of us look bad."

"Shit, Callahan my grandmother makes you look bad. Why don't you get over to the gym sometime?"

"Are you kidding?" Callahan pointed his cigarette at himself. "I'm a lover not a fighter."

Lester's expression changed as something occurred to him. He leaned back into Callahan's window and told him, "That reminds me, Gloria was asking about you."

John didn't sound very interested when he asked, "Is that right? What'd she say?"

"She said you don't come around to see her anymore."

"You got that right. Did she tell you why?"

"She said you came around all the time when she was at Pearl's house, but now that she's uptown you don't come around anymore."

John gestured toward Lester with cigarette. "You got that right, too. When she was at Pearl's, I could get a piece for two bucks. Now that she's uptown, she wants five dollars for it."

"You always were a big spender," said Lester sarcastically.

John punched the dashboard lighter. "I don't see any reason to throw away money. I let her know that I'd be glad to give her two bucks for it anytime she wanted."

"That's what she told me. She also said she'd sew the damned thing shut before you could have it for two dollars."

John chuckled and said, "You can tell her that the last time I had some, it could've used a couple stitches."

The lighter popped out, and John stuck it to the end of his cigarette.

Lester shook his head back and forth. "You're a real class act Callahan."

John spoke with the half of his mouth that wasn't lighting the cigarette and still managed to grin when he said. "That's what they tell me."

Lester waved for his brother and called back over his should, "You boys have a nice evening."

"Thanks fellas, you too."

They pretended to walk off to nowhere in particular, but I was sure they were patrolling in an organized fashion and would be back in a couple of minutes when Burns and Allen would be finished.

"Well," I started slowly, "I have to confess, you did handle that well."

"You sound surprised."

"I am."

John waited for me to clarify what I'd said, but I didn't. I finally asked, "So what's the deal with those guys?"

"Those muscleheads work for Jackie Banks. They're his primary bodyguards."

"At least you knew them; that seemed to help."

Callahan blew a plume of smoke at the window. "Shit, it wouldn't have helped a damned bit if they had any idea we knew it was Jackie Banks in that apartment."

"I noticed you danced around that."

John smiled. "When it comes to dancing around the truth, I can be Fred Astaire."

"I'm impressed. I can't lie worth a damn. Mike makes fun of me for it."

"Mike made fun of Charlie for the same reason; he couldn't lie for shit either. It wasn't in his nature." Callahan blew a cloud of smoke at the windshield and then tried to shoo it out the window with the back of his hand. It was wasted energy.

"I think that's the reason Mike took to you so quickly. You're a lot like Charlie."

"Really?"

"A *lot* like him. Charlie wasn't nearly as big and tough as you are, but he had the same inability to lie well and some kind of inner drive to try and do the right thing regardless of the cost."

My throat constricted and my eyes watered a little. I hadn't realized anyone thought of me that way. I certainly didn't. Everyone that had spoken of Charlie had spoken well of him and now I was being compared to him by his own brother. I didn't know what to say, so I didn't say anything.

Something caught Callahan's attention. He sat up quickly and gestured toward Evelyn Cantrell's apartment. "Something's happening over there."

"The lights had come on, and Mrs. Cantrell walked into the main room wearing her bathrobe and picked up the telephone.

"Oh yeah, this is hot and steamy," I said sarcastically.

John slapped his palms against the steering wheel. "Where's the hot burlesque show that everyone's been talking about. I've seen better action in the balcony at the movies."

I wanted to ask about balconies in movie theaters since that sounded interesting, but before I could, I picked up movement in the apartment window on my side of the car. The telescope slipped out of sight and a moment later the light around the edge of the blinds went out.

John noticed it as well. "It looks like your friends have given up on her too," he groused. "I don't blame them, there's nothing to see here."

Mrs. Cantrell hung up the phone and went back to the bedroom, turning the light out behind her.

Callahan and I both slumped back in the seat and listened to the last couple of minutes of the radio program, but we didn't laugh. As the announcer was giving one last commercial before the show's end, John pointed across my nose at the sidewalk. I turned my head and saw two men in trench coats standing on the sidewalk talking to each other in front of the apartment building on our right. They had their hats pulled down low, but I recognized them as the same two men I had seen when I had been there previously. I tried to remember what Callahan had called them.

"G-Men," I said as it popped into my head.

"Uh-huh," grunted Callahan. "Those look like the same two boys we saw before."

"They are."

"I thought maybe they were out chasing skirt when we saw them the other night, but now I'm thinking they're working."

"Working on what?"

John shrugged. "You got me." He gestured at me with his lit cigarette. "Unless you want to go hand-to-hand with that musclebound circus act you just met, we need to get going."

I didn't like the choices, but there was only one smart one. "I hate to run off, but I don't see any point tangling with those apes just to sit and stare at a dark window."

Callahan rubbed his chin with his fist. "I don't think so either, but what do we tell

Mike?"

"What do you mean?" I asked as I watched the G-Men head off between the buildings and disappear like they had before.

"We're supposed to be out here getting proof that Mrs. C. is having extramarital sessions with some guy or guys."

"Yeah, and it looks like she is."

"What do you base that on?"

"They went in the other room and turned the lights out."

"They sure did and I'm positive they were in there playing hide the sausage, but as far as we know for sure; they could have been holding midnight mass. We can't prove they weren't."

"Oh, I see what you mean." I thought for a moment and said, "It looks like we will need to come back."

"A man after my own heart," Callahan replied loudly.

He put the Studebaker in gear, wheeled around the cul-de-sac and cruised down the road.

CHAPTER 23

I was up early the next morning and went through my ritual of cleaning myself and my wounds. My face was looking a lot more normal, and the stitches at my scalp-Iine looked like they could come out. I decided I would try to get down to the doctor's office the next day if Mike didn't mind and *if* I could find the office. The stitches on my back and legs were doing a little better and weren't nearly as sore as they had been the previous day.

I got dressed and arrived at the breakfast table just a couple of minutes after Mike, but Esmerelda had used that couple of minutes to put food on the table and leave.

I could hardly wait until Roberto came to see her. I was now positive she had seen her loving boyfriend with his other girlfriend, so it was going to be up to her to choose whether she would run him off or forgive him; but either way, I would be glad to get things back to the way they had been just a couple of days earlier.

When I sat down I saw a guy in white painters overalls walk out of the dining room and into the living room. He had a paint brush in one hand and a tape measure in the other. I had no idea what he was trying to accomplish.

"Those guys start early," I said to Mike.

"Yeah, they've been at it for a while," he replied. "They're making good progress. The window's fixed, and the living room looks almost normal. They should be done by Saturday."

The breakfast was good. Huevos rancheros was always one of my favorites, and no one ever did it better than Mike's pretty Latin housekeeper.

I wanted to tell my news; but I figured the boss had news of his own, so I asked, "How did it go at the bar?"

The boss' eyes narrowed. "Did anybody ask where I was?"

"Just John."

"That's good, I was afraid someone might drop by looking for me and raise suspicions."

"So how did it go?" I repeated.

"It was as nice as a crappy little place in the middle of nowhere can be."

"They aren't putting her up at the Gifford Palace?" I was being facetious, but I was also thrilled that I could finally make a local reference to something.

"Not even close, but they are trying to make it as comfortable as they can. At least it's safe."

"How is she holding up," I asked.

"She's bored out of her mind and wants to come home."

"I can't say I blame her for that."

"Me neither, I hated to leave her," he said hoarsely. His eyes misted over as he turned to look at me, and with all the sincerity a human being was capable of mustering he said, "We need to find out who's doing this and stop them. I can't leave her again."

I couldn't think of anything stellar to say, so I nodded as reassuringly as I could.

Mike took a sip of his coffee and then his face lit up as a thought hit him. "Hey, what did your buddy, John, find at the morgue?"

"*My* buddy?"

"You're the one hanging out with him, watching women get undressed. What did he say?"

"He said the guy at the morgue was Shorty, his informant, and since you mentioned it we didn't see anybody take their clothes off."

"Shit on both counts," Mike hissed into his coffee cup.

"I grilled Callahan pretty hard about his informant, but he said he wasn't aware of any friends or acquaintances. He said the guy was just a street rat that showed up when he had some information to sell."

"That guy was fairly well-dressed and well-heeled for a street rat."

I had to rack my memory to recall that Mike had used the word "heeled" before, when he wanted to know if I was carrying a gun.

"I said the same thing about his clothes, but I didn't notice his gun."

"Custom, prewar 45 semi-automatic with ivory grips, like the ones Patton had on his pistols. That's a damned nice piece of hardware for a street rat."

I nodded in agreement. "John figured that he must have changed his ways, because Shorty didn't look that good anytime he had dealt with him."

The boss didn't ask anything else. I sat there looking at him waiting for the question; but it never came. He finally got tired of me staring at him and asked, "What?"

"Aren't you going to ask me if we saw anything last night?"

"You just said you didn't see anybody take their clothes off last night, so I'm trying to figure out where that 'cat that ate the canary look' on your face is coming from. I'm guessing you and John must have seen Mrs. Cantrell do *something* interesting last night."

"Actually she didn't do anything interesting. She went into the bedroom and turned the lights off."

Mike slid a cigarette out of the pack and fished in his shirt pocket for matches. "I'll mention that to her old man when I give him the bill. He'll be real happy."

"Probably not," I told him. "It's who she went in the bedroom *with* that's interesting."

"And that would be?"

"According to John, it was a guy named Jackie Banks."

Mike made a huffing noise like he had been punched in the stomach, and blew his match out before he could light his cigarette.

"Are you sure?" he asked in a very loud voice.

"The guy was moving quick with his collar up and hat down, but Callahan was sure of it."

"John's got the eye and memory for that sort of thing."

"Yes, he does," I agreed quickly.

"So if he says it's Jackie Banks -- then it's Jackie Banks." Mike lit his cigarette and asked, "Did you see anyone else?"

"A couple of professional thugs named..."

"Lester and Larry?"

"That's them."

"That helps confirm that it was Jackie you saw. These days he doesn't go anywhere without Mutt and Jeff with him. Did they give you any trouble?"

"I thought they were going to, but John handled them."

"You sound surprised."

"I didn't think John was the kind of guy to deal well with pressure, but he was smooth as silk with those guys."

Mike's head bobbed up and down. "When it comes to trouble, taking off like a jackrabbit is John's first impulse, but if you corner him he has an astonishing knack for dealing with it." He took a second to light his cigarette and then asked, "So they don't know you saw Jackie?"

"John told them we saw someone but didn't get a good look. He lies much better than I do."

"He can do that better than a lot of people. It was one thing he could do better than his brother Charlie."

"That's what he said."

"I'm glad you didn't have to tangle with those guys."

"*You're* glad!?" I hooted out.

Mike smiled. "Well I'm sure you're happy about it, too." He took a drag from his cigarette and said, "I've seen those guys in action. They have all the panache of a twenty-mule team performing Swan Lake, and they leave just as big a mess when they're finished." He pointed at me with the two fingers holding his cigarette. "But they usually get the job done."

I didn't have any trouble believing that and I started to say something, but I could see that Mike had finished talking and gone off into his thinking mode. His lips moved a little, but he wasn't saying anything. He looked up at the clock on the wall then snubbed out his cigarette in the green ceramic ashtray near his right hand.

An ashtray on the kitchen table was just one more of a million things I would have to get used to if I hung around the mid-twentieth century.

I didn't want to sit there and watch the boss smoke and drink coffee, so I cleared the dirty dishes from the table and started washing them. I was rinsing the last one when Mike stood up and put his coat and hat on. I grabbed mine and followed him to the car.

Twenty-six minutes later we were pulling up to the gates of Republic Aviation. It was a big place with a lot of three and four story red brick buildings interspersed between airplane hangars. Mike and I both had to show identification for them to let us through. The guard pointed to the security office, and we were able to park right in front of it next to the police car.

Lieutenant Briggs was already there with one foot on the front bumper and his elbow resting on his knee as he smoked a cigarette. He looked like he was posing for an ad in a magazine. Officers Muldoon and Jones were with him, but they didn't look quite so picturesque leaning against the side of the car with cigarettes sticking out of the corners of their mouths and their hats tipped back on their heads as they played Liar's Poker.

We got out of the car without anyone speaking. Mike walked over to Briggs and leaned down to light his cigarette from the one in the Lieutenant's hand as if that was what Briggs was there for.

Briggs stood up and headed for the front door causing Muldoon and Jones to rush and put away their dollar bills while they walked quickly to catch up. Mike and I followed them through door and were met by a woman who looked to be in her late fifties. She was wearing a blue dress, and had her mostly gray hair pulled back in a tight bun. She introduced herself as Lois, Mr. Gallagher's secretary. Briggs gave his name and rank and showed his badge. She didn't wait for any additional introductions, just spun on her heel and walked quickly down the hall.

At the end of the hall was a large office with a large wooden desk sitting opposite the door. In addition to the desk, there was a round table with four chairs, a credenza, and a filing cabinet. The room would have held a lot more, but that was all there was. The lack of furniture pointed up the fact that the carpet was pretty ratty and should have been replaced a long time ago.

Behind the desk sat a man in a gray suit. He looked to be in his mid-fifties, tall, fit, with dark hair that had swipes of gray running back from both temples. A younger man, maybe mid-forties, bald on top, wearing a blue coat and tan pants was standing next to the desk.

The two men watched us walk in and waited until we made a mob in front of the desk before speaking.

The man at the desk stood up and introduced himself as Henry Gallagher, Vice President of Security at Republic Aviation. He turned to the man next to the desk and introduced him as Bruce Laughlin, his Director of Security.

Briggs introduced himself and the rest of us. Gallagher and his Director didn't offer their hands. They just nodded as our names were called off.

The VP sat back down at the desk, but didn't offer anyone a chair. I was expecting him to be evasive or even hostile to our questions, but I quickly found out differently.

Briggs waded right in. "Do you know this man," he asked, as he handed over an 8x12 black and white photo of Max Winston.

Gallagher looked at it for only a second before he replied, "I believe that's Max Winston. He used to work for us." He handed the photo back and asked, "Is he in some kind of trouble?"

Briggs shook his head. "Actually, he's dead, but he was part of a crew that attacked Mr. Manzarek's wife, earlier this week."

The Security Chief looked over at Mike, and the big man nodded once in affirmation.

"I'm sorry to hear that, but I guess I'm not surprised."

"Why's that?"

"I took over this position right after the war, and he was one of the people that we had to let go.

"Why was that?" prompted Briggs.

"During the war we were short of labor just like everyone else. We did what we could to make up the deficiencies, pretty much the same as all the other businesses. We hired women, foreigners, vagabonds; you name it."

"Sounds like a formula for trouble."

"In all honesty, it worked pretty well, but working in Security, especially for a government contractor, requires a background check and the man whose job I took over was a little too lax about that part."

"Winston didn't have a criminal record," said Briggs. He spoke with conviction.

"No, but our investigation turned up that he was freelancing as hired muscle for a number of local criminal rings. Are you aware that he boxed professionally for a time?"

"I am," I whispered to Mike from the corner of my mouth. He shushed me out of the corner of his.

"Yeah, we turned that up," replied Briggs. He jotted something in his notebook and then asked,

"Didn't the government have something to say about your people not being cleared?"

Gallagher looked puzzled. "Like what?"

"Something like, 'we're going to cancel your government contracts if your people aren't cleared'."

Gallagher looked like one of those upper management types that didn't have a sense of humor, but that brought a smile to his face.

"I think you're laboring under an incorrect assumption. We don't have very many government contracts and the ones we do have are small and short lived."

Now it was Mike who looked puzzled. Even though it no longer made much sense, it was easy to figure out the boss was still fishing for the connection between Norma and the Senator.

The Big Man forged ahead, "Aren't you a DOD contractor?"

"We are, in the sense that we have a few, small, short-lived government contracts," Gallagher repeated in a fashion that suggested he was a little annoyed at having to do so.

"I was thinking more about during the war."

"It was pretty much the same then."

"My wife worked for Senator during the war. She said your people came through his office a number of times pitching ideas and chasing work."

Gallagher nodded. "We did. We just didn't get any."

Mike's frustration was obvious, and Gallagher tried to help him.

"I think I see what you're after. Since the men who attacked your wife came from here, you're thinking that maybe your wife saw or heard something, while she was working for the Senator."

"That's what I was thinking." Mike's lips wadded into a knot as he mulled something over, and then he went for broke. "I'll go ahead and ask you straight out, is there any chance this company pushed any money or favors in the Senator's direction in the hopes of getting any government work?"

I expected the question to bug him, but Gallagher fooled me again and smiled. "I don't blame you for asking, and I can see why you would; but surely you see the unlikelihood of it."

"Why is it unlikely," asked Briggs.

"It is unlikely we paid for government contracts, because we don't have any."

"Even during the war?" asked Mike.

"I'm talking about during the war." The smile left Gallagher's face, and it didn't take an expert in human emotions to see the disgust that replaced it. "During the war our sales people and engineers proposed program after program to Capitol Hill, and for whatever reasons; we never got anything but the scraps that other companies left behind. I didn't join the company until midyear of '44, so I wasn't here for most of that stuff. If there was anything going on under the table, I wouldn't have been privy to it. I couldn't say for sure that it didn't happen, but I know for a fact that if we paid anyone for favoritism, we never got it."

Briggs asked, "So the rumors about this place holding on by a thread..."

"...aren't rumors," finished Gallagher without hesitation.

We had pretty much ruled out the Norma/Senator/Republic connection when Ernest Dulay and Shorty's crew had tried to make off with Mike at Max Winston's house; but Mike had still gone poking around for an ember of hope that linked them together and now Gallagher had pissed on that too. The room was quiet for a moment as we processed the dead end we had run into.

Briggs finally broke the silence. "Let's get back to our mutual friend Max Winston. What did you do when you found out that he was moonlighting as an enforcer?"

"I fired him immediately."

"When did this happen?"

"Ahhh...let me think...it was sometime in late '45. I can pull the records and get the exact date if you want."

"Yeah, we'll need that."

Gallagher turned and looked at Lois. She jotted something down on a pad of spiral bound paper.

"You said, 'He was *one* of the people," that you had to let go. How many others were there?"

"That was a rough time; we had a real purge going. I let around fifteen people go in a month's time."

"Can you get us a list of those people," asked Briggs, and after a moment, "Actually, now that I'm thinking about it, can you get us a list of everyone that has worked for you since the war?"

On his face, I could see Gallagher tally up the time it was going to take to come up with that list, but he finally nodded and said he would. He cut his eyes toward the secretary, and she scribbled on her pad; then walked quickly out the door.

"How about this guy?" asked Briggs, pulling out another 8X10 black and white photo and handing it to the VP. It was a photo of the guy that had been killed the night Norma was attacked. Gallagher looked at it a moment and was obviously bothered by what he was seeing.

"Is this man dead?" he asked in a low voice.

"Yes he is," Briggs confirmed. "Do you know him?"

"Yes, I know him. May I ask why you're asking about him?"

"Along with Max Winston, he was part of the trio that attempted to kidnap Norma Manzarek last Sunday night. He was accidentally shot by one of the other three during the attempt."

The head of Republic Aviation's security didn't look happy at all. He sat looking at the picture for a little longer and finally said, "This man was working for us until last Friday. We have been wondering what happened to him as he didn't show up for work this week."

The atmosphere had been a little on the gloomy side until that moment. Suddenly the whole room perked up. From the way everyone behaved I assumed they had been laboring under the same assumption that I had, that Max Winston and anyone in cahoots with him had worked for Aviation Republic at one time, but was no longer employed there.

The police captain started asking questions for all of us. "Do you have a recent address for this guy?"

Gallagher twisted his lips together and then nodded. "We should have." There was a box the size of a shoe box on his desk with a row of switches sticking out of it. He pressed one of them down and said, "Would you see what personal information we have on Art Delgado?"

He let the switch up and the box replied, "Yes sir," in Lois' voice.

I knew about office intercoms, but I hadn't seen many of them. I wanted a closer look, but that was going to have to wait for another day.

Lois came walking back in with a manila folder that she passed to her boss. She turned around and went straight back out. I hadn't seen too much out of her personality-wise, but I sure couldn't fault her for efficiency.

Gallagher thumbed through it and then handed it to the Lieutenant. Briggs flipped it open and after looking at it for a moment he handed it to one of the officers.

"Has anyone else been missing since Friday?" asked Briggs.

The VP looked at the Director and Laughlin came to life. "No," he said. "We haven't noticed anyone else being out more than a day."

"Did this guy, Delgado, have any friends or hang out with anybody at the company?"

"I don't know," said Gallagher slowly. He turned to Laughlin again. "Bruce, do you know if he socialized with anyone from here?"

The director thought for a moment and said, "I've seen him in the cafeteria a couple of times. He was sitting with that little fellow...what's his name...I saw the guy just yesterday...Lynwood, Abner Lynwood."

The excitement showed in the police lieutenant's voice when he asked, "Is he here today?"

"He should be, yes," replied Laughlin.

"Now we're getting somewhere," whispered Mike.

The Lieutenant flipped his notepad shut and stated firmly, "We would like to speak with him right away,"

The two security men looked at each other, nodded their consent, and stood up.

"Where does he work?" asked Gallagher.

Laughlin squinted and thought for a second before he said, "Lynwood doesn't work for Security. I believe he's one of the maintenance crew, so he should be working out of B15."

We all nodded like we knew where that was, and Galllagher called down the hallway, "Lois!"

"I'll call the head of maintenance and tell him you're coming," she called back from an office doorway.

The head of security and his director walked down the hall to the front door, followed by Briggs and his people, and then Mike with me bringing up the rear.

I could hear Gallagher laying down the ground rules to Briggs as they walked.

"I want your reassurance that there won't be any improper accusations made or undue pressure put on this man. As far as we know his only crime is associating with a man that is alleged to have been part of a possible kidnapping."

Before the Lieutenant could answer, Laughlin came to a hard stop a couple of feet from the front door. He did it so quickly that the rest of the mob behind him bumped into each other.

The group un-bunched, and I could see Laughlin pointing out the window that made up the top half of the door. He was saying something softly to Gallagher and Briggs but I couldn't hear what it was. Briggs leaned his head over so that he could see out the same window from where he was standing, and then he gestured for Mike and me to come forward. As we walked up next to the Lieutenant, he pointed toward the window and asked in a soft voice, "Have either of you seen that guy across the street?"

Mike stepped to the side and looked and then shook his head. He stepped away, and I took my turn. Across the street from the security offices was another very similar brick building with windows surrounding it. Sticking out of the side of the building was a large water pipe and valve, and standing next to that was a small guy pretending to work on it. I don't know anything about plumbing, and normally I wouldn't have any idea if a guy working on a water valve was actually doing any real work or not, but this guy was so focused on watching the security building that his pretense of working on the valve was nowhere near credible. He kept stepping back and forth around the valve and pipe, but never took his eyes off of the building where our group was standing and watching him out the window. Every now and then he would rest his wrench on top of the pipe or poke at it a little. A couple of times he dropped the wrench altogether and still kept his eyes focused our way as he bent down and picked it up.

I twisted my head to look at Briggs. "That's the guy who was driving the car last Sunday night," I told him.

Laughlin cocked his head to look out the window again and then turned to Briggs. "That's Abner Lynwood. He looks like he's wearing the same clothes I saw him in yesterday. Should I just go out and tell him that we'd like to see him in here?"

"I don't think that's a good idea," replied Briggs. "You just heard an eye witness tell you that our friend out there was part of a kidnapping attempt. He knows we are here because he can see the squad car, and it obviously has him worried. If you invited him in here or if one of my officers walks outside and shows him any interest, we're going to have a foot race on our hands."

"We can lock the place down," suggested Gallagher. "I can call and have the gates closed."

The Lieutenant smiled. "That sounds like a wonderful idea, please do." He gave a stern look in Mike's direction and added, "Let us handle this." Mike lowered his head in a single nod, and then we waited to see how everything played out.

Apparently we weren't the only ones. Lois had come out of her office and was standing behind our group with her hands folded in front of her waiting for any instructions that might come her way. Gallagher turned toward her and she said, "I'll send the signal."

As she walked into her office Muldoon asked Briggs, "Why don't you just let me go out there and grab him?

Briggs snorted through his nose and looked at Muldoon as if the bulbous officer had lost his mind.

Muldoon looked surprised and a little offended. "You don't think I can catch him?"

Briggs snorted again. "Not unless he turns into a bottle of Four Roses."

"Very funny," grumbled the officer, turning red.

It was only funny for a moment, and then suddenly we were all in pain. The entire group jumped and clapped our hands to our ears as something that sounded very much like an air raid siren split open the quiet morning.

"What the hell is that?" Briggs yelled into Gallagher's face.

"That's the signal to close the gates," Gallagher yelled back.

"Oh that's subtle!" roared Mike.

Across the street, Abner Lynwood dropped his wrench and bolted like a gazelle. He must have made ten feet before the wrench hit the ground. He was heading out the way we had come in, toward the front gate.

I couldn't speak for Jones, but Briggs was right. There was no way Muldoon could catch him. The little guy could run.

"Go Jake!" yelled Mike without waiting for Briggs' permission. I took off as hard as I could go and burst through the front door. I didn't bother with the five or six concrete steps to the left or right leading down to street level. I vaulted the iron railing on the front and hit the street running. I was flying, but I could see I was going to have trouble catching this guy. In High School I had been considered fast for a football player, but Abner must have been one of those little track and field athletes who make it pointless for a guy like me to go out for the track team. My only saving grace was that I could at least keep him in sight.

Lynwood lost a little momentum as he turned to look behind him. His eyes got big when his fears were confirmed. There was actually somebody trying to run him down, somebody that had seen him trying to kidnap Norma Manzarek. Unfortunately for me the added fear put wings on the little man's feet, and he really put the heat to it. Up ahead I could see the guard at the gate talking on the phone and looking wildly around. Gallagher or maybe Lois must have been calling to let him know he had a runner headed his way.

The gate was closing but it was a big heavy iron thing sliding closed across a recessed rail, and it was taking forever. Lynwood must have known that and decided to make a break for it when the siren went off. His gamble had paid off. The gate wasn't going to close in time and Lynwood was going to clear it with seconds to spare.

The front gate was one leg of an intersection so once outside this guy had all the options right, left or straight. I didn't figure he would run headlong across the street so that narrowed it down to right or left. I was wondering if I could determine which way he was going to go and maybe I could take another path and cut him off.

That thought was up and gone in a couple of seconds. Lynwood reached the gatehouse, and the guard ran out to try and cut him off. The guard wasn't armed and he wasn't in any better shape than Muldoon. Lynwood did a quick shuffle and faked the fat bastard right out of his skivvies.

The little man shot through the gate and tasted freedom. I had been wrong about his direction. The light facing him was about to go green and cars were stopping on both sides. The little guy took advantage of it and bolted straight across the intersection. He was going way too fast to stop when he realized that the Chevrolet running the yellow light in the far lane was too. He spun on his heel, turning to face the oncoming vehicle, and I could see his mouth open, but whatever noise he made was drowned out by the sounds of blaring car horns and screaming tires. I came to a halt at the edge of the curb as the big car and little man collided. It wasn't a contest. The impact sent Lynwood pinwheeling through the air, and he landed on the other side of the traffic light. The big Chevy slid to a stop just under it.

I couldn't see him because my view was blocked by cars that had stopped for the light on my left. The cars didn't move when the light turned green. Everyone got out and ran to where Lynwood had landed. I didn't figure there was much use in hurrying, but I did anyway.

Lynwood's eyes were wide open and staring at the crowd of people that circled him and stared back. It only appeared that way. He was gone. His legs were bent up and twisted in impossible directions as was his right arm.

"Ah shit," wheezed Muldoon coming up behind me." He stood there for a moment, bent over with his hands on his thighs, breathing loudly and staring at the body in the street. He finally stood up and motioned for the other officer to go to the gatehouse and make a call.

"Ambulance?" asked the officer.

Muldoon   shook   his   head.

CHAPTER 24

According to his driver's license, Abner Lynwood was 28 years old and his residence was about twenty-minutes away. Mike wanted to go right away, but Briggs had to wait for the Coroner and wouldn't let us leave until he was sure we wouldn't get to Abner's place before him.

The late Mr. Lynwood had lived in a run-down apartment complex in an even more run-down part of the city. The streets were covered with cigarette butts, matches, and pieces of cardboard and paper that blew everywhere. I watched the paper cups and newspapers flying around, and I was reminded that even though this was New Egan, the wind blew the same way as it did in Chicago.

Trashcans were lined up against the side of the brick building, and all of them were overflowing with the lids placed on top of the mounds growing out of them. The walls had the powder black covering of a city that still burned coal for heat.

It was a four-story walkup and Briggs barked, "We're going to 303," as he headed up the stairs. Mike was right behind Briggs, and I brought up the rear behind Muldoon. It was bad enough I had to listen to him huff and wheeze most of the way up, but the view was the worst of it. I swore to never get behind him on the stairs again.

The flooring was wood on the third floor hallway. Years ago it was probably nice to look at, but now it was rough and worn and needed to be sanded down and refinished. Even in that rundown state, it would be worth a fortune as reclaimed lumber in the 21st century. In the middle of the 20th century, judging from the stains and smells; it was just a place to walk, spit, and urinate. Dirty beige paint was flaking and peeling from the walls.

We stopped in front of 303, and Briggs tried the door. It was locked.

"Well," said Briggs, stepping back and speaking thoughtfully, "I could send Muldoon down to the superintendent's apartment for the key."

We all looked over at Muldoon who was leaning against the wall trying to catch his breath.

"If you do, his death will be on your conscience," Mike told Briggs in a low voice.

My boss looked over at the door and placed the flat of his big hand just above the deadbolt. "Besides," he added, "the door's open." In a move that looked effortless, he pushed against the door.

I could hear the door frame cracking and splintering as he forced the deadbolt through it. The door swung open, and he motioned for Briggs to go first.

I heard Muldoon whisper, "Thank God," as he walked up behind me.

The apartment matched the hallway except it wasn't as well cleaned and maintained. It was an efficiency unit where you could pretty much stand in the middle of the room and see everything there was to see. Unfortunately, I didn't want to see what was there. Dirty dishes were piled in the small kitchen sink, and they littered all the flat surfaces in the room. Dirty clothes, newspapers, and what looked like unopened mail was strewn all over the floor. The wallpaper was loose and curling; and Cockroaches punctuated it in numerous places. I suspected this was because the rug was too threadbare to hide them, so they didn't try.

Mike looked around and said to me, "We should go out in the hall and let these fine officers do their job."

"You're all heart," barked Briggs. You didn't have any trouble sticking your nose in everything at Winston's house; but when it comes to a shithole like this you'll gladly hand it off to me."

"I figured you'd just give it to Muldoon and Jones," said Mike.

"And I will," the Lieutenant replied sharply. "Muldoon," he ordered, "you and Jones look around, and see if you find anything. I'll be in the hall smoking a cigarette if you need me."

We went into the hall and the thought crossed my mind that it might actually be healthier digging around in Abner's toilet of an apartment than smoking a cigarette.

Standing in the hallway we could hear Muldoon cursing everyone from Briggs to the Chief of Police to Abner Lynwood. After about forty-five minutes the swearing stopped, and the door opened.

Muldoon and Jones were both sweat and dust covered. Their hats were pushed back on their heads, and large wet patches showed through the dust on their uniforms. Jones was carrying a rolled up brown paper bag. He handed it to Briggs and said, "That was stuffed behind the radiator." He stepped back to try and dust himself off.

Briggs unrolled the bag to look inside, but before he could take a look Muldoon sounded off, "It's two hundred dollars and a Smith & Wesson 38."

That got my attention. I stepped over to Briggs who was still looking into the bag and asked him, "What was the name of the guy that got killed Sunday night. The guy at Republic Aviation called him Art something. "

"Art Delgado," answered Briggs without looking up.

"That's it," I replied softly. "I bet if you run a test, the bullets in Art's back will match bullets fired from this gun."

Briggs looked up, but he didn't seem excited. "I'll bet they will too, but I already have your word that Lynwood was the driver of the car so the only reason to check the gun out is to see if we can attach it to other crimes."

The new world I was living in kept throwing me curves. It had been a while since people had taken my word as gospel and not bothered to verify anything. I really enjoyed the feeling; and at that moment, I realized how much I had missed it.

Jones finally finished beating the dust out of his uniform and said, "I'm guessing the two hundred bucks are for the job they screwed up snatching Mrs. Manzarek."

"Yeah, that tracks," agreed Briggs.

Mike pointed his cigarette at Officer Jones, "Anything in there that links Lynwood to anybody else? "

The young man shook his head. "No sir, I couldn't find anything. The only mail is unpaid bills. Other than old newspapers, there are no other papers in the apartment. "He pushed his hat farther back on his head. "There's no phone in there, and I didn't see one downstairs when we came in. If he's calling anyone, he must be using the one at the drugstore on the corner. If he's talking to anyone from here, he's using his dirty laundry to signal in semaphore."

"There's plenty of it lying around," growled Muldoon.

Mike nodded. "We can go down and ask the guy at the drug counter if anyone there is taking messages for him." He said it without much conviction, so I figured it was a long shot.

It was all new to me. I wasn't used to living in a place where phones weren't plentiful. Even though I was staring right into the reality of it, it was hard to believe that making a phone call was so hard. It was one more thing the new century had all over the old one.

It was halfhearted, but we all went down to the corner drugstore and questioned the people that worked there. Lieutenant Briggs had Abner Lynwood's picture from his work file and showed it around. The people we talked to had seen Lynwood around, but no one had taken any messages for him or seen him with anyone or noticed the frequency he did or didn't make phone calls. It was just one more of a running string of dead ends.

"We have Art Delgado's address," said Briggs solemnly. It's only about ten minutes from here. He looked over at Mike, and the big man nodded.

Briggs left Muldoon to canvas the area and see if anybody knew Abner Lynwood or anything about him and then barked, "You're driving" at Jones as he headed for the car.

Mike and I didn't make any noise. I could tell the Boss was as depressed about the total lack of leads and clues as I was. We got into the Cadillac and followed the police to Delgado's place.

Art Delgado lived in a little better area than his partner. His apartment was half of a duplex and the owner who lived in the other half, opened Art's apartment for us. One look inside told us we were screwed. The apartment was Spartan to say the least. In the small living room there was one dull green vinyl covered recliner with a side table, a lamp, and a large standing radio. It all sat on top of a well-worn, but very clean oval rug. There was nothing on the kitchen counter. The only things in the cabinets were just enough cookware, flatware, and dinnerware for one lone bachelor. The only other item in the cabinets was a coffee pot.

"This guy even puts his coffee pot away!" Briggs yelped upon finding it.

The pantry had just enough groceries to last for two or three days, and it was the same for the refrigerator. The floor and counters were spotless, and there was only the faintest trace of dust which gave the appearance that Mr. Delgado had dusted just before he left the house Sunday night.

There was only a small nightstand and single bed in the bedroom. The bed was well-made, and the nightstand had a reading lamp on it, but there were no books or magazines anywhere.

"There's nothing under the bed," Muldoon announced, as he pulled up the bedspread. "No dust bunnies...nothing."

The small bathroom was the same. Everything was clean and the medicine cabinet held only toothpaste, a bottle of aspirin, a razor, and shaving cream -- in a tube no less.

The small closet in the bedroom had a small chest of drawers in it, and it held all of Art Delgado's unmentionables all clean and folded neatly with the socks rolled up.

"Marine or Navy," said Mike flatly when he looked in the drawer.

That would have been my call too. It is interesting how many telltale ways the military makes its mark on someone, even down to the way they fold their skivvies and socks.

Briggs dug into Delgado's work file and after studying it a moment announced, "Navy Seaman from 1932 to 1934."

There was a dirty laundry hamper, but it was empty. The rest of his clothes were hung neatly on the single closet rod, with two hats sitting on the shelf above them.

The small closet in the small hallway held all the towels and linens. There were two small waste-cans in the house, and a larger can on the back porch, which were all empty. The back porch also yielded a mop, bucket, broom, and some rags. That was it for Art Delgado's place.

We all took turns looking at what wasn't there, and Jones finally said, "It's clean...literally."

The owner was still standing there -- a slim, balding man in his early fifties. Briggs asked him, "Where are your trash cans?"

"They're around back," the man answered and pointed with his finger, but before we could get started he added, "The trash pickup was Monday."

I looked over at my boss. His head was down, staring at the floor, and his body posture suggested that he was as dejected as I was.

Muldoon started questioning the owner. Delgado had lived there for the last seven years, but other than being super punctual with the rent and meticulously clean, the landlord didn't know anything else about him.

Briggs had been going through the files while Muldoon was asking questions and he let us know, "Neither of these guys has any next of kin listed in their files."

The two best leads we had come across had just fizzled out right in front of us. Briggs told Jones to canvas the area and see if anybody knew anything, but none of us had high hopes of him turning up anything.

Mike nodded to Briggs who nodded back. We got in the car and drove away.

CHAPTER 25

My big boss got behind the wheel, fired the engine, shifted into gear, and punched in the cigarette lighter as he let out the clutch. As the car pulled away he said what we were both thinking.

"Whoever these guys are, they are way ahead of us. They've beaten us at every turn."

"We stopped them from kidnapping you and Norma," I offered weakly.

"Yeah, but that was you're doing. You're the wild card they weren't expecting. Without you this operation would have gone off like clockwork."

I wasn't so sure I was contributing that much to what was going on, and I didn't know what else to say, so I was glad when the lighter popped out.

Mike lit up, wagged the lighter like he was putting out a match and stuck it back in the dash.

"These guys not only make good moves; they clean up after themselves, and they do it really well."

"Is that unusual?" I asked.

"Damned right it is. Cleaning up on this level takes some serious brain power that most organizations, legal or illegal, don't have."

We spent the rest of the trip kicking the same old ideas and questions around, but we didn't get any farther than we were when we had gotten out of bed that morning.

Mike slid the Cadillac into the garage, and we went up to the kitchen.

The room smelled good, but there was no one there. A note on the refrigerator read, "Lunch is in the oven. I am seeing Roberto at 12:30."

Mike read the note and then looked around the kitchen as if he had never seen it.

"What's up with Esmerelda?" he asked aloud. "I thought she wasn't seeing Roberto until tonight."

I was hoping the question was rhetorical, but he turned and looked at me like he was hoping I had an answer.

"She's also usually here at mealtimes, but lately she's been throwing the chow on table and then running off to somewhere else.

I tried to think of something non-committal to say, and I even opened my mouth but before anything came out of it Mike said, "You know something, let's have it."

"You can see that on my face?" I squawked in a voice that was much higher pitched than I cared for.

"Are you shitting me? A blind man could read the look on your face with a cane." He didn't change tone or demeanor when he added, "Don't ever play cards."

He continued to look at me, waiting for an answer; and since I couldn't tell him anything but the truth, that's what I told him. I painted a quick picture of our trip to the hair dresser's and how I had seen Roberto getting cozy with the blonde woman.

My boss massaged his eyes with the forefinger and thumb of his big hand. "Where does she find these guys?" he asked in a low voice.

This time I was sure the question was rhetorical, so I went over to see what we had for lunch. The big pot on the stove was full of Mexican Meatball soup, so I went looking through the cabinets for bowls. I was hoping that Mike would notice that I was searching for something and help me out but he was lost in thought and not paying any attention to my rifling his kitchen cabinetry.

He wasn't looking at me when he asked, "You would think a woman that fine looking, hardworking and smart would attract a better class of guys, wouldn't you?"

I didn't know if I was supposed to be part of the conversation or not, but my response popped out before I knew I had given one. "I don't know why any man would run around on a woman like Esmerelda."

"You and me are coming from the same place on that one," returned Mike as he finally looked around and saw me. "What are you looking for?"

"Bowls for the soup."

"They're in the cabinet on your right." The boss sat down at the table, and I grabbed the bowls and began ladling soup into them."

Mike continued his musing as I fixed lunch. "The woman is even a fantastic cook," he said.

"She's also pretty damned handy with a shotgun," I added quickly.

"So you figure one of the girls at the beauty shop ratted out Roberto to Esmerelda?"

The question caught me by surprise. "Huh, no I figured she saw them together on the street."

"Are you kidding me?" roared Mike.

I started to answer, but before I could he asked, "Are you sure she saw him?"

"No, but she could have seen them, and she started acting funny right after that."

Mike had a look on his face like I had just told him there was a tornado headed toward the house.

"What's wrong?" I asked. The question ended up being ironic, because someone picked that exact moment to begin screaming.

"That's coming from the front of the house," yelled Mike, jumping up from the table and sending his chair flying into the wall.

The big man was closer to the doorway, but I was faster than he was and caught him at the opening to the living room. The scream cut the air again.

"That's not Esmerelda," roared the Boss. The painters had knocked off for lunch, but everything in the living room, including the carpet, was still covered for painting. Mike bulldozed through the room kicking cloth draped ottomans aside like they were shoeboxes.

"Pinche mamón!" howled a female voice from beyond the front door.

"*That's* Esmerelda," yelled Mike.

As we hit the front door the Big Man went to the right side and I went to the left. We both drew our guns, and Mike looked out the side window onto the front porch.

He only peeked out for a second; then with a disgusted look he holstered his gun and opened the front door. I followed him outside just in time to see Esmerelda hit Roberto in the head with a sawed-off baseball bat. Roberto let out the same scream we had heard before.

There was a pretty, but sturdy, wooden railing that ran around the perimeter of the porch. I could see that Roberto's right wrist was handcuffed to it. His left hand was going back and forth between fending off Esmerelda and rubbing his head.

The police officers were still on duty and came running around the house from both sides with their guns drawn. Mike caught their attention and waved them off. They nodded and went back to patrolling the grounds.

The Latina brought the slugger down on the crown of Roberto's head. It made a soft thunking sound, and he wailed again.

I had no doubt that the bat to the head hurt plenty, but I thought Roberto's screaming was a little feminine and way over the top.

Esmerelda was doing some screaming of her own. "Hijo de tu puta madre," she squalled as she brought the bat down again. This time Roberto moved out of the way of her swing and then kicked out sideways at her. He got close, and I started to move toward him; but Mike's big arm came up across my chest. When I looked up he just shook his head. It didn't take long to understand his reasoning.

Esmerelda was wearing a beautiful pair of red high-heeled pumps. She kicked one off and put her stocking foot on the ground. She grabbed her skirt with both hands, raised it high and then kicked out and drove the spiked heel of her other pump into Roberto's thigh. The Boss and I flinched involuntarily. Roberto screamed again, and I couldn't fault him for that one.

"Callate, pinche chillón!" Esmerelda screamed back.

"Esmerelda!" Mike's voice boomed.

Her head snapped up and her hair cascaded like dark clouds around a maelstrom of anger. Her eyes blazed from inside the storm, and she just stood there looking at us. I had heard people talk about women who were beautiful when they were angry. Esmerelda was one of those women, but she was already beautiful, so I have no way of describing what I was looking at. It made me ache way down deep.

"Do you always have to do this in front of the house?" asked Mike.

"She's done this before?" I blurted out in a surprised and stupid sounding voice.

"Right about this same time last year," said Mike.

Esmerelda didn't respond and turned her attention back to Roberto. She slipped her foot back into her shoe, then walked back and forth in a half-circle around her cheating boyfriend. In a low hissing voice she alternated cursing at him in Spanish and English.

The Boss and I just stood there as if we were spectators at a boxing match. For lack of something better, I finally asked, "Where did she get that bat?"

"I don't know, that's new," replied Mike. "Last time she beat a guy's eyes closed with

191

the big rolling pin from the kitchen."

"What was the problem with that guy?"

"He was running around on her."

I stopped watching the show and twisted my head to look at Mike. With all the sincerity I owned I repeated what I had asked in the kitchen, "Why would any man run around on a woman like her?"

The big man shook his head. "I don't know where she finds these guys."

"Should we do something?"

"Nah, in a minute or two, she'll get tired of beating on him. After that we can turn him loose."

I watched Roberto cower against the railing and said, "I don't guess they come back."

"Are you shitting me?" Mike hooted. "Would you?"

The Boss cocked his head to one side as if he was looking for something. "It's better than the time before last," he said.

"Better?"

"Yeah, that time I had to take a straight razor away from her."

"Where the hell did she get a straight razor?"

Mike grinned like he was telling a secret and said, "From her bathroom."

It took me a second to process what that meant and when the amazement struck me, I blurted out, "She shaves her legs with a straight razor?"

"Uh huh, she told me her grandfather gave it to her. It's a beautiful museum piece with Abalone handles." Mike smiled. "You should ask her to give you a shave sometime."

"That sounds like a good way to get my throat cut."

"If you were Roberto it would be."

"Bastardo!" snarled Esmerelda, as the bat bounced off Roberto's elbow.

Robert howled and tried to curl up in a ball.

She kicked him again and then, as the Boss had predicted, she spun on her heel and marched toward us. Mike and I stepped to either side of the doorway to allow her to pass.

She stopped and turned to face me. Her eyes burned, and somewhere inside; so did I.

"You knew," she said. Her voice was low and flat. It wasn't a question or even an accusation. It was statement.

"Yes," I said softly.

"I saw you on the street talking to him after I had already seen him with that woman. "

I lowered my head and nodded.

"And you weren't going to say anything."

"I told *him* to say something," I replied truthfully and still softly.

"Why?"

"I wanted to give him the chance to do the right thing. I told him to break it off with one of you, or I would break him in half and tell you myself."

"You thought I needed protecting."

I felt like a moron. "Well, I realize it seems stupid *now*."

"You're a fool," said the beautiful Latina, "Just like all the other men." She turned, went inside, and closed the door behind her.

We stood there for a moment, looking at the door. The doorknob was close enough to reach out and touch but Mike kept his hands in his pockets and said, "I hope she didn't lock it, I left my keys on the table."

"It   doesn't   matter,"   I   told   him.   "I   can   walk   under   it."

CHAPTER 26

We turned Roberto loose and he whimpered and limped to his car and drove off. We didn't bother to say anything to him. It seemed pointless after a beating with a sawed off bat and a bilingual cussing.

Fortunately, the front door was open. We went back and quietly sat down to eat our lunch.

We didn't know where Esmerelda had gone and neither of us had the guts to go look for her so we finished our lunch in silence. Afterwards, Mike went off to his office and I cleaned up the kitchen. When I was done I asked Mike if he needed anything. He said he didn't, so I told him I'd be in the guest house.

I went out the back door and down the short path to what I now called "my place". One of the policemen on duty was coming around the corner of the house, and I waved at him.

There were quite a few feet between the door and the corner of the house, so he had to yell, "Is everything okay?"

I figured his curiosity was killing him but I didn't feel happy enough about my position in the universe to stop and socialize about what had taken place on the front porch, so I called back, "Everything's fine, thanks."

I opened the door to my 1947 home and stepped inside. It was a comfortable little place and it gave me a good feeling when I was there. Over the last couple of nights, I had noticed how homey I found the little house. I called it that, because it wasn't just a detached guest room. It was actually a small house. It was also clean and quiet and I felt more at home there than any place I had been since I left for the Marines at eighteen.

I took off my hat and hung it on the hat rack just inside the doorway; and since there was a hanger there I hung my coat up too. I took a couple steps toward the kitchen table and looked at the brown paper bag that held the gun cleaning supplies. I considered it as something to kill time; but all the guns were clean so it would have been a waste. Esmerelda had agreed to do my laundry, so I didn't need to do that either…at least I hoped I didn't. At that moment it wasn't outside the realm of possibilities that she was pouring gasoline on my skivvies and lighting them on fire. "It could be worse," I thought. "I could be in them."

A small squeaking noise from behind me shot a jolt of adrenaline through my system, and I jerked the .45 out the shoulder holster and spun toward the sound. It was one of those noises that everyone has heard many times; but my system was on high alert and my mind couldn't move fast enough to identify it before I thumb cocked the pistol and drew a bead on the sound. It was a crying woman.

"Holy shit," I shrieked, pulling my arm back and pointing the pistol straight up. I lowered the hammer and replaced the weapon in the holster. "You scared the daylights out of me."

Esmerelda was sitting on the sofa holding a tissue to her right eye. "You're very fast with that gun," she sobbed. "Have you shot a lot of women?"

Her mascara ran down her face in little black rivers, and her eyes were horribly red; but that wasn't the worst part. Her emotional pain was tangible. I could feel it, all of it. I considered myself as sympathetic as the next guy, but I couldn't remember absorbing that much of anyone's pain before. "No," I said very softly, "I haven't shot a lot of women."

The tissue she was holding was soaking wet and useless. I looked around and didn't see any more, so I went into the bathroom and grabbed a handful of toilet paper and brought it out to her.

"Gracias," she said, accepting the new paper. I took her old wadded up tissue and sat down near her. I couldn't believe how much I wanted to help her, how much I wanted to take her sadness away; but all I could do was sit and watch her cry.

After a little while I asked, "Would you like a glass of water?"

She shook her head, and I sat and watched her cry some more.

It finally dawned on me that she might prefer being alone.

"You probably want to be alone." I began, but as I stood to leave she shook her head. I sat back down, but she didn't say anything so I didn't either.

I had never had much practice with a woman in this state. I wanted to console her, but I didn't have any good ideas on how to go about it. I had even less of an idea about what was politically correct. It made me feel better when I remembered that it would be a long time before someone coined the term politically correct. Score one for the twentieth century.

I reached out and touched her on the shoulder, but before I could say anything she made a loud wailing noise and fell over sideways into my lap with the side of her head resting on my leg. She continued to sob and after a moment, I put one hand on her shoulder and softly stroked her hair with the other. I was glad she was facing away from me so she wouldn't see the tears running down *my* face.

We sat that way for a long time, and after a while I realized that she had stopped moving and was breathing softly. I didn't want to wake her so I just sat there and tried not to move.

A few minutes went by and my eyes started to wander, looking around the room for something that would help me pass the time as I sat there. The radio wasn't too far away, and it caught my attention first. I would have enjoyed listening to music or even one of those radio programs which seemed to be growing on me, but I couldn't quite reach it from where I was sitting. Since I was likely to turn it on and blow the windows out before I got it adjusted, it was just as well. I smiled at the thought that I could work a computer but had trouble with a 70 year old AM radio.

I continued to look around the room in hopes of finding something interesting. There were a few magazines on the end table next to me and more on the coffee table in front of me. The coffee table was out of the question, but I thought I could get to one of the others if nothing else presented itself.

I was turning my head to check out the far end of the sofa, and I froze when Esmerelda made a snorting noise and almost woke herself up. She squirmed a little and then breathed softly again. I stayed frozen until I was sure she was sleeping and then I went back to looking around.

She was still dragging the shotgun around with her. It was leaning against the wall at the opposite end of the sofa. It was an older Remington pump, and I wondered how she had come by it. It was a pretty nice gun, maybe a little big for a small person, but she could make it do what she told it to do, so I didn't have any complaints.

The options available to occupy my time were extremely limited, so I finally reached over and slowly slipped the top magazine off the stack on my left. It was a copy of Life magazine from December of 1941. I laid it on the arm of the sofa and turned the pages with my left hand. The magazine was loaded with pictures which would have been nice except these pictures were from the bombing of Pearl Harbor. I rolled back the page to the cover again. The date was December 15th, 1941. The copy still lying on the table was December 8th. I could understand it, but it was still odd to be seeing it. I kept looking back and forth at the magazines to see if maybe I was missing something. Pearl Harbor was attacked on December 7th, but the magazine which came out the next day had apparently already gone to print. It published weekly so they didn't have stories and pictures until the December 15th issue. It was one more reminder that I was no longer in the Information Age.

I looked slowly through the old, but not so old photos. There wasn't anything I hadn't seen before, but everything seemed different now that I was actually among the men and women who lived through that time less than six years ago. In my world, the people who fought the Second World War were all people from a bygone generation. Thinking of it that way had seemed to make at least some sense in the 21st century as the war had started over seventy years earlier, but it always seemed like a war fought by old people, a war fought in black and white to the sound track of outdated music, a war that really didn't have anything to do with me or anyone of my generation. Now that I was here, walking and talking with the people that who served, it was obvious that there was no difference between the wars I knew and the one my Grandfather fought in. The real lesson was that the people were the same…the same as me. They were people who existed in full color, people whose music played when they turned on the radio, because it was popular and people who were young and filled with life and hope, way too much of which was left on battlefields in places they had never wanted to know and didn't want to remember, places they could barely pronounce and that no one gave a shit about when the battle was over. Dickens had called it when he said, "…it was a time very much like the present." The thought was amusing because, in my case it was the present.

I realized that I had even come to think about The War in much the same way as everyone around me, which meant that in my speech and in my mind I referred to it simply as, "The War."

I thumbed through the magazine and then I slowly managed to thumb my way through the other three that were on the table. It was sort of like reading through history books, because everything was about what I thought of as old news. The ads were selling old things, but the feeling was more like reading a how-to manual. Everything, even the advertisements, gave me a feel for how I should handle my surroundings, and it made the material much more important and personal.

I didn't want to move, but as I looked through the last magazine my leg went to sleep. I knew my only choice was to try and escape unnoticed. It took a while, but I managed to sneak out from under Esmerelda without waking her. I placed a pillow under her head and pulled a blanket out of the chest at the end of my bed and covered her up.

I slipped out and went back to the main house. I found Mike still in his office. When he looked up I asked him, "Didn't I see a library near here?"

"Yeah, it's one block over from the barbershop. That street is Fernwood."

Mike fished in his pocket and said, "Here take the Chevrolet," as he tossed me his car keys. "I don't need you for anything so you're off the hook this afternoon. Are you and John going to take another crack at catching Mrs. Cantrell *In flagrante delicto.*"

I figured that meant sex, and I also figured I could have gotten away with being ignorant and asking about it, but I was ignorant about so many other things I didn't want to ask. Unfortunately for me, my big boss could read my face like it was a teleprompter and said, "It means *in blazing offense.* In legal terms it has come to mean caught in the act of committing a crime. In common usage it has come to mean you've been caught with your lover in your arms and your drawers around your ankles.

Mike snapped his fingers as a thought occurred to him and said, "Speaking of being caught with your drawers down, the car needs gas." He fished in his pocket and came up with a five dollar bill and said, "Fill it up, would you?"

I could feel the big smile spreading across my face, and for a split second I almost laughed before it sunk in that he wasn't kidding. It took an act of will to keep my mouth from hanging open. I was actually going to take a car, big enough to double as an efficiency apartment, and fill it up with gas for five dollars. The twentieth century had its problems, but there were parts of it that I couldn't fault.

Mike didn't seem to notice my amusement. "Esmerelda normally has Thursday afternoons off, but I'm still expecting her to be back to fix dinner

"She's in the guest house," I told him.

"She is?" he asked in voice that suggested there was something going on. "What's she doing there?"

I didn't bother to respond to what he was implying. In a flat voice I said, "Crying herself to sleep on the sofa."

His face softened as he said, "Poor thing, did she say anything to you?

"She asked if I had shot a lot of women."

Mike's eyes narrowed. "Why in the hell would she…"

"I heard her crying and drew down on her."

"I think I've figured out why you don't have a girlfriend. Why in the hell would you…"

"I didn't know she was there until she made a noise, and I had the gun pointed before I realized it was her." It had seemed pretty straight forward when it happened, but saying it out loud to Mike made it sound a little weird and I said so.

"It's not that weird," the boss assured me. "I've scared the shit out of Norma a couple of times. And don't let Esmerelda make you feel guilty. On more than one occasion I've walked around a corner and found the working end of her shotgun."

That reminded me of the question I had wanted to ask so I did. "Is that really her shotgun? "

The boss smiled. "It is now. She commandeered it during a break-in we had a year or so ago."

"Commandeered it?"

"Yeah, some jackass was breaking into the house late one night and our favorite housekeeper heard him. Since that shotgun was still laying on the kitchen table where I had been cleaning it, she grabbed it and went after the guy."

"It wasn't as bad as the other day was it?"

"No, the gun wasn't even loaded, but she went after him just the same. He heard her jack the slide back and ran to get back out of the window before she got to him. "

"And…"

"He didn't make it. He was half in and half out when she stuck the barrel of that shotgun up his ass and told him not to move."

"I'm guessing he didn't."

"Would you?"

"Not for a million dollars," I replied sincerely.

"She never offered to give it back, and I never asked for it. So as far as I'm concerned, it's her shotgun."

"Works for me, no one is happier she has it than I am."

The boss started to say something, but then his face became more serious as he looked toward the back door and asked, "Does one of us need to go out and sit with her?"

"I don't think so. She fell asleep, so I covered her up and snuck out."

"That was nice of you."

"It seemed like the thing to do."

Mike nodded his agreement and then rubbed his chin as a thought occurred to him. "Since you're going out you might want to look around and find somewhere to have your evening meal. Even if Esmerelda's here, it doesn't mean dinner will be any good. She's a great cook, but when she's distracted she'll feed you a pine board with cheese on it…and she'll burn the board."

"Do you want me to pick up something for you?" I asked.

"Now that we're talking about it, I'm remembering the moss covered football I had to eat when she had boyfriend trouble last year. He reached for his wallet saying, "When dinnertime rolls around run over to Benny's and pick up an order of spaghetti and meatballs for me, and get whatever you want." He stuck his fingers into his wallet but then he pulled them back and said, "What am I thinking, you can just use the change from the fiver."

I wondered what kind of math they were teaching in the schools of the late forties if he thought I could fill up his battleship of a car with gas and then turn around and buy two spaghetti dinners with the same five dollar bill. It sounded too much like the

Reaganomics that my dad used to complain about. I started to get the feeling that my boss was hoping to start recouping some of the money he had spent on the clothes I kept destroying. That thought came with the additional one that it wouldn't be totally unfair if he did, so I tried to appear as if what he had said was perfectly normal, and I headed down to the garage.

I kept looking back over my shoulder as I made my way to the car. I was afraid Mike might follow me and be there when I tried to get the old monstrosity going. I had a pretty good idea about how to get it done, at least I hoped I did, but I wasn't so confident that I wanted someone to watch me while I tried it. Even if I was right, I knew I couldn't pull off looking nonchalant about it.

I got to the garage alone, opened the garage door, went over and sat in the car and tried to get up the nerve to start it and drive away. I had watched Esmerelda fire it up. She made it look easy, but she had a lot more practice than I did. I took one last look at the door to make sure Mike didn't come out and catch me trying to figure out how to do something as simple as starting a car.

Everything was pretty much in the same place as it would be on cars of the future. There were some obvious things missing: no air conditioning controls, GPS, electric windows or electric door locks. The radio took up most of the middle of the dashboard. The speaker was a big part of it, and it was only AM. There were also some additions that one wouldn't expect to find on a newer model. There was an extra pedal in the floorboard, to the right of the gas pedal. I had heard about starter pedals, but I had never used one so I crossed my fingers and continued to work through the process.

The shift lever was on the column just like an automatic shift lever, except this one was manual. I ran through what I thought to be the gear pattern but the car would have to be moving for me to prove I was right.

There were two knobs marked "T" and "C" under the radio, and I was desperately hoping that I understood how to use them. I had driven a couple of old vehicles with a choke, so I figured that would be the knob with the "C" on it. I knew that I needed the choke engaged if I wanted to start the car cold, so I pulled that one out of the dash until it stopped. I put the key in the ignition, which was under the radio, also. I turned it clockwise, but nothing happened. If I understood the operation correctly, and that was a big "if", then the key in this vehicle didn't start the car, it only allowed it to be started.

I put one foot on the brake and pushed the clutch in with the other. I moved the shift lever to what I hoped was neutral, and then changed feet and put my left foot on the brake. I moved my right foot over onto the starter pedal, but that left me without a foot to press the gas pedal when I tried to start the car. I was guessing that this was what the knob labeled "T" was for. If I had followed Esmerelda correctly, she had used the "T" knob to give the car gas while she stepped on the starter pedal. I figured that meant the "T" stood for throttle, but this was all conjecture and guesswork at that point. I swallowed, gritted my teeth, pulled the T-knob out a little bit and stepped on that extra pedal. The engine spun and made a sound like I thought a car engine should. It roared to life pretty quickly, and I lifted my foot off the starter pedal. I put my foot on the gas and pushed the T-knob back in.

I paused a moment to thank a higher power for my good fortune thus far, and then I pulled the shift lever into what I hoped was first gear and let off the clutch a little. I failed to give it enough gas, and the old heap started to move and then stalled and died. I swore at it through my teeth, but now that I knew how; I was able to get it started quickly and try again. It jumped a couple times as I tried to get used to the feel of the old clutch. I'd driven a few large military trucks in my time, and the old heap reminded me more of them than a car, so I treated it that way and that seemed to work better for both man and machine. I pulled onto the driveway and stopped to get out and close the garage, but I failed to put the car in neutral before I let out the clutch. It jumped and died, and I prayed that the boss wasn't watching out the window. I closed the garage door and fired the old clunker up again. This time I was able to get moving and stay moving. I headed down to the end of the street and took a left. When the car started to whine, I pushed in the clutch and shifted. The gear I went to behaved like I thought second gear should, so I called that a win. Third gear was the same way, and since I was pretty sure that reverse was straight up from first, three gears was all the old car had.

I had been really worried about getting the old vehicle to start and run, but after I came to the first stop-sign, I realized that getting the car to move wasn't the real problem. The old tin can had all the stopping power of a hot air balloon. I had forgotten that four wheel disc brakes wouldn't be standard until later in the twentieth century. Somewhere in the back of my mind, there was a vague memory of my grandfather telling me that the big cars of his day were rolling death traps. I checked the seat and the doors but if the car had ever had seat belts, someone had taken them out. Air bags were totally out of the question. If I was reading the situation correctly, all the cars on the road were big and heavy with no safety features and poor stopping power. I had also noticed that neither Mike's Cadillac nor this old Chevrolet had power steering. It was bad enough that the old heap handled like a parade float; but if you weren't moving, it took a lot of muscle to get the wheels to turn. Granddad's claim that it was a deathtrap might have been an understatement.

I watched for Fernwood and made a left. The library was just a little way down on the driver's side, and I pulled in. There were more cars than I expected in the parking lot. I had really not expected anyone to be around, but that was my futuristic thinking again. They weren't exactly overrun, but apparently the library in 1947 was a little more popular than it was in my time.

I parked the car and walked to the front of the building where there was a covered walkway leading up to the main door. Inside the walkway was a large bulletin board that was covered and layered with thumbtacked papers. The various papers were advertising for products, services, used cars, concerts, rooms for rent, jobs, and a ton of other stuff. There were very few with pictures, and the ones that did show an image were in black and white. There were also a lot of notices for events happening around town -- everything from church socials to sporting events. The World Series had ended the previous Monday, and since the New Egan Captains baseball team hadn't made it to the series, local baseball had been over for a while. Fortunately for avid sports fans the New Egan Admirals football team had a game coming up.

I stood and read a lot of the different notices and then I just stared at the board as a whole. "So this is what the internet used to look like," I mumbled to myself.

CHAPTER 27

I came out of the library with a brand new library card and two books, one about the war in the Pacific and the other about the war in Europe.

I had been worried that getting a library card was going to involve questions I couldn't answer or producing documentation that I didn't have, but the librarian, a sweet elderly woman with hazel eyes that actually sparkled when I asked for a library card, had simply asked for my driver's license and used it to type my name and address on the library card.

I was still leaning toward going back to the 21st century once we found out who it was terrorizing Mike and Norma, but it would be hard to say goodbye to little perks like that.

I had started reading my books inside. It was nice and quiet with no one around to bother me. I would have loved to stay and read a little longer, which was a first for me as I had never been much of an academic, But if Mike and I were going to have anything worthwhile to eat for dinner I needed to go get it.

I went out to the car and was able to get the old clunker started with a lot less effort than it took the first time and headed towards Benny's Barbershop, Pool Hall, Bar and Grill.

I cruised at an easy pace with my window down, listening to a song the radio announcer called, "Ole Buttermilk Sky". I really missed having a smart phone or MP3 player so that I could listen to whatever music I wanted, but I was trying to keep an open mind about the music in the late forties. A whole generation of people had enjoyed this music, so I thought there had to be something to it. That *something* could be really elusive.

The song was more Cowboy than Country, and I tried to take it on its own merit and not compare it with anything I already enjoyed. I wouldn't want to have admitted it to any of my future friends, but it was okay and I started drumming my hands on the wheel as it played. After a moment it finished and a group of harmonica players started in on a song called Peg O' My Heart. I started wishing someone would put Ole Buttermilk Sky back on. There were some things about 1947 that I wasn't ever going to like.

A little farther up the street I caught sight of a big two story concrete block building that had something resembling gas pumps in front of it, so I pulled in and parked in front of what turned out to be the only two pumps at the station. The big letters mounted on the front of the building read, "SINCLAIR", and the logo was the green silhouette of a dinosaur. I assumed it was the logo as it was painted on flattened glass globes that sat on top of the gas pumps.

I started to get out of the car to pump the gas, but before I could a guy yelled, "How are you doing this afternoon, Sir?" as he sprayed the windshield with window cleaner and started wiping it. From the rear of the car another guy yelled, "Regular or Ethel, sir?"

I was afraid I had pulled into some swanky gas station where the rich people go, and it ran through my mind that I might not be able to afford gas there. The price wasn't posted, so I was stuck for that one unless I asked.

I had no idea what Ethel was but Regular made me think it might be common.

I mentally flipped a coin and called out, "Regular."

"Fill it up?" the man asked as he pulled a nozzle and hose from one of the pumps and dragged it around behind the car.

Since the price wasn't posted, I was equally stuck up for that one too. I resigned myself to whatever happened and said, "Yes, please."

By this time, the first guy had finished cleaning the windshield and was pulling up the hood of the car. There was no switch or lever inside the car for me to pull, the guy just reached for something under the hood, and then raised it. The gas pump numbers were on wheels, and they spun as the gasoline was pumped. Every time it went past a gallon a little bell inside the pump made a dinging noise. It dinged a couple of times, and then the guy under the hood yelled, "You're oil is a quart low sir, would you like for me to top it off?"

My first thought had been, *"What's this guy looking for under the hood?"* Now that I knew the answer to that my next thought was, *"Where did the quart of oil go?"*, but that was way down the list of things that I had to worry about at that moment. It was still up to fate at that point, so I yelled back for him to go ahead.

While I was waiting I looked around for any scrap of information that would help, and I learned that Ethel was spelled "Ethyl" and something about the signs on the pumps made me think it cost extra so I was happy with my choice. I just hoped the car would run okay on Regular and didn't need whatever extras Ethyl had to offer.

I had started to sweat by the time the pump dinged its last ding and when the guy walked up to my window, I handed him the five dollar bill before he could say anything. I sat and stared out the newly cleaned windshield and hoped he wouldn't laugh.

Out of the corner of my eye, I could see him reach into his pants pocket and after a moment he said, "Your change, sir."

I took it without looking, and stuck the money, coins and all, in my shirt pocket. I smiled and thanked him and tried not to look as relieved as I felt.

I went through the routine of getting the car started and was pleased when it fired up and sounded the same as it had when I pulled up. It seemed to be running fine on Regular, so I looked to the heavens and said, "Thanks," before I put the car in gear and headed on down the road.

A couple blocks down the street I pulled the money from my pocket and glanced at it quickly. In my hand were two one-dollar bills and two quarters. That time I laughed out load.

I pulled into the last parking spot on the street about fifty feet from the doorway of the barbershop. I hopped out, and as I shut the door a car horn sounded from behind me.

I turned toward the noise and saw the horn blower was the driver of a big yellow cab.

The side of the cab read, "Eddie's Taxi Service."

. It was Eddie, the guy I had met at the Barbershop on my first full day in 1947.

"You got the last parking spot you bastard." He was grinning ear to ear as if he had just told the funniest joke in history

"That's Mister Bastard to you," I called back.

He pointed his finger at me, still grinning, and roared away. I headed past the door of the barbershop and the big window of the pool hall toward the door on the end marked "Benny's Bar and Grill."

As I passed the door of the Barbershop, I could see the place was already getting crowded. Guys were everywhere, standing in groups, sitting in unused Barber chairs, even leaning on the arms of the elevated shoeshine chair where some guy was getting his shoes done, and talking over the top of the head of the guy shining them. The pool hall was just as bad. When Mike had brought me here he had said that Benny Shapiro built the pool hall, barber shop and grill altogether to make sure he got everybody's money. From what I could tell, he was getting it.

Everyone was talking at once, about sports, about the weather, about the war, but mostly about nothing. It was thrilling to be there.

I could see Bert the Barber trying to elbow guys out of the way so he could finish cutting a customer's hair. I caught his eye and he yelled, "Hey Jake, have you ever seen a bigger bunch of worthless losers than this?" Before I could answer, somebody accidentally jostled Bert and got the barber's attention. He turned on the jostler and waved his shears in the guy's face. "Damnit Clem, if you make me screw this up, you'll have to learn to piss out of your ears." He snapped the scissors together for emphasis, and Clem raised his hands and backed away.

Everybody laughed, except Clem and the middle aged man in the barber chair who looked more than a little worried. I moved on down the sidewalk toward the smell of food.

I went past the Pool Hall and into the door on the end. I could barely get inside. Young men were everywhere. I picked out one or two women, but they were in the company of specific guys that held them tightly with one arm around the waist, to make sure no one made any mistakes or got any ideas.

Everybody seemed to be smiling and joking, and I couldn't help but think how everything *didn't* seem old or out of date to me. If I had been looking at an old black and white photo of this room full of people, I would have considered their clothes and hairstyles outdated. It would never have dawned on me that anyone in the picture was doing or saying anything interesting. Standing among them was completely different. Everything seemed perfectly natural. The fashions might not have been to my taste; but whatever it was, everyone was wearing it and truth be told it was growing on me. There was music playing in the background; and I wouldn't have cared for it in the 21st century, but it fit the moment like a glove.

My grandfather had shown me pictures of family and friends of this time period, and I remember telling him that I didn't like the way the women in the pictures did their hair. Now that I had walked some of the same streets as he had; I found that attractive women are attractive in any century, and I liked the hairstyles just fine.

My thoughts were happy thoughts, and the smiling faces around me made it easy. It would have been nice to think everyone in 1947 was happy; but I had come from the future, and it only took a cursory glance around the room to notice that some things were conspicuously absent. There were no Black, Asian or Latino young men present; or to make it easier to describe, there were only young, white males. It reminded me that a lot of people still had a lot of fights to fight before things would look different. If memory served, this was the year that Jackie Robinson started in Major League Baseball, and that meant there were going to be quite a few years before it became widely accepted in all the Major League and College sports. Television barely existed, so I had no idea how long it would be before ethnic performers made it into mainstream programming. Sports and entertainment were going to suck for a decade or two.

I was sorry it was going to take more than a few years before there would be any pretty ethnic women in a bar like this. On the other hand there weren't many women there at all. I was sure the sparsity of the fairer sex wasn't because of any discrimination, but was more likely due to the majority of women not wanting to be caught in the middle of a turbocharged sausage fest.

I elbowed my way to the counter and managed to order two spaghetti dinners to go. I also got extra garlic bread for each of us. After I paid the bill with the change I had left over from buying the gas, I still had twenty-three cents to put in my pocket. When I finally got over the amazement of doing that, I felt bad that I had thought Mike might be stiffing me for part of the bill. What he had actually done was loan me his car to go to the library and paid for my dinner.

It was funny to think that despite the fact my job duties included jumping through windows and being chased off the toilet by men with shotguns, I still enjoyed working for Mike. Maybe I really had needed the therapy the VA tried to give me.

While I waited for my dinner to be ready, I surveyed the area and saw Eddie standing just inside the open doorway to the Pool Hall section of Benny's. He had his hat tipped back on his head and was standing next to a table -- half leaning, half hanging on a pool cue. His posture made him look like he was trying to pull a bell rope. He had his eye on a game in progress, so I assumed he was waiting to play the winner. I didn't have anything better to do, so I walked over to say hello.

As I approached him he turned toward me, and with a big shit-eating grin he asked, "Hey Jake, have you jumped out any windows lately?"

"How does word about these things get around?" I asked in surprise.

"When a guy does *anything* with a woman who looks like Norma Manzarek everybody wants to talk about it."

"You do realize that there wasn't any fun involved? I jumped through a bay window, and I still have stitches across my back and legs to prove it.

"I'm telling you, I can find twenty-four guys, right now, that would trade places with you."

"You show me those twenty-four guys, and I'll show you two dozen idiots."

"Idiots we have in large supply, women with movie-star looks to jump out of windows with, not so much. Speaking of people that aren't too bright, you do know you're supposed to leave the other man's wife behind when you jump out of a window don't you?"

"So people keep telling me."

At that point one of the guys at the table sank his last ball, and Eddie moved in to rack a new game. I stood to watch for a few shots, but after Eddie's new opponent started to shoot; Eddie was pretty much free for the rest of the game, and he went back to hanging on his pool cue.

Something Mike had said came to mind and I asked Eddie, "Mike says that sometimes you hear things around town."

The cab driver looked around to see who might have overheard my remark, and when he saw that no one was paying any attention to the two of us he said, "Sometimes people inadvertently say things that I may or may not overhear."

He drew the corners of his mouth back in a big smile that almost went ear to ear and asked, "What did you think I may have overheard?"

"We're getting the word that maybe eight or ten guys from out of town have arrived, and we're trying to get a fix on them."

"Lots of tourists going in and out this burg," replied Eddie, still smiling. "Is there anything that might distinguish these particular guys?"

"We're told they're high caliber muscle and gun."

Eddie neither flinched nor blinked. He spoke as if I had asked him the spread on a football game.

"There are ten of them, eight from Detroit and two from St. Louis. The Detroit boys are spending their time at the Egan Arms, and the St. Louis duo is at the old Wilton Palace."

He waited for me to say something, and I wanted to; but for a moment I could only stand there with my mouth open and blink at him. We had been digging and clawing after dead end leads for days, and this guy had just nonchalantly spewed out more information than we had uncovered in total.

I finally managed to ask, "Do you know what their job is?"

Eddie shook his head. "It's a private job for some individual, and it's not one of the regular people that I would expect to put a crew like this together."

"Regular people?"

"Yeah, somebody like a Jackie Banks or a Paul Cantrell."

"Jules Epstein?"

Eddie snorted lightly through his nose, "Maybe in the old days, but he's got a big operation and has his own people working under a couple of psychos."

"Abe and Izzy."

His eyebrows went up. "You've met them?"

I nodded. "They tried to hire me."

"No shit?" He whistled softly and said, "Friend, you have my new found respect. They only hire top drawer talent."

"So it wasn't one of the regular bosses that called for the out of town boys?"

"Nah, it looks to be some rich guy that needed dirty work done. Maybe he wants some of his in-laws removed or needs to chase a bunch of squatters out of a tenement building."

He started to say something else, buth then something occurred to him and his face clouded over.

"Hey, has this got something to do with beautiful women and jumping out of windows?"

I really didn't know how much I should confide in Eddie but I couldn't think of anything to say.

My slow response told Eddie everything he needed to know. The look on his face was pure deep thought and made it appear as if his brain had gone into overdrive.

"So those guys are part of what you and Mike have been fighting off all week."

I gave up trying to respond to that and asked, "Do you know any more about these guys, like when they might do what they came to do?"

"Nope, other than showing up, these boys have been on the QT and stayed holed up."

His opponent finally missed a shot and Eddie picked up his cue. "Tell Mike I'm on the job, and not to worry about the meter running. Anybody messing with him is on my fighting side."

I didn't know what to say, so I simply thanked him. He turned to the table to line up a shot as the man at the counter called out my order. I nodded toward Eddie and weaved back through the crowd to get my dinner. I couldn't see much of the guy that had called my order, but there was a hand and arm holding a brown paper bag sticking out of the throng, so I took it and started for the exit. I didn't get far before a new voice yelled, "Phone call for Jake Kowalski, Jake Kowalski phone call!"

The voice belonged to a waiter that was at the far end of the counter holding the receiver part of the telephone against his chest and waving his other hand. I raised my arm to get his attention and started making my way in his direction. As I approached I could see how he held the phone in one hand and was covering the mouthpiece with the other.

"*No mute button in 1947,*" I thought.

I had intended to get the phone and step over to a bare spot next to the cigarette machine; but as I took it, I realized there was only enough cord to reach where I was standing. I stuck the phone to my ear and tried to say, "Hello," loud enough to be heard without yelling.

"Jake, this is Mike," the phone blurted out. "Have you already ordered dinner?"

"Yeah, I've got it in my hand," I said raising it up as if he could see it.

"Throw that shit in the garbage. Our favorite Mexican firebrand got a second wind and is cooking the best smelling Arroz con pollo that's ever been. Lose that spaghetti and get home as quick as you can."

Happily I barked, "Will do," and added "Mike I got some information from Eddie that might be useful."

"Then that's two reasons to get here fast, but be careful."

I told him I would and handed the phone back to the counterman without waiting for a reply.

I headed back through the pool hall and caught Eddie's attention. He was watching the winner of the last game become the winner of his game.

His smile was long gone. "I'm not having any luck tonight," he said as I approached.

"The hell you're not," I told him as I handed him the big paper bag, "Dinner's on me and Mike." Before he could ask I said, "We got a better offer."

CHAPTER 28

I parked the car in the garage and managed to shut the engine off without making the car jump. With that done, I shoved the gearshift up into reverse, as I had seen Mike do, and left it that way. I jumped out, closed the garage door, and headed for the kitchen.

I was pulling my coat and hat off as I came through the living room, and when I hit the kitchen I smelled what I can only describe as joy. Mike had told me right. If the Arroz con Pollo tasted like it smelled it was the best that had ever been.

"Sit down!" Mike's voice boomed out from the table. "She wouldn't feed me until you got here and she's been making me sit here and smell that for the last half-hour."

My butt was halfway to the chair when Esmerelda yelled, "Did you wash your hands?" She said it with a smile. She looked a lot different from the Esmerelda that had been upset with me earlier or the crying one in the guest house. She looked the same way the kitchen smelled.

I jumped up and headed for the sink. As I scooted past her I said, "Feed Mike before he eats the table."

She grabbed a pan and headed for the boss as I gave my hands a quick scrub and ran back to my seat. Mike's gorgeous housekeeper was already placing homemade tortillas next to the pile of chicken and rice on my plate.

Before I could begin eating I had to tell Mike, "I had a nice conversation with Eddie over at the pool hall. He knows where our friends from out of town are staying."

The big man was already eating and had a look of ecstasy on his face. I felt bad because the look was gone instantly.

He swallowed and asked, "Does he know how many there are?"

"He says there are ten of them, eight out of Detroit and two from St. Louis. He said the ones from Detroit are at a place called the...what was it...Egan Arms and the St. Louis boys were at the Wilton..."

"...Palace," Mike finished for me.

"That's it."

"Did he have anything else?"

"Not yet. He said that he was going to see what else he could find out and not to worry about the meter running. "

The Boss bobbed his head up and down softly. "Eddie's a stand-up guy, and this is good information." He caught me by the shoulder with one of his huge hands and said, "You did really well with this…thinking to ask Eddie. You earned your pay for the week."

"It's almost Friday; does that mean I get paid double?"

"I did mention the pay around here is mediocre, didn't I?"

"Yeah, you mentioned that."

"Eat up, your dinner's getting cold, and this food is to die for."

I didn't need to be told twice. I grabbed a fork and went at it.

I couldn't believe how good it was. "This is the best stuff I ever put in my mouth," I said, loud enough to make sure Esmerelda heard me. More quietly I told Mike, "It certainly isn't the moss covered football you were expecting."

"I don't know what you said to her, but she's been wearing a big happy face ever since she came back into the house."

"I don't think that's my doing. I didn't say anything. I just sat there while she cried herself to sleep."

"Well you must have made a good job of it."

I had a tortilla in one hand and a fork in the other, and I continued throwing food in my mouth with both of them. When I finally took a breath Mike asked, "Well, did you learn anything at the library?"

"I learned that it's pretty easy to get a library card."

"You don't aspire to much do you?"

"Hey, give me a break. Yesterday I couldn't even spell library."

"And today?"

"I still can't, but I have high hopes."

"It's in big letters mounted on the side of the building. A couple more trips and you should have it licked."

I was trying to swallow my dinner so I could make a smart-assed reply, but I was interrupted by yelling from the front of the house.

"Mike, Esmerelda is anybody home?" John Callahan called from the living room.

"How does he always know when we're having dinner," Mike asked around the tortilla he was stuffing in his face.

"More important than that," I questioned, "how did he get by the cops around the house?"

"That's my fault," said Mike swiping his mouth with a napkin. "Like an idiot, I told them he was okay and to let him through."

Esmerelda was standing at the edge of the table and waved her spoon at us.

"Stop acting like school boys. There's plenty of food here for everyone."

Mike raised his hands in surrender and yelled, "We're in the kitchen, John. Grab a plate and join us."

Callahan came through the doorway walking quickly. "You don't have to ask me more than once. That aroma is straight out of the heavens."

Esmerelda waved him to a chair with the same spoon she had threatened us with and then went to get another plate.

Callahan and I nodded at each other as he sat down, and I noticed his eyes looked a little better. They were both still black, but the color was starting to fade a little and he looked less like a raccoon than he had before.

"What do you know John?" asked Mike.

"Not much," said Callahan ruefully. "I've been chasing after shadows. People tell me they hear things, but none of them are panning out to be credible."

"Does that include the guys from out of town?"

"Whoops, I misspoke. That part's real. I've had several sources corroborate that story, but I can't get a line or their movements or even nail down what part of town they're hanging out in."

"We've got new intel on that," Mike told him. "Jake hooked up with Eddie and got a line on their whereabouts. They're holed up at the Wilton and the Egan Arms.

Callahan just stared at us with a blank look on his face. I couldn't tell if he was upset that he hadn't been able to dig that information up himself or if he was using the news he had just gotten to figure out something else.

Esmerelda broke the moment by sticking a plate of food in front of him.

Callahan's face came back to life and he said, "That's some good information. I've got to find out where Eddie's getting his tips."

He grabbed a knife and fork, and he didn't lose any more time digging in than Mike and I had. In between mouthfuls he asked Mike, "Was Eddie able to find out anything else?"

Mike looked at me and I answered, "No, that's all he had. He said he would do some more digging."

John's mouth was full so he nodded, but when he finally swallowed he asked, "How's Norma doing? Have you heard anything?"

From the corner of my eye I could see the Boss stop eating. He laid his fork down on his plate and took a breath before he spoke.

"Briggs said she's doing okay. She's bored and lonely, but she's okay."

"That's tough," Callahan sympathized, "but bored and lonely is better than being in harm's way. At least she's safe."

Mike was staring off into space. It didn't take a genius to know where his thoughts had gone.

"I suppose so," he finally replied, "but I don't know how much longer I can stand it without her here."

Callahan's face lit up like something had just occurred to him and he said, "I know where you're going with this Mike, and believe it or not I agree with you."

The Boss looked up at John. "You do?"

I had no idea what John was thinking or where Mike was *going*, but they seemed to be in sync, so I just ate and listened.

"I certainly do. To hell with all these damned cops and hiding out. It's time to go get that pretty woman and take her where no one can find her and just hole up until whatever the hell's going on stops going on."

Mike replied, "I certainly don't like being away from Norma this long."

Callahan nodded. "Of course not, and normally I'm not the guy that grabs the bull by the horns; but we have no idea who is after you two, or why, so I'm advocating blowing town and pulling the road up behind you."

Mike's eyes glazed over as his mind churned out ideas and scenarios. Finally he said, "I do know of a cabin overlooking a river in Idaho. No one could find us there, even with a map and a pack of bloodhounds."

Esmerelda was standing at the edge of the table listening to everything being said. She had her hands in the pockets of her apron, and I couldn't tell she was doing anything but listening until I noticed a Rosary bead pop out of the edge of her right hand apron pocket. It hung there by itself for a moment, and then it was joined by another one.

I thought that she might be onto something. Religious people have told me that it is comforting to lean on God when things are beyond the control of man, and I could have used a little comfort because everything had taken a giant step outside of my sphere of influence. I sat and watched and listened and hoped the pretty lady would say a prayer for both of us.

Mike finally let us off the hook. "However, what I was actually thinking was that now that we know where these guys are holed up, I should call Briggs and have New Egan's finest roust them and give them a good old-fashioned Police welcome."

John never actually stopped eating, but he did return to the blank look he had shown before and continued chewing. After a moment his mind stopped spinning and he said, "Yeah, that's a good idea. The boys in blue can break out the night sticks and rubber hoses and do their best Gene Krupa on these boys."

Callahan finally stopped talking around what he was eating and took the fork out of his mouth long enough to use it for emphasis when he gestured at Mike. "But don't wait too long. Something's up and the feeling I'm getting is that it's going to break loose sometime soon."

"I hear you, and I believe you," the Boss acknowledged; but he said nothing more about it, so I figured he was just going to mull it over and let everyone know what he decided in his own good time."

We worked on our dinners as if we were being paid to do it, but after a while we pushed our plates away and leaned back in our chairs.

Esmerelda had more if we wanted it, and she pointed her spoon as she interrogated us one-by-one about another helping. When the three of us had all declined, she announced, "In that case who wants to help me with the dishes."

That was John's cue. He jumped to his feet and bolted for the front door yelling, "I've got to get back and put my ear to the ground. Something's up, and I don't want these guys to get the drop on us."

We watched him leave and Mike just grinned and shook his head. I grabbed his plate and stacked it on top of mine, but when I tried to stand up Esmerelda put her hand on my shoulder and nudged me back down on the chair. She stood there with her hand on my shoulder until she heard the front door open and close.

"Who wants coffee and pie?" she asked in a conspiratorial voice.

"You have pie?" bellowed Mike. "Why didn't you say something? I'm full of chicken and rice."

"I didn't want to say anything with John sitting here. I only bought one pie at the store. If you don't want any…"

"I didn't say that. What kind of pie do you have?"

"Pecan, do you want ice cream on it?"

"You're an evil little woman. I'll have a slice a-la-mode and a cup of coffee."

She looked at me and I said, "I'll have the same. I'll clear these plates while you're doing that."

We both went at it and then the three of us met back at the table. The pie was a good finish to the dinner and the coffee, as always, was fantastic. Esmerelda's cooking weighed heavily in the plus column for living in the 20th century.

I kept thinking about what Bert the barber had said about being happy. Earlier might have been rough and later might be worse, but right then I was happy and I sipped my coffee and ate my pie slowly and made a point of enjoying the moment.

Mike was in a different place than I was, and he finished quickly and excused himself. He headed for his office, and the worried look returned to Esmerelda's face.

"This is very serious," she said softly.

"It's hard on both of them," I agreed. I walked the dessert dishes over to the sink and set them down next to it with the dinner plates.

She shook her head to indicate that I didn't understand.

"A lot of things have happened to Mike and Norma before, but I've never heard him talk about running away."

"It's not his style, and it wasn't really what he was thinking," I told her, but after a moment's thought I added, "It isn't a bad idea."

She leaned her head far to one side and looked at me strangely, as if she was buying me off a shelf and wondered if I came in another color.

"I didn't think you would be the kind to run away from trouble either."

"I like to think I'm not, but sometimes it's better to back up than go forward. John was right, we don't even know who our enemy is, so we don't know what he wants or where he's going to be coming from."

A stern look came over her face, and she gestured with her spoon when she said, "That's what you're here for, to keep Mike and Norma from getting hurt."

I tried to smile but I only got part way there. "There are only so many times that I'm going to be able to dodge a shotgun blast in an outhouse before I run out of luck."

"Maybe you should only use one if it has a big bay window."

"There's another thing I can't do much more of. I already look like a patchwork quilt."

She grinned wickedly. "You could do it a few more times."

"You have more faith in me than I do."

"You should have more faith in yourself. "

She looked up at me and placed her hand on the side of my face. It was warm and felt charged with energy.

"I know you will protect us," she said softly.

I wanted to say something. I wanted to *do* something, but her hand held me in place as much as it moved me.

In the same soft voice she asked, "Are you going to stay here?"

She removed her hand, but that side of my head was still warm and tingled from the touch.

"Why...why do you ask that?"

"You are...como se dice...conflicted. I think it is because you aren't from here, and you can't decide if you want to stay or not. "

I'm sure my heart actually skipped a couple of beats. At first I thought she had somehow found out about where I had come from. Then I realized she meant I wasn't from New Egan and more specifically, this small part of it. It was still a hell of a deduction on her part, and I wondered if this new world was ever going to stop surprising me as I asked, "How do you know that?"

"I don't know. There are things that you are hiding that I can't see, but I don't think they are bad things. I don't think you have the ability to hide bad things like Roberto did."

"Or the desire," I told her before I realized I was saying it.

Something flashed behind her eyes when I spoke, and then she asked again, "Are you going to stay here?"

There were a lot of things I wanted to say and a lot of things I couldn't say, but I finally said what I had to say, which was the truth.

"I don't know."

Half of me cheered from the relief of saying it aloud, and the other half cursed the first half for doing so.

She put her hand against my cheek again and looked at me with shimmering brown eyes that could dive into my soul and swim around in it.

"I hope you won't leave without saying goodbye."

I tried to smile and failed again. "I won't," I told her.

Her mouth curled up sweetly in a silent response, and she went back to washing the dishes. I helped her finish, and we cleaned the kitchen in silence. When we were done she hung her apron on a hook and left me standing alone trying to figure out what I wanted to do, and wondering why I felt like a piece of shit again.

I was only there for a moment when the ringing of the telephone disrupted my thoughts. Twentieth century phones had actual bells in them and sounded like old alarm clocks going off. You could hear them anywhere in the house which I assumed was the point.

I could hear the boss get up from somewhere he was sitting in the living room and lumber toward the ringing in his office.

"Manzarek," he boomed into the receiver.

I walked into the living room and could see him standing in the doorway of the office. His look was serious and the features on his face grew darker as the caller spoke.

"When?" asked the Boss.

I couldn't make out the words, but the tinny little speaker was buzzing in a fashion that let me know whoever he was talking to was speaking loudly and quickly.

"Okay," he said finally. "Thanks for the heads up."

I didn't think that he knew I was there, but as he hung up and turned toward me and said, "That was John. The new word on the street is that our out-of-town friends have found Norma's location, and they'll be moving on it sometime tonight."

"Shit," I hissed softly. "What's our move?"

"We're going to do just what we were talking about earlier. I'm going to go get Norma, and head to Idaho. They'll never find me where I'm going, and if they did I could see them coming for miles. "

I hated to hear him talk about leaving, but I couldn't blame him.

Mike bellowed, "Esmerelda," in the direction of the staircase, and she appeared almost instantly. When she hit the bottom step he said, "Please pack a bag for Norma and another one for her makeup and bathroom stuff. Also pack my bag as well."

Her eyes were sad, but she understood the need. "For how long?" she asked.

"For as long as you can cram into one suitcase for each of us. We need to move quickly. I want to be out of Illinois before anyone knows we're gone."

She nodded and headed back upstairs.

Mike turned to me and said, "The little alarm in the back of my head is ringing like school is out."

"I'll get the BAR," I said, and headed out the back door.

"I have to make a phone call. I'll meet you outside the garage," the big man called as the door   closed   behind   me.

CHAPTER 29

It was still daylight and we drove through a lousy part of the city that wasn't too far from the water. It was an industrial area, but it looked like a lot of the buildings were being used more for storage than for industry.

Mike turned toward one large multi-storied building that had all the windows broken; then cut across an empty parking lot with patches of grass growing up through the asphalt. He went around behind the building and cut off on a dirt road that twisted toward a small building with a much larger structure next to it. The larger one was around two-and-a-half to three stories tall and looked like it hadn't been in use for a while. It might have been a distribution warehouse or manufacturing facility in its time. There were a few doors of varying sizes around the ground level, but almost all of the windows ran around the top edge of the building.

The small building next to it was just that, a little place which had probably been the offices for whatever operation was taking place in the bigger one next to it. I wondered if it had gone out of business during the depression or maybe the owner had never returned from the war.

Those thoughts were followed by one of how quickly I seemed to be adjusting to the time period. I had assumed the Great Depression to be the odds-on favorite as the cause for any economic hardship and in my mind I had again thought of the Second World War as 'The War'. If I didn't get back home pretty soon, I was going to become accustomed to wearing a hat and paying pennies for gasoline.

We parked the car and walked up to the little building. Over on our left was a large overhead door on the large facility that was big enough to open and allow a transfer truck through, so I decided that's what it had been used for. The door was raised a couple of feet, and I could see the bumper of a Police Cruiser inside.

The area in front of the little building was mostly hard packed dirt with a little clump of grass here and there. We parked the car in the dirt, got out, and walked up to the building.

There was only one low step up to the four by four concrete slab that served as the front porch of the little place. Mike knocked firmly, but not loudly.

"Who is it?" asked the voice inside.

"Mike Manzarek," answered the Boss. "I brought my associate with me." From the corner of his mouth he said to me, "If I don't mention you, they assume I'm here under duress and come out blazing."

"Thanks for the mention," I said sincerely.

"Come on in," said the voice.

Mike twisted the knob and we stepped inside. The doorway opened into a room that looked like it took up most of the little building. The room was taken up by three large metal desks and a half-dozen assorted chairs scattered around. Since Norma was living there, my guess was that a small bedroom and bathroom made up the rest of it, and that was all there was.

The walls were all paneled with dark paneling that was most likely considered cheap and tacky in 1947, but would be sold for a fortune as *reclaimed* in the next century. The floor was black and white tile. Big sections of the paneling were covered with bulletin boards, and they were covered with old yellowing paper. It was a safe bet that the police department must have commandeered the place as it had been left and hadn't bothered to make any changes.

A large calendar was pinned to one of the bulletin boards. Inside a wide, growing, amber border the year "1942" was prominent. That answered my original question. The owner-operator was most likely still part of the real estate on a European or Pacific Island beach or just as likely at the bottom of an ocean.

There was another door straight across from the one we entered, and in front of that was one of the large desks with a policeman sitting behind it. He was facing toward the door we came through. He also had a dogleg shotgun laid on its side across the desk, which he was holding by the pistol grip. He wasn't exactly pointing it at us, but he wasn't exactly *not pointing* it, either.

I pulled the door closed behind me, and he continued to hold the shotgun and look at me. I was a new variable in the officer's complicated life, and it was obvious he was weighing the unknowns and the consequences of his actions in his head. I let him off the hook by unslinging the BAR and leaning it in the corner of the room.

He let go of the grip on the gun and said flatly, "Hi, Mike."

"Hi Billy Ray, sorry to bust in on you."

"No problem Mike, what's wrong?"

"You heard we had some company from out of town looking for Norma?"

"Yeah, the Captain called and gave us the scoop on that."

"We just got word that they know where this place is, and they intend to make a move tonight."

"Shit," growled Billy Ray. He stood quiet for a moment and said, "I need to call that in. Can you wait until the Captain gets here?"

Mike shook his head. "No, I've got a hideaway already picked out, and I intend to get there as fast as possible."

"Are you sure that's the way to go?" asked the officer.

"I'm sure it's not working the way we've been doing it."

The Policeman nodded his agreement, then gestured toward a doorway on our left and said, "Mrs. Manzarek is taking a shower. She should be done any minute now. He picked up his shotgun from the desktop and said, "I still need to call it in."

He gestured with his head and eyes toward the other building, so I assumed they were using the radio in the Police Cruiser. I didn't see a phone anywhere. I wasn't sure I was ever going to get used to that.

He continued, "I'll say we're making a change but I won't give any details in case someone is listening in. That will still bring the Captain out here. He's taking this one personally."

"That makes two of us," said Mike in a low throaty rumble.

Billy Ray put his hat on and hustled out the front door, Mike went through the side door, and I stood alone and watched paper age.

It was probably only a few minutes, but it seemed like a lot longer before the boss returned. My grandfather had all sorts of strange country sayings that he would spout out from time to time. One in particular was, "He had a smile that could blister a bull's ass at a thousand yards." In all honesty, I never paid much attention to him when he said things like that. I just chalked it up to goofy shit that old men say until I saw Mike Manzarek do it.

Norma walked out with her hair still wet from the shower. She was wearing slacks and a plain white shirt bent all out of shape from what the short sighted fashion designer had originally envisioned. Mike followed behind her with a smile that would have had all the bulls in a two-mile radius running for cover.

She walked to me and extended her hand; but it would have felt odd to shake it, so I grabbed her hand in both of mine and held it while I told her I was glad to see her and asked how she was doing.

Before she could answer Mike turned to me and said, "I'll get the car running and open the trunk. Grab her bags and bring her out as quickly as you can."

As he exited Norma finally said, "I'm fine. They're treating me well, and the food isn't too terrible."

I smiled weakly. "Now who's a bad liar," I asked her softly.

She returned the smile and said, "They do treat me well, but the food's awful. Please don't tell Mike as he's liable to go find whoever's been doing the cooking and fry him in his own skillet."

"You're probably right. I won't say a word."

"Mike said you found out that someone hired men from out of town to come after us?"

I nodded slowly.

"Any idea about who's pulling the strings?"

I probably should have been more discrete with saying how little we knew, but I didn't seem to have the desire to deceive her any more than I did Mike. I was also sure I didn't have the ability to deceive her any better than I could Esmerelda. I started talking as if she had flipped a switch on my mouth.

"We don't really know much of anything. Whoever's doing this has stayed ahead of us at every turn. They have either killed off the loose ends…or left me to do it."

"Are you referring to the gentleman you got into an altercation with in an outhouse?"

I felt my face get warm. "Mike told you about that?"

"He mentioned it.

"Yeah…by killing the guy that might have been able to tell us what's going on."

"If it makes you feel any better, Mike wasn't complaining when he told me. On the contrary, he said you saved his life."

"After he saved mine."

"He mentioned that, too," she said as her smile widened. "Humility is not one of his strong suits."

I nodded my head and told her, "Mike keeps saying that we are putting all the pieces together, but we still don't see a picture. Something must be missing."

My father had a saying about things like that. "When everything should work, but doesn't, something you believe to be true…isn't."

"If that's right, I'd sure like to know what it is."

"You two will figure it out. I have faith in you."

I continued to try and look pleased about the way things were going and I asked, "Can I help you pack?"

"No, I can get it, I just…wait a minute; I can use that green canvas bag that's in the trunk of the Cadillac. Would you get it for me?"

"Of course," I told her. I was happy to do anything other than around waiting for everyone else to do something.

I trotted out the front door, and as I stepped onto the concrete porch I realized that the area in front of the little building looked different. When we went inside, the Cadillac was the only thing there. Now I noticed there were five rather nasty looking men with guns standing in the dirt along with it.

I could see Officer Billy Ray lying on the ground about twelve feet away, at my 1:00 position. There were two other men off to my right about the same distance. The man at my 1:30 position was wearing jeans, a white t-shirt, and some kind of work cap. He was wiping a large knife with a handkerchief. I assumed that was the reason I could see the dirt darkening under Billy Ray. At my 2:00 position, the man standing in front of Big Knife was wearing khaki pants and a blue cotton work shirt. He was pointing a snub-nose .38 at Mike Manzarek.

There were two men standing in front of the Cadillac at my 12:00 position. One was wearing a dark coat, hat, and pants. He had both his hands in his pockets. Something about him made me think he was calling the shots.

The man next to him was a young fellow, with wavy brown hair, holding a .45 colt semi-automatic like the one in my shoulder holster. It was pointed at me. I felt like a moron for having walked out the door without the BAR.

The thought didn't last long. Another gentleman in overalls and a floppy felt hat came around the corner of the building on my left. He was average height and build and seemed a little nervous. Parts of his face kept twitching. This was made even worse as he was holding a beautiful Winchester 1901 10 gauge shotgun. It was a lever action gun and it would bring some serious money in seventy years, but the future I was worried about was much closer than that. If he pulled the trigger a whole lot of me would be all over Mike.

"Evening," said the Shot Caller in a casual tone. "Just stay where you are while we take care of a couple of things. He turned his head to the man next to him. "Jeff run inside and fetch the missus, would you?"

Mike turned his head and looked at me. I could see the fear in it, and I knew it wasn't for him.

Jeff trotted toward me, and as I was standing directly in front of the door, I stepped slowly to my left, so he would be able to walk past. As I did I heard a sound I had become quite familiar with in the last few days.

I looked over at Mike and tried to make my face express that something was about to happen, the same way he had when we had gotten off the elevator at Julius Epstein's place.

I couldn't put all the time and effort into it that I wanted to. In a split second I was going to be forced to make my move. The sound I heard was the bolt going back on the BAR.

Jeff walked past me and stepped into the open doorway.

"What in the…" he began, and I heard the bolt go home on the big gun.

I would have preferred to get farther from the doorway, but I didn't have the luxury. I wrapped my left hand around the end of Twitchy's gun barrel and twisted hard to my right, pulling him and the shotgun across my left side.

Twitchy yelled, the BAR roared and pieces of the door, the doorframe, and Jeff flew all over the place.

I knew these things were happening around me, but I wasn't able to stand and watch. I had become part of a much bigger process that was moving fast. As I twisted with Twitchy's shotgun barrel in my hand I tried to keep it pointed at the man holding the 38 on Mike.

I expected Twitchy would try to pull the gun away from me, and that would mean gripping it tighter and pulling back. I felt it buck before I heard the roar of the big gun. The barrel got hot under my hand as the gun fired.

The man with the 38 saw what I was doing, and if he could have had a second more he might have been able to dive into the dirt. Too bad for him, he didn't have it. The blast caught him just above the shoulders and blew the surprised look off his face.

Before Twitchy had a chance to cock the shotgun, I grabbed the barrel with both hands and dragged him toward me. He thought I was trying to take his toy away from him and he started to let go and back off, but I couldn't let him do that. I needed him. I grabbed him by the straps of his overhauls with one hand and pulled him to me. At that point he really started shaking and dropped his gun on the ground.

I turned to look for the Shot Caller. He had dropped to the dirt when the shooting started, and I figured he would be digging for a gun and come up shooting. Out of the corner of my eye I saw Mike get hold of Big Knife. He didn't even bother to take it away. He took Big Knife's hand, knife and all, and crammed it into the side of his head.

Shot Caller came up with a 9mm Luger, a real museum piece, and pointed it in my direction. I hoisted Twitchy up in front of me with my left arm and drew the .45 with my right.

The Luger started going off, and I started wishing Twitchy was bigger. He caught most of it, but one of the rounds took a chunk out of the brim on the side of my hat and another one cut into my coat and creased my rib cage just under my right arm. It burned like hell and I put a stop to the trouble with two shots from the .45. The rounds caught Shot Caller in the middle, and he fell to the dirt.

Twitchy had gone limp; and when I dropped him into an uncomfortable looking pile on the ground, he didn't move

Mike turned toward me and we both yelled, "Are you alright?" We saw that we were, and Mike wasted no time running toward the open door of the little building. As he did he yelled, "See if you can help Billy Ray...and keep watch, there's at least 3 more of these assholes running around."

I ran over and knelt down near the officer. I rolled him onto his back, and his lifeless eyes stared up at me. I closed them, and lowered my head for a moment. I had only known the guy for a few minutes, but I felt bad that he had gotten caught up in this mess. Mike and I knew we were walking around with targets on our backs, but this guy didn't deserve what happened to him.

My thoughts were interrupted when all hell broke loose inside the little building.

CHAPTER 30

"Mike!" I yelled as I jumped up and ran toward the small building.

A lot of sound and fury was coming from the structure, and the commotion was rising in intensity. It sounded as if the place was having its insides torn out.

I could hear Mike bellowing and cursing, and I could hear at least two more men in there with him. From them it sounded mostly like fear and pain.

I was running toward the front door, but before I could reach it, a man flew out of it. He landed in the dirt and rolled to within three feet of the Shot Caller's body. I thought he was going to lay there with the Shot Caller, but in an instant he was up and running toward the larger building.

"Get that son-of-a-bitch!" Mike's voice roared through the open door.

"I've got him," I yelled back. The guy was pretty solidly built, just over six feet. He ducked under the big overhead door and disappeared.

I ran to the door, peeked in, and looked from side to side. It was definitely some kind of manufacturing facility. Big cast iron machines and large heavy work tables dotted the room. An overhead head gantry wrapped around the roofline. I tried to raise the big rolling overhead door to let in a little more ligh, but it didn't move; so I ducked under it like the guy I was chasing.

It was still light outside, but the sun was on top of the horizon and visibility inside the big building wasn't optimal, to say the least. The facility was completely open on the inside with only steel trusses, and the overhead gantry between me and the roof. At one time everything had been covered in grease and dirt, but now the grease and dirt was covered with dust. Large windows right under the gantry circled the building and would have let in a lot of light earlier in the day, but it was getting gloomy, and as I picked my way between machines I was quickly deciding it was a stupid thing to be doing.

I made up my mind to turn around and go back. I had been foolish to chase that guy in here, and I stood a better chance of waiting for him, or them, to come out than I did trying to dig somebody out from behind all the machinery. I had no idea how many guys there were, I didn't know the layout and there were too many places for someone to hide. They could easily jump me from either side, and I wouldn't have any notice.

"Or they could be right behind me," I thought as I turned around and came face to face with the guy I had been chasing.

He had a brown shoe polish colored mop of hair that didn't look like it had seen a comb in a while. He was wearing a t-shirt and jeans, and was swinging a pipe at my head. I spun out of the way and the pipe missed my head and raked down my back. That normally would have been fine, but this time the stitches on my back let me know they didn't care for it. I lunged to the side and went twisting across the edge of a big steel table. There was a lot of stuff on the table, but everything was covered with muck and dust, and I was moving too quickly to be able to tell what anything was. I grabbed the first thing I could get my hand on. I couldn't stop to examine it, but I learned later that it was a pint can of gear grease.

Pipe Boy came down the side of the table after me. He swung again, but he telegraphed it and I threw my left arm up and blocked it without trying real hard. He tried to do the same when I brought my right arm around, but he was too slow. Even so, he was near my size, so I put everything I owned into burying the grease can into the side of his head. The pipe came out his hand as he fell away and landed on his side. He was still moving, and I wanted to put a stop to that. But before I could someone bounced a monkey wrench off the side of my head. It was big and orange and I saw it coming out of the corner of my eye and tried to get out of the way.

The fellow swinging the wrench was my old pal Skinny, the guy who had shot up Mike's house. I had moved enough to keep him from caving my skull in, but he still got a good piece of me. My shot up hat went rolling across the floor and stars flooded my eyes as I dropped to my knees. I grabbed the edge of the table and tried to get back on my feet, but Skinny gave my head another whack and the lights went out.

I regained consciousness with the sensation of being dragged across the floor. It hurt like hell, but I managed to open my eyes and raise my head a little. I could see that Pipe Boy and Skinny had hold of my ankles and were dragging me across the floor. The trip only lasted a few seconds, and the inside of my skull was swimming way too wildly for me to do anything about it.

They stopped in front of a large cage, maybe 6 x 6 and 7 feet tall, made up of corrugated metal with angle iron at the edges. At first I wondered why there was a cage in the middle of this factory and then my head finally cleared enough to realize that it was a tool crib. Through the large corrugated openings I could see industrial power tools, hoses, and belts hanging around the interior. It was grime and dust covered like everything else, and my new friends turned my legs loose and let my feet flop onto the floor next to it.

I could feel blood trickling down the sides of my head and neck. I was pretty sure they had reopened the wound from my pal Lenny's dental work and probably made some new ones.

I started to draw my knees under me with the intention of trying to stand; but before I could, I caught something in my peripheral vision coming toward me. It was Pipe Boy. He had traded his pipe for a .45 semi-automatic. He kicked me in the thigh and yelled, "Get up, Asshole!"

The kick caught me off guard, and I half grunted and half snarled as I bounced against the big cage and dropped on my face. It popped into my thoughts that where he had kicked me was one of the few places I hadn't been hurting. My head whirled like it was in a blender, and I was having trouble focusing. In addition to that, the stitches on my back were still pissed off from the pipe bouncing across them.

I was face down on the floor with my head rolled to one side, facing the big fenced-in box, and I noticed that this side of the cage didn't go all the way to the floor. It was only a couple of inches, but I could see under the edge of it with no problem. There was a lot of accumulated trash on the floor inside the big box, mostly metal shavings, cigarette butts, and a couple of dead cockroaches. There was also a piece of threaded rod, a little less than four inches long and little under a half inch in diameter lying just under the edge. I put my hands down and attempted to rise up again, but this time my fingers went under the edge of the cage.

I struggled to get -- technically stagger -- to my feet, and I made it; but everything in my skull decided to take a quick spin around the inside of my head and my knees buckled. I fell forward and reached out to catch the wall of the cage, which I almost missed. I stabbed the fingers of my left hand through the corrugated openings and caught myself before I pitched off into the floor on my right. I flopped against the side of the big box, hanging by my left arm, and tried to get my footing. I pulled myself upright and put the right side of my face against the corrugated metal as I shoved the pocket of my shoulder against the corner for support. I twisted my head around to the left enough to see that there was a big work table about five feet from the front of the cage. Pipe Boy was a little to my left, half sitting, half leaning against the table's edge facing the cage. His head was turned, and I could see the red circular ring on his temple where I had caught him with the grease can. Skinny was a little farther to the left, standing at the end of the table. Both of them were looking to their right at something that wasn't me.

I attempted to turn my head that way, and my knees buckled again. I was still hanging on to the cage, so I didn't fall far. I must have gotten Pipe Boy's attention back for the moment, because I heard him snort-laugh as I caught myself.

It took me a moment, but I was finally able to pull my body mostly upright. After I had managed to maintain that position for a few seconds I slowly twisted my head around to my right.

Standing just a foot or two back from the front of the tool crib were two more big goons I had never seen. The first goon was about three feet away. He was over six feet tall, thick and muscular with a dirty blonde crewcut. The second one was maybe an additional three feet farther from the cage, about the same height and weight but not quite as muscular. He was balding prematurely and trying to hide it with a bad comb-over. From where I was standing, I was looking at them in three-quarter profile. I couldn't see much behind them. They had turned the lights on in the front area, so we were all lit up; but it was dark and gloomy past the edge of the light where the goons were.

They weren't paying any attention to me either, and I assumed they were looking at whatever had the other two's attention. I had to get a surer footing and better hold on the cage so I could twist around and see what they were looking at. In the process I managed to slip one hand down to see if the .45 was still in its holster. It wasn't. I figured that was the one Pipe Boy had in his hand.

When I finally got my head twisted around I could see Mike Manzarek, standing about six feet in front of the Goons. On his right was a large steel table covered with an assortment of wrenches. To his rear there were a number of wooden pallets with 30 gallon drums loaded on them. His left side, the one between him and me, was clear, and in his right hand he was holding some little chubby guy, maybe five-seven or five-eight, by the collar. Mike was talking and he was using his hands when he spoke, just as he would if they were empty. The little guy was being waved around like a sports pennant, and the two big goons were finding it pretty amusing.

"Are you going to let him keep jerking me around?" squealed the little man.

Mike's voice boomed, "I found the little shit in my wife's bedroom. That makes his ass mine."

"He's got you there, Orville," said the goon closest to me. He smiled and nodded as if Mike had correctly recited the rules from a book.

Orville's arms were flying all over the place, but he managed to get his hand inside his coat. At that point Mike caught him by the front of the coat with both hands and lifted off the floor until he was looking directly down into his eyes.

In a low basso profundo the big man said, "You jerk that gun out, and I'll beat you to death with it."

Orville slid his empty hand out of his jacket, and Mike lowered him to the floor.

"Besides," the second goon chimed in, "we're through with your ass anyway. We know damned well it was you that skimmed the take from that last job. Ferguson told us it was you."

"Hey, Jake," Mike called out, suddenly, as if we were standing on his front porch having a conversation.

It caught me by surprise, but I tried to go along with him.

"Yeah, Mike," I replied, attempting to sound as casual.

"How are you doing over there?"

"I've got a bit of a headache, but I'm good." That made both of the guys behind me snort

"Glad to hear it. I wanted to ask you something, did John Callahan ever mention a guy named Dunbar to you?"

That was an odd enough question when my head was clear, but now I had to try and think as everything swam around. I thought over the last few days and about the conversations John and I had in the car. "That name sounds familiar...Bill...Glen...no...Ben...Ben Dundar...he gave some guy with a name like that a ride to the bus station. John said he was part of your old platoon, and they talked about you and Charlie."

"Yeah, that's what I thought. "

I had no idea where this was going, so I just stood and tried to steady myself as the Boss played it out.

"Did I ever tell you how Charlie Callahan died?" he asked abruptly.

That took me off balance as much as the first question, but I tried to keep working with him.

I hesitated, trying to think of something clever to say, but I finally replied simply, "No, you just said he...died badly."

Mike lit a cigarette and the light from the match emphasized the fact that the dark gloom surrounding our little area.

"You guys'll like this story," he said directly to the goons as he wagged his big hand to extinguish the match and then let the little stick fly off onto the floor. He spoke as if he were holding court at the barber shop, and everyone seemed amused at the way Orville was being flapped around at the end of the boss' arm.

Mike took a long drag off his cigarette, and as he blew out the smoke he said, "It was just after the Cicely landing. Ten of us parachuted in one night for what was supposed to be a reconnaissance mission. The planned target was just outside of enemy lines, but as usual we didn't get anywhere near the target."

The thought went through my head that he had said; "Cicely landing" and no one needed any more detail than that. Even the criminals had participated in the war.

The Boss took another pull on his cigarette and spoke as if he didn't have a care in the world. The goons on my right seemed to be interested and stood quietly listening. I didn't have the energy or the will to turn my head back around to see what the other two were doing.

"We ended up behind, way behind, enemy lines with only eight of us still alive. Lieutenant Ross broke his neck on landing, and we never did find Staff Sargent Winslow. That left me in charge."

The big man looked down at Orville, who stared back with the same unchanging, frightened look on his face. Mike blew smoke into it and continued.

The Boss used Orville to gesture at the goons. "You guys know the drill; we're in enemy territory and trying to get out as fast as we can. Of course we're doing most of our traveling at night and were cutting back across the Italian country side, trying to take the shortest route to the coast."

Mike's big hand had been the only thing holding Orville erect, but at that point he set him down on a nearby shipping crate, allowing him to sit and nurse his wounds.

"We ended up in a little Italian town...what the hell's the name of that place?" He was quiet for a moment and then shook his head. "It doesn't matter. The place had been busted up pretty good. It was mostly abandoned, torn down and cratered out from the bombing runs that went before the landing."

He looked off toward the windows on the tops of the high walls. The external light was almost gone, but Mike was somewhere else reliving a moment in time that I had once thought only old men remembered.

"We were headed down the edges of the main street when we noticed there was a group of small vehicles coming from the other direction. We thought it was a German or Italian reconnaissance unit, like ours, so we grabbed the quickest shelter we could find and settled in to wait them out."

He massaged his forehead with his big hand as if it hurt to bring up the memory.

"We were on top of a bombed out corner Bistro. What had been a second story apartment was now one big roofless room with not a lot left of the two front walls."

"Not much of a hideout," I offered lamely, trying to hold up my end of whatever the boss was trying to accomplish.

"It was a sorry little shithole and a lousy hiding spot," he confirmed. "We hunkered in the back corner in the shadows, but if anyone had bothered to look for us they sure as hell would have found us. We weren't too worried about it at first, but then we discovered that what we thought was a reconnaissance unit was actually the front end of an armored column."

"Oh shit," the goon closest to me said as a smile crossed his face.

"You got that right. We were going to be there for a while. "

"German or Italian?" the other goon asked

"German. They were moving back from the landing area and taking everything with them. We watched radio antennas and the tops of tanks and halftracks go by forever."

He flicked the ashes off his cigarette onto the top of Orville's head. The smaller man just sat and said nothing.

"The main road was actually on a high broad rise that ran straight through the town. If you turned off that road in front of our little Bistro, you would go down a steep hill for a couple of blocks before hitting another street that ran parallel to the big one. That road couldn't quite be seen from the main road, but we could see it if we peeked out from where we were hiding. I sent Charlie Callahan and Whiskey Lewis in that direction to see if they could find us a way out of there without the Germans getting wind that we were there."

I was having trouble believing that everyone was just sitting around listening and interacting with the Boss telling a story, but there we were.

"Obviously, they couldn't just walk down the street."

First goon nodded like that made perfect sense to him.

"The main road was broad and the hill was steep, but you still had to be a fair ways down the incline before you were invisible to the main road. I'm still not sure you couldn't see it from the top of a Tiger Tank, but if they could see the bottom of the hill they didn't give it any notice.

Charlie and Whiskey went through an opening in the back wall where we were hiding. That led into another building and from there it was in and out of windows and across rooftops all the way down to the bottom of the hill. It took them, at best, ten or twelve minutes to get there."

"At the intersection at the bottom of the hill there was one lone streetlight that was still working. We could see it if we peeked around the corner. He looked down at the floor and actually chuckled. "Wouldn't you know that two blocks past that street light was the last working whorehouse in a twenty mile radius?"

I thought, "A place like that would draw traffic," and then realized that I had said it aloud.

"It did. A big Kraut Major and his aide were leaving Madam Maria Dimuccio's, we learned her name the next day, and they were coming down that side street when we saw them walk into the light. They passed on through, and we couldn't see where our boys were. After a moment the Germans walked back into the light prodding Charlie and Whiskey with their Lugers. We never did find out any details, but somehow they had gotten the drop on Callahan and Lewis, who most likely thought they were on the street alone and weren't paying close attention to what was behind them. The aide made Lewis get down on his knees with his hands behind his head, but the big Major had other plans for Charlie."

I admit that I was curious, but I wasn't so curious that I wanted to hear what came next. I said nothing.

Mike looked around as he said, "I'm not sure I can explain this." He reached down and caught Orville by the back of his coat. "I'll need a visual aid."

"Wh...wh...what the hell are you doing," stammered the smaller man.

"That big German picked Charlie up like this." He hefted chubby little Orville effortlessly and then brought his free arm up behind the little man's legs and gathered him up as if he was going to carry him.

"The Major used a big piece of drainage pipe that was sitting upright next to a wall on the edge of the road." He took a couple steps and said, "This thirty gallon drum will do just fine."

The drum he was talking about was sitting on top of a couple of palates and pushed against the front wall of the big building. It was empty, and the top was missing. He lowered Orville's legs into the open drum and let him stand there.

Mike's face had a look of sadness that I was sure wasn't for Orville. Orville's face had an unhappy look that I'm sure was.

"That German was at least my size, but looking back, I believe he was actually a little bigger." He sighed. "It doesn't really matter. What matters is that he reached over and did this."

Mike put his hand on Orville's chest and leaned over pinning him against the wall. The little man didn't like it much, and he grabbed the boss' wrist and forearm and tried to move them. He might as well have tried to fly.

Mike had the appearance of a man doing nothing more than leaning against a lamppost, but the simplicity of what was happening was deceiving.

The big man used his free hand to take a slow, easy drag off his cigarette and said, "When you're caught in this position, you think the problem is that a big man has his hand and weight on your chest, and it hurts. It takes a few seconds to realize -- that isn't the problem.

Orville must have already discovered the problem, because his eyes had become wide and round and terrified.

"The problem," said Mike, turning his head to look at the squirming man, "is you can't breathe."

The little man squirmed and thrashed at Mike's arm. He was pinned against the wall by the boss supporting most of his weight, and his feet drummed impotently at the inside of the barrel.

I don't think Mike saw any of it. He was looking at something else that happened somewhere else.

Softly Mike said, "We could see it from where we were hiding, but we couldn't do a damned thing about it. Any of us could have taken a shot that would have blown that big Kraut bastard's head off, but that would have brought that armored column down on us. If I had been alone, I would have done it; and the consequences be damned, but I couldn't fire off a round that would kill everyone else with me.

Orville's mouth kept opening and closing like a fish out of water, as he tried in vain to take a breath. The terrified look on his face was accentuated by the cords that stood out on his neck as his head begged for the oxygen his body wouldn't allow him to take in. His legs began kicking slower and slower and finally they stopped altogether, and his eyes rolled back in his head.

Mike leaned back and gripped him by the collar and pulled him out of the barrel. He put him on the floor like he was setting down a suitcase. I thought the guy was dead, but after a few seconds he coughed a little and then rubbed his chest.

The Boss rubbed his forehead and then wiped his eyes. The memory was doing almost as much damage as he was, but he went on.

"I sent Paul Winslow and Jax Jackson over the rooftops to try and help them, but it took too long to get down there without being seen. "

"After the Major was done with the Charlie, his aide had Lewis lower his hands. Then he threw a piano-wire garrote over his head and began strangling him.

The boss stopped for a moment and looked down at his cigarette, studying it as if he had never seen it before. When he looked up he added, "The son-of-a-bitch put his knee between Whiskey's shoulder blades and hauled back on the wire like he was stopping a twenty mule team."

He paused again and after a moment, in a quiet voice, he said, "By the time Winslow and Jackson got there they were both dead."

Mike took the last drag off his cigarette and exhaled the smoke slowly through his nose. His eyes misted over as he spoke. "Before the war, Winslow had a job as a lifeguard down on Daytona Beach. He worked on Charlie for a long time, but it was too late."

I didn't know what to say or do, so I just stood there and felt bad about two men I had never known, who had technically died eighty years earlier. I had always viewed the Second World War as something my grandfather had done for a few years before he went back to farming. I don't know why I had failed to realize that the war they fought shaped their lives and changed their destinies as much as anyone who had ever fought a war. In their hearts and minds they were still fighting it.

After a moment Mike continued. "The only good thing was that when Jackson and Winslow went hunting for those Nazis, they surprised them the same way they had surprised Charlie and Whiskey.

They were out of sight from us when they caught up to them, but Jax busted the aide's skull with the butt of his M1 carbine. When the big Major tried to intervene, Paul jumped on his back and opened his neck from ear to ear with that Number One Randall he carried all over Europe."

He took his cigarette and crushed what was left of it against the side of the barrel that had held Orville. He stared for a moment at the mark it left and then flipped the butt toward a corner of the room.

"The next morning the Germans were gone and we buried Charlie and Whiskey in a pretty little cemetery just outside that damned little town that I never can remember the name of."

Mike ran his big hand through his hair. "I never wanted to tell John that his brother died that way. I wasn't trying to keep any secrets from him; I just thought it would hurt him even worse if he knew, but it looks like he took it completely different than I expected."

The Boss stared into the gloom between the two big goons in front of him and said, "You blame me for it, don't you John?"

It was probably only a few seconds, but it seemed like a long time before something finally moved in the thick shadow behind the two goons, and with the sound of shuffling footsteps John Callahan stepped between the two men and stood in front of them. He was holding Norma by the hair and had a revolver stuck to the side of her head.

CHAPTER 31

John's voice had a nervous edge to it when he replied, "Why shouldn't I blame you? You're the reason Charlie's dead. You actually sat and watched a man torture my brother to death without doing a damned thing about it."

"*Well that explains why Mike was able to ramble on like that,*" I thought. "*The Boss must have figured that Callahan would want to hear him tell the story.*" The thing I was having trouble figuring out was how Mike had figured out it was Callahan.

Fortunately, I wasn't the only one who wanted to know that.

"When did you know it was me," John asked.

"When I walked out the door into that pack of thugs."

Callahan sneered a smug little sneer and his arm moved around as Norma squirmed, but he kept a tight rein on her hair.

"You were the only one who knew where we were going," Mike finished.

John's sneer turned into a full blown hateful grin. "I should have thought of that bit a lot sooner."

Mike nodded. "It was a good move. You called and said the hiding place had been compromised, and when we came running you just followed us down here." The big man's face was a solid mask of disgust. "You had already set us up with the idea about running away and hiding. I didn't even bother to check for a tail, because I believed that whoever was after Norma already knew where she was being hidden."

John's smug look returned. "When it comes right down to it, you're a pretty gullible fellow."

"I'm sorry Mike," Norma half-talked, half-shrieked as Callahan moved her around by the hair. "He said to come with him, and I thought he was on our side."

"It's not your fault, Baby," said Mike in a low voice, and then to John, "I can't believe I didn't see it sooner, a guy with a photographic memory who couldn't identify a picture of a man he had worked with." He rubbed his chin and asked, "Who killed Max Winston?"

"I did," Callahan said proudly.

Mike made a pig-like grunting noise through his nose. "You...you piss in your pants when the wind changes direction."

John's face wadded up and turned red. "Maybe I'm not as big a coward as you think I am," he snapped.

"The hell you're not. You even fieldstripped your cigarettes because you were smoking a different brand than Winston's other visitors and you didn't want anyone to have a clue that you were ever there."

Callahan was perspiring heavily, and he wiped at the moisture on his chin with back of his gun hand before he told Mike, "It was when I was stripping that last cigarette that I decided I was only going to do business with one guy. Starting the next morning I went through Shorty to gather a new team to collect you at Max's house."

There was humor in his voice when Mike replied, "That partnership didn't last long."

The anger flashed for a moment in Callahan's eyes and he shook Norma by the hair. She tried not to squeal out loud, but she wasn't able to hold it in. She made enough noise to cause Mike's face to cloud over.

"Yeah," admitted Callahan, "you're boy there cut him in half, and I had to use Kurt to bring these gentlemen in from other parts of the country."

"Since the cut-rate help you were getting from your old buddies at Republic Aviation wasn't making it."

"You may be a big man in this town, but I think your reputation is mostly gas," John snarled. Spittle flew off his lips as he yelled, "The amateurs would have been fine if you were by yourself!"

He looked toward me, but I was as happy to needle him as Mike so I chimed in, "You really want to give me credit for that? The way I remember it was Shorty and Pencil-Neck," I gestured toward Skinny with my head, "got themselves shot up and run off by the maid."

Pipe Boy took a step forward and kicked me in the back of my left knee. The kneecap banged into the cage and when that leg buckled, the other one went with it. I lost my grip on the cage and dropped to floor on my knees.

My pain seemed to bring John a little pleasure, and he sounded more cheerful when he told Mike, "So since your boy...and the maid...kept mucking things up, I shelled out for professional help. They were pricey but I think you'll admit they were worth it."

Mike crossed his arms and looked at John as if he were appraising him. "So you murdered Max Winston. Where did you find the guts to do that...with a knife yet?"

Callahan shrugged a little. "It took a lot of liquid courage, and I didn't plan on doing it with a knife. I pulled a gun on Winston, but I had trouble pulling the trigger, and he walked up and slapped it out of my hand. He grabbed me by the collar and said he was going to kill me. At that point I panicked. There was a rusty kitchen knife lying on the little table next to the door, and in desperation I grabbed it and stuck it in him. Even with that knife sticking out of him, and me hanging onto it, he still damned near beat me to death."

"That's where those black eyes and bruises came from," offered Mike.

"Yeah, I can't get over you two buying into that story about me fighting with two big men over a loose piece of ass."

Callahan turned to watch as I grappled with the front of the cage and finally managed to haul myself back up to an unsteady standing position. From the look on his face, I got the impression that he enjoyed any and all pain or discomfort on my part.

Mike asked, "Why didn't you let your guys know that Jake was at the house last

Monday?   It doesn't make any sense to hire a bunch of guys just to let them walk into a surprise."

"That was a little miscommunication between me and Shorty," replied John.

"*Apparently, everyone called that guy Shorty*," I thought.

"I had told Shorty that someone would be watching the house, and I thought that he understood it would be me doing the watching. I was waiting for him to show up so I could let him know that there was one more in the house to take care of, but Shorty had already sent the driver, Kurt, over there," he gestured with his head toward Pipe Boy, "to deal with whoever was watching the house."

Mike grinned. "So you actually got sapped by your own guy?"

Kurt raised his hands and shrugged.

""Yup," John admitted, "nobody but Shorty knew who had hired them. It wasn't any fun, but it did help me keep up a good front."

"That it did," agreed Mike.

The puzzle was finally together, but it didn't make me any happier. We were outnumbered, outgunned; and even if we had a fighting chance; I didn't have much left in me. I couldn't tell if I had a concussion, or if the last few days were finally catching up with me. The stitches on my back still burned from where Pipe Boy, Kurt, hit me; and my head throbbed from the pounding with the wrench. There was a chance that I could, if I got lucky, take out Kurt and Skinny. But there was no way I could do anything with the pair of goons standing behind John, and he still held Norma with a gun to her head.

Callahan asked Mike, "Are you done playing for time or do you have other stories you want to tell?"

The Big Man replied, "Norma doesn't have anything to do with any of this, John. Do whatever you want with me, but let her go. I'm begging you."

"You let my brother die and took him away from me. I'm going to do the same with her. I'm going to blow her pretty head off, and you can stand there and watch."

"I couldn't save Charlie's life," Mike said softly. "I've spent a lot of nights thinking about it, and more than one night I've woken up screaming out his name; but I couldn't save him."

"You didn't even try; you just sat and watched it. Dunbar told me everything."

"If he told you everything, then you have to know that I couldn't do any more than I did without it costing the lives of everyone else."

"Then that's what you should have done. "

"It occurred to me, it really did. Charlie was my friend and I thought hard about taking the shot that might have saved him; but would have killed everyone else, and I couldn't bring myself to do it."

"You mean it would have killed you. You let Charlie die to save your own ass."

"You can't possibly believe that."

"That's exactly what I believe, because that's what happened. Mighty Mike Manzarek chickened out and stayed hidden in the shadows while Charlie Callahan died a slow death."

The boss' eyes narrowed and I could see the cords stand out on his neck when he growled, "Fine, then shoot me and have done with it, but let Norma go."

"It's not the same. You took something from me, and I'm going to take something from you. That's the way it works."

Way down deep I knew I couldn't stand there and watch him kill Norma, but there was no way I could stop him either. I felt my fist constrict around the threaded rod. With some luck I might be able to damage Kurt really badly, maybe even get a piece of Skinny before one of the goons blew a hole in me. The little old man had been right after all, I wasn't going to live to see the weekend.

The goons' attention was still focused on Mike and John. I watched them as I started to take slow deep breaths in an effort to clear my head and gather whatever strength I had left.

The goon closest to me had his gun in hand and looked to be the one most alert and aware of his surroundings. He would most likely be the one to put a bullet in my back when I made my move. So be it.

Mentally I started a count to three with the intention of breaking Kurt's face on four, and most likely dying on five. I had gotten to two when the goon closest to me made an odd face. The look stayed on his face for a moment, and then his head tilted back. I thought he might be looking at something around the roofline, but then his legs gave way and he dropped toward the floor. He didn't quite go all the way down, because something caught him by the shirt collar and stopped him from falling.

Isaiah "The Ice Pick" Goldberg stood there holding him with a grin on his face that looked like he had just won big at the track.

The second goon saw the first one drop and jerked a big revolver from a shoulder holster, but before he could get it pointed, Izzy raised a sawed-off double barrel shotgun with his free hand and let the guy have it.

The stock on the gun had been cut down to a pistol grip, and the barrel had been sawed off to around twelve inches; so the shot pattern wasn't any more tightly grouped than a herd of monkeys. Unfortunately, for the second goon, he wasn't very far away. The blast caught him mostly around the head and he flew backwards and slammed into a big piece of machinery and slid to the floor.

With the cage blocking his view, Kurt had missed what happened to the first goon; but the roar of the twelve-gauge got his attention.

"What the...," he began, but he wasn't able to finish the sentence.

As the shotgun went off, my fist balled into a hard knot around the little threaded rod, and I spun counter-clockwise as fast and hard as I thought my body could stand it. Kurt was stepping to the side to get a bead on Izzy, but he saw me coming and tried to bring the .45 around to draw down on me instead. I caught him in the jaw before he could go far. The gun went down, but it also went off. I felt the round plow down the side of my left thigh. It burned like hell, but the burst of adrenaline cleared my head and almost made me grateful for the pain.

I felt bones shatter when I connected with Kurt's jaw. I was sure that none of them were mine, but fighting was something I knew well, and I could tell I wasn't going to have full use my right hand for a couple of days. The pain from the jolt shot up my right arm as Kurt struck the table he had been leaning on. He pitched forward across it and tried to hang on, but slid off onto the floor.

My momentum carried me into the table as well. I tried to hang on to the little threaded rod, but whether it was inability or spiteful revenge for the damage I had done to it, my hand wouldn't obey my command and the rod dropped to the floor. I slammed against the edge of the table, and the fresh wound on my leg didn't like it. It felt like a bolt of lightning struck my left side. I howled and scrambled toward Skinny at the end of the table.

Kurt had gone down, but he wasn't out. That was unfortunate for him since he was laying on the floor between me and Skinny. I staggered forward, still howling, and caught Kurt between the legs with my right foot. Blood and saliva bubbled out his mouth as he yelled and tried to rise up, but my left foot came down on his face. I plowed my way down the edge of the table, stomping all over him and dragging my left arm in an attempt to harvest whatever was on the table and use it to beat Skinny to death.

Skinny's eyes widened as he realized his life was on the line. He had the BAR slung over his shoulder, but there would be no getting to that before I got to him. He went for the revolver in his shoulder holster, but he was scared and having trouble figuring out why the gun wouldn't move. It was because the strap holding the gun in place was still snapped shut. I could see the recognition on his face when he discovered what the problem was. He would have it loose in another second, but I charged toward him, still dredging the table top with my left hand. The table was covered with small combination wrenches and it finally dawned on me that wrenches were what this place had produced... monkey, stilson, combination, box end, whatever. It was just my luck that the table was covered with small ones when what I needed was a large monkey wrench. It was just then that a big one, the size of my thigh, went spinning past my ear and hit skinny in the face. I assumed that it was thrown by my big boss...overhand.

Skinny's head snapped back sharply without changing the trajectory of the wrench which flew past him into the darkness. Skinny flipped over backwards and landed on his head.

Despite a broken jaw and my stomping all over him, Kurt was still wiggling around on the floor. The work table he was laying half-under was a shop made item with structural I-Beams for legs. I finally just stepped to the side and kicked his head into one of them. It made a dull "bong" sound and Kurt stopped wiggling.

I turned quickly to see what Callahan was doing. It looked like Izzy had been holding his attention and John was just now finding out that his other two boys had been done in by me and the Boss' big pipe wrench.

Izzy was reloading his sawed-off shotgun in an extremely casual and non-hurried manner.

The look on Callahan's face changed as he realized that he could still take his revenge, but his chances of getting out alive afterwards were dwindling fast. If he had planned on getting out past Izzy that idea fizzled out when someone called out from the gloom in the back of the building.

"You know, I don't think this place is safe," said the voice.

I didn't think there was ever a time when I would be able to say it, but I sure was glad to see Abe "The Axe" Weinfarb step out of the shadows. He was carrying a camping axe in one hand, and walking and talking as if he were out strolling around the park.

"It's not safe at all," he said again. "The guy that was guarding the back door of this place has come to an awful end."

He had been so busy making his entrance that until that moment he hadn't seen John holding a gun to Norma's head.

"Aw John what are you doing over there?"

"He's the one behind it all," confirmed Izzy as he slapped the barrels shut on the shotgun.

"So he's the one who called and told Big Mike we were out to get him?"

Izzy's head bobbed up and down. "Yeah, and then he called and did the same to us."

Abe made a little clicking noise with his tongue. "Johnny, I am really sorry to be hearing this."

"You psychos stay away from me," snarled John. He turned back and forth in a half-circle trying to keep an eye on everyone at the same time. Norma shrieked as he twisted his hand in her hair.

I managed to move closer, but when I did Callahan spun around to face me, holding the pretty woman between us.

"You come any closer I'll blow her head off," he wailed in a way that led me to believe he was coming completely off the rails. I knew what I needed to do, but I couldn't do it with him looking right at me.

"Orville," Mike's big voice boomed in the building. "I'll give you five hundred dollars to pull that pistol out and shoot this son-of-a-bitch!"

The little man cleared leather almost instantly, and Mike roared as he realized the little man was going to fire without regard for the fact that John was still using Norma for a shield.

Fortunately, Callahan still held Norma between him and me, so Orville had a clearer shot. He was also a pretty good shot. The round got close and took Callahan's hat off his head.

Unfortunately for the smaller man, John turned out to be the better gunman. "Orville, you asshole!" he yelled swinging his pistol around and firing. The little man caught the round in the center of his chest. The pistol dropped from his hand and he fell forward on top of it.

I could tell by the look on his face that John understood, almost instantly, that he had made a grievous tactical error.

With the last strength I owned I grabbed the edge of the table for leverage, jumped into the air, and kicked Norma in the chest. She screamed when she saw it coming, but it was cut short when the bottom of my foot smashed into her breast bone.

She slammed into John and he yelled as they both flew backwards. On a good day I could have moved fast enough to be on top of them when they fell, which is what I wanted to do, but this wasn't a good day. I hobbled towards them as they staggered and flopped backwards, but I was moving way too slow. As luck would have it they flew backwards into the waiting arms of Izzy and Abe.

Abe grabbed John's gun arm by the wrist and Izzy got the other one. Norma fell to the floor in front of them. Izzy stuck his shotgun up against John's head, and Abe put the axe to John's throat.

Callahan let go of his gun, and it fell to the floor in front of Norma. Abe bent down to get it. When he did, Izzy noticed that no one was standing on the other side of Callahan so he blew John's head in that direction by snapping both triggers on the little double-barrel.

The concussion was much louder and more intense than it had been the first time, and the air was fogged with gun smoke and little bits and pieces that had been John Callahan. Despite the cloud of human gore, I rushed forward to see about Norma.

Even before the sound of the gun receded, Abe started yelling at Izzy.

"Gahldamnit Iz, what have I told you about that. You got that shit all over me." He was trying to brush the little bits of red and gray pieces of gore off his shoulders and upper back. A fine spray of blood had gotten on everything.

I made it to Norma first and raised her up by the shoulders and propped her up with my leg under her.

She groaned and then rubbed the center of her chest. I tried to brush the mess out of her hair as best I could.

"You kick very hard," she said softly.

"I'm sorry," I told her.

"Do you always apologize when you save people's lives?" she asked. The corners of her mouth bent up slightly.

I had a feeling of deja-vu, and then became cognizant that this was the way I was sitting with her on the sidewalk in front of the diner not long after I had arrived in this world.

She must have understood the same thing as she said, "We have to stop meeting like this, my husband will find out."

"I'm already wise to the two of you," Mike told her softly, leaning over my shoulder.

I squirmed out of the way and he picked up his wife with the same ease I would pick up a small bird. He cradled her into his arms and whispered softly to her.

I went over and stood with Abe and Izzy. The three of us just watched for a moment and then I went over to the Squad Car and used the radio to call the Police.

CHAPTER 32

The Police were on their way, and while we were waiting, I had a few things to ask Mike. We wanted to sit in the office area, but between being shot up by Norma, and broken up by Mike, and the three men he was fighting; it was more comfortable to sit on the concrete pad in front of the small office building.

We dragged the only unbroken wooden chair outside for Norma to sit on but she wouldn't have any part of it. She sat with Mike and me on the edge of the concrete pad, snuggled up under Mike's arm.

"So the phone call you made before we left the house was to Jules Epstein?" I asked.

Mike nodded.

"How did you know we would need Abe and Izzy?"

"I didn't. Something about that phone call from John made me feel uneasy. Too many things weren't lining up. I just had a funny feeling that things were going sideways, so I went for broke.

"That must have been a major league funny feeling," I mused. "You called a group of mentally questionable assassins and told them where the safe-house was."

He grinned. "Some people are broker than others."

"How did you know Abe and Izzy would be enough help?"

"I didn't. I just asked Jules for help. I had no idea he would send in the first string."

"I'm glad he did," I told him sincerely. "We really owe them."

"I'm guessing they mentioned that before they left."

"Over and over."

"It looks like you took care of everybody in the office building," I told him, looking back over my shoulder toward the doorway. "There are two of them still lying in the floor. How did they get the drop on you?"

"That was my own stupid fault," Mike replied. "After I bounced that one guy out the door, I was able to take care of the other two. Then I went in the bedroom to see if Norma was still in there, but all I found was Orville."

"What was he doing? "

"He was being a damned decoy. I walked in the room and got hold of him with the intention of rattling his head like a maraca until he told me where Norma was, but just as I grabbed him one of those other guys stuck a gun in my back and marched me to the same place you ended up. Speaking of which, how's your head."

"It's knotty as a pine board, and it hurts; but I think it will be alright."

It was then a big black car came around from the side of the larger building and headed out toward the main road.

"That Lincoln is a good looking car," said Mike as he watched the red tail lights move away.

We had conferred with Abe and Izzy and they preferred not to have to deal with anyone from law enforcement, so we told our sanity challenged guardian angels they could take off and we would leave their contribution out of the story when the police arrived.

Mike turned toward me and said, "Jules takes good care of his people. Are you sure you don't want to take Abe and Izzy up on their offer?"

"There doesn't seem to be much difference between working for them and working for you," I said bluntly. "The guys working for them tried to kill us; the guy working for you tried to kill us. I'm thinking I should look around for a safe job, like bullfighting or shark dentistry."

Mike made a guffaw noise way back in his throat. "I can't believe I didn't see through John sooner. When his version and your version of Shorty diverged it should have set off the alarm bells."

"Don't beat yourself up; we all wanted to think the best of him. Even when Eddie came up with more information off the top of his head than Callahan had given us all week, we still didn't think to look in that direction."

Since Briggs had been in charge of the safe-house, he and his people were the ones dispatched. That was good news. We were omitting the presence of Abe and Izzy, and that left quite a few gaping holes in the story we were telling.

The Captain showed up with Muldoon and Jones and while the two lower ranking officers worked the scene, he got the story from Mike.

We had gone over our story quickly, just before the Police arrived. We found that it was easy enough to account for everything that happened before we went into the larger manufacturing building, because we had been on our own. After that our story didn't hold water.

I stood with Norma while Briggs took down Mike's version of what happened.

"This story has more holes in it that I have knots on my head," I said quietly to Norma.

"Don't worry," she said, squeezing my forearm for reassurance. "Mike has a knack for making these things work."

"This one's going to take a miracle," I told her.

It was at that moment that Briggs shouted, "Bullshit!"

"Sometimes it's a harder sell than others," she whispered.

The Police Captain was looking at his notebook and had pushed his hat back so he could scratch his head. "You're telling me these guys got into a big fight and ended up killing each other."

Mike nodded.

"You realize that the guy you claim started it, died from an icepick in the back?"

"Yeah, I'm not sure how that happened," Mike falsely confessed.

Briggs made a growling noise. "Shit, let's try a different tack; why did they start fighting?"

Mike stopped to think, and Briggs asked, "You actually have to think about that?"

"Well you want an accurate story don't you?"

"I don't want a story at all," barked Briggs.

"As I recall," began Mike, "they claimed the little guy had skimmed money from a job they pulled."

"That's true," I offered.

"Well at least there's one part that is," snarled the Captain, as he turned his face to make sure I could see the nasty look on it.

I decided it would probably be best to stay out of it, so I went back to being quiet and listening.

Briggs continued to try and weave our web of lies into something that made sense. "Uh huh, so you said the first guy killed the second guy with a sawed off shotgun."

"That's right."

"So why can't we find the shotgun?"

The Boss started to answer and then got some unexpected relief when Muldoon showed up and interrupted him.

"What have you got Muldoon", Briggs asked him.

"There's a guy out back who looks like he was killed with a cleaver or a hatchet."

"Was there another body around?"

"No sir, just the one body."

"So who killed that guy," Briggs asked in exasperation.

"I didn't see that happen," Mike said truthfully.

Briggs took off his hat and ran his hand through his hair. "Let me see if I can summarize this."

Mike leaned in to show he was listening intently.

"After stabbing himself in the back with an icepick, the first guy shot the second one with a gun that doesn't exist and all this because another guy had skimmed money from a previous job."

"So far, so good," Mike assured him.

"At the same time this is going down you and Jake took out two of the other guys."

"Yup."

"And lastly, Callahan gets into it with the guy that did the skimming and they shoot each other."

"Yup."

"All the while, some guy out back is doing himself in with a hatchet."

"That sounds right."

Briggs closed his eyes and slowly shook his head. "You know the little guy doing the skimming was only packing a 32 caliber revolver."

"Lots of power in those little guns," said Mike.

Callahan's head is missing!" Briggs roared.

Mike shrugged.

"So you're sticking to this story?"

"Yes."

The Captain pointed at his notebook. "You are actually telling me this is what happened."

The Boss shook his head. "I thought you understood; I'm not telling what happened, I'm telling you what *needs* to have happened."

The Captain looked at Mike, then at Muldoon, and then he flipped his notebook shut and yelled for Officer Jones.

"Yes, sir," yelled Jones as he came through the big overhead door.

"We're done here, Jones."

"I still haven't found the shotgun."

"There wasn't one," Briggs told him. "John Callahan was killed with a 32 caliber revolver."

Officer Jones' loyalty was unquestionable. "I understand sir…lots of power in those little guns."

I was impressed. That little stunt wouldn't have worked in 2017. The twentieth century had its upside.

We spent the next few hours watching the officers examine, and sometimes adjust, the crime scene. Ambulances and Coroner Wagons came and went, and somewhere in the traffic the medical examiner checked me out.

"I'm not used to working on live bodies," he said, shining a light into my eye.

I told him, "If I look the way I feel, there shouldn't be too much difference."

"You do, and you're right," he said without any trace of humor.

He informed me that Kurt's bullet had just grazed my leg and it didn't need stitches, so he cleaned out the wound and dressed it. He also let me know I didn't have a concussion, and I didn't appear to have a cracked skull, as far as he could tell. But he was insistent that I should go to a real hospital and see a real doctor to get a real opinion.

The doctor also informed me they had found the other officer that had been guarding Norma. I figured there must have been at least two of them on duty, but I had never seen the other one. The doctor told me he had been walking patrol around the building and they had jumped him and put him out of commission with a tire-iron to the head. He was hurt pretty badly but they expected him to recover.

Considering what had happened to Billy Ray, I put that down in the good news column and whispered my quick thanks heavenward.

It was between 2:00 and 3:00 in the morning when we finally got home

Esmerelda met us at the door and went into a frenzied display of welcome for Norma that involved hugging, laughing, crying and lots of excited Spanish that I couldn't catch a word of.

Mike finally decided it was enough and bodily removed Norma, with Esmerelda going down the hallway after them, still crying and laughing.

Mike called back to me over his shoulder. "Jake, you're off tomorrow. Rest up and enjoy the day."

I hobbled to my little house in the back and lay down on the bed with the intention of resting for a moment before cleaning up, but that didn't happen. I nodded off almost instantly.

Before I could get into a deep sleep I felt something pulling me back to consciousness, and through the foggy haze I realized that someone was pulling my pants off.

My head felt like it weighed 100 pounds, but I managed to lift it up to see Esmerelda tugging on the ends of my pants legs.

She said, "You can't go to sleep with your dirty clothes on, cochino."

I didn't have the strength, will, or energy to argue with her. I lowered my head and she finished dragging my pants. I hoped my skivvies hadn't gone with them, but I didn't have anything left to care or to look.

She rolled me onto my side and dragged the bed covers down and then back over me. She stood over me and bent down. "You did a good job saving Norma. Goodnight, cochino."

Through nearly-closed eyes I could see her smile and see her dark hair cascading around her face, hanging towards me.

I heard someone say, "You're beautiful," and my eyes closed, and the darkness swallowed me whole.

When I woke up there was sunlight coming in the windows, and it came in at a pretty high angle. Everything from the crown of my head to my ankles hurt. It took a few minutes to decide if I was going to lay there and hurt or get up and hurt somewhere else.

I finally managed to get out of bed, shower, and shave. I gave myself a good going over and paid special attention to the new wounds on my head. I flexed my right hand and found out that I could actually use it. I wouldn't be able to get a hard grip on anything for a couple of days, but I would be able to pick up loose change and zip my pants, so I considered myself lucky.

The wounds on my back and legs and the older ones on my head were closed up, so the stitches could be taken out. Since we had gotten our biggest problem out of the way, it looked like a good day to ask Mike for time to go see Doctor Hebert and have him remove the stitches and check out the new gouges in my skull while he was at it.

I finally got dressed and wandered over to the kitchen. On the way out I noticed the clock said it was just before noon.

When I came in the door I could see Mike was still sitting at the table reading his paper.

Norma was sitting next to him writing something in a big book. She smiled when she saw me. "Good morning, Jake. You look a little better than you did last night."

"Thanks, I feel a little better. How's everything going this morning?"

"We wouldn't know. We only beat you here by about ten minutes."

She closed the book, stood up, and motioned for me to sit down. I did, and she brought me a cup of coffee.

As she was doing this she told me, "I was so glad that I didn't have to eat any more Police food, that I sent Esmerelda to the market to get something special for dinner tonight. That means that I'm doing lunch. Mike and I decided we would still eat breakfast. Does that work for you?"

"Yes, ma'am it does," I said earnestly.

"It's nothing special, just eggs and bacon."

I had eaten at enough military chow halls to be able to proclaim, "Home cooked eggs and bacon are always special."

Norma headed toward the stove and I asked, "Are you writing your memoirs?" I pointed at the book she had left on the table.

She tied an apron around her waist and said, "That's the company ledger. I have to keep up with accounts payable and receivable and chase after the delinquents. Your boss is too busy fighting and hanging out with gangsters to do the menial grunt work."

A voice behind the newspaper said, "Useless bum."

"Can I help with anything?" I offered.

"Yes," she said, cracking eggs into a skillet. "As soon as you are feeling better, I need for you to go look at a naked woman."

"I'm not busy," said Mike's newspaper.

"If I catch you looking at another naked woman, you'll wear this skillet for a hat."

Mike folded his paper as he replied, "Speaking of which, Jake's hat has a bullet hole in it."

"Wait a minute," I squawked. "Let's not gloss over this naked woman thing."

Norma smiled. "We still need to finish up the job for Paul Cantrell. You just need to spend one more evening, whenever you feel like going back over there," she added quickly, "to see if anything happens or not."

"We know she's keeping Jackie Banks company with the curtains drawn and the lights out," I said. "Do we want to report that?"

"That's a good question. Mike, what do you think?"

The Boss rubbed his chin and thought for a moment. "Callahan already told Banks' goons that he and Jake saw someone go into the apartment, but they didn't know who it was. I think we should stick with that story."

"It might keep a gang war from starting," Norma agreed. She topped off my coffee and stood looking at Mike.

"Maybe, maybe not," he replied, "but we were hired to see if she was doing anything with anybody. That's all we need to report. If Cantrell wants to dig deeper he can, but that will keep us out of the middle of things if trouble breaks out."

Norma concurred. "I can stand being away from trouble for a while."

"Amen," Mike and I offered up at the same time.

Norma headed back to the stove, and Mike went back to his original thought. "As I was saying, you're hat has a bullet hole in it."

"So does my coat...and pants," I added.

Mike made a face. "I'm thinking your day off would be a good time to run over and get a new hat...and coat...and pants. What do you think?"

I agreed that sounded like a good idea.

"Do you remember where we got the first one?"

I thought for a second and told him I did.

"Good, I already called and told them you would be there this afternoon. You can run over there after your doctor's appointment."

"I have a doctor's appointment?"

"1:30 at Dr. Hebert's office." Mike pushed a piece of paper towards me. "I drew you a map."

As I looked at the map Mike added, "Don't worry, we'll hold dinner for you if we need to."

I nodded and said, "Okay," and then I asked, "Can I just go get the hat right after I see the doctor?"

Mike look puzzled and his face wadded up. "That's what I figured you would do?"

"If the appointment is at 1:30, why would I be late for dinner?"

Mike and Norma both started laughing. "Well," began Mike, "you might not be, but I wouldn't bet on it." He rubbed his chin and looked at me questioningly. "You have been to see a doctor before, haven't you?"

I didn't have a clue what he was talking about but I said, "Oh yeah, I see what you mean."

"Unless you like reading five year old magazines, you might want to take a book," Norma suggested, as she brought the eggs, bacon and toast to the table.

The breakfast was good and I told her so, but it wasn't as good as Esmerelda's cooking. I wasn't sure if it was the cooking or just her presence that made it better, and I didn't want to think too hard about it. That caused me to remember that I still wasn't sure about what I was going to tell the little old man when he came back.

Mike unfolded his paper and said, "Esmerelda's got the Caddy so you can take the Chevy. The keys are in it."

He threw the paper up in front of his face, so I didn't bother to respond. I took my dishes to the sink and started washing the ones that were already there. Norma was glad to have the help, and she swept and cleaned elsewhere. By the time I was done, it was a just before 1:00; so I grabbed the little map that Mike had made and headed to the garage.

I got the old Chevrolet rolling with what I hoped would pass for a practiced ease. It was a little chilly outside, but I rolled the window down anyway and enjoyed the cool air coming into the car. I got to the doctor's office between five and ten minutes early and sat down to wait.

Two hours later I understood what Mike and Norma had been laughing about. Norma had been right, there were no new magazines to read, only very old ones. As I sat there looking at a five year old copy of Life, I listened to the conversations of the other people in the waiting room. I slowly came to the understanding that, as much as going to the doctor's office in the twenty-first century sucked, going in the twentieth-century was exponentially worse.

Judging from what I was hearing, the doctor could have been at a number of places -- the hospital, someone's home, lunch or even another doctor's office. No one in the waiting room had any idea if the doctor was on premises or where he was, if he wasn't.

An hour later I finally got in to see him. He removed the stitches from my old wounds and redressed the ones the medical examiner had patched up. He checked out my head and said it wasn't broken.

Just about the time he was done it dawned on me that I would need to pay him. I had gotten so used to the military or the VA handling my medical needs, that it hadn't crossed my mind before then.

I asked about the cost and he said he had already been instructed to send the bill to Mike's house.

"I hope you know you work for a good man," said Hebert as he washed his hands.

"I do know that," I replied sincerely.

The doctor turned and headed out of the examination room. He didn't break stride, but as he exited the doorway he called back from the hall, "Take good care of him."

"I will," I said to no one.

I left the doctor's office and got into the car to drive to the men's store where I had gotten my hat on Monday. I was finding it hard to believe it was only Friday.

It was pleasant to think that despite the little old man's predictions, I had made it this far. I had spent a lot of my time, in the doctor's waiting room thinking about what I would tell him the next time I saw him.

All-in-all I'd made a pretty good first week of it there in 1947, and I really liked working for Mike and Norma. I also liked Esmerelda's cooking. Truth be told, I liked everything about Esmerelda but I didn't figure she felt the same about me since she spent quite a bit of time telling me what a buffoon I was or calling me a cochino. Despite the fact that I had meddled in her affairs with Roberto, we seemed to have shared a moment afterwards; so I felt like we were on good terms. It was also true she had said I did a good job helping Norma, or had I dreamt that?

I missed a lot of things the twenty-first century had to offer; the internet, color television, cell phones, and cars that were designed to at least try not to kill me. 1940's radio was a lot more interesting and entertaining than I thought it would be, but it couldn't compete with watching a good movie on HDTV.

I pulled up in front of the clothing store and went in to see Mickey Crowley, the fellow I had met when I bought my original clothes. He shook my hand like we were old friends, and I could see him checking out the wounds on my head.

You look like you've healed up a little since I first saw you, but isn't that bandage on top of your head new?

"Yeah, it's been a rough week for my face and head," I told him.

"I'm told that's one of the hazards when you work with Mike."

That piqued my curiosity. "You've known some of the other guys."

"Only one; I met him when I was working here before the war started. You're the first one he's hired since the war ended."

I wasn't sure I really wanted to know, but I asked, "What happened to the other guy?"

Crowley smiled. "Nothing tragic. He was like you and came in with bumps and bruises, but he quit working for Mike because he got married. His wife didn't want him doing work that she thought was dangerous. He sells insurance over in Detroit, but I see him every now and then."

I was glad to hear the good news. "So there is life after this job."

Crowley shook his head. "Not according to him. He said if he had it to do again, he would run the wife off and keep the job. "

"That's some recommendation."

"They don't come any better. You work for a great guy."

"I agree, I told him."

I looked at the hat he had handed me, but I didn't know beans about buying the right hat, so I just asked him. "Is this the one I want?"

"It is."

"Then I'll take it. I also need a coat and pants to replace the ones I just bought from you."

Crowley was already pulling them off the rack. "Mike mentioned that. I believe these are like the ones you bought."

They were and I asked him, "How much do I owe you?"

"It's already paid for, but Mike did say he wanted us to have your next hat made out of his old Army helmet."

"It wouldn't be a bad idea. I'm having a little trouble keeping my clothes presentable."

Mickey spread his arms wide. "We're always here for you,"

"I have no doubt."

He whistled cheerfully while he pulled down the box for my hat. I wasn't sure why he was taking such care to make sure I had the box the hat came in but I didn't want to appear as ignorant as I was, so I took it with a smile and left.

I went back home, parked the car, and went around the back to my little place to wash up before dinner. I scrubbed my face and hands and checked the bandages on my head. Everything seemed to be in place. I hung my coat in the closet, and I was going to throw the hat box in the garbage on the way up to the big house, but after a closer inspection I discovered that the box was actually a special storage container. The hat actually went in upside down and the box was made to protect it. I put the hat in it, and stuck the box on the shelf in the closet.

I could smell the steaks broiling before I opened the back door to the kitchen. I went in expecting to see Esmerelda, but it was only Norma.

"Have a seat Jake," dinner's almost ready.

"Esmerelda's not here?" I asked.

"No, she had a date for the movies, so I told her I would get dinner so she could make the early show."

A beautiful woman doesn't have to spend her evenings alone, so I had no right to expect anything different; but the new information caught me by surprise and created a lump in my stomach.

"Going to the early movie will give her and some lucky guy more time to make out down the street," I thought unhappily.

My head kept telling me that I had no hold on the woman and that I barely knew her, but something inside told me differently, and that something was in pain. I continued telling myself that I didn't have all the facts, and she could be out with a guy for any number of reasons; but my emotions had taken over and wouldn't allow my mind to think of any.

I took a deep breath and tried to concentrate on the good part of the moment, and not the part that I didn't know that much about and had zero control over. There certainly was a lot to enjoy. I was alive, which was against the odds; and I was sitting in a room smelling home cooked steaks. That was a lot to be thankful for, and I tried to push the rest out of my mind. After all, Esmerelda wasn't the first woman to be friendly but disinterested in me.

Norma cracked the oven door to check the steaks and fanned the smoke away as she said, "I hope you like ribeye."

"Who doesn't like ribeye?" I asked.

Norma asked, "What are your plans for the evening?"

"Well, going on a date with your gorgeous latin housekeeper is out."

I made a conscious effort to push that thought out and said, "I figured I would go and see what Mrs. Cantrell is up to."

"Jake, when I said we needed to have you to go watch her for one more night, I didn't mean tonight. You've more than earned yourself a rest."

I tried to sound upbeat and motivated when I told her, "I appreciate that; but I don't have anything special planned, and I'd like to put that project to bed."

"What are you putting to bed," asked Mike as he came through the doorway.

"Evelyn Cantrell," said Norma.

To me he said, "You do understand we're only paying you to watch her?"

Norma pulled a pan of sizzling steaks from the broiler and called out, "Sit down and behave, Groucho. Dinner's ready"

Dinner was excellent. It's hard to beat a good steak and baked potato. I could see Mike felt the same way. I assumed the steaks had been his idea.

I helped Norma clean up the kitchen, and then I took the car and drove off to put my project to bed.

CHAPTER 33

I pulled up on the far side of the big cul-de-sac and turned the car off. The weather had taken a sharp turn for the worse, and it got chilly almost immediately. I pulled my coat tighter and watched my breath vaporize. If I hung around, I could see that I would need a heavy coat. New Egan might not look like Chicago, but I had no doubt the winters were identical.

Mrs. Cantrell was already home. She was doing what she had done the last time I saw her, lounging on the sofa, sipping a drink, and reading a book. It wasn't much fun to watch, but I did it anyway and hoped for better things to come. That went on for a little over an hour, and all the while it just kept getting colder. I bounced around as much as I could and tried to stay warm. I remembered that my grandfather hadn't been the only one to tell me it was a bad idea to run the heaters on these old cars when they aren't moving, as they sometimes let the exhaust into the interior.

There were so many things he had told me that I wished I could remember, but unfortunately, that one stuck, so I sat in the cold and watched a pretty woman read a book.

The windshield kept fogging over until I couldn't see out, so for something like the twentieth time I took my sleeve and wiped it as clear as I could. As I was doing that, I saw her jump up and go quickly to the end of sofa. She reached down and came up with a telephone handset. She spoke and then listened for a moment. Her face grew unhappy, and it looked like she stamped her foot. She slapped the handset down on the phone in a huff and stood there staring at it. After a moment she picked it up again and called someone. It was a quick call, similar to the one we had seen her make before. After she hung up, she went into another room and flipped off the light in the living room. The big window went black.

It had been boring enough watching her read a book, but sitting in the cold looking at a dark window was beyond dull. I heard a door close somewhere past the passenger side of the car so I scooted over and wiped the window to see out.

The two G-Men were making their exit just as they had done before. They had their hats pulled down, their coat collars turned up, and they were carrying large brief cases. I found it odd that they had come out just after Evelyn Cantrell's phone call, just exactly as they had before. I watched them walk down the sidewalk and disappear over the grassy knoll.

Nothing else was going on, so I sat in the cold and tried to find something interesting on the radio. According to the advertisements, I had missed the "The Lone Ranger" which had come on earlier. I ended up listening to something else, but I don't remember what it was. It didn't hold my attention, but I couldn't blame it on the radio. I was still trying to figure out what to do with my future. I had my share of problems in the twenty-first century, but it had finally dawned on me that they were of my own making, just like all the therapists had told me they were.

Mike was great to work for, but I figured there must be similar jobs in the future. Then again, why go looking for something I already had. It was also pretty cool hanging out with "The Greatest Generation", but I missed a lot of the technology of the future.

I would have liked to factor Esmerelda into the equation, but it appeared that I wasn't as interesting to her as she was to me. She didn't owe me anything and there was nothing between us other than my feelings for her, so I had no right to be bothered that she was out with someone else. On the other hand, I would have been lying if I said I wasn't bothered. I thought that we had shared a moment together, but it looked like she thought of me as more of a friend and that was sure death to a future that held any chance for me. She could cry on my lap and even pull my pants off; but when it came to other things she was out with some lucky guy, and I was left sitting in the cold hoping that a woman I didn't know would pull her clothes off for me.

I checked to see if there was something more interesting on the radio, but I wasn't having much luck. I was watching the little pointer slide across the lighted dial and noticed that my hand was shaking from the cold. My grandfather's warning about the heaters in old cars kept running through my head, but I gave up and finally decided to chance it. I reached for the heater controls and almost jumped out of my skin when someone rapped on the driver's side window.

I sat bolt upright and when I wiped the fog off the glass, I found myself looking right into the gorgeous face of Evelyn Cantrell. She motioned for me to roll the window down, and I complied.

"Why are you watching me," she asked. She didn't sound angry; she seemed to just be making conversation.

I stared at her with my mouth hanging open to the cold. I couldn't believe I had been spotted before I even got going. *"I really suck at this,"* I thought to myself.

She had one of her furs on, maybe mink, and her arms were crossed to bring it close against the cold. "Did you hear me? Why have you and your friend been watching me?"

Now that she was close, I could see she really was a pretty woman. She had a face I would expect to see in a magazine. She had beautiful waves of dark brown hair that she had pulled around to one side of her head and it partially covered and shaded the right side of her face. The effect was incredible, but what was really striking about her was her voice. I don't normally pay attention to the way a woman's voice sounds, but Mrs. Cantrell's was amazing. It was rough, but it was also low and sexy. It's hard to describe, but if a bottle of sipping whiskey could talk, it would sound like Evelyn Cantrell.

"You're not any of my husband's people, so he must have hired you. Are you private investigators?"

It took me a second to recover from the surprise, but I worked my jaw up and down a couple of times and finally blurted out, "I…uh…I'm not at liberty to say."

"How long does he want you to watch me?"

"I don't know what you're talking about."

"You already said you're a private detective, and that means my husband hired you."

"I said, 'I wasn't at liberty to say'."

"Besides a private dick, who would say that?"

"*I'm being outmaneuvered by an ex- stripper. I really, really suck at this.*"

I don't remember what I tried to say after that, but when I tried to say it my teeth chattered.

She frowned at me and asked, "Why are you sitting out here without an overcoat? Where's your friend with the Studebaker?"

"He had somewhere else to go," I lied through clicking teeth.

"Are you just going to sit here and freeze to death?"

"*Apparently,*" I thought, but I replied, "I was just leaving."

"Bullshit," she said softly.

She watched me shiver for a moment then grudgingly she said, "C'mon, I can't let you sit out here and die of hypothermia. You can come inside and keep me company while you watch me." She turned around and headed around the big cul-de-sac to her apartment.

I wasn't completely out of options. There are ways to get warm in emergency situations, but none of them ever involved following a beautiful woman into her apartment. I hopped out of the car and started to follow her when she turned and said, "You probably shouldn't leave your car parked here with no one in it."

I opened my mouth to tell her it wouldn't fit in my pocket, but she continued, "Go back out to the intersection and take a left and the first left after that. That will take you to the parking lot just over that knoll." She pointed to where the G-Men had disappeared and I nodded as I got back in the car.

I felt a little foolish, but I had the time to kill, and I didn't have a better idea. Maybe I would learn something and maybe I wouldn't, but I certainly didn't have a better idea than spending a warm evening with a beautiful woman.

I was hoping to get some heat from the car as I drove around to the parking lot, but I never got the heater to blow anything but cold air. There were a lot of inefficiencies on these old cars, and the heaters looked to be another one of them.

I parked the car, and then wandered around for a couple of minutes before I found the walkway leading to her place. The door was not quite closed, so I pushed it open and then turned around to see if anyone was watching. I didn't see anything obvious, but it wouldn't have mattered if I did. I could feel the warm air coming through the doorway and after that there was no turning back. I did look to see if the shades were drawn before I stepped into the living room. The room looked much nicer than it did from outside. She had made it kind of homey, and it had a warm feeling to it, of which I was very sensitive to at that moment.

I hadn't been able to see it from the window, but the sofa was a big, overstuffed, fluffy looking piece of furniture. She motioned toward it, and I sat down. She took my hat and threw an afghan in my lap with a nice sweeping movement. I thanked her and wrapped myself in the afghan.

She went into the kitchen and yelled back, "Do you want something to drink?"

"What do you have?" I was hoping for something that was served boiling.

"I normally have wine, but I drank my last glass this evening. Now, I have gin and scotch."

Before I could answer she added, "It's rotgut that some of my husband's associates had left over from prohibition. It's still around, because nobody wanted it. The gin is really foul. It tastes like it was made from old socks."

"I'll have the scotch," I said quickly.

"She came out of the kitchen holding two glasses with scotch in them. "I keep the gin around because it does have one redeeming quality," she said as she handed me one of the glasses.

"What does it have going for it," I asked, taking the glass and sampling it.

"In comparison, it makes this nasty scotch seem drinkable."

I made a choking sound as the liquor cauterized my throat shut. It wasn't possible the gin could be worse than this. She had said, "foul," but the sour battery acid in my glass was beyond that. My face wadded up like I was sucking on an electrified lemon, and I willed myself not to spit the stuff across the room. It was just as well. I was having enough trouble keeping up with things without dulling my senses. I set the glass on the table.

Mrs. Cantrell didn't seem to have any problem with it and she didn't sip it either. I assumed this had more than a little something to do with her whiskey voice. She went back into the kitchen and came back dragging a dining chair. She turned the chair to face me and sat down. When she crossed her legs her foot just missed touching my leg. I could tell from the look on her face that she crossed them knowing I would watch her do it. I willed myself not to look and failed.

She took another hard pull on her drink and then asked me, "So how long did he tell you to watch me?"

I tried hard to think of something clever or evasive but couldn't come up with anything. I didn't want to tell her the truth, but she seemed to know enough of it already so I couldn't see how it would hurt.

"We don't have a time limit," I said, finally.

"What, you're just going to watch me for the next twenty years?"

"We are just supposed to watch and see if you have any...," I began but I ran out of juice at that point.

"Gentleman callers?"

"Right."

"Well, what have you seen?"

"Mostly, we've seen you sit on the couch and read a book."

"You haven't seen anything else?"

I figured I might as well stop trying to act like I was good at this and just tell her the truth.

"We saw some guy come in a couple of days ago."

"Did you see who it was?"

"No, he had his hat pulled down and his collar up. It could have been anyone."

She seemed surprised. "That's all you've seen?"

"That's it," I told her honestly.

"Where the hell have you guys been? Early last week, I forgot to close the blinds, and I had my blouse off before I realized it. I drew a crowd like you wouldn't believe."

"I'd believe it."

There was a group outside my window for the next three or four nights, hoping for another show and don't get me started on the rumors going around and what people were claiming I was doing in front of that big window.

Suddenly, her face lit up. "That's the reason Paul hired you to watch me, wasn't it? He heard those rumors and wanted to know if they were true?"

"Well…," I began, but I could tell by the look on her face that anything I could fabricate wasn't going to be believed.

"Why doesn't he just come and look for himself," she asked.

I took a deep breath and shifted nervously. The wounds where the stitches had been removed were warming up and starting to itch.

"He said something about hoping the stories weren't true and in case they were, he wanted us to go look because he couldn't bear watching you with another man."

I hadn't noticed that her accent had been fairly Midwestern and rather neutral, but it went straight to Brooklyn when she was aggravated. "Gahdamn airsole! I can't believe he pulls that, 'I love her so much I can't bear to look' crap."

Paul Cantrell had already shown me he didn't give a shit if I existed or not, but I did my best to be a standup guy.

"He seemed sincere," I said flatly.

She took another hit off her glass and stood up. "He can be as sincere as he wants. It didn't keep him from putting his hands and pecker all over the Hat Check Girl at the Shang Hai Club, or the Cigarette Girl, for that matter."

I thought I knew what a Hatcheck Girl was, but I pulled out my pencil and piece of paper and wrote it down anyway.

My writing caught her attention. "You also keep tabs on who he's screwing?"

"Not really, this is just to help me keep track of things."

"Well if you're trying to keep track of who Paul Cantrell has been sleeping with, you'll need a bigger piece of paper."

She took off her fur and threw it at the other end of the sofa. Judging by her appearance, she must have just tossed her mink over the top of her nightgown when she went out to talk to me. What she was wearing under the fur wouldn't have passed for scandalous in the 21st century, but it looked like something a 1940's woman would sleep in if she wasn't interested in sleeping alone. It was a pretty color of pink and cut down low in the front. You couldn't see through it but it was silky and it stuck to her in all sorts of wonderful ways. All manner of warning bells went off in my head, and suddenly I wasn't cold anymore.

She sat back down and crossed her legs again. I saw it coming a lot sooner this time and willed myself to look away, but my neck no longer took orders from my head. My temperature was rising, and I was powerless to do anything about it. She owned me, and she knew it.

In a moment of clarity I asked, "Where's your boyfriend this evening?"

"He called just a little bit ago and said he was catching the train out of town."

"There's a phrase you don't hear much in the twenty-first century."

It seemed odd that a woman as pretty as she was would just stay home, so I asked her why she hadn't gone out.

"I thought about it but," she began, and then finished by holding up her glass and saying, "I've been drinking this swill all evening, and I might get into all kinds of trouble if I went out."

"That makes sense."

"I went in and changed clothes and then I remembered you were still sitting out there watching."

I knew where the story went from there so I asked, "You said your boyfriend was catching the train out of town?"

"That's right, and he's not really my boyfriend."

"Just a friend?"

"No, he's more like...a job." She grunted and fingered the side of her glass. I could have watched her do that all day.

"He doesn't mean anything to you?" I didn't care, but Mrs. Cantrell's sex life had suddenly become the focal point of all my attention.

"Not really. I started sleeping with him because I knew it would really make my husband mad."

"Madder than sleeping with anyone else?"

"Oh yeah. The man I've been sleeping with is Jackie Banks." She looked at me to see if the name registered. I tried to act like it didn't and she asked, "Have you heard of him?"

"No, but I'm new in town."

"Well, you don't have to live here long to know Jackie Banks' name. He's the guy my husband wants to be.

She took her toe and prodded my right calf. I managed not to moan by gritting my teeth.

"Who are you working for?" she asked.

If I had given any thought to the question I would have decided that there was no reason to hide that information, but I didn't give it any thought. She asked and I answered, "Mike Manzerek."

She owned me.

"Big Mike Manzerek," she said dreamily, taking her already low voice down a note or two. She used the rim of the glass to toy with her lower lip.

"You know him?" I asked, surprised.

"Everybody knows Big Mike," she answered, squirming in her seat. "There are a lot of women out there who would like to know him better."

"Anyone in particular," I asked, watching her wiggle in the chair.

"There's no hope for me," she said into her glass. She took another hit and added, "Not with that walking heart attack he has for a wife. With a beautiful woman like that, there's no chance he would stray away from home."

I shouldn't have spoken at all, but my body had long ago stopped taking commands from my brain. "You're a beautiful woman…," I blurted out before I realized that I didn't want to finish the sentence.

She finished it for me. "…and my husband still strayed off." She took another drink and managed to swirl that vile crap around in her mouth as she sat there thinking.

"I'm sorry," I told her.

"That's all right. It's sweet of you to say I'm beautiful." She ran her foot up and down the inside of my calf. My eyes half closed, and my mouth half opened. With the tiny shred of dignity I had left, I tried not to make a sound. I succeeded, but I knew it was my last victory.

She looked at me for a moment and then a mischievous look crossed her face. "So what were you expecting to see in the window?"

"We heard the rumors you were talking about," I told her honestly.

"I'm a modern woman," she announced into her glass, "but I'm not that modern." She laughed as if she had said something really funny.

I had no idea of how to reply to that, but I didn't have to. She stood up and grabbed my hand. "If anything was going to happen, it would happen in here." She headed toward the room where we had seen her go with Jackie Banks.

"This is where things would definitely happen," I thought as she pulled me into her bedroom.

There was no mistaking it for anything but a woman's bedroom, what wasn't wooden furniture was pink and that included the curtains, the pillows, the bedspread and some of the wallpaper.

She let go of my hand and wrapped hers in the lapels of my coat. She looked up at me and asked, "So what do you want to watch me do?"

I didn't need an engraved invitation. I bent down and kissed her. She tasted like that nasty scotch, so it wasn't nearly as pleasant as I thought it was going to be. Fortunately, that didn't slow her down any. She undid the buttons on my coat, pulled it down from my shoulders and tossed it onto a chair partially covered by a pink afghan. She did the same thing with my shirt and she took her time about it.

As she pulled my shirt down I told her, "I'm kind of beat up."

She didn't seem to care about that and she ignored the myriad of purple and black bruises on my torso as she ran her hands down my chest and the muscles on my stomach. I don't know if she noticed something or if what I had said got through to her whiskey soaked brain, but after a moment she placed her hands on my sides and guided me to turn around.

For what seemed like a long time she said nothing and then, softly, almost to herself, "Shit, you're the one. You're the guy that jumped out of the window with Norma Manzarek."

"Yes," I whispered back to her.

She ran her fingers over a couple of the newly unstitched wounds and the sensation felt nice, but it reminded me of when Esmerelda had cleaned the wounds and rubbed the ointment on them. I tried to push the thought away and I didn't expect for it to be any problem, but it just kept getting worse. I thought of how Esmerelda had looked standing in the doorway of the bathroom screaming, when she found me on my first day, and how cute she was with the BAR slung over her shoulder. I even thought of how intensely beautiful she was when she was angry with Roberto and then me.

Evelyn guided me to turn back around, but it was too late. I had realized that I didn't want to be there anymore. I wanted to be with someone else even if she didn't want to be with me. I felt like a total moron and I had no clue what I was going to do, but I knew I couldn't stay there.

I didn't figure I could make Evelyn Cantrell understand what I was thinking and feeling, but I did figure it was okay to tell a married woman, especially one married to a gangster, that I didn't want to sleep with her.

I opened my mouth to tell her just that, but the noise of a key fumbling in the lock of the front door saved me the trouble.

Before I could say, "Who's that?" Evelyn Cantrell had shoved my shirt, coat, hat and gun into my arms and was pushing me into the closet.

"That's Jackie," she hissed pushing my head down and shoving me in between the dresses and coats.

"I thought you said he was leaving town."

"That's what he said, but he's the only one with a key."

She closed the closet doors, flipped off the bedroom light and went to the living room.

"Surprise," said a male voice.

"Yes it is," she replied. "I thought you were leaving town."

"I had a last minute change of plans, so I get to spend the evening with you instead of riding a train." There was a pause and the male voice said, "If you don't have other plans."

"The only plans I had for this evening were to read a book and drink my nasty scotch," she lied.

The male voice chuckled. "I thought you might be down to that, so I brought good wine and good scotch."

Mrs. Cantrell's low husky voice said, "Oh, you sweet man. You are a life saver."

She was a much better liar than me. Anyone listening to the conversation, other than myself, would never have suspected there was a man hiding in the closet.

I heard the sound of glasses clinking together, so I figured I was going to be in the closet for a while. I sat down on top of a bunch of shoes and did my best to put my shirt and coat back on.

I couldn't see much from where I was sitting. The doors on the closet were actually two bi-fold doors and the space between them was almost the width of my little finger, so I could peep through that. The doors were slatted but the slats angled down from my side so if I looked through them I could only see the floor. When the light was on, the opening between the doors gave me a pretty good view of the center of the bed but not much else. Now that the light was off, I couldn't see much of anything.

I hated to admit it, but I was more than a little scared. I didn't mind the darkness, but hiding in the closet of the girlfriend of a known gangster seemed like a real good way to peg out a Dumbass-o-meter. That was bad enough, but then I remembered that Jackie Banks traveled with those two gorillas who found us sitting in John's car a couple of nights ago, and that didn't do anything to alleviate my anxiety.

I did the only thing I could. I sat quietly in the dark, and waited for someone to leave or go to sleep. It seemed like days passed before Evelyn and Jackie left the living room and came into the bedroom.

I had been looking forward to it, because that would mean I was closer to going home. I had high hopes that Jackie Banks was a quick two-stroker that fell asleep afterwards but the way my luck had been running for the past few days he was more likely one of these guys that spends all night running through the Kama Sutra.

As it turned out, Jackie was a pretty ordinary guy. I know this for a fact, because he liked to do it with the lights on, and from my hidey-hole; I had a wonderful view of his hairy ass.

They went at it for a while and when they were done I was hoping he would roll over and go to sleep, but instead he rolled over, and they both lit up a cigarette.

Neither of them said much and I could see Mrs. Cantrell staring at the crack between the closet doors as I stared back at her.

After they were done with their cigarettes, they started things up again and about a half hour later Jackie rolled over and this time he did go to sleep. He was still laying half on top of Evelyn, but she raised her head up and motioned with her eyes that I should get the hell out. I didn't need any extra urging. When she saw the door opening she laid her head back down and I eased the door open just a little, checking to make sure it didn't squeak or make some other kind of noise. I had only gotten the crack a little wider but it allowed me to see a little more of the room.

I could see the right hand side of the bed, the nightstand and the muzzles of two Thompson   Submachine   Guns.

CHAPTER 34

I reached for the .45 in my shoulder holster, but I was too late. The twin guns roared in unison, ripping into the bed and the couple in it. Pieces of sheets, mattress, feathers, blood and people flew into the air and filled the room with gore and trash.

I jerked the .45 out of the holster with the intent of rushing into the room and I prayed to God there wasn't a third person out there that would make me eat the end of a Tommy Gun. In the split second it took to get my gun out the two Thompsons strayed away from the bed and started tearing up the room. They were both sporting hundred round drums, so they had plenty of ammunition to play with.

The guy closest to me spun around and chewed into the wall where I was. It was a good thing I was still in a crouch as the torrent of lead came across the middle of the closet and the top halves of the doors turned into kindling. I fell sideways into the closet floor. The closet rod and all the clothes came down on top of me.

I was buried under a pile of silk dresses and fine furs which was my good fortune, since the top half of the closet was now open to the world. I hated not doing anything, but my choices were limited. If I stirred and made a sound or the pile of clothes showed any movement, I'd get the full attention of those Thompsons. I lay still and tried not to breathe loudly.

I didn't have to wait long. I heard one of the men say, "That's it, let's go." I could hear their footsteps exit the room and then nothing.

I got up as fast as I could dig myself out. I needed to get out of that room quickly. Those submachine guns made a hell of a racket, and as soon as people decided it was safe they would come looking. I looked over at the bed, but there was nothing I could do. Evelyn Cantrell and Jackie Banks lay side by side with open eyes that could no longer see. Their bodies were riddled with bullets, and the top of the bed was almost completely red. The room was a shambles with bullet holes in all four walls and the ceiling. There had been a nice window with pretty curtains that looked out on the front lawn of the apartment; but now the glass was shot out, and the curtains were covered with blood and gore.

I had trouble taking my eyes off of Mrs. Cantrell. She had been a pretty woman and she had been sweet to me. I was sorry for what had happened to her, and I was sorry I hadn't been able to stop it.

I had to suck up my feelings and get moving. I could already hear people out on the lawn in front of the apartment. I ran into the hallway and through the nearest door. It was the bathroom, just as pink as the bedroom had been. There was no other door and the window was small, so I ran to the next room. That room was a bedroom on the back side of the apartment, and the window was big enough to escape through, so I did. It was an old sash style, and I threw it open to the top, climbed out, and dropped onto a large grassy area. Maybe thirty yards away was another set of apartments under construction with no one living there. I went in that direction in a fast walk, but just before I got up a good head of steam something caught me across the neck and jerked me off my feet. Landing in the grass was much better than landing on hard dirt or concrete, but I was still sore from the night before. My whole body let out one big throbbing ache when I hit the ground.

I lay in the cold grass and considered staying there until I quit hurting, but that was a luxury option I couldn't afford. I rose up and looked around but there was no one there. I didn't really expect there to be. I was fairly certain that whatever had clotheslined me had been stationary, but I still got up slowly, scanning the area. There was no one around as I got to my feet so I brushed myself off and started to move toward the construction again. I had only taken a couple of steps when I came across the culprit that had knocked me on my butt.

There was a cord stretched across the lawn about neck high. I turned and looked to see where the cord was coming from, and saw that it was attached to what looked like a crucifix with the top piece cut off. It was about a half a foot shorter than me; just a large "T" silhouetted in the moonlight. I followed the cord in the other direction to another big "T". The "T's" were about twenty feet apart, and there were at least two more cords attached to the crossbars connecting the "T's",. I stared at the rig for a moment and then almost laughed out loud. I had literally been clotheslined... by a clothesline.

I made a mental note to keep an eye out for these things in the future. Then I ducked under the lines and headed toward the construction. I went on the other side of where the new apartments were going up and started to weave my way back to where I had parked the car.

I needed to talk to the police. I hadn't had much of a view from the closet, but when I had opened the door just a little bit; I had seen the men that had killed Mrs. Cantrell and her lover, or whatever she wanted to call him.

Putting aside my feelings for the death of Mrs. Cantrell, I could say I had accomplished everything I had been assigned and more. I could now say that I knew Evelyn Cantrell had been sleeping with someone, and I could positively identify that someone as Jackie Banks. I could also identify their killers, and that information needed to be in someone's hands who could make use of it.

I came off the far side of the knoll and down to the parking area where my car was and waited for the law to show up. It was even colder than when I had gone inside, so I didn't give a second thought to firing up the car and seeing if I could get some heat out of it. It took a while, but just as warm air started flowing out I heard the sirens coming down the street on the other side of the knoll and into the cul-de-sac. I could also see the glow of blue lights over the top of the grassy rise.

I hated to leave the heat, but I got out of the car and headed over the knoll to tell the

A Different Place to Die

cops who had killed Evelyn and Jackie.

There was a large crowd in the cul-de-sac. Three police cars were pulled up to the curb with their headlights and spotlights shining on the front of Evelyn's apartment. I assumed that no one lived in the apartment above her since it was still dark. The blue lights going round and round gave everything a disco effect. Just then the blue lights were joined by the red lights of ambulances pulling up. There was a lot of horn blowing and yelling as the ambulances tried to move through the crowd, but they didn't make any headway until four of the officers came over and moved the crowd for them.

I had almost as hard a time as the ambulances, threading my way through the mob of people. Everyone was standing in the cold in their bathrobes and pajamas with coats thrown over them, trying to get a glimpse at whatever had happened inside that apartment.

The far reaching effects of The War were still being felt. As I wound my way through the mob I heard more than one guy say, "I know damned well what Thompson Submachine Guns sound like, and those were Thompsons."

There was a small group of Police officers standing behind their parked vehicles, and I finally managed to get within ten feet of them when two people I didn't expect to see popped out of the crowd on the other side.

"Make way...FBI, clear a path...FBI!" It was the same two G-Men that had been watching Evelyn Cantrell's apartment. They had their badges out and were waving them around as they shouted. They went up to the group of Police officers and announced very loudly, "We saw what happened officers; we saw the two men who killed that couple."

The Policemen waved them to come in closer, but the two men continued to speak with voices loud enough to be heard by everyone in a twelve foot radius.

"Did you recognize either of the men?" asked one Policeman.

"We certainly did," said the first G-Man. "They were Joey Gardell and Vic Hogan."

"Those are Paul Cantrell's people," replied one of the officers.

"That's right," the second G-Man confirmed.

At that point the group of men gathered closer and started speaking with lower voices. I could only make out a couple of phrases about how much trouble this was going to cause, but I couldn't catch anything else.

It didn't look like there was anything else I could learn, and there was no point in trying to stay to tell my story, so I turned my collar up, pulled my hat down, and made my way back to the car as quickly as possible.

CHAPTER 35

I drove home but I barely remembered doing it. Someone had opened a can of worms, and I was knee deep in it.

I parked the car and went upstairs. Everyone had already gone to bed, but I figured I had better wake up the boss and tell him the story as soon as possible. I went up the stairs and into the living room before it dawned on me that I didn't know where Mike and Norma's bedroom was. I knew Esmerelda's was upstairs somewhere; but I had never gotten a tour of the big house, so I had no idea where anybody slept.

I was wondering if Mike snored, and if he did could I locate him that way. I was saved the trouble of trying when I heard the sound of a key in the front door. Since whoever it was used a key I figured they were okay; but it had been a rough week and a real bad night, so I put my hand on the .45 as I watched the door open.

Esmerelda came in and turned on the light, then squealed and jumped when she realized I was standing in the dark with my hand on my gun.

"Estupido! You scared me," she barked putting her hand to her heart.

"I'm sorry," I told her. She looked nice. She always looked nice, but she wasn't as well dressed or fixed up as she had been when she went out with Roberto. I decided she must only dress up for her real boyfriends, and this new guy hadn't made the cut yet. I smiled when I saw that her dress was on right side out.

"Why are you standing in the dark? Are you waiting to shoot someone?"

"No," I said in a low voice. "I've had enough of that tonight."

Her face clouded over. "What happened?" she asked, and then I could see recognition in her eyes. "Hay Dios mio! That's where all those sirens were going?"

"You heard those?"

"Si, the radio said that some people had been murdered, but they weren't sure how many."

"Two," I informed her.

She looked at me with fear in her eyes. "Did you murder them?"

"Did I…no, I didn't murder them. What kind of guy do you think I am?"

She put her hands on her hips and stared at me like I was an idiot."

I was a little put out, and then it came to me that she had a point. "Okay, that's fair," I admitted, "but I didn't kill anyone."

"Who's killing someone?" boomed Mike's voice from the hallway.

The Boss stepped out of the hallway closing and tying his bathrobe. It was white terrycloth and I was wondering where in the world he found one that big when he asked, "What's happened?"

Before I could answer Norma stepped out and stood beside him.

I took a deep breath and said, "Evelyn Cantrell's dead." That was more than I wanted to tell, but it was only half the news so I added, "So's Jackie Banks."

Norma gasped and Esmerelda crossed herself.

Mike's eyes narrowed. He asked, "How?"

"Two guys machine gunned her bedroom."

"Shit," Mike hissed. "Did you see who it was when they went in?"

I knew this line of questioning would be coming, and I hadn't been looking forward to it but I thought it would be best to lean into it and get it over with. "To be honest," I didn't see them until they came into the bedroom."

His eyes narrowed. "What were you doing in the bedroom?"

I sighed and said, "Hiding in the closet."

"Cochino!" yelled Esmerelda.

"This is a long story, isn't it?" asked Mike.

"Longer than I want it to be."

The big man rubbed his face and then turned to Esmerelda. "As long as we're all up, would you mind putting on a pot of coffee?"

To me he said, "Take off your hat and coat, grab a seat, and start from the beginning."

I did as I was instructed and took a seat at the kitchen table. Mike and Norma did the same. They both had amused looks on their faces that didn't help the way I felt at all.

"Okay," said Mike, "start at the beginning."

I went into the story about how Evelyn Cantrell had known about John and me watching and had invited me into her apartment. I tried to play up the part about the lousy liquor she served and tried to underplay the part where I had my shirt off in her bedroom, but no one was fooled.

I told them about Jackie showing up unannounced and about Mrs. Cantrell stuffing me into the closet with my clothes.

"She might have saved your life," said Mike. "Jackie doesn't travel light and he comes with an entourage."

"That occurred to me," I told him. I wondered, again, why I hadn't seen Jackie's gorillas anywhere.

I finished the story by telling about the killing of Mrs. Cantrell and Banks, my escape through another bedroom window and then waiting for the police to arrive. I left out the part about the clothesline since it was equal parts irrelevant and embarrassing.

"So you told the Police this story?" asked Norma.

I shook my head. I tried to, but when I went to tell them I found two other guys were already there, claiming to have been eyewitnesses to the murder.

"Had you ever seen these guys before?"

"Yeah, they were the same G-men that Callahan and I saw watching from the other apartment."

Esmerelda brought cups and started pouring hot water in them.

"So these guys…" Mike began and then looked at Esmerelda. "Is that instant coffee?"

"Of course it is. Do you want to wait for real coffee?"

Mike made a sour face and held up his mug for Esmerelda to fill.

I was thinking Esmerelda would pass me a cup, but she went back to the stove so I stood up and got one for myself. I stirred it, took a sip, and then wished I hadn't bothered. That was one more plus in the twenty-first century column. In the future I would have already been drinking a cup of decent coffee instead of whatever the hell was in the cup I was holding.

Mike went back to his original questioning. "So these guys claimed to have witnessed the murders?"

"They did."

"Why would they lie about that?" asked Norma?"

"They weren't lying," I told her.

Mike was the first to understand what I was saying, and when he did; he sprayed coffee across the top of his cup. "Are you shitting me? The FBI killed Cantrell and Banks?"

Esmerelda grabbed a rag and started cleaning up the mess Mike had just made as I told him, "They were telling the truth about witnessing the crime. They were there."

Mike wiped the coffee off his face and said, "I don't suppose they confessed to that?"

"Not even close. They gave the cops the names of two men I had never heard of. One was Joey Gardell and the other was…what did they say…Vic Hogan."

"Ah, damn, this just keeps getting worse."

"You know these guys?"

"We do," Norma replied. "Those are two of Paul Cantrell's lieutenants."

"Oh great, that means those two guys not only murdered Mrs. Cantrell…"

"…they also framed her husband," Mike finished.

For the next few minutes the three of us sat at the table not talking, and not drinking our lousy coffee.

"I'm not sure what to do with this," Mike said quietly and then looked at me. "I believe everything you're saying, but your word alone won't cut it if two of J. Edgar's boys are claiming different."

"That's the way I figured it too. That's the reason I didn't stay around when I saw them."

Mike nodded. "You're safe for the moment, since no one knows you saw what happened. If they find out you were there, you're liable to get the full attention of people you'd rather not know."

We sat in silence a little longer and finally Norma said, "Let's go to bed and sleep on it. As Mike said, your anonymity is keeping you safe, so there's no reason to rush at this headlong."

I looked around for Esmerelda, but she had disappeared. I gave up and decided to go home and go to bed. I had started through the laundry room, headed for the back door, when I heard Norma call me. I turned around and saw her standing next to the breakfast table by herself, waving a piece of paper at me.

I walked back to her. She handed me the paper and said, "This is your first week's check."

"Thank you," I told her as I folded it and put it in my pocket without looking at it.

Norma looked amused. "You don't want to make sure the numbers are right?"

"You and Mike have treated me very well since I've been here." I tapped my pocket. "I'm sure this is fine."

"That's a wonderful gesture, but I hope you will let me know if you find out different."

"I will, thanks."

"Before you go, I wanted to ask you about something."

"What's that?"

"Esmerelda mentioned you might not be staying."

"I do have some things to sort out before I can make permanent plans." It was vague, but it was honest.

"Well, Mike and I wanted you to know that you have a job here as long as you want it. Hopefully, it won't be as exciting as this week. It might even involve mundane everyday chores but you've proved your worth, and nothing would please us more than keeping you around."

"You're very kind," I told her. "I expect to have an answer very soon."

"Let us know when you do." She smiled her movie-star smile and then called out "Good night," over her shoulder as she left the kitchen.

I went out through the back door and then down to my little home. I opened the door, flipped on the light and hung up my hat and coat. The coat was a little wrinkled from being wadded up, but at least it had made it through the evening in one piece. Considering what it and I had been through that evening, I counted it as a personal best.

I went to the sink and got a glass of water to wash the miserable coffee taste out of my mouth, and then into the living room to sit down and take my shoes off. I usually turned on the TV at times like these, but that was impossibility; so I turned on the radio and sat down and waited for it to warm up. The station came up and was playing soft, orchestra music. It wasn't my first choice, but it wasn't annoying or abrasive, so I let it play. I assumed it was music to sleep by and I would be glad to do just that.

I pulled the check out of my pocket and looked at it. It was made out for twenty dollars. I would have laughed, except I had already done the math, and it was what I was expecting. On the surface it would have appeared woefully inadequate for a week of getting shot at, cut up, and beat on, but anyone in a combat zone could say the same.

I tended to think about it in a different way. Twenty dollars a week, after taxes, came to around a thousand dollars a year. If you took that number and factored in that I was also receiving room and board, which included Esmerelda's fine cooking and lodging in a very nice guest house, then I was looking at approximately three thousand dollars worth of annual salary and benefits.

If I took into account that my employer had also covered my medical bills and most of my clothing costs, I was doing a little better than 3K a year. Since, according to the magazines I had been reading, a good wage for 1947 was a little over three thousand dollars a year, I was doing pretty well.

In addition to all that I actually enjoyed the job so that didn't leave anything to complain about.

I leaned back on the sofa and thought again of how much the little house felt like home. The whole train of thought brought back Bert the Barber's advice on paying attention to when you're happy.

I did feel happy, but I didn't feel like I should be after the week I had just had, not to mention having to stand on the sidelines while Esmerelda went out with someone else. I figured I would know when I was happy, but was it even possible to be happy after an extremely rough week that had ended by witnessing a double homicide while hiding in a closet. It didn't seem likely but, then again, Bert claimed to have found happiness in the Argonne forest in World War I. If a guy could be happy there, he could be happy anywhere.

I looked down at the glass in my hand. It was just clear water, and I could see the floor through the bottom. There was something odd about it, and I just kept looking at it. It suddenly hit me that I had spent a lot of time looking for answers at the bottom of a glass, and the answer I was looking for was actually at the bottom of this one.

It was past midnight on a Friday night, and I was drinking a glass of water. I had heard people say that laughing while you're alone is a sign of insanity, but I laughed out loud and enjoyed it. At least I finally knew the answer, and I was amazed at the relief that came over me.

I decided it was time to get up and get ready for bed, but before I could, someone next to me said, "Hello."

I squawked out a sound that I'm embarrassed to admit was a little more feminine than masculine. I twisted my head toward the sound of the voice that had suddenly appeared next to me. It was the ugly little old man.

"Hello," he repeated.

"Hello," I replied. "You surprised me. I didn't know when to expect you."

"Yeah, that's the way it works in this business," he said nonchalantly.

I was going to ask what business that was, but he spoke first.

"There's nothing good on the radio this time of night, is there?"

I shook my head and he said, "I guess you probably miss television."

"A little, but not nearly as much as I thought I would. Some of these radio programs are pretty good."

"Just wait until Sunday. That's when Jack Benny comes on. You're in for a treat, assuming you're going to stay, or course."

I opened my mouth to respond to him, but again he spoke before I could.

"Well, I have to confess, you've accomplished something I didn't think you could."

He looked at me like I should know what he was talking about, but it took me a moment before I looked over at the clock on the wall. It was just before 1:00 in the morning.

"I lived to see the weekend."

"You did, and I'm impressed."

I smiled and told him, "There was more than one time I didn't think I was going to make it."

"None the less, you made it; and I don't mind telling you that I didn't think you were smart enough or clever enough to make it happen."

That took that wind out of my moment. "You don't mind telling me that?" I asked flatly.

"Not a bit."

He had walked over to the radio and was winding away at the knobs, searching for a station he liked better. Punching a button to scan for another radio station was one more thing that was far into the future.

He found a different station playing the same soft music and gave up searching.

"So," he said turning around to face me, "what have you decided?"

"I've spent a lot of time thinking about that," I said honestly.

"I'm sure that's true. What have you come up with?"

"I think I might be able to make a life here."

"That's the secret to it all," replied the old man. "Everyone goes looking for happiness, but the truth is, you have to make it yourself."

"Yeah, the guy at the barbershop said pretty much the same thing."

The old man nodded. "You can learn a lot from Bert."

He seemed to know everything else, so I figured it shouldn't surprise me that he knew Bert, the Barber. Since he had all the information, I thought I should ask him, "So you think I could be happy here?"

"It's up to you whether you enjoy your life or not. You can do it on your old world, or you can do it here. It doesn't matter."

"I kind of like it here."

"So you'll be staying?"

I smiled. "Why not, it's just different place to die."

"Or a different place to live," replied the old man.

At that, he turned and walked to the front door. As he opened it he said, "You should go back up to the main house."

"Everybody went to bed already."

The old man lowered his head slightly and shook it slowly back and forth. "It was just advice; ignore it if you wish."

He walked through the doorway and left it open. I went to it and looked outside, but I knew I wouldn't see him.

I felt like a dumbass, but I went back up to the main house. Everything looked dark except for a dim light in the kitchen. I was guessing that someone had left the light on over the stove. I didn't expect to get in. The doors were most likely locked, and I wasn't even sure that the key I had used to get into the front door would open the back door. It and the key to the guest house were the only ones I had.

It began to collect in my consciousness that I had just signed on to this new world and I barely had a toehold in it.

I tried the back door knob. It twisted, and the door came open. I went in through the laundry room and then into the kitchen. I had been correct; the light above the stove was on. It was a good-sized kitchen, not including the breakfast area, so most of the room was in darkness. There was also a little bit of moonlight coming in from the window, but I couldn't see anything. I didn't want to turn on the kitchen lights, so I decided to just turn off the stove light and go back to my place.

I walked to the stove, switched off the light, and stood there wondering about what I was going to do in the morning. I had spent the week being worried about the big picture of my future, and I had no idea what I was going to do tomorrow.

My eyes adjusted to the darkness as I stood there, and I began to see more and more of the room. The pale moonlight from the window sucked away most of the color and everything became an off-shade of white, gray and what I would call blue simply because it wasn't really black.

I turned to leave, but as I walked by the breakfast area I heard a small squeaking sound. It was a sound I had heard many times before and I had heard this particular one very recently. This time I didn't draw down on it.

I went toward the noise and found Esmerelda sitting at the breakfast table. I was standing between her and the moon, so when I moved around to the side I could make out her features in the sparse light. She was sitting at the table with a tissue to her nose. I assumed the bluish black smears under her eyes were where her mascara had run. The tears running down her face glistened in the moonlight.

I sat down next to her. The pain I had felt before came back to me. She was in pain and for some reason I neither understood nor questioned that meant I was in pain.

"What's wrong," I asked softly.

"She shook her head, but didn't say anything."

A thought suddenly occurred to me and I asked, "He didn't hurt you did he?"

The question surprised her and she asked, "Who?"

"The guy you were out with, the guy that took you to the movies, did he hurt you?"

"Who told you I went out with a man?"

"Norma said you had a date to go to the movies."

"Si, with Esperanza and Violet."

Now I was the one surprised. "Esperanza and Violet?"

"Si, mis amigas from the beauty shop."

"Oh," I said, sure that I looked as foolish as I felt.

Her squeaking voice returned as she said, "You had a much more exciting night than me."

"I suppose so, but I wish I had been at the movies with you," I told her honestly.

"I'm sure that wouldn't have been as good as sleeping with a burlesque dancer."

A thought crept into my head, but I was afraid to believe it. Was she actually crying because she thought I had gotten in bed with Evelyn Cantrell? I wanted it to be true so badly I couldn't trust my judgement.

I knew it was crazy. I hadn't known her very long, and I didn't even know her well but something inside of me was tied to her so I went for broke.

In a low quiet voice I told the crying woman, "I wasn't going to sleep with her."

"Liar," she squeaked through her tissue filled hands.

"When have you seen me lie and get away with it?"

I reached out and put my fingertips under her chin and turned her head to face me. I looked her in the eyes and said, "I had every intention of going to bed with her, but when we got to the bedroom I couldn't stop thinking about this crazy woman I just met.

"What crazy woman?"

"She's a housekeeper."

Esmerelda cocked her head a little to the side to look at me and asked, "Is she a cook too?"

"Yes, she's a wonderful cook."

She lowered the tissue to her lap. Her eyes were still wet, but her face didn't show pain anymore when she asked, "Why were you thinking of her?"

"I don't know. I barely know her, but I really like her. She's fun and interesting..."

"Is she pretty?"

I looked as deep into her eyes as the light would allow and said, "She's incredibly beautiful."

"Really?" she asked softly.

"I know it sounds insane. I don't even know what she thinks of me," I told her. "She calls me a pig and a clown and..."

"...estupido."

"And estupido, but I knew I couldn't spend time with a burlesque dancer or anyone else until I found out if I had a chance with this woman."

I continued to look into her eyes, and she looked back into mine. I hoped she could see the truth in them.

"I was just about to tell Mrs. Cantrell I couldn't stay with her when Jackie Banks showed up and she stuffed me into the closet."

"I'm glad you didn't get killed," said Esmerelda. She gave her nose one last wipe and put the tissue in the pocket of her apron.

"That makes two of us."

She wiped the hair back from her face and pushed the tears off her cheek with the back of her hand. "I must look awful," she said as a smile appeared beneath her mascara smeared eyes.

"I've never seen you look awful," I told her.

"Now I know you're lying. The first time I saw you I looked terrible."

"You were worried about how you looked?" I squawked in surprise. "I was bloody and naked, lying in a bathtub!"

A little laugh bubbled out of her and she said, "That's true, you didn't look too good."

I reached over and took her hand and asked softly, "What are you doing tomorrow?"

She smiled and replied, "Tomorrow I have to go to the market and cook breakfast, lunch and dinner."

"Oh," I said as reality set back in.

"And you have to go find out why those men killed Evelyn Cantrell."

That answered my question about what to do in my near future and I nodded. "Yeah, I guess I do."

Esmerelda leaned closer to me. "But...you can take me to the movies tomorrow night...if you want."

265

"I want that very much."

Her face was very close to mine and she asked, "Does this mean you are going to stay?"

I cupped my hand around the back of her neck. "Yes it does."

She smiled. "The people around here are kind of old fashioned, but I think you will like it."

"I'm sure I will. I've started to like things that are old fashioned."

Our lips touched in the moonlight and a fire that I knew would never go out, swept through me.

The little old man had said it was simply a different place to die, and someday I would do that in this new world; but before that happened I would live and I would be happy. It was my job to make sure of it.

Tracy E Johnson

ACKNOWLEDGEMENTS

I want to thank my good friends Hank Wilbanks and Alf Gill for their continuous support and willingness to listen to me read chapter drafts over the telephone. Their help cannot be overstated.

I also need to thank my brother-in-law, Jose Padilla, who graciously took on the job as one of the proofreaders and corrected my Spanish.

Proofreading brings me to my mother whose input on punctuation was a great help.

And my sister, Gail, who was willing to give my manuscript the once over, but I was in a hurry and ran away with it before she got very far.

Thank you all.